"Monstrous!" the Spirit of Mara roared. The God's huge face convulsed with anger, and he strode directly toward the horse of the sleep-spelled Princess Ce'Nedra. "I will rend thy flesh, daughter of Nedra. I will sink thee in torment and terror all the days of thy life!"

"That's enough, Mara. Stop!" The voice was Garion's. He slid from his horse to approach the giant figure. "Your vengeance stops here, Mara," his voice said. "You will not touch her."

"I *will* have her!" Mara howled.

"No," Garion's voice replied. "You *won't*!"

The God raised an arm to strike. Garion felt a vast touch on his mind. Then a dreadful recognition began to dawn in Mara's weeping eyes. His arm fell. "Give her to me," he pleaded.

"No."

Mara fell back. "I must submit," the God said hoarsely. Then he bowed to Garion, his ravaged face strangely humble. He turned away and buried his face in his hands, weeping uncontrollably.

Also by David Eddings

THE BELGARIAD

Book One: **PAWN OF PROPHECY**

Book Two: **QUEEN OF SORCERY**

Book Three: **MAGICIAN'S GAMBIT**

Book Four: **CASTLE OF WIZARDRY***

Book Five: **ENCHANTED END GAME***

Published by Ballantine Books

*Forthcoming

Book Three of The Belgariad

MAGICIAN'S GAMBIT

DAVID EDDINGS

A Del Rey Book

BALLANTINE BOOKS • NEW YORK

A Del Rey Book
Published by Ballantine Books

Library of Congress Catalog Card Number: 82-91075

ISBN 0-345-30077-7

Manufactured in the United States of America

First Edition: June 1983

Cover art by Laurence Schwinger

For Dorothy,
who has the enduring grace to put up with Eddings men,
and for Wayne,
for reasons we both understand but could never be put into words.

Prologue

Being an Account of how Gorim sought a God for his People and of how he found UL upon the sacred Mountain of Prolgu.
—based upon *The Book of Ulgo* and other fragments

AT THE BEGINNING of Days, the world was spun out of darkness by the seven Gods, and they also created beasts and fowls, serpents and fishes, and lastly Man.

Now there dwelt in the heavens a spirit known as UL who did not join in this creation. And because he withheld his power and wisdom, much that was made was marred and imperfect. Many creatures were unseemly and strange. These the younger Gods sought to unmake, so that all upon the world might be fair.

But UL stretched forth his hand and prevented them, saying: "What you have wrought you may not unmake. You have torn asunder the fabric and peace of the heavens to bring forth this world as a plaything and an entertainment. Know, however, that whatsoever you make, be it ever so monstrous, shall abide as a rebuke for your folly. In the day that one thing which you have made is unmade, *all* shall be unmade."

The younger Gods were angered. To each monstrous or unseemly thing they had made they said: "Go thou unto UL and let *him* be thy God." Then from the races of men, each God chose that people which pleased him. And when there were yet peoples who had no God, the younger Gods drove

them forth and said: "Go unto UL, and *he* shall be your God."
And UL did not speak.

For long and bitter generations, the Godless Ones wandered
and cried out unheard in the wastelands and wilderness of the
West.

Then there appeared among their numbers a just and righteous man named Gorim. He gathered the multitudes before
him and spoke to them: "We wither and fall as the leaves from
the rigors of our wanderings. Our children and our old men
die. Better it is that only one shall die. Therefore, stay here
and rest upon this plain. I will search for the God named UL
so that we may worship him and have a place in this world."

For twenty years, Gorim sought UL, but in vain. Yet the
years passed, his hair turned gray, and he wearied of his search.
In despair, he went up onto a high mountain and cried in a
great voice to the sky: "No more! I will search no longer. The
Gods are a mockery and deception, and the world is a barren
void. There is no UL, and I am sick of the curse and affliction
of my life."

The Spirit of UL heard and replied: "Why art thou wroth
with me, Gorim? Thy making and thy casting out were none
of my doing."

Gorim was afraid and fell upon his face. And UL spoke
again, saying: "Rise, Gorim, for I am not thy God."

Gorim did not arise. "O my God," he cried, "hide not thy
face from thy people who are sorely afflicted because they are
outcast and have no God to protect them."

"Rise, Gorim," UL repeated, "and quit this place. Cease
thy complaining. Seek thou a God elsewhere and leave me in
peace."

Still Gorim did not rise. "O my God," he said, "I will still
abide. Thy people hunger and thirst. They seek thy blessing
and a place where they may dwell."

"Thy speech wearies me," UL said and he departed.

Gorim remained on the mountain, and the beasts of the field
and fowls of the air brought him sustenance. For more than a
year he remained. Then the monstrous and unseemly things

which the Gods had made came and sat at his feet, watching him.

The Spirit of UL was troubled. At last he appeared to Gorim. "Abidest thou still?"

Gorim fell on his face and said: "O my God, thy people cry unto thee in their affliction."

The Spirit of UL fled. But Gorim abode there for another year. Dragons brought him meat, and unicorns gave him water. And again UL came to him, asking: "Abidest thou still?"

Gorim fell on his face. "O my God," he cried, "thy people perish in the absence of thy care." And UL fled from the righteous man.

Another year passed while nameless, unseen things brought him food and drink. And the Spirit of UL came to the high mountain and ordered: "Rise, Gorim."

From his prostrate position, Gorim pleaded: "O my God, have mercy."

"Rise, Gorim," UL replied. He reached down and lifted Gorim up with his hands. "I am UL—thy God. I command thee to rise and stand before me."

"Then wilt thou be my God?" Gorim asked. "And God unto my people?"

"I am thy God and the God of thy people also," UL said.

Gorim looked down from his high place and beheld the unseemly creatures which had cared for him in his travail. "What of these, O my God? Wilt thou be God unto the basilisk and the minotaur, the Dragon and the chimera, the unicorn and the thing unnamed, the winged serpent and the thing unseen? For these are also outcast. Yet there is beauty in each. Turn not your face from them, O my God, for in them is great worthiness. They were sent to thee by the younger Gods. Who will be their God if you refuse them?"

"It was done in my despite," UL said. "These creatures were sent unto me to bring shame upon me that I had rebuked the younger Gods. I will in no wise be God unto monsters."

The creatures at Gorim's feet moaned. Gorim seated himself on the earth and said: "Yet will I abide, O my God."

"Abide if it please thee," UL said and departed.

It was even as before. Gorim abode, the creatures sustained him, and UL was troubled. And before the holiness of Gorim, the Great God repented and came again. "Rise, Gorim, and serve thy God." UL reached down and lifted Gorim. "Bring unto me the creatures who sit before thee and I will consider them. If each hath beauty and worthiness, as thou sayest, then I will consent to be their God also."

Then Gorim brought the creatures before UL. The creatures prostrated themselves before the God and moaned to beseech his blessing. UL marveled that he had not seen the beauty of each creature before. He raised up his hands and blessed them, saying: "I am UL and I find beauty and worthiness in each of you. I will be your God, and you shall prosper, and peace shall be among you."

Gorim was glad of heart and he named the high place where all had come to pass *Prolgu*, which means "Holy Place." Then he departed and returned to the plain to bring his people unto their God. But they did not know him, for the hands of UL had touched him, and all color had fled, leaving his body and hair as white as new snow. The people feared him and drove him away with stones.

Gorim cried unto UL: "O my God, thy touch has changed me, and my people know me not."

UL raised his hand, and the people were made colorless like Gorim. The Spirit of UL spoke to them in a great voice: "Hearken unto the words of your God. This is he whom you call Gorim, and he has prevailed upon me to accept you as my people, to watch over you, provide for you, and be God over you. Henceforth shall you be called UL-Go in remembrance of me and in token of his holiness. You shall do as he commands and go where he leads. Any who fail to obey him or follow him will I cut off to wither and perish and be no more."

Gorim commanded the people to take up their goods and their cattle and follow him to the mountains. But the elders of the people did not believe him, nor that the voice had been the voice of UL. They spoke to Gorim in despite, saying: "If you are the servant of the God UL, perform a wonder in proof of it."

Gorim answered: "Behold your skin and hair. Is that not wonder enough for you?"

They were troubled and went away. But they came to him again, saying: "The mark upon us is because of a pestilence which you brought from some unclean place and no proof of the favor of UL."

Gorim raised his hands, and the creatures which had sustained him came to him like lambs to a shepherd. The elders were afraid and went away for a time. But soon they came again, saying: "The creatures are monstrous and unseemly. You are a demon sent to lure the people to destruction, not a servant of the Great God UL. We have still seen no proof of the favor of UL."

Now Gorim grew weary of them. He cried in a great voice: "I say to the people that they have heard the voice of UL. I have suffered much in your behalf. Now I return to Prolgu, the holy place. Let him who would follow me do so; let him who would not remain." He turned and went toward the mountains.

Some few people went with him, but the greater part of the people remained, and they reviled Gorim and those who followed him: "Where is this wonder which proves the favor of UL? We do not follow or obey Gorim, yet neither do we wither and perish."

Then Gorim looked upon them in great sadness and spoke to them for the last time: "You have besought a wonder from me. Then behold this wonder. Even as the voice of UL said, you are withered like the limb of a tree that is cut off. Truly, this day you have perished." And he led the few who followed him into the mountains and to Prolgu.

The multitude of the people mocked him and returned to their tents to laugh at the folly of those who followed him. For a year they laughed and mocked. Then they laughed no more, for their women were barren and bore no children. The people withered and in time they perished and were no more.

The people who followed Gorim came with him to Prolgu. There they built a city. The Spirit of UL was with them, and they dwelt in peace with the creatures who had sustained Gorim.

Gorim lived for many lifetimes; and after him, each High Priest of UL was named Gorim and lived to a great age. For a thousand years, the peace of UL was with them, and they believed it would last forever.

But the evil God Torak stole the Orb that was made by the God Aldur, and the war of men and Gods began. Torak used the Orb to break the earth asunder and let in the sea, and the Orb burned him horribly. And he fled into Mallorea.

The earth was maddened by her wounding, and the creatures which had dwelt in peace with the people of Ulgo were also maddened by that wounding. They rose against the fellowship of UL and cast down the cities and slew the people, until few remained.

Those who escaped fled to Prolgu, where the creatures dared not follow for fear of the wrath of UL. Loud were the cries and lamentations of the people. UL was troubled and he revealed to them the caves that lay under Prolgu. The people went down into the sacred caves of UL and dwelt there.

In time, Belgarath the Sorcerer led the king of the Alorns and his sons into Mallorea to steal back the Orb. When Torak sought to pursue, the wrath of the Orb drove him back. Belgarath gave the Orb to the first Rivan King, saying that so long as one of his descendants held the Orb, the West would be safe.

Now the Alorns scattered and pushed southward into new lands. And the peoples of other Gods were troubled by the war of Gods and men and fled to seize other lands which they called by strange names. But the people of UL held to the caverns of Prolgu and had no dealings with them. UL protected them and hid them, and the strangers did not know that the people were there. For century after century, the people of UL took no note of the outer world, even when that world was rocked by the assassination of the last Rivan King and his family.

But when Torak came ravening into the West, leading a mighty army through the lands of the children of UL, the Spirit of UL spoke with the Gorim. And the Gorim led forth his people in stealth by night. They fell upon the sleeping army and wreaked mighty havoc. Thus the army of Torak was weakened and fell in defeat before the armies of the West at a place called Vo Mimbre.

Then the Gorim girded himself and went forth to hold council with the victors. And he brought back word that Torak had been gravely wounded. Though the evil God's body was stolen away and hidden by his disciple Belzedar, it was said that Torak would lie bound in a sleep like death itself until a descendant of the Rivan line should again sit upon the throne at Riva—which meant never, since it was known that no descendants of that line lived.

Shocking as the visit of the Gorim to the outer world had been, no harm seemed to come of it. The children of UL still prospered under the care of their God and life went on almost as before. It was noticed that the Gorim seemed to spend less time studying *The Book of Ulgo* and more searching through moldy old scrolls of prophecy. But a certain oddity might be expected of one who had gone forth from the caverns of UL into the world of other peoples.

Then a strange old man appeared before the entrance to the caverns, demanding to speak with the Gorim. And such was the power of his voice that the Gorim was summoned. Then, for the first time since the people had sought safety in the caverns, one who was not of the people of UL was admitted. The Gorim took the stranger into his chambers and remained closeted with him for days. And thereafter, the strange man with the white beard and tattered clothing appeared at long intervals and was welcomed by the Gorim.

It was even reported once by a young boy that there was a great gray wolf with the Gorim. But that was probably only some dream brought on by sickness, though the boy refused to recant.

The people adjusted and accepted the strangeness of their Gorim. And the years passed, and the people gave thanks to their God, knowing that they were the chosen people of the Great God UL.

Part One

MARAGOR

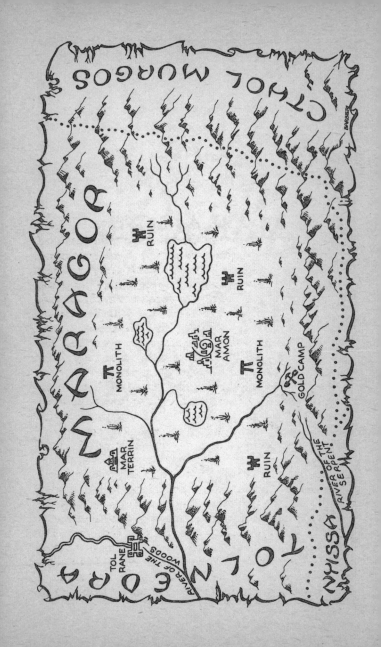

Chapter One

HER IMPERIAL HIGHNESS, Princess Ce'Nedra, jewel of the House of Borune and the loveliest flower of the Tolnedran Empire, sat cross-legged on a sea chest in the oak-beamed cabin beneath the stern of Captain Greldik's ship, nibbling thoughtfully on the end of a tendril of her coppery hair as she watched the Lady Polgara attend to the broken arm of Belgarath the Sorcerer. The princess wore a short, pale-green Dryad tunic, and there was a smudge of ash on one of her cheeks. On the deck above she could hear the measured beat of the drum that paced the oar strokes of Greldik's sailors as they rowed upstream from the ash-choked city of Sthiss Tor.

It was all absolutely dreadful, she decided. What had begun as merely another move in the interminable game of authority and rebellion against it that she had been playing with her father, the Emperor, for as long as she could remember had suddenly turned deadly serious. She had never really intended for things to go this far when she and Master Jeebers had crept from the Imperial Palace in Tol Honeth that night so many weeks ago. Jeebers had soon deserted her—he had been no more than a temporary convenience, anyway—and now she was caught up with this strange group of grim-faced people from the north in a quest she could not even understand. The Lady Polgara, whose very name sent a chill through the princess, had rather bluntly informed her in the Wood of the Dryads that the game was over and that no evasion, wheedling, or coaxing would alter the fact that she, Princess Ce'Nedra, *would*

stand in the Hall of the Rivan King on her sixteenth birthday—
in chains if necessary. Ce'Nedra knew with absolute certainty
that Lady Polgara had meant exactly that, and she had a momentary vision of being dragged, clanking and rattling in her
chains, to stand in total humiliation in that grim hall while
hundreds of bearded Alorns laughed at her. That had to be
avoided at any cost. And so it had been that she had accompanied them—not willingly, perhaps—but never openly re-
bellious. The hint of steel in Lady Polgara's eyes always seemed
to carry with it the suggestion of manacles and clinking chains,
and that suggestion cowed the princess into obedience far more
than all the Imperial power her father possessed had ever been
able to do.

Ce'Nedra had only the faintest idea of what these people
were doing. They seemed to be following someone or something, and the trail had led them here into the snake-infested
swamps of Nyissa. Murgos seemed to be somehow involved,
throwing frightful obstacles in their path, and Queen Salmissra
also seemed to take an interest, even going so far as to have
young Garion abducted.

Ce'Nedra interrupted her musing to look across the cabin
at the boy. Why would the queen of Nyissa want him? He was
so *ordinary*. He was a peasant, a scullion, a nobody. He was
a nice enough boy, certainly, with rather plain, sandy hair that
kept tumbling down across his forehead, making her fingers
itch to push it back. He had a nice enough face—in a plain
sort of way—and he was somebody she could talk to when
she was lonely or frightened, and somebody she could fight
with when she felt peevish, since he was only slightly older
than she was. But he completely refused to treat her with the
respect due her—he probably didn't even know how. Why all
this excruciating interest in him? She pondered that, looking
thoughtfully at him.

She was doing it again. Angrily she jerked her eyes from
his face. Why was she always watching him? Each time her
thoughts wandered, her eyes automatically sought out his face,
and it wasn't really that exciting a face to look at. She had

even caught herself making up excuses to put herself into places where she could watch him. It was stupid!

Ce'Nedra nibbled at her hair and thought and nibbled some more, until once again her eyes went back to their minute study of Garion's features.

"Is he going to be all right?" Barak, the Earl of Trellheim, rumbled, tugging absently at his great red beard as he watched the Lady Polgara put the finishing touches on Belgarath's sling.

"It's a simple break," she replied professionally, putting away her bandages. "And the old fool heals fast."

Belgarath winced as he shifted his newly splinted arm. "You didn't have to be so rough, Pol." His rust-colored old tunic showed several dark mud smears and a new rip, evidence of his encounter with a tree.

"It had to be set, father," she told him. "You didn't want it to heal crooked, did you?"

"I think you actually enjoyed it," he accused.

"Next time you can set it yourself," she suggested coolly, smoothing her gray dress.

"I need a drink," Belgarath grumbled to the hulking Barak.

The Earl of Trellheim went to the narrow door. "Would you have a tankard of ale brought for Belgarath?" he asked the sailor outside.

"How is he?" the sailor inquired.

"Bad-tempered," Barak replied. "And he'll probably get worse if he doesn't get a drink pretty soon."

"I'll go at once," the sailor said.

"Wise decision."

This was yet another confusing thing for Ce'Nedra. The noblemen in their party all treated this shabby-looking old man with enormous respect; but so far as she could tell, he didn't even have a title. She could determine with exquisite precision the exact difference between a baron and a general of the Imperial Legions, between a grand duke of Tolnedra and a crown prince of Arendia, between the Rivan Warder and the king of the Chereks; but she had not the faintest idea where sorcerers fit in. The materially oriented mind of Tolnedra refused even to admit that sorcerers existed. While it was quite true that Lady Polgara, with titles from half the kingdoms of the West, was the most respected woman in the world, Belgarath was a vagabond, a vagrant—quite frequently a public nuisance. And Garion, she reminded herself, was his grandson.

"I think it's time you told us what happened, father," Lady Polgara was saying to her patient.

"I'd really rather not talk about it," he replied shortly.

She turned to Prince Kheldar, the peculiar little Drasnian nobleman with the sharp face and sardonic wit, who lounged on a bench with an impudent expression on his face. "Well, Silk?" she asked him.

"I'm sure you can see my position, old friend," the prince apologized to Belgarath with a great show of regret. "If I try to keep secrets, she'll only force things out of me—unpleasantly, I imagine."

Belgarath looked at him with a stony face, then snorted with disgust.

"It's not that I *want* to say anything, you realize."

Belgarath turned away.

"I knew you'd understand."

"The story, Silk!" Barak insisted impatiently.

"It's really very simple," Kheldar told him.

"But you're going to complicate it, right?"

"Just tell us what happened, Silk," Polgara said.

The Drasnian sat up on his bench. "It's not really much of a story," he began. "We located Zedar's trail and followed it down into Nyissa about three weeks ago. We had a few encounters with some Nyissan border guards—nothing very serious. Anyway, the trail of the Orb turned east almost as soon as it crossed the border. That was a surprise. Zedar had been headed for Nyissa with so much single-mindedness that we'd both assumed that he'd made some kind of arrangement with Salmissra. Maybe that's what he wanted everybody to think. He's very clever, and Salmissra's notorious for involving herself in things that don't really concern her."

"I've attended to that," Lady Polgara said somewhat grimly.

"What happened?" Belgarath asked her.

"I'll tell you about it later, father. Go on, Silk."

Silk shrugged. "There isn't a great deal more to it. We followed Zedar's trail into one of those ruined cities up near the old Marag border. Belgarath had a visitor there—at least he said he did. *I* didn't see anybody. At any rate, he told me that something had happened to change our plans and that we were going to have to turn around and come on downriver to Sthiss Tor to rejoin all of you. He didn't have time to explain much more, because the jungles were suddenly alive with Murgos—either looking for us or for Zedar, we never found out which. Since then we've been dodging Murgos and Nyissans both—traveling at night, hiding—that sort of thing. We sent a messenger once. Did he ever get through?"

"The day before yesterday," Polgara replied. "He had a fever, though, and it took a while to get your message from him."

Kheldar nodded. "Anyway, there were Grolims with the Murgos, and they were trying to find us with their minds. Belgarath was doing something to keep them from locating us that way. Whatever it was must have taken a great deal of concentration, because he wasn't paying too much attention to where he was going. Early this morning we were leading the horses through a patch of swamp. Belgarath was sort of stumbling along with his mind on other things, and that was when the tree fell on him."

"I might have guessed," Polgara said. "Did someone make it fall?"

"I don't think so," Silk answered. "It might have been an old deadfall, but I rather doubt it. It was rotten at the center. I tried to warn him, but he walked right under it."

"All right," Belgarath said.

"I *did* try to warn you."

"Don't belabor it, Silk."

"I wouldn't want them to think I didn't try to warn you," Silk protested.

Polgara shook her head and spoke with a profound note of disappointment in her voice. *"Father!"*

"Just let it lie, Polgara," Belgarath told her.

"I dug him out from under the tree and patched him up as

best I could," Silk went on. "Then I stole that little boat and we started downriver. We were doing fine until all this dust started falling."

"What did you do with the horses?" Hettar asked. Ce'Nedra was a little afraid of this tall, silent Algar lord with his shaved head, his black leather clothing, and his flowing black scalp lock. He never seemed to smile, and the expression on his hawklike face at even the mention of the word "Murgo" was as bleak as stone. The only thing that even slightly humanized him was his overwhelming concern for horses.

"They're all right," Silk assured him. "I left them picketed where the Nyissans won't find them. They'll be fine where they are until we pick them up."

"You said when you came aboard that Ctuchik has the Orb now," Polgara said to Belgarath. "How did that happen?"

The old man shrugged. "Beltira didn't go into any of the details. All he told me was that Ctuchik was waiting when Zedar crossed the border into Cthol Murgos. Zedar managed to escape, but he had to leave the Orb behind."

"Did you speak with Beltira?"

"With his mind," Belgarath answered.

"Did he say why the Master wants us to go to the Vale?"

"No. It probably never occurred to him to ask. You know how Beltira is."

"It's going to take months, father," Polgara objected with a worried frown. "It's two hundred and fifty leagues to the Vale."

"Aldur wants us to go there," he answered. "I'm not going to start disobeying him after all these years."

"And in the meantime, Ctuchik's got the Orb at Rak Cthol."

"It's not going to do him any good, Pol. Torak himself couldn't make the Orb submit to him, and he tried for over two thousand years. I know where Rak Cthol is; Ctuchik can't hide it from me. He'll be there with the Orb when I decide to go take it away from him. I know how to deal with *that* magician." He said the word "magician" with a note of profound contempt in his voice.

"What's Zedar going to be doing all that time?"

"Zedar's got problems of his own. Beltira says that he's moved Torak from the place where he had him hidden. I think we can depend on him to keep Torak's body as far away from Rak Cthol as he possibly can. Actually, things have worked out rather well. I was getting a little tired of chasing Zedar anyway."

Ce'Nedra found all this a bit confusing. Why were they all so caught up in the movements of a strangely named pair of Angarak sorcerers and this mysterious jewel which everyone seemed to covet? To her, one jewel was much the same as another. Her childhood had been surrounded by such opulence that she had long since ceased to attach much importance to ornaments. At the moment, her only adornment consisted of a pair of tiny gold earrings shaped like little acorns, and her fondness for them arose not so much from the fact that they were gold but rather from the tinkling sound the cunningly contrived clappers inside them made when she moved her head.

All of this sounded like one of the Alorn myths she'd heard from a storyteller in her father's court years before. There had been a magic jewel in that, she remembered. It was stolen by the God of the Angaraks, Torak, and rescued by a sorcerer and some Alorn kings who put it on the pommel of a sword kept in the throne room at Riva. It was somehow supposed to protect the West from some terrible disaster that would happen if it were lost. Curious—the name of the sorcerer in the legend was Belgarath, the same as that of this old man.

But that would make him thousands of years old, which was ridiculous! He must have been named after the ancient myth hero—unless he'd assumed the name to impress people.

Once again her eyes wandered to Garion's face. The boy sat quietly in one corner of the cabin, his eyes grave and his expression serious. She thought perhaps that it was his seriousness that so piqued her curiosity and kept drawing her eyes to him. Other boys she had known—nobles and the sons of nobles—had tried to be charming and witty, but Garion never tried to joke or to say clever things to try to amuse her. She was not entirely certain how to take that. Was he such a lump that he didn't know how he was supposed to behave? Or perhaps he knew but didn't care enough to make the effort. He might at least *try*—even if only occasionally. How could she possibly deal with him if he was going to refuse flatly to make a fool of himself for her benefit?

She reminded herself sharply that she was angry with him. He had said that Queen Salmissra had been the most beautiful woman he had ever seen, and it was far, far too early to forgive him for such an outrageous statement. She was definitely going to have to make him suffer extensively for *that* insulting lapse. Her fingers toyed absently with one of the curls cascading down the side of her face, her eyes boring into Garion's face.

The following morning the ashfall that was the result of a massive volcanic eruption somewhere in Cthol Murgos had diminished sufficiently to make the deck of the ship habitable again. The jungle along the riverbank was still partially obscured in the dusty haze, but the air was clear enough to breathe, and Ce'Nedra escaped from the sweltering cabin below decks with relief.

Garion was sitting in the sheltered spot near the bow of the ship where he usually sat and he was deep in conversation with Belgarath. Ce'Nedra noted with a certain detachment that he had neglected to comb his hair that morning. She resisted her immediate impulse to go fetch comb and brush to rectify the situation. She drifted instead with artful dissimulation to a place along the rail where, without seeming to, she could conveniently eavesdrop.

"—It's always been there," Garion was saying to his grandfather. "It used to just talk to me—tell me when I was being childish or stupid—that sort of thing. It seemed to be off in one corner of my mind all by itself."

Belgarath nodded, scratching absently at his beard with his good hand. "It seems to be completely separate from you," he observed. "Has this voice in your head ever actually done anything? Besides talk to you, I mean?"

Garion's face grew thoughtful. "I don't think so. It tells me how to do things, but I think that I'm the one who has to do them. When we were at Salmissra's palace, I think it took me out of my body to go look for Aunt Pol." He frowned. "No," he corrected. "When I stop and think about it, it told me how to do it, but I was the one who actually did it. Once we were out, I could feel it beside me—it's the first time we've ever been separate. I couldn't actually see it, though. It *did* take over for a few minutes, I think. It talked to Salmissra to smooth things over and to hide what we'd been doing."

"You've been busy since Silk and I left, haven't you?"

Garion nodded glumly. "Most of it was pretty awful. I burned Asharak. Did you know that?"

"Your Aunt told me about it."

"He slapped her in the face," Garion told him. "I was going to go after him with my knife for that, but the voice told me to do it a different way. I hit him with my hand and said 'burn.' That's all—just 'burn'—and he caught on fire. I was going to put it out until Aunt Pol told me he was the one who killed my mother and father. Then I made the fire hotter. He begged me to put it out, but I didn't do it." He shuddered.

"I tried to warn you about that," Belgarath reminded him gently. "I told you that you weren't going to like it very much after it was over."

Garion sighed. "I should have listened. Aunt Pol says that once you've used this—" He floundered, looking for a word.

"Power?" Belgarath suggested.

"All right," Garion assented. "She says that once you've used it, you never forget how, and you'll keep doing it again and again. I wish I *had* used my knife instead. Then this thing in me never would have gotten loose."

"You're wrong, you know," Belgarath told him quite calmly. "You've been bursting at the seams with it for several months now. You've used it without knowing it at least a half dozen times that I know about."

Garion stared at him incredulously.

"Remember that crazy monk just after we crossed into Tolnedra? When you touched him, you made so much noise that I thought for a moment you'd killed him."

"You said Aunt Pol did that."

"I lied," the old man admitted casually. "I do that fairly often. The whole point, though, is that you've always had this ability. It was bound to come out sooner or later. I wouldn't feel too unhappy about what you did to Chamdar. It was a little exotic perhaps—not exactly the way I might have done it— but there was a certain justice to it, after all."

"It's always going to be there, then?"

"Always. That's the way it is, I'm afraid."

The Princess Ce'Nedra felt rather smug about that. Belgarath had just confirmed something she herself had told Garion. If the boy would just stop being so stubborn, his Aunt and his grandfather and of course she herself—all of whom knew much better than he what was right and proper and good for him— could shape his life to their satisfaction with little or no difficulty.

"Let's get back to this other voice of yours," Belgarath suggested. "I need to know more about it. I don't want you carrying an enemy around in your mind."

"It's not an enemy," Garion insisted. "It's on our side."

"It might seem that way," Belgarath observed, "but things aren't always what they seem. I'd be a lot more comfortable if I knew just exactly what it is. I don't like surprises."

The Princess Ce'Nedra, however, was already lost in thought. Dimly, at the back of her devious and complex little mind, an idea was beginning to take shape—an idea with very interesting possibilities.

Chapter Two

THE TRIP UP to the rapids of the River of the Serpent took the better part of a week. Although it was still swelteringly hot, they had all by now grown at least partially accustomed to the climate. Princess Ce'Nedra spent most of her time sitting on deck with Polgara, pointedly ignoring Garion. She did, however, glance frequently his way to see if she could detect any signs of suffering.

Since her life was entirely in the hands of these people, Ce'Nedra felt keenly the necessity for winning them over. Belgarath would be no problem. A few winsome little-girl smiles, a bit of eyelash fluttering, and a spontaneous-seeming kiss or two would wrap him neatly around one of her fingers. That particular campaign could be conducted at any time she felt it convenient, but Polgara was a different matter. For one thing, Ce'Nedra was awed by the lady's spectacular beauty. Polgara was flawless. Even the white lock in the midnight of her hair was not so much a defect as it was a sort of accent— a personal trademark. Most disconcerting to the princess were Polgara's eyes. Depending on her mood, they ranged in color from gray to a deep, deep blue and they saw through everything. No dissimulation was possible in the face of that calm, steady gaze. Each time the princess looked into those eyes, she seemed to hear the clink of chains. She definitely had to get on Polgara's good side.

"Lady Polgara?" the princess said one morning as they sat

together on deck, while the steaming, gray-green jungle slid by on either bank and the sweating sailors labored at their oars.

"Yes, dear?" Polgara looked up from the button she was sewing on one of Garion's tunics. She wore a pale blue dress, open at the throat in the heat.

"What *is* sorcery? I was always told that such things didn't exist." It seemed like a good place to start the discussion.

Polgara smiled at her. "Tolnedran education tends to be a bit one-sided."

"Is it a trick of some kind?" Ce'Nedra persisted. "I mean, is it like showing people something with one hand while you're taking something away with the other?" She toyed with the laces on her sandals.

"No, dear. It's nothing at all like that."

"Exactly how much can one do with it?"

"We've never explored that particular boundary," Polgara replied, her needle still busy. "When something has to be done, we do it. We don't bother worrying about whether we can or not. Different people are better at different things, though. It's somewhat on the order of some men being better at carpentry while others specialize in stonemasonry."

"Garion's a sorcerer, isn't he? How much can he do?" Now why had she asked *that*?

"I was wondering where this was leading," Polgara said, giving the tiny girl a penetrating look.

Ce'Nedra blushed slightly.

"Don't chew on your hair, dear," Polgara told her. "You'll split the ends."

Ce'Nedra quickly removed the curl from between her teeth.

"We're not sure what Garion can do yet," Polgara continued. "It's probably much too early to tell. He seems to have talent. He certainly makes enough noise whenever he does something, and that's a fair indication of his potential."

"He'll probably be a very powerful sorcerer then."

A faint smile touched Polgara's lips. "Probably so," she replied. "Always assuming that he learns to control himself."

"Well," Ce'Nedra declared, "we'll just have to teach him to control himself then, won't we?"

Polgara looked at her for a moment, and then she began to laugh.

Ce'Nedra felt a bit sheepish, but she also laughed.

Garion, who was standing not far away, turned to look at them. "What's so funny?" he asked.

"Nothing you'd understand, dear," Polgara told him.

He looked offended and moved away, his back stiff and his face set.

Ce'Nedra and Polgara laughed again.

When Captain Greldik's ship finally reached the point where rocks and swiftly tumbling water made it impossible to go any farther, they moored her to a large tree on the north bank, and the party prepared to go ashore. Barak stood sweating in his mail shirt beside his friend Greldik, watching Hettar oversee the unloading of the horses. "If you happen to see my wife, give her my greetings," the red-bearded man said.

Greldik nodded. "I'll probably be near Trellheim sometime during the coming winter."

"I don't know that you need to tell her that I know about her pregnancy. She'll probably want to surprise me with my son when I get home. I wouldn't want to spoil that for her."

Greldik looked a little surprised. "I thought you enjoyed spoiling things for her, Barak."

"Maybe it's time that Merel and I made peace with each other. This little war of ours was amusing when we were younger, but it might not be a bad idea to put it aside now— for the sake of the children, if nothing else."

Belgarath came up on deck and joined the two bearded Chereks. "Go to Val Alorn," he told Captain Greldik. "Tell Anheg where we are and what we're doing. Have him get word to the others. Tell them that I absolutely forbid their going to war with the Angaraks just now. Ctuchik has the Orb at Rak Cthol, and if there's a war, Taur Urgas will seal the borders of Cthol Murgos. Things are going to be difficult enough for us without that to contend with."

"I'll tell him," Greldik replied doubtfully. "I don't think he'll like it much, though."

"He doesn't have to like it," Belgarath said bluntly. "He just has to do it."

Ce'Nedra, standing not far away, felt a little startled when she heard the shabby-looking old man issuing his peremptory commands. How could he speak so to sovereign kings? And what if Garion, as a sorcerer, should someday have a similar authority? She turned and gazed at the young man who was helping Durnik the smith calm an excited horse. He didn't *look* authoritative. She pursed her lips. A robe of some kind might help, she thought, and maybe some sort of book of magic in his hands—and perhaps just the hint of a beard. She narrowed her eyes, imagining his so robed, booked and bearded.

Garion, obviously feeling her eyes on him, looked quickly in her direction, his expression questioning. He was so *ordinary*. The image of this plain, unassuming boy in the finery she had concocted for him in her mind was suddenly ludicrous. Without meaning to, she laughed. Garion flushed and stiffly turned his back on her.

Since the rapids of the River of the Serpent effectively blocked all further navigation upriver, the trail leading up into the hills was quite broad, indicating that most travelers struck out overland at that point. As they rode up out of the valley in the midmorning sunlight, they passed rather quickly out of the tangled jungle growth lining the river and moved into a hardwood forest that was much more to Ce'Nedra's liking. At the crest of the first rise, they even encountered a breeze that seemed to brush away the sweltering heat and stink of Nyissa's festering swamps. Ce'Nedra's spirits lifted immediately. She considered the company of Prince Kheldar, but he was dozing in his saddle, and Ce'Nedra was just a bit afraid of the sharp-nosed Drasnian. She recognized immediately that the cynical, wise little man could probably read her like a book, and she didn't really care for that idea. Instead she rode forward along the column to ride with Baron Mandorallen, who led the way, as was his custom. Her move was prompted in part by the desire to get as far away from the steaming river as possible, but there was more to it than that. It occurred to her that this might be an excellent opportunity to question this Arendish nobleman about a matter that interested her.

"Your Highness," the armored knight said respectfully as she pulled her horse in beside his huge charger, "dost think it prudent to place thyself in the vanguard thus?"

"Who would be so foolish as to attack the bravest knight in the world?" she asked with artful innocence.

The baron's expression grew melancholy, and he sighed.

"And why so great a sigh, Sir Knight?" she bantered.

"It is of no moment, your Highness," he replied.

They rode along in silence through the dappled shade where insects hummed and darted and small, scurrying things skittered and rustled in the bushes at the side of the trail. "Tell me," the princess said finally, "have you known Belgarath for long?"

"All my life, your Highness."

"Is he highly regarded in Arendia?"

"Highly regarded? Holy Belgarath is the paramount man in the world! Surely thou knowest that, Princess."

"I'm Tolnedran, Baron Mandorallen," she pointed out. "Our familiarity with sorcerers is limited. Would an Arend describe Belgarath as a man of noble birth?"

Mandorallen laughed. "Your Highness, holy Belgarath's birth is so far lost in the dim reaches of antiquity that thy question has no meaning."

Ce'Nedra frowned. She did not particularly like being laughed at. "Is he or is he not a nobleman?" she pressed.

"He is Belgarath," Mandorallen replied, as if that explained everything. "There are hundreds of barons, earls by the score, and lords without number, but there is only one Belgarath. All men give way to him."

She beamed at him. "And what about Lady Polgara?"

Mandorallen blinked, and Ce'Nedra saw that she was going too fast for him. "The Lady Polgara is revered above all women," he said in puzzled response. "Highness, could I but know the direction of thine inquiry, I might provide thee with more satisfactory response."

She laughed. "My dear Baron, it's nothing important or serious—just curiosity, and a way to pass the time as we ride."

Durnik the smith came forward at a trot just then, his sorrel horse's hoofbeats thudding on the packed earth of the trail. "Mistress Pol wants you to wait for a bit," he told them.

"Is anything wrong?" Ce'Nedra asked.

"No. It's just that there's a bush not far from the trail that she recognized. She wants to harvest the leaves—I think they have certain medicinal uses. She says it's very rare and only found in this part of Nyissa." The smith's plain, honest face was respectful as it always was when he spoke of Polgara. Ce'Nedra had certain private suspicions about Durnik's feelings, but she kept them to herself. "Oh," he went on, "she said to warn you about the bush. There might be others around. It's about a foot tall and has very shiny green leaves and a little purple flower. It's deadly poisonous—even to touch."

"We will not stray from the trail, Goodman," Mandorallen assured him, "but will abide here against the lady's permission to proceed."

Durnik nodded and rode on back down the trail.

Ce'Nedra and Mandorallen pulled their horses into the shade of a broad tree and sat waiting. "How do the Arends regard Garion?" Ce'Nedra asked suddenly.

"Garion is a good lad," Mandorallen replied, somewhat confused.

"But hardly noble," she prompted him.

"Highness," Mandorallen told her delicately, "thine education, I fear, hath led thee astray. Garion is of the line of Belgarath and Polgara. Though he hath no rank such as thou and I both have, his blood is the noblest in the world. I would give precedence to him without question should he ask it of me—which he would not, being a modest lad. During our sojourn at the court of King Korodullin at Vo Mimbre, a young countess pursued him most fervently, thinking to gain status and prestige by marriage to him."

"Really?" Ce'Nedra asked with a hard little edge coming into her voice.

"She sought betrothal and trapped him often with blatant invitation to dalliance and sweet conversation."

"A *beautiful* countess?"

"One of the great beauties of the kingdom."

"I see." Ce'Nedra's voice was like ice.

"Have I given offense, Highness?"

"It's not important."

Mandorallen sighed again.

"What is it now?" she snapped.

"I perceive that my faults are many."

"I thought you were supposed to be the perfect man." She regretted that instantly.

"Nay, Highness. I am marred beyond thy conception."

"A bit undiplomatic, perhaps, but that's no great flaw—in an Arend."

"Cowardice is, your Highness."

She laughed at the notion. "Cowardice? You?"

"I have found that fault in myself," he admitted.

"Don't be ridiculous," she scoffed. "If anything, your fault lies in the other direction."

"It is difficult to believe, I know," he replied. "But I assure thee with great shame that I have felt the grip of fear upon my heart."

Ce'Nedra was baffled by the knight's mournful confession. She was struggling to find some proper reply when a great crashing rush burst out of the undergrowth a few yards away. With a sudden start of panic, her horse wheeled and bolted. She caught only the briefest glimpse of something large and tawny leaping out of the bushes at her—large, tawny, and with a great gaping mouth. She tried desperately to cling to her saddle with one hand and to control her terrified horse with the other, but its frantic flight took him under a low branch, and she was swept off its back to land unceremoniously in the middle of the trail. She rolled to her hands and knees and then froze as she faced the beast that had so clumsily burst forth from concealment.

She saw at once that the lion was not very old. She noted that, though his body was fully developed, he had only a half-grown mane. Clearly, he was an adolescent, unskilled at hunting. He roared with frustration as he watched the fleeing horse disappear back down the trail, and his tail lashed. The princess felt a momentary touch of amusement—he was so young, so awkward. Then her amusement was replaced by irritation with this clumsy young beast who had caused her humiliating un-horsing. She rose to her feet, brushed off her knees, and looked at him sternly. "Shoo!" she said with an insistent flip of her hand. She was, after all, a princess, and he was only a lion—a very young and foolish lion.

The yellow eyes fell on her then and narrowed slightly. The lashing tail grew suddenly quite still. The young lion's eyes widened with a sort of dreadful intensity, and he crouched, his belly going low to the ground. His upper lip lifted to reveal his very long, white teeth. He took one slow step toward her, his great paw touching down softly.

"Don't you dare," she told him indignantly.

"Remain quite still, Highness," Mandorallen warned her in a deathly quiet voice. From the corner of her eye she saw him slide out of his saddle. The lion's eyes flickered toward him with annoyance.

Carefully, one step at a time, Mandorallen crossed the in-tervening space until he had placed his armored body between the lion and the princess. The lion watched him warily, not seeming to realize what he was doing until it was too late. Then, cheated of another meal, the cat's eyes went flat with rage. Mandorallen drew his sword very carefully; then, to Ce'Nedra's amazement, he passed it back hilt-first to her. "So that thou shalt have means of defending thyself, should I fail to withstand him," the knight explained.

Doubtfully, Ce'Nedra took hold of the huge hilt with both hands. When Mandorallen released his grip on the blade, how-ever, the point dropped immediately to the ground. Try though she might, Ce'Nedra could not even lift the huge sword.

Snarling, the lion crouched even lower. His tail lashed fu-riously for a moment, then stiffened out behind him. "Man-dorallen, look out!" Ce'Nedra screamed, still struggling with the sword.

The lion leaped.

Mandorallen flung his steel-cased arms wide and stepped forward to meet the cat's charge. They came together with a resounding crash, and Mandorallen locked his arms around the beast's body. The lion wrapped his huge paws around Mandorallen's shoulders and his claws screeched deafeningly as they raked the steel of the knight's armor. His teeth grated and ground as he gnawed and bit at Mandorallen's helmeted head. Mandorallen tightened his deadly embrace.

Ce'Nedra scrambled out of the way, dragging the sword behind her, and stared wide-eyed with fright at the dreadful struggle.

The lion's clawing became more desperate, and great, deep scratches appeared on Mandorallen's armor as the Mimbrate's arms tightened inexorably. The roars became yowls of pain, and the lion struggled now not to fight or kill, but to escape. He wriggled and thrashed and tried to bite. His hind paws came up to rake furiously on Mandorallen's armored trunk. His yowls grew more shrill, more filled with panic.

With a superhuman effort, Mandorallen jerked his arms together. Ce'Nedra heard the cracking of bones with a sickening clarity, and an enormous fountain of blood erupted from the cat's mouth. The young lion's body quivered, and his head dropped. Mandorallen unclenched his locked hands, and the dead beast slid limply from his grasp to the ground at his feet.

Stunned, the princess stared at the stupendous man in blood-smeared and clawed armor standing before her. She had just witnessed the impossible. Mandorallen had killed a lion with no weapon but his mighty arms—and all for her! Without knowing why, she found herself crowing with delight. "Mandorallen!" She sang his name. "You are *my* knight!"

Still panting from his efforts, Mandorallen pushed up his visor. His blue eyes were wide, as if her words had struck him with a stunning impact. Then he sank to his knees before her. "Your Highness," he said in a choked voice, "I pledge to thee here upon the body of this beast to be thy true and faithful knight for so long as I have breath."

Deep inside her, Ce'Nedra felt a profound sort of click— the sound of two things, fated from time's beginning to come together, finally meeting. Something—she did not know exactly what—but something very important had happened there in that sun-dappled glade.

And then Barak, huge and imposing, came galloping up the trail with Hettar at his side and the others not far behind. "What happened?" the big Cherek demanded, swinging down from his horse.

Ce'Nedra waited until they had all reined in to make her announcement. "The lion there attacked me," she said, trying to make it sound like an everyday occurrence. "Mandorallen killed him with his bare hands."

"I was in fact wearing these, Highness," the still-kneeling knight reminded her, holding up his gauntleted fists.

"It was the bravest thing I've ever seen in my life," Ce'Nedra swept on.

"Why are you down on your knees?" Barak asked Mandorallen. "Are you hurt?"

"I have just made Sir Mandorallen my very own knight," Ce'Nedra declared, "and as is quite proper, he knelt to receive that honor from my hands." From the corner of her eye she saw Garion in the act of sliding down from his horse. He was scowling like a thundercloud. Silently, Ce'Nedra exulted. Leaning forward then, she placed a sisterly kiss on Mandorallen's brow. "Rise, Sir Knight," she commanded, and Mandorallen creaked to his feet.

Ce'Nedra was enormously pleased with herself.

The remainder of the day passed without incident. They crossed a low range of hills and came down into a little valley as the sun settled slowly into a cloudbank off to the west. The valley was watered by a small stream, sparkling and cold, and they stopped there to set up their night's encampment. Mandorallen, in his new role as knight-protector, was suitably attentive, and Ce'Nedra accepted his service graciously, casting occasional covert glances at Garion to be certain that he was noticing everything.

Somewhat later, when Mandorallen had gone to see to his horse and Garion had stomped off to sulk, she sat demurely on a moss-covered log congratulating herself on the day's accomplishments.

"You're playing a cruel game, Princess," Durnik told her bluntly from the spot a few feet away where he was building a fire.

Ce'Nedra was startled. So far as she could remember, Durnik had never spoken directly to her since she had joined the party. The smith was obviously uncomfortable in the presence of royalty and, indeed, seemed actually to avoid her. Now, however, he looked straight into her face, and his tone was reproving.

"I don't know what you're talking about," she declared.

"I think you do." His plain, honest face was serious, and his gaze was steady.

Ce'Nedra lowered her eyes and flushed slowly.

"I've seen village girls play this same game," he continued. "Nothing good ever comes of it."

"I'm not trying to hurt anybody, Durnik. There isn't really anything of that sort between Mandorallen and me—we both know that."

"Garion doesn't."

Ce'Nedra was amazed. "Garion?"

"Isn't that what it's all about?"

"Of course not!" she objected indignantly.

Durnik's look was profoundly skeptical.

"Such a thing never entered my mind," Ce'Nedra rushed on. "It's absolutely absurd."

"Really?"

Ce'Nedra's bold front collapsed. "He's so stubborn," she complained. "He just won't do anything the way he's supposed to."

"He's an honest boy. Whatever else he is or might become, he's still the plain, simple boy he was at Faldor's farm. He doesn't know the rules of the gentry. He won't lie to you or flatter you or say things he doesn't really feel. I think something very important is going to happen to him before very long— I don't know what—but I do know it's going to take all his strength and courage. Don't weaken him with all this childishness."

"Oh, Durnik," she said with a great sigh. "What am I going to do?"

"Be honest. Say only what's in your heart. Don't say one thing and mean another. That won't work with him."

"I know. That's what makes it all so difficult. He was raised one way, and I was raised another. We're never going to get along." She sighed again.

Durnik smiled, a gentle, almost whimsical smile. "It's not all that bad, Princess," he told her. "You'll fight a great deal at first. You're almost as stubborn as he is, you know. You were born in different parts of the world, but you're not really all that different inside. You'll shout at each other and shake your fingers in each others' faces; but in time that will pass, and you won't even remember what you were shouting about. Some of the best marriages I know of started that way."

"Marriage!"

"That's what you've got in mind, isn't it?"

She stared at him incredulously. Then she suddenly laughed. "Dear, dear Durnik," she said. "You don't understand at all, do you?"

"I understand what I see," he replied. "And what I see is a young girl doing everything she possibly can to catch a young man."

Ce'Nedra sighed. "That's completely out of the question, you know—even if I felt that way—which of course I don't."

"Naturally not." He looked slightly amused.

"Dear Durnik," she said again, "I can't even allow myself such thoughts. You forget who I am."

"That isn't very likely," he told her. "You're usually very careful to keep the fact firmly in front of everybody."

"Don't you know what it means?"

He looked a bit perplexed. "I don't quite follow."

"I'm an Imperial Princess, the jewel of the Empire, and I *belong* to the Empire. I'll have absolutely no voice in the decision about whom I'm going to marry. That decision will be made by my father and the Council of Advisers. My husband will be rich and powerful—probably much older than I am—and my marriage to him will be to the advantage of the Empire and the House of Borune. I probably won't even be consulted in the matter."

Durnik looked stunned. "That's outrageous!" he objected.

"Not really," she told him. "My family has the right to protect its interests, and I'm an extremely valuable asset to the Borunes." She sighed again, a forlorn little sigh. "It might be nice, though—to be able to choose for myself, I mean. If I could, I might even look at Garion the way you seem to think I have been looking—even though he's absolutely impossible. The way things are, though, all he can ever be is a friend."

"I didn't know," he apologized, his plain, practical face melancholy.

"Don't take it so seriously, Durnik," she said lightly. "I've always known that this was the way things have to be."

A large, glistening tear, however, welled into the corner of her eye, and Durnik awkwardly put his work-worn hand on her arm to comfort her. Without knowing why, she threw her arms around his neck, buried her face in his chest, and sobbed.

"There, there," he said, clumsily patting her shaking shoulder. "There, there."

Chapter Three

GARION DID NOT sleep well that night. Although he was young and inexperienced, he was not stupid, and Princess Ce'Nedra had been fairly obvious. Over the months since she had joined them, he had seen her attitude toward him change until they had shared a rather specialized kind of friendship. He liked her; she liked him. Everything had been fine up to that point. Why couldn't she just leave it alone? Garion surmised that it probably had something to do with the inner workings of the female mind. As soon as a friendship passed a certain point—some obscure and secret boundary—a woman quite automatically became overwhelmed by a raging compulsion to complicate things.

He was almost certain that her transparent little game with Mandorallen had been aimed at *him*, and he wondered if it might not be a good idea to warn the knight to spare him more heartbreak in the future. Ce'Nedra's toying with the great man's affections was little more than the senseless cruelty of a spoiled child. Mandorallen must be warned. His Arendish thick-headedness might easily cause him to overlook the obvious.

And yet, Mandorallen *had* killed the lion for her. Such stupendous bravery could quite easily have overwhelmed the flighty little princess. What if her admiration and gratitude had pushed her over the line into infatuation? That possibility, coming to Garion as it did in those darkest hours just before dawn, banished all possibility of further sleep. He arose the next morning sandy-eyed and surly and with a terrible worry gnawing at him.

As they rode out through the blue-tinged shadows of early morning with the slanting rays of the newly risen sun gleaming on the treetops above them, Garion fell in beside his grandfather, seeking the comfort of the old man's companionship. It was not only that, however. Ce'Nedra was riding demurely with Aunt Pol just ahead, and Garion felt very strongly that he should keep an eye on her.

Mister Wolf rode in silence, looking cross and irritable, and he frequently dug his fingers under the splint on his left arm.

"Leave it alone, father," Aunt Pol told him without turning around.

"It itches."

"That's because it's healing. Just leave it alone."

He grumbled about that under his breath.

"Which route are you planning to take to the Vale?" she asked him.

"We'll go around by way of Tol Rane," he replied.

"The season's moving on, father," she reminded him. "If we take too long, we'll run into bad weather in the mountains."

"I know that, Pol. Would you rather cut straight across Maragor?"

"Don't be absurd."

"Is Maragor really all that dangerous?" Garion asked.

Princess Ce'Nedra turned in her saddle and gave him a withering look. "Don't you know *anything*?" she asked him with towering superiority.

Garion drew himself up, a dozen suitable responses to that coming to mind almost at once.

Mister Wolf shook his head warningly. "Just let it pass," the old man told him. "It's much too early to start in on that just now."

Garion clenched his teeth together.

They rode for an hour or more through the cool morning, and Garion gradually felt his temper improving. Then Hettar rode up to speak with Mister Wolf. "There are some riders coming," he reported.

"How many?" Wolf asked quickly.

"A dozen or more—coming in from the west."

"They could be Tolnedrans."

"I'll see," Aunt Pol murmured. She lifted her face and closed her eyes for a moment. "No," she said. "Not Tolnedrans. Murgos."

Hettar's eyes went flat. "Do we fight?" he asked with a dreadful kind of eagerness, his hand going to his sabre.

"No," Wolf replied curtly. "We hide."

"There aren't really that many of them."

"Never mind, Hettar," Wolf told him. "Silk," he called ahead, "there are some Murgos coming toward us from the west. Warn the others and find us all a place to hide."

Silk nodded curtly and galloped forward.

"Are there any Grolims with them?" the old man asked Aunt Pol.

"I don't think so," she answered with a small frown. "One of them has a strange mind, but he doesn't seem to be a Grolim."

Silk rode back quickly. "There's a thicket off to the right," he told them. "It's big enough to hide in."

"Let's go, then," Wolf said.

The thicket was fifty yards back among the larger trees. It appeared to be a patch of dense brush surrounding a small hollow. The ground in the hollow was marshy, and there was a spring at its center.

Silk had swung down from his horse and was hacking a thick bush off close to the ground with his short sword. "Take cover in here," he told them. "I'll go back and brush out our tracks." He picked up the bush and wormed his way out of the thicket.

"Be sure the horses don't make any noise," Wolf told Hettar.

Hettar nodded, but his eyes showed his disappointment.

Garion dropped to his knees and wormed his way through the thick brush until he reached the edge of the thicket; then he sank down on the leaves covering the ground to peer out between the gnarled and stumpy trunks.

Silk, walking backward and swinging his bush, was sweeping leaves and twigs from the forest floor over the tracks they had made from the trail to the thicket. He was moving quickly, but was careful to obliterate their trail completely.

From behind him, Garion heard a faint snap and rustle in the leaves, and Ce'Nedra crawled up and sank to the ground at his side. "You shouldn't be this close to the edge of the brush," he told her in a low voice.

"Neither should you," she retorted.

He let that pass. The princess had a warm, flowerlike smell; for some reason, that made Garion very nervous.

"How far away do you think they are?" she whispered.

"How would I know?"

"You're a sorcerer, aren't you?"

"I'm not that good at it."

Silk finished brushing away the tracks and stood for a moment studying the ground as he looked for any trace of their passage he might have missed. Then he burrowed his way into the thicket and crouched down a few yards from Garion and Ce'Nedra.

"Lord Hettar wanted to fight them," Ce'Nedra whispered to Garion.

"Hettar always wants to fight when he sees Murgos."

"Why?"

"The Murgos killed his parents when he was very young. He had to watch while they did it."

She gasped. "How awful!"

"If you children don't mind," Silk said sarcastically, "I'm trying to listen for horses."

Somewhere beyond the trail they had just left, Garion heard the thudding sound of horses' hooves moving at a trot. He sank down deeper into the leaves and watched, scarcely breathing.

When the Murgos appeared, there were about fifteen of them, mail-shirted and with the scarred cheeks of their race. Their leader, however, was a man in a patched and dirty tunic and with coarse black hair. He was unshaven, and one of his eyes was out of line with its fellow. Garion knew him.

Silk drew in a sharp breath with an audible hiss. "Brill," he muttered.

"Who's Brill?" Ce'Nedra whispered to Garion.

"I'll tell you later," he whispered back. "Shush!"

"Don't shush me!" she flared.

A stern look from Silk silenced them.

Brill was talking sharply to the Murgos, gesturing with short, jerky movements. Then he raised his hands with his fingers widespread and stabbed them forward to emphasize what he was saying. The Murgos all nodded, their faces expressionless, and spread out along the trail, facing the woods and the thicket where Garion and the others were hiding. Brill moved farther up the trail. "Keep your eyes open," he shouted to them. "Let's go."

The Murgos started to move forward at a walk, their eyes searching. Two of them rode past the thicket so close that Garion could smell the sweat on their horses' flanks.

"I'm getting tired of that man," one of them remarked to the other.

"I wouldn't let it show," the second one advised.

"I can take orders as well as any man," the first one said,

"but that one's beginning to irritate me. I think he would look better with a knife between his shoulder blades."

"I don't think he'd like that much, and it might be a little hard to manage."

"I could wait until he was asleep."

"I've never seen him sleep."

"Everybody sleeps—sooner or later."

"It's up to you," the second replied with a shrug, "but I wouldn't try anything rash—unless you've given up the idea of ever seeing Rak Hagga again."

The two of them moved on out of earshot.

Silk crouched, gnawing nervously at a fingernail. His eyes had narrowed to slits, and his sharp little face was intent. Then he began to swear under his breath.

"What's wrong, Silk?" Garion whispered to him.

"I've made a mistake," Silk answered irritably. "Let's go back to the others." He turned and crawled through the bushes toward the spring at the center of the thicket.

Mister Wolf was seated on a log, scratching absently at his splinted arm. "Well?" he asked, looking up.

"Fifteen Murgos," Silk replied shortly. "And an old friend."

"It was Brill," Garion reported. "He seemed to be in charge."

"Brill?" The old man's eyes widened with surprise.

"He was giving orders and the Murgos were following them," Silk said. "They didn't like it much, but they were doing what he told them to do. They seemed to be afraid of him. I think Brill's something more than an ordinary hireling."

"Where's Rak Hagga?" Ce'Nedra asked.

Wolf looked at her sharply.

"We heard two of them talking," she explained. "They said they were from Rak Hagga. I thought I knew the names of all the cities in Cthol Murgos, but I've never heard of that one."

"You're sure they said Rak Hagga?" Wolf asked her, his eyes intent.

"I heard them too," Garion told him. "That was the name they used—Rak Hagga."

Mister Wolf stood up, his face suddenly grim. "We're going to have to hurry then. Taur Urgas is preparing for war."

"How do you know that?" Barak asked him.

"Rak Hagga's a thousand leagues south of Rak Goska, and the southern Murgos are never brought up into this part of the world unless the Murgo king is on the verge of going to war with someone."

"Let them come," Barak said with a bleak smile.

"If it's all the same to you, I'd like to get our business attended to first. I've got to go to Rak Cthol, and I'd prefer not to have to wade through whole armies of Murgos to get there." The old man shook his head angrily. "What *is* Taur Urgas thinking of?" he burst out. "It's not time yet."

Barak shrugged. "One time's as good as another."

"Not for *this* war. Too many things have to happen first. Can't Ctuchik keep a leash on that maniac?"

"Unpredictability is part of Taur Urgas' unique charm," Silk observed sardonically. "He doesn't know himself what he's going to do from one day to the next."

"Knowest thou the king of the Murgos?" Mandorallen inquired.

"We've met," Silk replied. "We're not fond of each other."

"Brill and his Murgos should be gone by now," Mister Wolf said. "Let's move on. We've got a long way to go, and time's starting to catch up with us." He moved quickly toward his horse.

Shortly before sundown they went through a high pass lying in a notch between two mountains and stopped for the night in a little glen a few miles down on the far side.

"Keep the fire down as much as you can, Durnik," Mister Wolf warned the smith. "Southern Murgos have sharp eyes and they can see the light from a fire from miles away. I'd rather not have company in the middle of the night."

Durnik nodded soberly and dug his firepit somewhat deeper than usual.

Mandorallen was attentive to the Princess Ce'Nedra as they set up for the night, and Garion watched sourly. Though he had violently objected each time Aunt Pol had insisted that he serve as Ce'Nedra's personal attendant, now that the tiny girl had her knight to fetch and carry for her, Garion felt somehow that his rightful position had in some way been usurped.

"We're going to have to pick up our pace," Wolf told them after they had finished a meal of bacon, bread, and cheese. "We've got to get through the mountains before the first storms hit, and we're going to have to try to stay ahead of Brill and his Murgos." He scraped a space clear on the ground in front of him with one foot, picked up a stick and began sketching a map in the dirt. "We're here." He pointed. "Maragor's directly ahead of us. We'll circle to the west, go through Tol Rane, and then strike northeast toward the Vale."

"Might it not be shorter to cross Maragor?" Mandorallen suggested, pointing at the crude map.

"Perhaps," the old man replied, "but we won't do that unless we have to. Maragor's haunted, and it's best to avoid it if possible."

"We are not children to be frightened of insubstantial shades," Mandorallen declared somewhat stiffly.

"No one's doubting your courage, Mandorallen," Aunt Pol told him, "but the spirit of Mara wails in Maragor. It's better not to offend him."

"How far is it to the Vale of Aldur?" Durnik asked.

"Two hundred and fifty leagues," Wolf answered. "We'll be a month or more in the mountains, even under the best conditions. Now we'd better all get some sleep. Tomorrow's likely to be a hard day."

Chapter Four

WHEN THEY ROSE the next morning as the first pale hint of light was appearing on the eastern horizon, there was a touch of silvery frost on the ground and a thin scum of ice around the edges of the spring at the bottom of the glen. Ce'Nedra, who had gone to the spring to wash her face, lifted a leaf-thin shard from the water and stared at it.

"It's much colder up in the mountains," Garion told her as he belted on his sword.

"I'm aware of that," she replied loftily.

"Forget it," he said shortly and stamped away, muttering.

They rode down out of the mountains in the bright morning sunlight, moving at a steady trot. As they rounded a shoulder of outcropping rock, they saw the broad basin that had once been Maragor, the District of the Marags, stretching out below them. The meadows were a dusty autumn green, and the streams and lakes sparkled in the sun. A tumbled ruin, looking tiny in the distance, gleamed far out on the plain.

Princess Ce'Nedra, Garion noticed, kept her eyes averted, refusing even to look.

Not far down the slope below them, a cluster of crude huts and lopsided tents lay in a steep gully where a frothy creek had cut down through the rocks and gravel. Dirt streets and paths wandered crookedly up and down the sides of the gully, and a dozen or so ragged-looking men were hacking somewhat dispiritedly at the creek bank with picks and mattocks, turning the water below the shabby settlement a muddy yellow brown.

41

"A town?" Durnik questioned. "Out here?"

"Not exactly a town," Wolf replied. "The men in those settlements sift gravel and dig up the streambanks, looking for gold."

"Is there gold here?" Silk asked quickly, his eyes bright.

"A little," Wolf said. "Probably not enough to make it worth anyone's time to look for it."

"Why do they bother, then?"

Wolf shrugged. "Who knows?"

Mandorallen and Barak took the lead, and they moved down the rocky trail toward the settlement. As they approached, two men came out of one of the huts with rusty swords in their hands. One, a thin, unshaven man with a high forehead, wore a greasy Tolnedran jerkin. The other, much taller and bulkier, was dressed in the ragged tunic of an Arendish serf.

"That's far enough," the Tolnedran shouted. "We don't let armed men come in here until we know what their business is."

"You're blocking the trail, friend," Barak advised him. "You might find that unhealthy."

"One shout from me will bring fifty armed men," the Tolnedran warned.

"Don't be an idiot, Reldo," the big Arend told him. "That one with all the steel on him is a Mimbrate knight. There aren't enough men on the whole mountain to stop him, if he decides to go through here." He looked warily at Mandorallen. "What're your intentions, Sir Knight?" he asked respectfully.

"We are but following the trail," Mandorallen replied. "We have no interest in thy community."

The Arend grunted. "That's good enough for me. Let them pass, Reldo." He slid his sword back under his rope belt.

"What if he's lying?" Reldo retorted. "What if they're here to steal our gold?"

"What gold, you jackass?" the Arend demanded with contempt. "There isn't enough gold in the whole camp to fill a thimble—and Mimbrate knights don't lie. If you want to fight with him, go ahead. After it's over, we'll scoop up what's left of you and dump you in a hole someplace."

"You've got a bad mouth, Berig," Reldo observed darkly. "And what do you plan to do about it?"

The Tolnedran glared at the larger man and then turned and walked away, muttering curses.

Berig laughed harshly, then turned back to Mandorallen. "Come ahead, Sir Knight," he invited. "Reldo's all mouth. You don't have to worry about him."

Mandorallen moved forward at a walk. "Thou art a long way from home, my friend."

Berig shrugged. "There wasn't anything in Arendia to keep me, and I had a misunderstanding with my lord over a pig. When he started talking about hanging, I thought I'd like to try my luck in a different country."

"Seems like a sensible decision." Barak laughed.

Berig winked at him. "The trail goes right on down to the creek," he told them, "then up the other side behind those shacks. The men over there are Nadraks, but the only one who might give you any trouble is Tarlek. He got drunk last night, though, so he's probably still sleeping it off."

A vacant-eyed man in Sendarian clothing shambled out of one of the tents. Suddenly he lifted his face and howled like a dog. Berig picked up a rock and shied it at him. The Sendar dodged the rock and ran yelping behind one of the shacks. "One of these days I'm going to do him a favor and stick a knife in him," Berig remarked sourly. "He bays at the moon all night long."

"What's his problem?" Barak asked.

Berig shrugged. "Crazy. He thought he could make a dash into Maragor and pick up some gold before the ghosts caught him. He was wrong."

"What did they do to him?" Durnik asked, his eyes wide.

"Nobody knows," Berig replied. "Every so often somebody gets drunk or greedy and thinks he can get away with it. It wouldn't do any good, even if the ghosts didn't catch you. Anybody coming out is stripped immediately by his friends. Nobody gets to keep any gold he brings out, so why bother?"

"You've got a charming society here," Silk observed wryly.

Berig laughed. "It suits me. It's better than decorating a tree in my lord's apple orchard back in Arendia." He scratched absently at one armpit. "I guess I'd better go do some digging," he sighed. "Good luck." He turned and started toward one of the tents.

"Let's move along," Wolf said quietly. "These places tend to get rowdy as the day wears on."

"You seem to know quite a bit about them, father," Aunt Pol noticed.

"They're good places to hide," he replied. "Nobody asks any questions. I've needed to hide a time or two in my life."

"I wonder why?"

They started along the dusty street between the slapped-together shacks and patched tents, moving down toward the roiling creek.

"Wait!" someone called from behind. A scruffy-looking Drasnian was running after them, waving a small leather pouch. He caught up with them, puffing. "Why didn't you wait?" he demanded.

"What do you want?" Silk asked him.

"I'll give you fifty pennyweight of fine gold for the girl," the Drasnian panted, waving his leather sack again.

Mandorallen's face went bleak, and his hand moved toward his sword hilt.

"Why don't you let me deal with this, Mandorallen?" Silk suggested mildly, swinging down from his saddle.

Ce'Nedra's expression had first registered shock, then outrage. She appeared almost on the verge of explosion before Garion reached her and put his hand on her arm. "Watch," he told her softly.

"How dare—"

"Hush. Just watch. Silk's going to take care of it."

"That's a pretty paltry offer," Silk said, his fingers flicking idly.

"She's still young," the other Drasnian pointed out. "She obviously hasn't had much training yet. Which one of you owns her?"

"We'll get to that in a moment," Silk replied. "Surely you can make a better offer than that."

"It's all I've got," the scruffy man answered plaintively, waving his fingers, "and I don't want to go into partnership with any of the brigands in this place. I'd never get to see any of the profits."

Silk shook his head. "I'm sorry," he refused. "It's out of the question. I'm sure you can see our position."

Ce'Nedra was making strangled noises.

"Be quiet," Garion snapped. "This isn't what it seems to be."

"What about the older one?" the scruffy man suggested, sounding desperate. "Surely fifty pennyweight's a good price for her."

Without warning Silk's fist lashed out, and the scruffy Drasnian reeled back from the apparent blow. His hand flew to his mouth, and he began to spew curses.

"Run him off, Mandorallen," Silk said quite casually.

The grim-faced knight drew his broadsword and moved his warhorse deliberately at the swearing Drasnian. After one startled yelp, the man turned and fled.

"What did he say?" Wolf asked Silk. "You were standing in front of him, so I couldn't see."

"The whole region's alive with Murgos," Silk replied, climbing back on his horse. "Kheran says that a dozen parties of them have been through here in the last week."

"You *knew* that animal?" Ce'Nedra demanded.

"Kheran? Of course. We went to school together."

"Drasnians like to keep an eye on things, Princess," Wolf told her. "King Rhodar has agents everywhere."

"That awful man is an agent of King Rhodar?" Ce'Nedra asked incredulously.

Silk nodded. "Actually Kheran's a margrave," he said. "He has exquisite manners under normal circumstances. He asked me to convey his compliments."

Ce'Nedra looked baffled.

"Drasnians talk to each other with their fingers," Garion explained. "I thought everybody knew that."

Ce'Nedra's eyes narrowed at him.

"What Kheran actually said was, 'Tell the red-haired wench

that I apologize for the insult,'" Garion informed her smugly. "He needed to talk to Silk, and he had to have an excuse."

"Wench?"

"His word, not mine," Garion replied quickly.

"You know this sign language?"

"Naturally."

"That'll do, Garion," Aunt Pol said firmly.

"Kheran recommends that we get out of here immediately," Silk told Mister Wolf. "He says that the Murgos are looking for somebody—us, probably."

From the far side of the camp there were sudden angry voices. Several dozen Nadraks boiled out of their shanties to confront a group of Murgo horsemen who had just ridden up out of a deep gully. At the forefront of the Nadraks hulked a huge, fat man who looked more animal than human. In his right hand he carried a brutal-looking steel mace. "Kordoch!" he bellowed. "I told you I'd kill you next time you came here."

The man who stepped out from among the Murgo horses to face the hulking Nadrak was Brill. "You've told me a lot of things, Tarlek," he shouted back.

"This time you get what's coming to you, Kordoch," Tarlek roared, striding forward and swinging his mace.

"Stay back," Brill warned, stepping away from the horses. "I don't have time for this right now."

"You don't have any time left at all, Kordoch—for anything."

Barak was grinning broadly. "Would anyone like to take this opportunity to say good-bye to our friend over there?" he said. "I think he's about to leave on a very long journey."

But Brill's right hand had dipped suddenly inside his tunic. With a flickering movement, he whipped out a peculiar-looking triangular steel object about six inches across. Then, in the same movement, he flipped it, spinning and whistling, directly at Tarlek. The flat steel triangle sailed, flashing in the sun as it spun, and disappeared with a sickening sound of shearing bone into the hulking Nadrak's chest. Silk hissed with amazement.

Tarlek stared stupidly at Brill, his mouth agape and his left hand going to the spurting hole in his chest. Then his mace slid out of his right hand, his knees buckled, and he fell heavily forward.

"Let's get out of here!" Mister Wolf barked. "Down the creek! Go!"

They plowed into the rocky streambed at a plunging gallop, and the muddy water sprayed out from under their horses' hooves. After several hundred yards they turned sharply to scramble up a steep gravel bank.

"That way!" Barak shouted, pointing toward more level ground. Garion did not have time to think, only to cling to his horse and try to keep up with the others. Faintly, far behind, he could hear shouts.

They rode behind a low hill and reined in for a moment at Wolf's signal. "Hettar," the old man said, "see if they're coming."

Hettar wheeled his horse and loped up to a stand of trees on the brow of the hill.

Silk was muttering curses, his face livid.

"What's your problem now?" Barak demanded.

Silk kept on swearing.

"What's got him so worked up?" Barak asked Mister Wolf.

"Our friend's just had a nasty shock," the old man answered. "He misjudged somebody—so did I, as a matter of fact. That weapon Brill used on the big Nadrak is called an adder-sting."

Barak shrugged. "It looked like just an odd-shaped throwing knife to me."

"There's a bit more to it than that," Wolf told him. "It's as sharp as a razor on all three sides, and the points are usually dipped in poison. It's the special weapon of the Dagashi. That's what has got Silk so upset."

"I should have known," Silk berated himself. "Brill's been a little too good all along to be just an ordinary Sendarian footpad."

"Do you know what they're talking about, Polgara?" Barak asked.

"The Dagashi are a secret society in Cthol Murgos," she told him. "Trained killers—assassins. They answer only to

Ctuchik and their own elders. Ctuchik's been using them for centuries to eliminate people who get in his way. They're very efficient."

"I've never been that curious about the peculiarities of Murgo culture," Barak replied. "If they want to creep around and kill each other, so much the better." He glanced up the hill quickly to find out if Hettar had seen anything behind them. "That thing Brill used might be an interesting toy, but it's no match for armor and a good sword."

"Don't be so provincial, Barak," Silk said, beginning to regain his composure. "A well-thrown adder-sting can cut right through a mail shirt; if you know how, you can even sail it around corners. Not only that, a Dagashi could kill you with his hands and feet, whether you're wearing armor or not." He frowned. "You know, Belgarath," he mused, "we might have been making a mistake all along. We assumed that Asharak was using Brill, but it might have been the other way around. Brill has to be good, or Ctuchik wouldn't have sent him into the West to keep an eye on us." He smiled then, a chillingly bleak little smile. "I wonder just how good he is." He flexed his fingers. "I've met a few Dagashi, but never one of their best. That might be very interesting."

"Let's not get sidetracked," Wolf told him. The old man's face was grim. He looked at Aunt Pol, and something seemed to pass between them.

"You're not serious," she said.

"I don't think we've got much choice, Pol. There are Murgos all around us—too many and too close. I don't have any room to move—they've got us pinned right up against the southern edge of Maragor. Sooner or later, we're going to get pushed out onto the plain anyway. At least, if we make the decision ourselves, we'll be able to take some precautions."

"I don't like it, father," she stated bluntly.

"I don't care much for it myself," he admitted, "but we've got to shake off all these Murgos or we'll never make it to the Vale before winter sets in."

Hettar rode back down the hill. "They're coming," he re-

ported quietly. "And there's another group of them circling in
from the west to cut us off."

Wolf drew in a deep breath. "I think that pretty well decides
it, Pol," he said. "Let's go."

As they passed into the belt of trees dotting the last low line
of hills bordering the plain, Garion glanced back once. A half
dozen dust clouds spotted the face of the miles-wide slope above
them. Murgos were converging on them from all over the
mountains.

They galloped on into the trees and thundered through a
shallow draw. Barak, riding in the lead, suddenly held up his
hand. "Men ahead of us," he warned.

"Murgos?" Hettar asked, his hand going to his sabre.

"I don't think so," Barak replied. "The one I saw looked
more like some of those we saw back at the settlement."

Silk, his eyes very bright, pushed his way to the front. "I've
got an idea," he said. "Let me talk to them." He pushed his
horse into a dead run, plunging directly into what seemed to
be an ambush. "Comrades!" he shouted. "Get ready! They're
coming—and they've got the gold!"

Several shabby-looking men with rusty swords and axes
rose from the bushes or stepped out from behind trees to sur-
round the little man. Silk was talking very fast, gesticulating,
waving his arms and pointing back toward the slope looming
behind them.

"What's he doing?" Barak asked.

"Something devious, I imagine," Wolf replied.

The men surrounding Silk looked dubious at first, but their
expressions gradually changed as he continued to talk excitedly.
Finally he turned in his saddle to look back. He jerked his arm
in a broad, overhead sweep. "Let's go!" he shouted. "They're
with us!" He spun his horse to scramble up the graveled side
of the gully.

"Don't get separated," Barak warned, shifting his shoulders
under his mail shirt. "I'm not sure what he's up to, but these
schemes of his sometimes fall apart."

They pounded down through the grim-looking brigands and

up the side of the gully on Silk's heels. "What did you say to them?" Barak shouted as they rode.

"I told them that fifteen Murgos had made a dash into Maragor and come out with three heavy packs of gold." The little man laughed. "Then I said that the men at the settlement had turned them back and that they were trying to double around this way with the gold. I told them that we'd cover this next gully if they'd cover that one back there."

"Those scoundrels will swarm all over Brill and his Murgos when they try to come through," Barak suggested.

"I know." Silk laughed. "Terrible, isn't it?"

They rode on at a gallop. After about a half mile, Mister Wolf raised his arm, and they all reined in. "This should be far enough," he told them. "Now listen very carefully, all of you. These hills are alive with Murgos, so we're going to have to go into Maragor."

Princess Ce'Nedra gasped, and her face turned deathly pale.

"It will be all right, dear," Aunt Pol soothed her.

Wolf's face was grimly serious. "As soon as we ride out onto the plain, you're going to start hearing certain things," he continued. "Don't pay any attention. Just keep riding. I'm going to be in the lead and I want you all to watch me very closely. As soon as I raise my hand, I want you to stop and get down off your horses immediately. Keep your eyes on the ground and don't look up, no matter what you hear. There are things out there that you don't want to see. Polgara and I are going to put you all into a kind of sleep. Don't try to fight us. Just relax and do exactly what we tell you to do."

"Sleep?" Mandorallen protested. "What if we are attacked? How may we defend ourselves if we are asleep?"

"There isn't anything alive out there to attack you, Mandorallen," Wolf told him. "And it isn't your body that needs to be protected; it's your mind."

"What about the horses?" Hettar asked.

"The horses will be all right. They won't even see the ghosts."

"I can't do it," Ce'Nedra declared, her voice hovering on the edge of hysteria. "I *can't* go into Maragor."

"Yes, you can, dear," Aunt Pol told her in that same calm, soothing voice. "Stay close to me. I won't let anything happen to you."

Garion felt a sudden profound sympathy for the frightened little girl, and he drew his horse over beside hers. "I'll be here, too," he told her.

She looked at him gratefully, but her lower lip still trembled, and her face was very pale.

Mister Wolf took a deep breath and glanced once at the long slope behind them. The dust clouds raised by the converging Murgos were much closer now. "All right," he said, "let's go." He turned his horse and began to ride at an easy trot down toward the mouth of the gully and the plain stretching out before them.

The sound at first seemed faint and very far away, almost like the murmur of wind among the branches of a forest or the soft babble of water over stones. Then, as they rode farther out onto the plain, it grew louder and more distinct. Garion glanced back once, almost longingly at the hills behind them. Then he pulled his horse close in beside Ce'Nedra's and locked his eyes on Mister Wolf's back, trying to close his ears.

The sound was now a chorus of moaning cries punctuated by occasional shrieks. Behind it all, and seeming to carry and sustain all the other sounds, was a dreadful wailing—a single voice surely, but so vast and all-encompassing that it seemed to reverberate inside Garion's head, erasing all thought.

Mister Wolf suddenly raised his hand, and Garion slid out of his saddle, his eyes fixed almost desperately on the ground. Something flickered at the edge of his vision, but he refused to look.

Then Aunt Pol was speaking to them, her voice calm, reassuring. "I want you to form a circle," she told them, "and take each others' hands. Nothing will be able to enter the circle, so you'll all be safe."

Trembling in spite of himself, Garion stretched out his hands. Someone took his left, he didn't know who; but he instantly knew that the tiny hand that clung so desperately to his right was Ce'Nedra's.

Aunt Pol stood in the center of their circle, and Garion could feel the force of her presence there washing over all of them. Somewhere outside the circle, he could feel Wolf. The old man was doing something that swirled faint surges through Garion's veins and set off staccato bursts of the familiar roaring sound.

The wailing of the dreadful, single voice grew louder, more intense, and Garion felt the first touches of panic. It was not going to work. They were all going to go mad.

"Hush, now," Aunt Pol's voice came to him, and he knew that she spoke inside his mind. His panic faded, and he felt a strange, peaceful lassitude. His eyes grew heavy, and the sound of the wailing grew fainter. Then, enfolded in a comforting warmth, he fell almost at once into a profound slumber.

Chapter Five

GARION WAS NOT exactly sure when it was that his mind shook off Aunt Pol's soft compulsion to sink deeper and deeper into protective unawareness. It could not have been long. Falteringly, like someone rising slowly from the depths, he swam back up out of sleep to find himself moving stiffly, even woodenly, toward the horses with the others. When he glanced at them, he saw that their faces were blank, uncomprehending. He seemed to hear Aunt Pol's whispered command to "sleep, sleep, sleep," but it somehow lacked the power necessary to compel him to obey.

There was to his consciousness, however, a subtle difference. Although his mind was awake, his emotions seemed not to be. He found himself looking at things with a calm, lucid detachment, uncluttered by those feelings which so often churned his thoughts into turmoil. He knew that in all probability he should tell Aunt Pol that he was not asleep, but for some obscure reason he chose not to. Patiently, he began to sort through the notions and ideas surrounding that decision, trying to isolate the single thought which he knew must lie behind the choice not to speak. In his search, he touched that quiet corner where the other mind stayed. He could almost sense its sardonic amusement.

"Well?" he said silently to it.

"I see that you're finally awake," the other mind said to him.

"No," Garion corrected rather meticulously, "actually a part of me is asleep, I think."

"That was the part that kept getting in the way. We can talk now. We have some things to discuss."

"Who are you?" Garion asked, absently following Aunt Pol's instructions to get back on his horse.

"I don't actually have a name."

"You're separate from me, though, aren't you? I mean, you're not just another part of me, are you?"

"No," the voice replied, "we're quite separate."

The horses were moving at a walk now, following Aunt Pol and Mister Wolf across the meadow.

"What do you want?" Garion asked.

"I need to make things come out the way they're supposed to. I've been doing that for a very long time now."

Garion considered that. Around him the wailing grew louder, and the chorus of moans and shrieks became more distinct. Filmy, half-formed tatters of shape began to appear, floating across the grass toward the horses. "I'm going to go mad, aren't I?" he asked somewhat regretfully. "I'm not asleep like the others are, and the ghosts will drive me mad, won't they?"

"I doubt it," the voice answered. "You'll see some things you'd probably rather not see, but I don't think it will destroy your mind. You might even learn some things about yourself that will be useful later on."

"You're very old, aren't you?" Garion asked as the thought occurred to him.

"That term doesn't have any meaning in my case."

"Older than my grandfather?" Garion persisted.

"I knew him when he was a child. It might make you feel better to know that he was even more stubborn than you are. It took me a very long time to get him started in the direction he was supposed to go."

"Did you do it from inside his mind?"

"Naturally."

Garion noted that his horse was walking obliviously through one of the filmy images that was taking shape in front of him. "Then he knows you, doesn't he—if you were in his mind, I mean?"

"He didn't know I was there."

"I've always known you were there."

"You're different. That's what we need to talk about."

Rather suddenly, a woman's head appeared in the air directly in front of Garion's face. The eyes were bulging, and the mouth was agape in a soundless scream. The ragged, hacked-off stump of its neck streamed blood that seemed to dribble off into nowhere. "Kiss me," it croaked at him. Garion closed his eyes as his face passed through the head.

"You see," the voice pointed out conversationally. "It's not as bad as you thought it was going to be."

"In what way am I different?" Garion wanted to know.

"Something needs to be done, and you're the one who's going to do it. All the others have just been in preparation for you."

"What is it exactly that I have to do?"

"You'll know when the time comes. If you find out too soon, it might frighten you." The voice took on a somewhat wry note. "You're difficult enough to manage without additional complications."

"Why are we talking about it then?"

"You need to know *why* you have to do it. That might help you when the time comes."

"All right," Garion agreed.

"A very long time ago, something happened that wasn't supposed to happen," the voice in his mind began. "The universe came into existence for a reason, and it was moving toward that purpose smoothly. Everything was happening the way it was supposed to happen, but then something went wrong. It wasn't really a very big thing, but it just happened to be in the right place at the right time—or perhaps in the wrong place at the wrong time might be a better way to put it. Anyway, it changed the direction of events. Can you understand that?"

"I think so," Garion replied, frowning with the effort. "Is it like when you throw a rock at something but it bounces off something else instead and goes where you don't want it to go—like the time Doroon threw that rock at the crow and it hit a tree limb and bounced off and broke Faldor's window instead?"

"That's exactly it," the voice congratulated him. "Up to that point there had always been only one possibility—the original one. Now there were suddenly two. Let's take it one step further. If Doroon—or you—had thrown another rock very quickly and hit the first rock before it got to Faldor's window, it's possible that the first rock might have been knocked back to hit the crow instead of the window."

"Maybe," Garion conceded doubtfully. "Doroon wasn't really that good at throwing rocks."

"I'm much better at it than Doroon," the voice told him. "That's the whole reason I came into existence in the first place. In a very special way, you are the rock that I've thrown. If you hit the other rock just right, you'll turn it and make it go where it was originally intended to go."

"And if I don't?"

"Faldor's window gets broken."

The figure of a naked woman with her arms chopped off and a sword thrust through her body was suddenly in front of Garion. She shrieked and moaned at him, and the stumps of her arms spurted blood directly into his face. Garion reached up to wipe off the blood, but his face was dry. Unconcerned, his horse walked through the gibbering ghost.

"We have to get things back on the right course," the voice

went on. "This certain thing you have to do is the key to the whole business. For a long time, what was supposed to happen and what was actually happening went off in different directions. Now they're starting to converge again. The point where they meet is the point where you'll have to act. If you succeed, things will be all right again; if you don't, everything will keep going wrong, and the purpose for which the universe came into existence will fail."

"How long ago was it when this started?"

"Before the world was made. Even before the Gods."

"Will I succeed?" Garion asked.

"I don't know," the voice replied. "I know what's supposed to happen—not what will. There's something else you need to know too. When this mistake occurred, it set off two separate lines of possibility, and a line of possibility has a kind of purpose. To have a purpose, there has to be awareness of that purpose. To put it rather simply, that's what I am—the awareness of the original purpose of the universe."

"Only now there's another one, too, isn't there?" Garion suggested. "Another awareness, I mean—one connected with the other set of possibilities."

"You're even brighter than I thought."

"And wouldn't it want things to keep going wrong?"

"I'm afraid so. Now we come to the important part. The spot in time where all this is going to be decided one way or another is getting very close, and you've got to be ready."

"Why me?" Garion asked, brushing away a disconnected hand that appeared to be trying to clutch at his throat. "Can't somebody else do it?"

"No," the voice told him. "That's not the way it works. The universe has been waiting for you for more millions of years than you could even imagine. You've been hurtling toward this event since before the beginning of time. It's yours alone. You're the only one who can do what needs to be done, and it's the most important thing that will ever happen—not just in this world but in all the worlds in all the universe. There are whole races of men on worlds so far away that the light from their suns will never reach this world, and they'll cease to exist if you fail. They'll never know you or thank you, but their entire existence depends on you. The other line of possibility leads to absolute chaos and the ultimate destruction of the universe, but you and I lead to something else."

"What?"

"If you're successful, you'll live to see it happen."

"All right," Garion said. "What do I have to do—now, I mean?"

"You have enormous power. It's been given to you so that you can do what you have to do, but you've got to learn how to use it. Belgarath and Polgara are trying to help you learn, so stop fighting with them about it. You've got to be ready when the time comes, and the time is much closer than you might think."

A decapitated figure stood in the trail, holding its head by the hair with its right hand. As Garion approached, the figure raised the head. The twisted mouth shrieked curses at him.

After he had ridden through the ghost, Garion tried to speak to the mind within his mind again, but it seemed to be gone for the moment.

They rode slowly past the tumbled stones of a ruined farmstead. Ghosts clustered thickly on the stones, beckoning and calling seductively.

"A disproportionate number seem to be women," Aunt Pol observed calmly to Mister Wolf.

"It was a peculiarity of the race," Wolf replied. "Eight out of nine births were female. It made certain adjustments necessary in the customary relationships between men and women."

"I imagine you found that entertaining," she said dryly.

"The Marags didn't look at things precisely the way other races do. Marriage never gained much status among them. They were quite liberal about certain things."

"Oh? Is that the term for it?"

"Try not to be so narrow-minded, Pol. The society functioned; that's what counts."

"There's a bit more to it than that, father," she said. "What about their cannibalism?"

"That was a mistake. Somebody misinterpreted a passage

in one of their sacred texts, that's all. They did it out of a sense of religious obligation, not out of appetite. On the whole, I rather liked the Marags. They were generous, friendly, and very honest with each other. They enjoyed life. If it hadn't been for the gold here, they'd probably have worked out their little aberration."

Garion had forgotten about the gold. As they crossed a small stream, he looked down into the sparkling water and saw the butter-yellow flecks glittering among the pebbles on the bottom.

A naked ghost suddenly appeared before him. "Don't you think I'm beautiful?" she leered. Then she took hold of the sides of the great slash that ran up her abdomen, pulled it open and spilled out her entrails in a pile on the bank of the stream.

Garion gagged and clenched his teeth together.

"Don't think about the gold!" the voice in his mind said sharply. "The ghosts come at you through your greed. If you think about gold, you'll go mad."

They rode on, and Garion tried to push the thought of gold out of his mind.

Mister Wolf, however, continued to talk about it. "That's always been the problem with gold. It seems to attract the worst kind of people—the Tolnedrans in this case."

"They were trying to stamp out cannibalism, father," Aunt Pol replied. "That's a custom most people find repugnant."

"I wonder how serious they'd have been about it if all that gold hadn't been lying on the bed of every stream in Maragor."

Aunt Pol averted her eyes from the ghost of a child impaled on a Tolnedran spear. "And now no one has the gold," she said. "Mara saw to that."

"Yes," Wolf agreed, lifting his face to listen to the dreadful wail that seemed to come from everywhere. He winced at a particularly shrill note in the wailing. "I wish he wouldn't scream so loud."

They passed the ruins of what appeared to have been a temple. The white stones were tumbled, and grass grew up among them. A broad tree standing nearby was festooned with hanging bodies, twisting and swinging on their ropes. "Let us down," the bodies murmured. "Let us down."

"Father!" Aunt Pol said sharply, pointing at the meadow beyond the fallen temple. "Over there! Those people are real."

A procession of robed and hooded figures moved slowly through the meadow, chanting in unison to the sound of a mournfully tolling bell supported on a heavy pole they carried on their shoulders.

"The monks of Mar Terrin," Wolf said. "Tolnedra's conscience. They aren't anything to worry about."

One of the hooded figures looked up and saw them. "Go back!" he shouted. He broke away from the others and ran toward them, recoiling often from things Garion could not see. "Go back!" he cried again. "Save yourselves! You approach the very center of the horror. Mar Amon lies just beyond that hill. Mara himself rages through its haunted streets!"

Chapter Six

THE PROCESSION OF monks moved on, the sound of their chanting and slowly tolling bell growing fainter as they crossed the meadow. Mister Wolf seemed deep in thought, the fingers of his good hand stroking his beard. Finally he sighed rather wryly. "I suppose we might as well deal with him here and now, Pol. He'll just follow us if we don't."

"You're wasting your time, father," Aunt Pol replied. "There's no way to reason with him. We've tried before."

"You're probably right," he agreed, "but we should try at least. Aldur would be disappointed if we didn't. Maybe when he finds out what's happening, he'll come around to the point where we can at least talk to him."

A piercing wail echoed across the sunny meadow, and Mister Wolf made a sour face. "You'd think that he'd have shrieked himself out by now. All right, let's go to Mar Amon." He turned his horse toward the hill the wild-eyed monk had pointed out to them. A maimed ghost gibbered at him from the air in front of his face. "Oh, stop that!" he said irritably. With a startled flicker, the ghost disappeared.

There had perhaps been a road leading over the hill at some time in the past. The faint track of it was dimly visible through the grass, but the thirty-two centuries which had passed since the last living foot had touched its surface had all but erased it. They wound to the top of the hill and looked down into the ruins of Mar Amon. Garion, still detached and unmoved, perceived and deduced things about the city he would not have otherwise noted. Though the destruction had been nearly total, the shape of the city was clearly evident. The street—for there was only one—was laid out in a spiral, winding in toward a broad, circular plaza in the precise center of the ruins. With a peculiar flash of insight, Garion became immediately convinced that the city had been designed by a woman. Men's minds ran to straight lines, but women thought more in terms of circles.

With Aunt Pol and Mister Wolf in the lead and the rest following in wooden-faced unconsciousness, they started down the hill to the city. Garion rode at the rear, trying to ignore the ghosts rising from the earth to confront him with their nudity and their hideous maiming. The wailing sound which they had heard from the moment they had entered Maragor grew louder, more distinct. The wail had sometimes seemed to be a chorus, confused and distorted by echos, but now Garion realized that it was one single, mighty voice, filled with a grief so vast that it reverberated through all the kingdom.

As they approached the city, a terrible wind seemed to come up, deadly chill and filled with an overpowering charnel-house stench. As Garion reached automatically to draw his cloak tighter about him, he saw that the cloak did not in any way react to that wind, and that the tall grass through which they rode did not bend before it. He considered it, turning it over in his mind as he tried to close his nostrils to the putrid stench of decay and corruption carried on that ghostly wind. If the wind did not move the grass, it could not be a real wind. Furthermore, if the horses could not hear the wails, they could not be real wails either. He grew colder and he shivered, even as he told himself that the chill—like the wind and the grief-laden howling—was spiritual rather than real.

Although Mar Amon, when he had first glimpsed it from the top of the hill, had appeared to be in total ruin, when they entered the city Garion was startled to see the substantial walls of houses and public buildings surrounding him; and some-where not far away he seemed to hear the sound of laughing children. There was also the sound of singing off in the distance.

"Why does he keep doing this?" Aunt Pol asked sadly. "It doesn't do any good."

"It's all he has, Pol," Mister Wolf replied.

"It always ends the same way, though."

"I know, but for a little while it helps him forget."

"There are things we'd all like to forget, father. This isn't the way to do it."

Wolf looked admiringly at the substantial-seeming houses around them. "It's very good, you know."

"Naturally," she said. "He's a God, after all—but it's still not good for him."

It was not until Barak's horse inadvertently stepped directly through one of the walls—disappearing through the solid-looking stone and then reemerging several yards farther down the street—that Garion understood what his Aunt and grandfather were talking about. The walls, the buildings, the whole city was an illusion—a memory. The chill wind with its stink of corruption seemed to grow stronger and carried with it now the added reek of smoke. Though Garion could still see the sunlight shining brightly on the grass, it seemed for some reason that it was growing noticeably darker. The laughter of children and the distant singing faded; instead, Garion heard screams.

A Tolnedran legionnaire in burnished breastplate and plumed helmet, as solid-looking as the walls around them, came running down the long curve of the street. His sword dripped blood, his face was fixed in a hideous grin, and his eyes were wild.

Hacked and mutilated bodies sprawled in the street now, and there was blood everywhere. The wailing climbed into a piercing shriek as the illusion moved on toward its dreadful climax.

The spiral street opened at last into the broad circular plaza at the center of Mar Amon. The icy wind seemed to howl through the burning city, and the dreadful sound of swords chopping through flesh and bone seemed to fill Garion's entire mind. The air grew even darker.

The stones of the plaza were thick with the illusory memory of uncounted scores of Marag dead lying beneath rolling clouds of dense smoke. But what stood in the center of the plaza was not an illusion, nor even a ghost. The figure towered and seemed to shimmer with a terrible presence, a reality that was in no way dependent upon the mind of the observer for its existence. In its arms it held the body of a slaughtered child that seemed somehow to be the sum and total of all the dead of haunted Maragor; and its face, lifted in anguish above the body of that dead child, was ravaged by an expression of inhuman grief. The figure wailed; and Garion, even in the half-somnolent state that protected his sanity, felt the hair on the back of his neck trying to rise in horror.

Mister Wolf grimaced and climbed down from his saddle. Carefully stepping over the illusions of bodies littering the plaza, he approached the enormous presence. "Lord Mara," he said, respectfully bowing to the figure.

Mara howled.

"Lord Mara," Wolf said again. "I would not lightly intrude myself upon thy grief, but I must speak with thee."

The dreadful face contorted, and great tears streamed down the God's cheeks. Wordlessly, Mara held out the body of the child and lifted his face and wailed.

"Lord Mara!" Wolf tried once again, more insistent this time.

Mara closed his eyes and bowed his head, sobbing over the body of the child.

"It's useless, father," Aunt Pol told the old man. "When he's like this, you can't reach him."

"Leave me, Belgarath," Mara said, still weeping. His huge voice rolled and throbbed in Garion's mind. "Leave me to my grief."

"Lord Mara, the day of the fulfillment of the prophecy is at hand," Wolf told him.

"What is that to me?" Mara sobbed, clutching the body of the child closer. "Will the prophecy restore my slaughtered children to me? I am beyond its reach. Leave me alone."

"The fate of the world hinges upon the outcome of events which will happen very soon, Lord Mara," Mister Wolf insisted. "The kingdoms of East and West are girding for the last war, and Torak One-Eye, thy accursed brother, stirs in his slumber and will soon awaken."

"Let him awaken," Mara replied and bowed down over the body in his arms as a storm of fresh weeping swept him.

"Wilt thou then submit to his dominion, Lord Mara?" Aunt Pol asked him.

"I am beyond his dominion, Polgara," Mara answered. "I will not leave this land of my murdered children, and no man or God will intrude upon me here. Let Torak have the world if he wants it."

"We might as well leave, father," Aunt Pol said. "Nothing's going to move him."

"Lord Mara," Mister Wolf said to the weeping God, "we have brought before thee the instruments of the prophecy. Wilt thou bless them before we go?"

"I have no blessings, Belgarath," Mara replied. "Only curses for the savage children of Nedra. Take these strangers and go."

"Lord Mara," Aunt Pol said firmly, "a part is reserved for thee in the working-out of the prophecy. The iron destiny which compels us all compels thee as well. Each must play that part laid out for him from the beginning of days, for in the day that the prophecy is turned aside from its terrible course, the world will be unmade."

"Let it be unmade," Mara groaned. "It holds no more joy for me, so let it perish. My grief is eternal, and I will not abandon it, though the cost be the unmaking of all that has been made. Take these children of the prophecy and depart."

Mister Wolf bowed with resignation, turned, and came back toward the rest of them. His expression registered a certain hopeless disgust.

"Wait!" Mara roared suddenly. The images of the city and its dead wavered and shimmered away. "What is this?" the God demanded.

Mister Wolf turned quickly.

"What hast thou done, Belgarath?" Mara accused, suddenly towering into immensity. "And thou, Polgara. Is my grief now an amusement for thee? Wilt thou cast my sorrow into my teeth?"

"My Lord?" Aunt Pol seemed taken aback by the God's sudden fury.

"Monstrous!" Mara roared. "Monstrous!" His huge face convulsed with rage. In terrible anger, he strode toward them and then stopped directly in front of the horse of Princess Ce'Nedra. "I will rend thy flesh!" he shrieked at her. "I will fill thy brain with the worms of madness, daughter of Nedra. I will sink thee in torment and horror for all the days of thy life."

"Leave her alone!" Aunt Pol said sharply.

"Nay, Polgara," he raged. "Upon her will fall the brunt of my wrath." His dreadful, clutching fingers reached out toward the uncomprehending princess, but she stared blankly through him, unflinching and unaware.

The God hissed with frustration and whirled to confront Mister Wolf. "Tricked!" he howled. "Her mind is asleep."

"They're all asleep, Lord Mara," Wolf replied. "Threats and horrors don't mean anything to them. Shriek and howl until the sky falls down; she cannot hear thee."

"I will punish thee for this, Belgarath," Mara snarled, "and Polgara as well. You will all taste pain and terror for this arrogant despite of me. I will wring the sleep from the minds of these intruders, and they will know the agony and madness I will visit upon them all." He swelled suddenly into vastness.

"That's enough! Mara! Stop!" The voice was Garion's, but Garion knew that it was not he who spoke.

The Spirit of Mara turned on him, raising his vast arm to strike, but Garion felt himself slide from his horse to approach the vast threatening figure. "Your vengeance stops here, Mara," the voice coming from Garion's mouth said. "The girl is bound to *my* purpose. You will not touch her." Garion realized with a certain alarm that he had been placed between the raging God and the sleeping princess.

"Move out of my way, boy, lest I slay thee," Mara threatened.

"Use your mind, Mara," the voice told him, "if you haven't howled it empty by now. You know who I am."

"I *will* have her!" Mara howled. "I will give her a multitude of lives and tear each one from her quivering flesh."

"No," the voice replied, "you *won't*."

The God Mara drew himself up again, raising his dreadful arms; but at the same time, his eyes were probing—and more than his eyes. Garion once again felt a vast touch on his mind as he had in Queen Salmissra's throne room when the Spirit of Issa had touched him. A dreadful recognition began to dawn in Mara's weeping eyes. His raised arms fell. "Give her to me," he pleaded. "Take the others and go, but give the Tolnedran to me. I beg it of thee."

"No."

What happened then was not sorcery—Garion knew it instantly. The noise was not there nor that strange, rushing surge that always accompanied sorcery. Instead, there seemed to be a terrible pressure as the full force of Mara's mind was directed crushingly at him. Then the mind within his mind responded. The power was so vast that the world itself was not large enough to contain it. It did not strike back at Mara, for that dreadful collision would have shattered the world, but it stood rather, calmly unmoved and immovable against the raging torrent of Mara's fury. For a fleeting moment, Garion shared the awareness of the mind within his mind, and he shuddered back from its immensity. In that instant, he saw the birth of uncounted suns swirling in vast spirals against the velvet blackness of the void, their birth and gathering into galaxies and ponderously turning nebulae encompassing but a moment. And beyond that, he looked full in the face of time itself—seeing its beginning and its ending in one awful glimpse.

Mara fell back. "I must submit," he said hoarsely, and then he bowed to Garion, his ravaged face strangely humble. He turned away and buried his face in his hands, weeping uncontrollably.

"Your grief will end, Mara," the voice said gently. "One day you will find joy again."

"Never," the God sobbed. "My grief will last forever."

"Forever is a very long time, Mara," the voice replied, "and only *I* can see to the end of it."

The weeping God did not answer, but moved away from them, and the sound of his wailing echoed again through the ruins of Mar Amon.

Mister Wolf and Aunt Pol were both staring at Garion with stunned faces. When the old man spoke, his voice was awed. "Is it possible?"

"Aren't you the one who keeps saying that anything is possible, Belgarath?"

"We didn't know you could intervene directly," Aunt Pol said.

"I nudge things a bit from time to time—make a few suggestions. If you think back carefully, you might even remember some of them."

"Is the boy aware of any of this?" she asked.

"Of course. We had a little talk about it."

"How much did you tell him?"

"As much as he could understand. Don't worry, Polgara, I'm not going to hurt him. He realizes how important all this is now. He knows that he needs to prepare himself and that he doesn't have a great deal of time for it. I think you'd better leave here now. The Tolnedran girl's presence is causing Mara a great deal of pain."

Aunt Pol looked as if she wanted to say more, but she glanced once at the shadowy figure of the God weeping not far away and nodded. She turned to her horse and led the way out of the ruins.

Mister Wolf fell in beside Garion after they had remounted to follow her. "Perhaps we could talk as we ride along," he suggested. "I have a great many questions."

"He's gone, Grandfather," Garion told him.

"Oh," Wolf answered with obvious disappointment.

It was nearing sundown by then, and they stopped for the night in a grove about a mile away from Mar Amon. Since they had left the ruins, they had seen no more of the maimed ghosts. After the others had been fed and sent to their blankets, Aunt Pol, Garion, and Mister Wolf sat around their small fire. Since the presence in his mind had left him, following the meeting with Mara, Garion had felt himself sinking deeper toward sleep. All emotion was totally gone now, and he seemed no longer able to think independently.

"Can we talk to the—other one?" Mister Wolf asked hopefully.

"He isn't there right now," Garion replied.

"Then he isn't always with you?"

"Not always. Sometimes he goes away for months—sometimes even longer. He's been there for quite a long while this time—ever since Asharak burned up."

"Where exactly is he when he's with you?" the old man asked curiously.

"In here." Garion tapped his head.

"Have you been awake ever since we entered Maragor?" Aunt Pol asked.

"Not exactly awake," Garion answered. "Part of me was asleep."

"You could see the ghosts?"

"Yes."

"But they didn't frighten you?"

"No. Some of them surprised me, and one of them made me sick."

Wolf looked up quickly. "It wouldn't make you sick now though, would it?"

"No. I don't think so. Right at first I could still feel things like that a little bit. Now I can't."

Wolf looked thoughtfully at the fire as if looking for a way to phrase his next question. "What did the other one in your head say to you when you talked together?"

"He told me that something had happened a long time ago that wasn't supposed to happen and that I was supposed to fix it."

Wolf laughed shortly. "That's a succinct way of putting it," he observed. "Did he say anything about how it was going to turn out?"

"He doesn't know."

Wolf sighed. "I'd hoped that maybe we'd picked up an advantage somewhere, but I guess not. It looks like both prophecies are still equally valid."

Aunt Pol was looking steadily at Garion. "Do you think you'll be able to remember any of this when you wake up again?" she asked.

"I think so."

"All right then, listen carefully. There are two prophecies, both leading toward the same event. The Grolims and the rest of the Angaraks are following one; we're following the other. The event turns out differently at the end of each prophecy."

"I see."

"Nothing in either prophecy excludes anything that will happen in the other *until* they meet in that event," she continued. "The course of everything that follows will be decided by how that event turns out. One prophecy will succeed; the other will fail. Everything that *has* happened and *will* happen comes together at that point and becomes one. The mistake will be erased, and the universe will go in one direction or the other, as if that were the direction it had been going from its very beginning. The only real difference is that something that's very important will never happen if we fail."

Garion nodded, feeling suddenly very tired.

"Beldin calls it the theory of convergent destinies," Mister

Wolf said. "Two equally possible possibilities. Beldin can be very pompous sometimes."

"It's not an uncommon failing, father," Aunt Pol told him.

"I think I'd like to sleep now," Garion said.

Wolf and Aunt Pol exchanged a quick glance. "All right," Aunt Pol said. She rose and took him by the arm and led him to his blankets.

After she had covered him, drawing the blankets up snugly, she laid one cool hand on his forehead. "Sleep, my Belgarion," she murmured.

And he did that.

Part Two

THE VALE
OF ALDUR

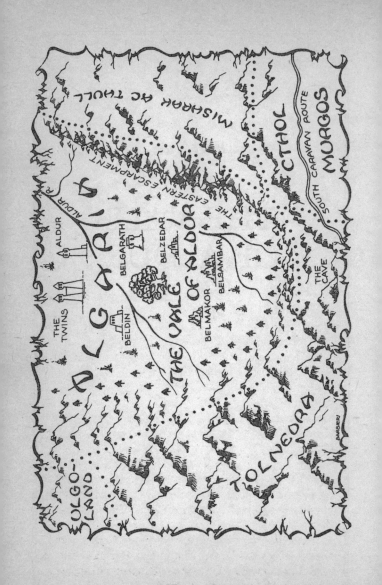

Chapter Seven

THEY WERE ALL standing in a circle with their hands joined when they awoke. Ce'Nedra was holding Garion's left hand, and Durnik was on his right. Garion's awarenss came flooding back as sleep left him. The breeze was fresh and cool, and the morning sun was very bright. Yellow-brown foothills rose directly in front of them and the haunted plain of Maragor lay behind.

Silk looked around sharply as he awoke, his eyes wary. "Where are we?" he asked quickly.

"On the northern edge of Maragor," Wolf told him, "about eighty leagues east of Tol Rane."

"How long were we asleep?"

"A week or so."

Silk kept looking around, adjusting his mind to the passage of time and distance. "I guess it was necessary," he conceded finally.

Hettar went immediately to check the horses, and Barak began massaging the back of his neck with both hands. "I feel as if I've been sleeping on a pile of rocks," he complained.

"Walk around a bit," Aunt Pol advised. "That will work the stiffness out."

Ce'Nedra had not removed her hand from Garion's, and he wondered if he should mention it to her. Her hand felt very warm and small in his and, on the whole, it was not unpleasant. He decided not to say anything about it.

73

Hettar was frowning when he came back. "One of the pack mares is with foal, Belgarath," he said.

"How long has she got to go?" Wolf asked, looking quickly at him.

"It's hard to say for sure—no more than a month. It's her first."

"We can break down her pack and distribute the weight among the other horses," Durnik suggested. "She'll be all right if she doesn't have to carry anything."

"Maybe." Hettar sounded dubious.

Mandorallen had been studying the yellowed foothills directly ahead. "We are being watched, Belgarath," he said somberly, pointing at several wispy columns of smoke rising toward the blue morning sky.

Mister Wolf squinted at the smoke and made a sour face. "Gold-hunters, probably. They hover around the borders of Maragor like vultures over a sick cow. Take a look, Pol."

But Aunt Pol's eyes already had that distant look in them as she scanned the foothills ahead. "Arends," she said, "Sendars, Tolnedrans, a couple of Drasnians. They aren't very bright."

"Any Murgos?"

"No."

"Common rabble then," Mandorallen observed. "Such scavengers will not impede us significantly."

"I'd like to avoid a fight if possible," Wolf told him. "These incidental skirmishes are dangerous and don't really accomplish anything." He shook his head with disgust. "We'll never be able to convince them that we're not carrying gold out of Maragor, though, so I guess there's no help for it."

"If gold's all they want, why don't we just give them some?" Silk suggested.

"I didn't bring all that much with me, Silk," the old man replied.

"It doesn't have to be real," Silk said, his eyes bright. He went to one of the packhorses, came back with several large pieces of canvas, and quickly cut them into foot-wide squares. Then he took one of the squares and laid a double handful of gravel in its center. He pulled up the corners and wrapped a stout piece of cord around them, forming a heavy-looking pouch. He hefted it a few times. "Looks about like a sackful of gold, wouldn't you say?"

"He's going to do something clever again," Barak said.

Silk smirked at him and quickly made up several more pouches. "I'll take the lead," he said, hanging the pouches on their saddles. "Just follow me and let me do the talking. How many of them are up there, Polgara?"

"About twenty," she replied.

"That will work out just fine," he stated confidently. "Shall we go?"

They mounted their horses and started across the ground toward the broad mouth of a dry wash that opened out onto the plain. Silk rode at the front, his eyes everywhere. As they entered the mouth of the wash, Garion heard a shrill whistle and saw several furtive movements ahead of them. He was very conscious of the steep banks of the wash on either side of them.

"I'm going to need a bit of open ground to work with," Silk told them. "There." He pointed with his chin at a spot where the slope of the bank was a bit more gradual. When they reached the spot, he turned his horse sharply. "Now!" he barked. "Ride!"

They followed him, scrambling up the bank and kicking up a great deal of gravel; a thick cloud of choking yellow dust rose in the air as they clawed their way up out of the wash.

Shouts of dismay came from the scrubby thornbushes at the upper end of the wash, and a group of rough-looking men broke out into the open, running hard up through the knee-high brown grass to head them off. A black-bearded man, closer and more desperate than the rest, jumped out in front of them, brandishing a rust-pitted sword. Without hesitation, Mandorallen rode him down. The black-bearded man howled as he rolled and tumbled beneath the churning hooves of the huge warhorse.

When they reached the hilltop above the wash, they gathered in a tight group. "This will do," Silk said, looking around at the rounded terrain. "All I need is for the mob to have enough room to think about casualties. I definitely want them to be thinking about casualties."

An arrow buzzed toward them, and Mandorallen brushed it almost contemptuously out of the air with his shield.

"Stop!" one of the brigands shouted. He was a lean, pock-marked Sendar with a crude bandage wrapped around one leg, wearing a dirty green tunic.

"Who says so?" Silk yelled back insolently.

"I'm Kroldor," the bandaged man announced importantly. "Kroldor the robber. You've probably heard of me."

"Can't say that I have," Silk replied pleasantly.

"Leave your gold—and your women," Kroldor ordered. "Maybe I'll let you live."

"If you get out of our way, maybe we'll let *you* live."

"I've got fifty men," Kroldor threatened, "all desperate, like me."

"You've got twenty," Silk corrected. "Runaway serfs, cowardly peasants, and sneak thieves. My men are trained warriors. Not only that, we're mounted, and you're on foot."

"Leave your gold," the self-proclaimed robber insisted.

"Why don't you come and take it?"

"Let's go!" Kroldor barked at his men. He lunged forward. A couple of his outlaws rather hesitantly followed him through the brown grass, but the rest hung back, eyeing Mandorallen, Barak, and Hettar apprehensively. After a few paces, Kroldor realized that his men were not with him. He stopped and spun around. "You cowards!" he raged. "If we don't hurry, the others will get here. We won't get any of the gold."

"I'll tell you what, Kroldor," Silk said. "We're in kind of a hurry, and we've got more gold than we can conveniently carry." He unslung one of his bags of gravel from his saddle and shook it suggestively. "Here." Negligently he tossed the bag into the grass off to one side. Then he took another bag and tossed it over beside the first. At his quick gesture the others all threw their bags on the growing heap. "There you are, Kroldor," Silk continued. "Ten bags of good yellow gold that you can have without a fight. If you want more, you'll have to bleed for it."

The rough-looking men behind Kroldor looked at each other and began moving to either side, their eyes fixed greedily on the heap of bags lying in the tall grass.

"Your men are having thoughts about mortality, Kroldor," Silk said dryly. "There's enough gold there to make them all rich, and rich men don't take unnecessary risks."

Kroldor glared at him. "I won't forget this," he growled.

"I'm sure you won't," Silk replied. "We're coming through now. I suggest that you get out of our way."

Barak and Hettar moved up to flank Mandorallen, and the three of them started deliberately forward at a slow, menacing walk.

Kroldor the robber stood his ground until the last moment, then turned and scurried out of their path, spouting curses.

"Let's go," Silk snapped.

They thumped their heels to their horses' flanks and charged through at a gallop. Behind them, the outlaws circled and then broke and ran toward the heap of canvas bags. Several ugly little fights broke out almost immediately, and three men were down before anyone thought to open one of the bags. The howls of rage could be heard quite clearly for some distance.

Barak was laughing when they finally reined in their horses after a couple of miles of hard riding. "Poor Kroldor." He chortled. "You're an evil man, Silk."

"I've made a study of the baser side of man's nature," Silk replied innocently. "I can usually find a way to make it work for me."

"Kroldor's men are going to blame him for the way things turned out," Hettar observed.

"I know. But then, that's one of the hazards of leadership."

"They might even kill him."

"I certainly hope so. I'd be terribly disappointed in them if they didn't."

They pushed on through the yellow foothills for the rest of the day and camped that night in a well-concealed little canyon where the light from their fire would not betray their location to the brigands who infested the region. The next morning they started out early, and by noon they were in the mountains.

They rode on up among the rocky crags, moving through a thick forest of dark green firs and spruces where the air was cool and spicy. Although it was still summer in the lowlands, the first signs of autumn had begun to appear at the higher elevations. The leaves on the underbrush had begun to turn, the air had a faint, smoky haze, and there was frost on the ground each morning when they awoke. The weather held fair, however, and they made good time.

Then, late one afternoon after they had been in the mountains for a week or more, a heavy bank of clouds moved in from the west, bringing with it a damp chill. Garion untied his cloak from the back of his saddle and pulled it around his shoulders as he rode, shivering as the afternoon grew colder.

Durnik lifted his face and sniffed at the air. "We'll have snow before morning," he predicted.

Garion could also smell the chill, dusty odor of snow in the air. He nodded glumly.

Mister Wolf grunted. "I knew this was too good to last." Then he shrugged. "Oh, well," he added, "we've all lived through winters before."

When Garion poked his head out of the tent the next morning, an inch of snow lay on the ground beneath the dark firs. Soft flakes were drifting down, settling soundlessly and concealing everything more than a hundred yards away in a filmy haze. The air was cold and gray, and the horses, looking very dark under a dusting of snow, stamped their feet and flicked their ears at the fairy touch of the snowflakes settling on them. Their breath steamed in the damp cold.

Ce'Nedra emerged from the tent she shared with Aunt Pol with a squeal of delight. Snow, Garion realized, was probably a rarity in Tol Honeth, and the tiny girl romped through the soft drifting flakes with childish abandon. He smiled tolerantly until a well-aimed snowball caught him on the side of the head. Then he chased her, pelting her with snowballs, while she dodged in and out among the trees, laughing and squealing. When he finally caught her, he was determined to wash her face with snow, but she exuberantly threw her arms around his neck and kissed him, her cold little nose rubbing against his cheek and her eyelashes thick with snowflakes. He didn't realize the full extent of her deceitfulness until she had already poured a handful of snow down the back of his neck. Then she broke free and ran toward the tents, hooting with laughter, while he tried to shake the snow out of the back of his tunic before it all melted.

By midday, however, the snow on the ground had turned to slush, and the drifting flakes had become a steady, unpleasant drizzle. They rode up a narrow ravine under dripping firs while a torrentlike stream roared over boulders beside them.

Mister Wolf finally called a halt. "We're getting close to the western border of Cthol Murgos," he told them. "I think it's time we started to take a few precautions."

"I'll ride out in front," Hettar offered quickly.

"I don't think that's a very good idea," Wolf replied. "You tend to get distracted when you see Murgos."

"I'll do it," Silk said. He had pulled his hood up, but water still dripped from the end of his long, pointed nose. "I'll stay about half a mile ahead and keep my eyes open."

Wolf nodded. "Whistle if you see anything."

"Right." Silk started off up the ravine at a trot.

Late that afternoon, the rain began to freeze as it hit, coating the rocks and trees with gray ice. They rounded a large outcropping of rock and found Silk waiting for them. The stream had turned to a trickle, and the walls of the ravine had opened out onto the steep side of a mountain. "We've got about an hour of daylight left," the little man said. "What do you think? Should we go on, or do you want to drop back down the ravine a bit and set up for the night?"

Mister Wolf squinted at the sky and then at the mountainside ahead. The steep slope was covered with stunted trees, and the timberline lay not far above them. "We have to go around this and then down the other side. It's only a couple of miles. Let's go ahead."

Silk nodded and led out again.

They rounded the shoulder of the mountain and looked down into a deep gorge that separated them from the peak they had crossed two days before. The rain had slackened with the approach of evening, and Garion could see the other side of the gorge clearly. It was no more than half a mile away, and his eyes caught a movement near the rim. "What's that?" He pointed.

Mister Wolf brushed the ice out of his beard. "I was afraid of that."

"What?"

"It's an Algroth."

With a shudder of revulsion, Garion remembered the scaly, goat-faced apes that had attacked them in Arendia. "Hadn't we better run?" he asked.

"It can't get to us," Wolf replied. "The gorge is at least a mile deep. The Grolims have turned their beasts loose, though. It's something we're going to have to watch out for." He motioned for them to continue.

Faintly, distorted by the wind that blew perpetually down the yawning gorge, Garion could hear the barking yelps of the Algroth on the far side as it communicated with the rest of its pack. Soon a dozen of the loathsome creatures were scampering along the rocky rim of the gorge, barking to one another and keeping pace with the party as they rode around the steep mountain face toward a shallow draw on the far side. The draw led away from the gorge; after a mile, they stopped for the night in the shelter of a grove of scrubby spruces.

It was colder the next morning and still cloudy, but the rain had stopped. They rode on back down to the mouth of the draw and continued following the rim of the gorge. The face on the other side fell away in a sheer, dizzying drop for thousands of feet to the tiny-looking ribbon of the river at the bottom. The Algroths still kept pace with them, barking and yelping and looking across with a dreadful hunger. There were other things as well, dimly seen back among the trees on the other side. One of them, huge and shaggy, seemed even to have a human body, but its head was the head of a beast. A herd of swift-moving animals galloped along the far rim, manes and tails tossing.

"Look," Ce'Nedra exclaimed, pointing. "Wild horses."

"They're not horses," Hettar said grimly.

"They look like horses."

"They may look like it, but they aren't."

"Hrulgin," Mister Wolf said shortly.

"What's that?"

"A Hrulga is a four-legged animal—like a horse—but it has fangs instead of teeth, and clawed feet instead of hooves."

"But that would mean—" The princess broke off, her eyes wide.

"Yes. They're meat-eaters."

She shuddered. "How dreadful."

"That gorge is getting narrower, Belgarath," Barak growled. "I'd rather not have any of those things on the same side with us."

"We'll be all right. As I remember, it narrows down to about a hundred yards and then widens out again. They won't be able to get across."

"I hope your memory hasn't failed you."

The sky above looked ragged, tattered by a gusty wind. Vultures soared and circled over the gorge, and ravens flapped from tree to tree, croaking and squawking to one another. Aunt Pol watched the birds with a look of stern disapproval, but said nothing.

They rode on. The gorge grew narrower, and soon they could see the brutish faces of the Algroths on the other side clearly. When the Hrulgin, manes tossing in the wind, opened their mouths to whinny to each other, their long, pointed teeth were plainly visible.

Then, at the narrowest point of the gorge, a party of mail-shirted Murgos rode out onto the opposite precipice. Their horses were lathered from hard riding, and the Murgos themselves were gaunt-faced and travel-stained. They stopped and waited until Garion and his friends were opposite them. At the very edge, staring first across the gorge and then down at the river far below, stood Brill.

"What kept you?" Silk called in a bantering tone that had a hard edge just below the surface. "We thought perhaps you'd gotten lost."

"Not very likely, Kheldar," Brill replied. "How did you get across to that side?"

"You go back that way about four days' ride," Silk shouted, pointing back the way they had come. "If you look very carefully, you'll find the canyon that leads up here. It shouldn't take you more than a day or two to find it."

One of the Murgos pulled a short bow out from beneath his left leg and set an arrow to it. He pointed the arrow at Silk, drew back the string and released. Silk watched the arrow calmly as it fell down into the gorge, spinning in a long, slow-looking spiral. "Nice shot," he called.

"Don't be an idiot," Brill snapped at the Murgo with the bow. He looked back at Silk. "I've heard a great deal about you, Kheldar," he said.

"One has developed a certain reputation," Silk replied modestly.

"One of these days I'll have to find out if you're as good as they say."

"That particular curiosity could be the first symptom of a fatal disease."

"For one of us, at least."

"I look forward to our next meeting, then," Silk told him. "I hope you'll excuse us, my dear fellow—pressing business, you know."

"Keep an eye out behind you, Kheldar," Brill threatened. "One day I'll be there."

"I always keep an eye out behind me, Kordoch," Silk called back, "so don't be too surprised if I'm waiting for you. It's been wonderful chatting with you. We'll have to do it again—soon."

The Murgo with the bow shot another arrow. It followed his first into the gorge.

Silk laughed and led the party away from the brink of the precipice. "What a splendid fellow," he said as they rode away. He looked up at the murky sky overhead. "And what an absolutely beautiful day."

The clouds thickened and grew black as the day wore on. The wind picked up until it howled among the trees. Mister Wolf led them away from the gorge which separated them from Brill and his Murgos, moving steadily toward the northeast.

They set up for the night in a rock-strewn basin just below the timberline. Aunt Pol prepared a meal of thick stew; as soon as they had finished eating, they let the fire go out. "There's no point in lighting beacons for them," Wolf observed.

"They can't get across the gorge, can they?" Durnik asked.

"It's better not to take chances," Wolf replied. He walked away from the last few embers of the dying fire and looked out into the darkness. On an impulse, Garion followed him.

"How much farther is it to the Vale, Grandfather?" he asked.

"About seventy leagues," the old man told him. "We can't make very good time up here in the mountains."

"The weather's getting worse, too."

"I noticed that."

"What happens if we get a real snowstorm?"

"We take shelter until it blows over."

"What if—"

"Garion, I know it's only natural, but sometimes you sound a great deal like your Aunt. She's been saying 'what if' to me since she was about seventeen. I've gotten terribly tired of it over the years."

"I'm sorry."

"Don't be sorry. Just don't do it any more."

Overhead in the pitch-blackness of the blustery sky, there was a sudden, ponderous flap as of enormous wings.

"What's that?" Garion asked, startled.

"Be still!" Wolf stood with his face turned upward. There was another great flap. "Oh, that's sad."

"What?"

"I thought the poor old brute had been dead for centuries. Why don't they leave her alone?"

"What is it?"

"It doesn't have a name. It's big and stupid and ugly. The Gods only made three of them, and the two males killed each other during the first mating season. She's been alone for as long as I can remember."

"It sounds huge," Garion said, listening to the enormous wings beat overhead and peering up into the darkness. "What does it look like?"

"She's as big as a house, and you really wouldn't want to see her."

"Is she dangerous?"

"Very dangerous, but she can't see too well at night." Wolf sighed. "The Grolims must have chased her out of her cave and put her to hunting for us. Sometimes they go too far."

"Should we tell the others about her?"

"It would only worry them. Sometimes it's better not to say anything."

The great wings flapped again, and there was a long, despairing cry from the darkness, a cry filled with such aching loneliness that Garion felt a great surge of pity welling up in him.

Wolf sighed again. "There's nothing we can do," he said. "Let's go back to the tents."

Chapter Eight

THE WEATHER CONTINUED raw and unsettled as they rode for the next two days up the long, sloping rise toward the snow-covered summits of the mountains. The trees became sparser and more stunted as they climbed and finally disappeared entirely. The ridgeline flattened out against the side of one of the mountains, and they rode up onto a steep slope of tumbled rock and ice where the wind scoured continually.

Mister Wolf paused to get his bearings, looking around in the pale afternoon light. "That way," he said finally, pointing. A saddleback stretched between two peaks, and the sky beyond roiled in the wind. They rode up the slope, their cloaks pulled tightly about them.

Hettar came forward with a worried frown on his hawk face. "That pregnant mare's in trouble," he told Wolf. "I think her time's getting close."

Without a word Aunt Pol dropped back to look at the mare, and her face was grave when she returned. "She's no more than a few hours away, father," she reported.

Wolf looked around. "There's no shelter on this side."

"Maybe there'll be something on the other side of the pass," Barak suggested, his beard whipping in the wind.

Wolf shook his head. "I think it's the same as this side. We're going to have to hurry. We don't want to spend the night up here."

As they rode higher, occasional spits of stinging sleet pelted them, and the wind gusted even stronger, howling among the rocks. As they crested the slope and started through the saddle, the full force of the gale struck them, driving a tattered sleet squall before it.

"It's even worse on this side, Belgarath," Barak shouted over the wind. "How far is it down to the trees?"

"Miles," Wolf replied, trying to keep his flying cloak pulled around him.

"The mare will never make it," Hettar said. "We've got to find shelter."

"There isn't any," Wolf stated. "Not until we get to the trees. It's all bare rock and ice up here."

Without knowing why he said it—not even aware of it until he spoke—Garion made a shouted suggestion. "What about the cave?"

Mister Wolf turned and looked sharply at him. "What cave? Where?"

"The one in the side of the mountain. It isn't far." Garion knew the cave was there, but he did not know how he knew.

"Are you sure?"

"Of course. It's this way." Garion turned his horse and rode up the slope of the saddle toward the vast, craggy peak on their left. The wind tore at them as they rode, and the driving sleet half-blinded them. Garion moved confidently, however. For some reason every rock about them seemed absolutely familiar, though he could not have said why. He rode just fast enough to stay in front of the others. He knew they would ask questions, and he didn't have any answers. They rounded a shoulder of the peak and rode out onto a broad rock ledge. The ledge curved along the mountainside, disappearing in the swirling sleet ahead.

"Where art thou taking us, lad?" Mandorallen shouted to him.

"It's not much farther," Garion yelled back over his shoulder.

The ledge narrowed as it curved around the looming granite face of the mountain. Where it bent around a jutting cornice, it was hardly more than a footpath. Garion dismounted and led his horse around the cornice. The wind blasted directly into his face as he stepped around the granite outcrop, and he had to put his hand in front of his face to keep the sleet from blinding him. Walking that way, he did not see the door until it was almost within reach of his hands.

The door in the face of the rock was made of iron, black and pitted with rust and age. It was broader than the gate at Faldor's farm, and the upper edge of it was lost in the swirling sleet.

Barak, following close behind him, reached out and touched the iron door. Then he banged on it with his huge fist. The door echoed hollowly. "There *is* a cave," he said back over his shoulder to the others. "I thought that the wind had blown out the boy's senses."

"How do we get inside?" Hettar shouted, the wind snatching away his words.

"The door's as solid as the mountain itself," Barak said, hammering with his fist again.

"We've got to get out of this wind," Aunt Pol declared, one of her arms protectively about Ce'Nedra's shoulders.

"Well, Garion?" Mister Wolf asked.

"It's easy," Garion replied. "I just have to find the right spot." He ran his fingers over the icy iron, not knowing just what he was looking for. He found a spot that felt a little different. "Here it is." He put his right hand on the spot and pushed lightly. With a vast, grating groan, the door began to move. A line that had not even been visible before suddenly appeared like a razor-cut down the precise center of the pitted iron surface, and flakes of rust showered from the crack, to be whipped away by the wind.

Garion felt a peculiar warmth in the silvery mark on the palm of his right hand where it touched the door. Curious, he stopped pushing, but the door continued to move, swinging open, it seemed, almost in response to the presence of the mark on his palm. It continued to move even after he was no longer touching it. He closed his hand, and the door stopped moving.

He opened his hand, and the door, grating against stone, swung open even wider.

"Don't play with it, dear," Aunt Pol told him. "Just open it."

It was dark in the cave beyond the huge door, but it seemed not to have the musty smell it should have had. They entered cautiously, feeling at the floor carefully with their feet.

"Just a moment," Durnik murmured in a strangely hushed voice. They heard him unbuckling one of his saddlebags and then heard the rasp of his flint against steel. There were a few sparks, then a faint glow as the smith blew on his tinder. The tinder flamed, and he set it to the torch he had pulled from his saddlebag. The torch sputtered briefly, then caught. Durnik raised it, and they all looked around at the cave.

It was immediately evident that the cave was not natural. The walls and floor were absolutely smooth, almost polished, and the light of Durnik's torch reflected back from the gleaming surfaces. The chamber was perfectly round and about a hundred feet in diameter. The walls curved inward as they rose, and the ceiling high overhead seemed also to be round. In the precise center of the floor stood a round stone table, twenty feet across, with its top higher than Barak's head. A stone bench encircled the table. In the wall directly opposite the door was a circular arch of a fireplace. The cave was cool, but it did not seem to have the bitter chill it should have had.

"Is it all right to bring in the horses?" Hettar asked quietly.

Mister Wolf nodded. His expression seemed bemused in the flickering torchlight, and his eyes were lost in thought.

The horses' hooves clattered sharply on the smooth stone floor as they were led inside, and they looked around, their eyes wide and their ears twitching nervously.

"There's a fire laid in here," Durnik said from the arched fireplace. "Shall I light it?"

Wolf looked up. "What? Oh—yes. Go ahead."

Durnik reached into the fireplace with his torch, and the wood caught immediately. The fire swelled up very quickly, and the flames seemed inordinately bright.

Ce'Nedra gasped. "The walls! Look at the walls!" The light from the fire was somehow being refracted through the crystalline structure of the rock itself, and the entire dome began to glow with a myriad of shifting colors, filling the chamber with a soft, multihued radiance.

Hettar had moved around the circle of the wall and was peering into another arched opening. "A spring," he told them. "This is a good place to ride out a storm."

Durnik put out his torch and pulled off his cloak. The chamber had become warm almost as soon as he had lighted the fire. He looked at Mister Wolf. "You know about this place, don't you?" he asked.

"None of us has ever been able to find it before," the old man replied, his eyes still thoughtful. "We weren't even sure it still existed."

"What is this strange cave, Belgarath?" Mandorallen asked.

Mister Wolf took a deep breath. "When the Gods were making the world, it was necessary for them to meet from time to time to discuss what each of them had done and was going to do so that everything would fit together and work in harmony—the mountains, the winds, the seasons and so on." He looked around. "This is the place where they met."

Silk, his nose twitching with curiosity, had climbed up onto the bench surrounding the huge table. "There are bowls up here," he said. "Seven of them—and seven cups. There seems to be some kind of fruit in the bowls." He began to reach out with one hand.

"Silk!" Mister Wolf told him sharply. "Don't touch anything."

Silk's hand froze, and he looked back over his shoulder at the old man, his face startled.

"You'd better come down from there," Wolf said gravely.

"The door!" Ce'Nedra exclaimed.

They all turned in time to see the massive iron door gently swinging closed. With an oath, Barak leaped toward it, but he was too late. Booming hollowly, it clanged shut just before his hands reached it. The big man turned, his eyes filled with dismay.

"It's all right, Barak," Garion told him. "I can open it again."

Wolf turned then and looked at Garion, his eyes questioning. "How did you know about the cave?" he asked.

Garion floundered helplessly. "I don't know. I just did. I think I've known we were getting close to it for the last day or so."

"Does it have anything to do with the voice that spoke to Mara?"

"I don't think so. He doesn't seem to be there just now, and my knowing about the cave seemed to be different somehow. I think it came from me, not him, but I'm not sure how. For some reason, it seems that I've always known this place was here—only I didn't think about it until we started to get near it. It's awfully hard to explain it exactly."

Aunt Pol and Mister Wolf exchanged a long glance. Wolf looked as if he were about to ask another question, but just then there was a groan at the far end of the chamber.

"Somebody help me," Hettar called urgently. One of the horses, her sides distended and her breath coming in short, heaving gasps, stood swaying as if her legs were about to give out from under her. Hettar stood at her side, trying to support her. "She's about to foal," he said.

They all turned then and went quickly to the laboring mare. Aunt Pol immediately took charge of the situation, giving orders crisply. They eased the mare to the floor, and Hettar and Durnik began to work with her, even as Aunt Pol filled a small pot with water and set it carefully in the fire. "I'll need some room," she told the rest of them pointedly as she opened the bag which contained her jars of herbs.

"Why don't we all get out of your way?" Barak suggested, looking uneasily at the gasping horse.

"Splendid idea," she agreed. "Ce'Nedra, you stay here. I'll need your help."

Garion, Barak, and Mandorallen moved a few yards away and sat down, leaning back against the glowing wall, while Silk and Mister Wolf went off to explore the rest of the chamber. As he watched Durnik and Hettar with the mare and Aunt Pol and Ce'Nedra by the fire, Garion felt strangely abstracted. The cave had drawn him, there was no question of that, and even now it was exerting some peculiar force on him. Though the situation with the mare was immediate, he seemed unable to focus on it. He had a strange certainty that finding the cave was only the first part of whatever it was that was happening. There was something else he had to do, and his abstraction was in some way a preparation for it.

"It is not an easy thing to confess," Mandorallen was saying somberly. Garion glanced at him. "In view of the desperate nature of our quest, however," the knight continued, "I must openly acknowledge my great failing. It may come to pass that this flaw of mine shall in some hour of great peril cause me to turn and flee like the coward I am, leaving all your lives in mortal danger."

"You're making too much of it," Barak told him.

"Nay, my Lord. I urge that you consider the matter closely to determine if I am fit to continue in our enterprise." He started to creak to his feet.

"Where are you going?" Barak asked.

"I thought to go apart so that you may freely discuss this matter."

"Oh, sit down, Mandorallen," Barak said irritably. "I'm not going to say anything behind your back I wouldn't say to your face."

The mare, lying close to the fire with her head cradled in

Hettar's lap, groaned again. "Is that medicine almost ready, Polgara?" the Algar asked in a worried voice.

"Not quite," she replied. She turned back to Ce'Nedra, who was carefully grinding up some dried leaves in a small cup with the back of a spoon. "Break them up a little finer, dear," she instructed.

Durnik was standing astride the mare, his hands on her distended belly. "We may have to turn the foal," he said gravely. "I think it's trying to come the wrong way."

"Don't start on that until this has a chance to work," Aunt Pol told him, slowly tapping a grayish powder from an earthen jar into her bubbling pot. She took the cup of leaves from Ce'Nedra and added that as well, stirring as she poured.

"I think, my Lord Barak," Mandorallen urged, "that thou hast not fully considered the import of what I have told thee."

"I heard you. You said you were afraid once. It's nothing to worry about. It happens to everybody now and then."

"I cannot live with it. I live in constant apprehension, never knowing when it will return to unman me."

Durnik looked up from the mare. "You're afraid of being afraid?" he asked in a puzzled voice.

"You cannot know what it was like, good friend," Mandorallen replied.

"Your stomach tightened up," Durnik told him. "Your mouth was dry, and your heart felt as if someone had his fist clamped around it?"

Mandorallen blinked.

"It's happened to me so often that I know exactly how it feels."

"Thou? Thou art among the bravest men I have ever known."

Durnik smiled wryly. "I'm an ordinary man, Mandorallen," he said. "Ordinary men live in fear all the time. Didn't you know that? We're afraid of the weather, we're afraid of powerful men, we're afraid of the night and the monsters that lurk in the dark, we're afraid of growing old and of dying. Sometimes we're even afraid of living. Ordinary men are afraid almost every minute of their lives."

"How can you bear it?"

"Do we have any choice? Fear's a part of life, Mandorallen, and it's the only life we have. You'll get used to it. After you've put it on every morning like an old tunic, you won't even notice it any more. Sometimes laughing at it helps—a little."

"Laughing?"

"It shows the fear that you know it's there, but that you're going to go ahead and do what you have to do anyway." Durnik looked down at his hands, carefully kneading the mare's belly. "Some men curse and swear and bluster," he continued. "That does the same thing, I suppose. Every man has to come up with his own technique for dealing with it. Personally, I prefer laughing. It seems more appropriate somehow."

Mandorallen's face became gravely thoughtful as Durnik's words slowly sank in. "I will consider this," he said. "It may be, good friend, that I will owe thee more than my life for thy gentle instruction."

Once more the mare groaned, a deep, tearing sound, and Durnik straightened and began rolling up his sleeves. "The foal's going to have to be turned, Mistress Pol," he said decisively. "And soon, or we'll lose the foal and the mare both."

"Let me get some of this into her first," she replied, quenching her boiling pot with some cold water. "Hold her head," she told Hettar. Hettar nodded and firmly wrapped his arms around the laboring mare's head. "Garion," Aunt Pol said, as she spooned the liquid between the mare's teeth, "why don't you and Ce'Nedra go over there where Silk and your grandfather are?"

"Have you ever turned a foal before, Durnik?" Hettar asked anxiously.

"Not a foal, but calves many times. A horse isn't that much different from a cow, really."

Barak stood up quickly. His face had a slight greenish cast to it. "I'll go with Garion and the princess," he rumbled. "I don't imagine I'd be much help here."

"And I will join thee," Mandorallen declared. His face was also visibly pale. "It were best, I think, to leave our friends ample room for their midwifery."

Aunt Pol looked at the two warriors with a slight smile on her face, but said nothing.

Garion and the others moved rather quickly away.

Silk and Mister Wolf were standing beyond the huge stone table, peering into another of the circular openings in the shimmering wall. "I've never seen fruits exactly like those," the little man was saying.

"I'd be surprised if you had," Wolf replied.

"They look as fresh as if they'd just been picked." Silk's hand moved almost involuntarily toward the tempting fruit.

"I wouldn't," Wolf warned.

"I wonder what they taste like."

"Wondering won't hurt you. Tasting might."

"I *hate* an unsatisfied curiosity."

"You'll get over it." Wolf turned to Garion and the others. "How's the horse?"

"Durnik says he's going to have to turn the foal," Barak told him. "We thought it might be better if we all got out of the way."

Wolf nodded. "Silk!" he admonished sharply, not turning around.

"Sorry." Silk snatched his hand back.

"Why don't you just get away from there? You're only going to get yourself in trouble."

Silk shrugged. "I do that all the time anyway."

"Just do it, Silk," Wolf told him firmly. "I can't watch over you every minute." He slipped his fingers up under the dirty and rather ragged bandage on his arm, scratching irritably. "That's enough of that," he declared. "Garion, take this thing off me." He held out his arm.

Garion backed away. "Not me," he refused. "Do you know what Aunt Pol would say to me if I did that without her permission?"

"Don't be silly. Silk, you do it."

"First you say to stay out of trouble, and then you tell me to cross Polgara? You're inconsistent, Belgarath."

"Oh, here," Ce'Nedra said. She took hold of the old man's arm and began picking at the knotted bandage with her tiny fingers. "Just remember that this was your idea. Garion, give me your knife."

Somewhat reluctantly, Garion handed over his dagger. The princess sawed through the bandage and began to unwrap it. The splints fell clattering to the stone floor.

"What a dear child you are." Mister Wolf beamed at her and began to scratch at his arm with obvious relief.

"Just remember that you owe me a favor," she told him.

"She's a Tolnedran, all right," Silk observed.

It was about an hour later when Aunt Pol came around the table to them, her eyes somber.

"How's the mare?" Ce'Nedra asked quickly.

"Very weak, but I think she'll be all right."

"What about the baby horse?"

Aunt Pol sighed. "We were too late. We tried everything, but we just couldn't get him to start breathing."

Ce'Nedra gasped, her little face suddenly a deathly white. "You're not going to just give up, are you?" She said it almost accusingly.

"There's nothing more we can do, dear," Aunt Pol told her sadly. "It took too long. He just didn't have enough strength left."

Ce'Nedra stared at her, unbelieving. "*Do* something!" she demanded. "You're a sorceress. Do something!"

"I'm sorry, Ce'Nedra, that's beyond our power. We can't reach beyond that barrier."

The little princess wailed then and began to cry bitterly. Aunt Pol put her arms comfortingly about her and held her as she sobbed.

But Garion was already moving. With absolute clarity he now knew what it was that the cave expected of him, and he responded without thinking, not running or even hurrying. He walked quietly around the stone table toward the fire.

Hettar sat cross-legged on the floor with the unmoving colt in his lap, his head bowed with sorrow and his manelike scalp lock falling across the spindle-shanked little animal's silent face.

"Give him to me, Hettar," Garion said.

"Garion! No!" Aunt Pol's voice, coming from behind him, was alarmed.

Hettar looked up, his hawk face filled with deep sadness.

"Let me have him, Hettar," Garion repeated very quietly.

Wordlessly Hettar raised the limp little body, still wet and glistening in the firelight, and handed it to Garion. Garion knelt and laid the foal on the floor in front of the shimmering fire. He put his hands on the tiny ribcage and pushed gently. "Breathe," he almost whispered.

"We tried that, Garion," Hettar told him sadly. "We tried everything."

Garion began to gather his will.

"Don't do that, Garion," Aunt Pol told him firmly. "It isn't possible, and you'll hurt yourself if you try."

Garion was not listening to her. The cave itself was speaking to him too loudly for him to hear anything else. He focused his every thought on the wet, lifeless body of the foal. Then he stretched out his right hand and laid his palm on the un-blemished, walnut-colored shoulder of the dead animal. Before him there seemed to be a blank wall—black and higher than anything else in the world, impenetrable and silent beyond his comprehension. Tentatively he pushed at it, but it would not move. He drew in a deep breath and hurled himself entirely into the struggle.

"Live," he said.

"Garion, stop."

"Live," he said again, throwing himself deeper into his effort against that blackness.

"It's too late now, Pol," he heard Mister Wolf say from somewhere. "He's already committed himself."

"Live," Garion repeated, and the surge he felt welling up out of him was so vast that it drained him utterly. The glowing walls flickered and then suddenly rang as if a bell had been struck somewhere deep inside the mountain. The sound shim-mered, filling the air inside the domed chamber with a vibrant ringing. The light in the walls suddenly flared with a searing brightness, and the chamber was as bright as noon.

The little body under Garion's hand quivered, and the colt

drew in a deep, shuddering breath. Garion heard the others gasp as the sticklike little legs began to twitch. The colt inhaled again, and his eyes opened.

"A miracle," Mandorallen said in a choked voice.

"Perhaps even more than that," Mister Wolf replied, his eyes searching Garion's face.

The colt struggled, his head wobbling weakly on his neck. He pulled his legs under him and began to struggle to his feet. Instinctively, he turned to his mother and tottered toward her to nurse. His coat, which had been a deep, solid brown before Garion had touched him, was now marked on the shoulder with a single incandescently white patch exactly the size of the mark on Garion's palm.

Garion lurched to his feet and stumbled away, pushing past the others. He staggered to the icy spring bubbling in the opening in the wall and splashed water over his head and neck. He knelt before the spring, shaking and breathing hard for a very long time. Then he felt a tentative, almost shy touch on his elbow. When he wearily raised his head, he saw the now steadier colt standing at his side and gazing at him with adoration in its liquid eyes.

Chapter Nine

THE STORM BLEW itself out the next morning, but they stayed in the cave for another day after the wind had died down to allow the mare to recover and the newborn colt to gain a bit more strength. Garion found the attention of the little animal disturbing. It seemed that no matter where he went in the cave, those soft eyes followed him, and the colt was continually nuzzling at him. The other horses also watched him with a kind of mute respect. All in all it was a bit embarrassing.

On the morning of their departure, they carefully removed all traces of their stay from the cave. The cleaning was spontaneous, neither the result of some suggestion or of any discussion, but rather was something in which they all joined without comment.

"The fire's still burning," Durnik fretted, looking back into the glowing dome from the doorway as they prepared to leave.

"It will go out by itself after we leave," Wolf told him. "I don't think you could put it out anyway—no matter how hard you tried."

Durnik nodded soberly. "You're probably right," he agreed.

"Close the door, Garion," Aunt Pol said after they had led their horses out onto the ledge outside the cave.

Somewhat self-consciously, Garion took hold of the edge of the huge iron door and pulled it. Although Barak with all his great strength had tried without success to budge the door, it moved easily as soon as Garion's hand touched it. A single tug was enough to set it swinging gently closed. The two solid edges came together with a great, hollow boom, leaving only a thin, nearly invisible line where they met.

Mister Wolf put his hand lightly on the pitted iron, his eyes far away. Then he sighed once, turned, and led them back along the ledge the way they had come two days before.

Once they had rounded the shoulder of the mountain, they remounted and rode on down through the tumbled boulders and patches of rotten ice to the first low bushes and stunted trees a few miles below the pass. Although the wind was still brisk, the sky overhead was blue, and only a few fleecy clouds raced by, appearing strangely close.

Garion rode up to Mister Wolf and fell in beside him. His mind was filled with confusion by what had happened in the cave, and he desperately needed to get things straightened out. "Grandfather," he said.

"Yes, Garion?" the old man answered, rousing himself from his half-doze.

"Why did Aunt Pol try to stop me? With the colt, I mean?"

"Because it was dangerous," the old man replied. "Very dangerous."

"Why dangerous?"

"When you try to do something that's impossible, you can pour too much energy into it; and if you keep trying, it can be fatal."

"Fatal?"

Wolf nodded. "You drain yourself out completely, and you don't have enough strength left to keep your own heart beating."

"I didn't know that." Garion was shocked.

Wolf ducked as he rode under a low branch. "Obviously."

"Don't you keep saying that *nothing* is impossible?"

"Within reason, Garion. Within reason."

They rode on quietly for a few minutes, the sound of their horses' hooves muffled by the thick moss covering the ground under the trees.

"Maybe I'd better find out more about all this," Garion said finally.

"That's not a bad idea. What was it you wanted to know?"

"Everything, I guess."

Mister Wolf laughed. "That would take a very long time, I'm afraid."

Garion's heart sank. "Is it that complicated?"

"No. Actually it's very simple, but simple things are always the hardest to explain."

"That doesn't make any sense," Garion retorted, a bit irritably.

"Oh?" Wolf looked at him with amusement. "Let me ask you a simple question, then. What's two and two?"

"Four," Garion replied promptly.

"Why?"

Garion floundered for a moment. "It just is," he answered lamely.

"But why?"

"There isn't any why to it. It just is."

"There's a why to everything, Garion."

"All right, why is two and two four then?"

"I don't know," Wolf admitted. "I thought maybe you might."

They passed a dead snag standing twisted and starkly white against the deep blue sky.

"Are we getting anywhere?" Garion asked, even more confused now.

"Actually, I think we've come a very long way," Wolf replied. "Precisely what was it you wanted to know?"

Garion put it as directly as he knew how. "What is sorcery?"

"I told you that once already. The Will and the Word."

"That doesn't really mean anything, you know."

"All right, try it this way. Sorcery is doing things with your mind instead of your hands. Most people don't use it because at first it's much easier to do things the other way."

Garion frowned. "It doesn't seem hard."

"That's because the things you've been doing have come out of impulse. You've never sat down and thought your way through something—you just do it."

"Isn't it easier that way? What I mean is, why not just do it and not think about it?"

"Because spontaneous sorcery is just third-rate magic— completely uncontrolled. Anything can happen if you simply turn the power of your mind loose. It has no morality of its own. The good or the bad of it comes out of *you*, not out of the sorcery."

"You mean that when I burned Asharak, it was me and not the sorcery?" Garion asked, feeling a bit sick at the thought.

Mister Wolf nodded gravely. "It might help if you remember that you were also the one who gave life to the colt. The two things sort of balance out."

Garion glanced back over his shoulder at the colt, who was frisking along behind him like a puppy. "What you're saying is that it can be either good or bad."

"No," Wolf corrected. "By itself it has nothing to do with good or bad. And it won't help you in any way to make up your mind how to use it. You can do anything you want to with it—almost anything, that is. You can bite the tops off all the mountains or stick the trees in the ground upside down or turn all the clouds green, if you feel like it. What you have to decide is whether you *should* do something, not whether you *can* do it."

"You said *almost* anything," Garion noted quickly.

"I'm getting to that," Wolf said. He looked thoughtfully at a low-flying cloud—an ordinary-looking old man in a rusty tunic and gray hood looking at the sky. "There's one thing that's absolutely forbidden. You can never destroy anything—not ever."

Garion was baffled by that. "I destroyed Asharak, didn't I?"

"No. You killed him. There's a difference. You set fire to him, and he burned to death. To destroy something is to try to uncreate it. That's what's forbidden."

"What would happen if I *did* try?"

"Your power would turn inward on you, and you'd be obliterated in an instant."

Garion blinked and then suddenly went cold at the thought of how close he had come to crossing that forbidden line in his encounter with Asharak. "How do I tell the difference?" he asked in a hushed voice. "I mean, how do I go about explaining that I only meant to kill somebody and not destroy him?"

"It's not a good area for experimentation," Wolf told him. "If you really want to kill somebody, stick your sword in him. Hopefully you won't have occasion to do that sort of thing too often."

They stopped at a small brook trickling out of some mossy stones to allow their horses to drink.

"You see, Garion," Wolf explained, "the ultimate purpose of the universe is to create things. It will not permit you to come along behind it *un*creating all the things it went to so much trouble to create in the first place. When you kill somebody, all you've really done is alter him a bit. You've changed him from being alive to being dead. He's still there. To uncreate him, you have to will him out of existence entirely. When you feel yourself on the verge of telling something to 'vanish' or 'go away' or 'be not,' you're getting very close to the point

of self-destruction. That's the main reason we have to keep
our emotions under control all the time."

"I didn't know that," Garion admitted.

"You do now. Don't even try to unmake a single pebble."

"A pebble?"

"The universe doesn't make any distinction between a pebble and a man." The old man looked at him somewhat sternly.
"Your Aunt's been trying to explain the necessity for keeping
yourself under control for several months now, and you've
been fighting her every step of the way."

Garion hung his head. "I didn't know what she was getting
at," he apologized.

"That's because you weren't listening. That's a great failing
of yours, Garion."

Garion flushed. "What happened the first time *you* found
out you could—well—do things?" he asked quickly, wanting
to change the subject.

"It was something silly," Wolf replied. "It usually is, the
first time."

"What was it?"

Wolf shrugged. "I wanted to move a big rock. My arms
and back weren't strong enough, but my mind was. After that
I didn't have any choice but to learn to live with it because,
once you unlock it, it's unlocked forever. That's the point where
your life changes and you have to start learning to control
yourself."

"It always gets back to that, doesn't it?"

"Always," Wolf said. "It's not as difficult as it sounds,
really. Look at Mandorallen." He pointed at the knight, who
was riding with Durnik. The two of them were in a deep
discussion. "Now, Mandorallen's a nice enough fellow—honest, sincere, toweringly noble—but let's be honest. His mind
has never been violated by an original thought—until now.
He's learning to control fear, and learning to control it is forcing
him to think—probably for the first time in his whole life. It's
painful for him, but he's doing it. If Mandorallen can learn to
control fear with that limited brain of his, surely *you* can learn

the same kind of control over the other emotions. After all, you're quite a bit brighter than he is."

Silk, who had been scouting ahead, came riding back to join them. "Belgarath," he said, "there's something about a mile in front of us that I think you'd better take a look at."

"All right," Wolf replied. "Think about what I've been saying, Garion. We'll talk more about it later." Then he and Silk moved off through the trees at a gallop.

Garion pondered what the old man had told him. The one thing that bothered him the most was the crushing responsibility his unwanted talent placed upon him.

The colt frisked along beside him, galloping off into the trees from time to time and then rushing back, his little hooves pattering on the damp ground. Frequently he would stop and stare at Garion, his eyes full of love and trust.

"Oh, stop that," Garion told him.

The colt scampered away again.

Princess Ce'Nedra moved her horse up until she was beside Garion. "What were you and Belgarath talking about?" she asked.

Garion shrugged. "A lot of things."

There was immediately a hard little tightening around her eyes. In the months that they had known each other, Garion had learned to catch those minute danger signals. Something warned him that the princess was spoiling for an argument, and with an insight that surprised him he reasoned out the source of her unspoken belligerence. What had happened in the cave had shaken her badly, and Ce'Nedra did not like to be shaken. To make matters even worse, the princess had made a few coaxing overtures to the colt, obviously wanting to turn the little animal into her personal pet. The colt, however, ignored her completely, fixing all his attention on Garion, even to the point of ignoring his own mother unless he was hungry. Ce'Nedra disliked being ignored even more than she disliked being shaken. Glumly, Garion realized how small were his chances of avoiding a squabble with her.

"I certainly wouldn't want to pry into a private conversation," she said tartly.

"It wasn't private. We were talking about sorcery and how to keep accidents from happening. I don't want to make any more mistakes."

She turned that over in her mind, looking for something offensive in it. His mild answer seemed to irritate her all the more. "I don't believe in sorcery," she said flatly. In the light of all that had recently happened, her declaration was patently absurd, and she seemed to realize that as soon as she said it. Her eyes hardened even more.

Garion sighed. "All right," he said with resignation, "was there anything in particular you wanted to fight about, or did you just want to start yowling and sort of make it up as we go along?"

"Yowling?" Her voice went up several octaves. *"Yowling?"*

"Screeching, maybe," he suggested as insultingly as possible. As long as the fight was inevitable anyway, he determined to get in a few digs at her before her voice rose to the point where she could no longer hear him.

"SCREECHING?" she screeched.

The fight lasted for about a quarter of an hour before Barak and Aunt Pol moved forward to separate them. On the whole, it was not very satisfactory. Garion was a bit too preoccupied to put his heart into the insults he flung at the tiny girl, and Ce'Nedra's irritation robbed her retorts of their usual fine edge. Toward the end, the whole thing had degenerated into a tedious repetition of "spoiled brat" and "stupid peasant" echoing endlessly back from the surrounding mountains.

Mister Wolf and Silk rode back to join them. "What was all the yelling?" Wolf asked.

"The children were playing," Aunt Pol replied with a withering look at Garion.

"Where's Hettar?" Silk asked.

"Right behind us," Barak said. He turned to look back toward the packhorses, but the tall Algar was nowhere to be seen. Barak frowned. "He was just there. Maybe he stopped for a moment to rest his horse or something."

"Without saying anything?" Silk objected. "That's not like him. And it's not like him to leave the packhorses unattended."

"He must have some good reason," Durnik said.

"I'll go back and look for him," Barak offered.

"No," Mister Wolf told him. "Wait a few minutes. Let's not get scattered all over these mountains. If anybody goes back, we'll all go back."

They waited. The wind stirred the branches of the pines around them, making a mournful, sighing sound. After several moments, Aunt Pol let out her breath almost explosively. "He's coming." There was a steely note in her voice. "He's been entertaining himself."

From far back up the trail, Hettar appeared in his black leather clothing, riding easily at a loping canter with his long scalp lock flowing in the wind. He was leading two saddled but riderless horses. As he drew nearer, they could hear him whistling rather tunelessly to himself.

"What have you been doing?" Barak demanded.

"There were a couple of Murgos following us," Hettar replied as if that explained everything.

"You might have asked me to go along," Barak said, sounding a little injured.

Hettar shrugged. "There were only two. They were riding Algar horses, so I took it rather personally."

"It seems that you always find some reason to take it personally where Murgos are concerned," Aunt Pol said crisply.

"It does seem to work out that way, doesn't it?"

"Didn't it occur to you to let us know you were going?" she asked.

"There were only two," Hettar said again. "I didn't expect to be gone for very long."

She drew in a deep breath, her eyes flashing dangerously.

"Let it go, Pol," Mister Wolf told her.

"But—"

"You're not going to change him, so why excite yourself about it? Besides, it's just as well to discourage pursuit." The old man turned to Hettar, ignoring the dangerous look Aunt Pol leveled at him. "Were the Murgos some of those who were with Brill?" he asked.

Hettar shook his head. "No. Brill's Murgos were from the south and they were riding Murgo horses. These two were northern Murgos."

"Is there a visible difference?" Mandorallen asked curiously.

"The armor is slightly different, and the southerners have flatter faces and they're not quite so tall."

"Where did they get Algar horses?" Garion asked.

"They're herd raiders," Hettar answered bleakly. "Algar horses are valuable in Cthol Murgos, and certain Murgos make a practice of creeping down into Algaria on horse-stealing expeditions. We try to discourage that as much as possible."

"These horses aren't in very good shape," Durnik observed, looking at the two weary-looking animals Hettar was leading. "They've been ridden hard, and there are whip cuts on them."

Hettar nodded grimly. "That's another reason to hate Murgos."

"Did you bury them?" Barak asked.

"No. I left them where any other Murgos who might be following could find them. I thought it might help to educate any who come along later."

"There are some signs that others have been through here, too," Silk said. "I found the tracks of a dozen or so up ahead."

"It was to be expected, I suppose," Mister Wolf commented, scratching at his beard. "Ctuchik's got his Grolims out in force, and Taur Urgas is probably having the region patrolled. I'm sure they'd like to stop us if they could. I think we should move on down into the Vale as fast as possible. Once we're there, we won't be bothered any more."

"Won't they follow us into the Vale?" Durnik asked, looking around nervously.

"No. Murgos won't go into the Vale—not for any reason. Aldur's Spirit is there, and the Murgos are desperately afraid of him."

"How many days to the Vale?" Silk asked.

"Four or five, if we ride hard," Wolf replied.

"We'd better get started then."

Chapter Ten

THE WEATHER, WHICH had seemed on the brink of winter in the higher mountains, softened back into autumn as they rode down from the peaks and ridges. The forests in the hills above Maragor had been thick with fir and spruce and heavy undergrowth. On this side, however, the dominant tree was the pine, and the undergrowth was sparse. The air seemed drier, and the hillsides were covered with high, yellow grass.

They passed through an area where the leaves on the scattered bushes were bright red; then, as they moved lower, the foliage turned first yellow, then green again. Garion found this reversal of the seasons strange. It seemed to violate all his perceptions of the natural order of things. By the time they reached the foothills above the Vale of Aldur, it was late summer again, golden and slightly dusty. Although they frequently saw evidences of the Murgo patrols which were crisscrossing the region, they had no further encounters. After they crossed a certain undefined line, there were no more tracks of Murgo horses.

They rode down beside a turbulent stream which plunged over smooth, round rocks, frothing and roaring. The stream was one of several forming the headwaters of the Aldur River, a broad flow running through the vast Algarian plain to empty into the Gulf of Cherek, eight hundred leagues to the northwest.

The Vale of Aldur was a valley lying in the embrace of the two mountain ranges which formed the central spine of the continent. It was lush and green, covered with high grass and dotted here and there with huge, solitary trees. Deer and wild horses grazed there, as tame as cattle. Skylarks wheeled and dove, filling the air with their song. As the party rode out into the valley, Garion noticed that the birds seemed to gather wherever Aunt Pol moved, and many of the braver ones even settled on her shoulders, warbling and trilling to her in welcome and adoration.

"I'd forgotten about that," Mister Wolf said to Garion. "It's going to be difficult to get her attention for the next few days."

"Oh?"

"Every bird in the Vale is going to stop by to visit her. It happens every time we come here. The birds go wild at the sight of her."

Out of the welter of confused bird sound it seemed to Garion that faintly, almost like a murmuring whisper, he could hear a chorus of chirping voices repeating, "Polgara. Polgara. Polgara."

"Is it my imagination, or are they actually talking?" he asked.

"I'm surprised you haven't heard them before," Wolf replied. "Every bird we've passed for the last ten leagues has been babbling her name."

"Look at me, Polgara, look at me," a swallow seemed to say, hurling himself into a wild series of swooping dives around her head. She smiled gently at him, and he redoubled his efforts.

"I've never heard them talk before," Garion marveled.

"They talk to her all the time," Wolf said. "Sometimes they go on for hours. That's why she seems a little abstracted sometimes. She's listening to the birds. Your Aunt moves through a world filled with conversation."

"I didn't know that."

"Not many people do."

The colt, who had been trotting rather sedately along behind Garion as they had come down out of the foothills, went wild with delight when he reached the lush grass of the Vale. With an amazing burst of speed, he ran out over the meadows. He rolled in the grass, his thin legs flailing. He galloped in long, curving sweeps over the low, rolling hills. He deliberately ran at herds of grazing deer, startling them into flight and then plunging along after them. "Come back here!" Garion shouted at him.

"He won't hear you," Hettar said, smiling at the little horse's antics. "At least, he'll pretend that he doesn't. He's having too much fun."

"Get back here right now!" Garion projected the thought a bit more firmly than he'd intended. The colt's forelegs stiffened, and he slid to a stop. Then he turned and trotted obediently back to Garion, his eyes apologetic. "Bad horse!" Garion chided.

The colt hung his head.

"Don't scold him," Wolf said. "You were very young once yourself."

Garion immediately regretted what he had said and reached down to pat the little animal's shoulder. "It's all right," he apologized. The colt looked at him gratefully and began to frisk through the grass again, although staying close.

Princess Ce'Nedra had been watching him. She always seemed to be watching him for some reason. She would look at him, her eyes speculative and a tendril of her coppery hair coiled about one finger and raised absently to her teeth. It seemed to Garion that every time he turned around she was watching and nibbling. For some reason he could not quite put his finger on, it made him very nervous. "If he were mine, *I* wouldn't be so cruel to him," she accused, taking the tip of the curl from between her teeth.

Garion chose not to answer that.

As they rode down the valley, they passed three ruined towers, standing some distance apart and all showing signs of great antiquity. Each of them appeared to have originally been about sixty feet high, though weather and the passage of years had eroded them down considerably. The last of the three looked as if it had been blackened by some intensely hot fire.

"Was there some kind of war here, Grandfather?" Garion asked.

"No," Wolf replied rather sadly. "The towers belonged to

my brothers. That one over there was Belsambar's, and the one near it was Belmakor's. They died a long time ago."

"I didn't think sorcerers ever died."

"They grew tired—or maybe they lost hope. They caused themselves no longer to exist."

"They killed themselves?"

"In a manner of speaking. It was a little more complete than that, though."

Garion didn't press it, since the old man appeared to prefer not to go into details. "What about the other one—the one that's been burned? Whose tower was that?"

"Belzedar's."

"Did you and the other sorcerers burn it after he went over to Torak?"

"No. He burned it himself. I suppose he thought that was a way to show us that he was no longer a member of our brotherhood. Belzedar always liked dramatic gestures."

"Where's *your* tower?"

"Farther on down the Vale."

"Will you show it to me?"

"If you like."

"Does Aunt Pol have her own tower?"

"No. She stayed with me while she was growing up, and then we went out into the world. We never got around to building her one of her own."

They rode until late afternoon and stopped for the day beneath an enormous tree which stood alone in the center of a broad meadow. The tree quite literally shaded whole acres. Ce'Nedra sprang out of her saddle and ran toward the tree, her deep red hair flying behind her. "He's beautiful!" she exclaimed, placing her hands with reverent affection on the rough bark.

Mister Wolf shook his head. "Dryads. They grow giddy at the sight of trees."

"I don't recognize it," Durnik said with a slight frown. "It's not an oak."

"Maybe it's some southern species," Barak suggested. "I've never seen one exactly like it myself."

"He's very old," Ce'Nedra said, putting her cheek fondly against the tree trunk, "and he speaks strangely—but he likes me."

"What kind of tree is it?" Durnik asked. He was still frowning, his need to classify and categorize frustrated by the huge tree.

"It's the only one of its kind in the world," Mister Wolf told him. "I don't think we ever named it. It was always just the tree. We used to meet here sometimes."

"It doesn't seem to drop any berries or fruit or seeds of any kind," Durnik observed, examining the ground beneath the spreading branches.

"It doesn't need them," Wolf replied. "As I told you, it's the only one of its kind. It's always been here—and always will be. It feels no urge to propagate itself."

Durnik seemed worried about it. "I've never heard of a tree with no seeds."

"It's a rather special tree, Durnik," Aunt Pol said. "It sprouted on the day the world was made, and it will probably stand here for as long as the world exists. It has a purpose other than reproducing itself."

"What purpose is that?"

"We don't know," Wolf answered. "We only know that it's the oldest living thing in the world. Maybe that's its purpose. Maybe it's here to demonstrate the continuity of life."

Ce'Nedra had removed her shoes and was climbing up into the thick branches, making little sounds of affection and delight.

"Is there by any chance a tradition linking Dryads with squirrels?" Silk asked.

Mister Wolf smiled. "If the rest of you can manage without us, Garion and I have something to attend to."

Aunt Pol looked questioningly at him.

"It's time for a little instruction, Pol," he explained.

"We can manage, father," she said. "Will you be back in time for supper?"

"Keep it warm for us. Coming, Garion?"

The two of them rode in silence through the green meadows

with the golden afternoon sunlight making the entire Vale warm and lovely. Garion was baffled by Mister Wolf's curious change of mood. Always before, there had been a sort of impromptu quality about the old man. He seemed frequently to be making up his life as he went along, relying on chance, his wits, and his power, when necessary, to see him through. Here in the Vale, he seemed serene, undisturbed by the chaotic events taking place in the world outside.

About two miles from the tree stood another tower. It was rather squat and round and was built of rough stone. Arched windows near the top faced out in the directions of the four winds, but there seemed to be no door.

"You said you'd like to visit my tower," Wolf said, dismounting. "This is it."

"It isn't ruined like the others."

"I take care of it from time to time. Shall we go up?"

Garion slid down from his horse. "Where's the door?" he asked.

"Right there." Wolf pointed at a large stone in the rounded wall.

Garion looked skeptical.

Mister Wolf stepped in front of the stone. "It's me," he said. "Open."

The surge Garion felt at the old man's word seemed commonplace—ordinary—a household kind of surge that spoke of something that had been done so often that it was no longer a wonder. The rock turned obediently, revealing a sort of narrow, irregular doorway. Motioning for Garion to follow, Wolf squeezed through into the dim chamber beyond the door.

The tower, Garion saw, was not a hollow shell as he had expected, but rather was a solid pedestal, pierced only by a stairway winding upward.

"Come along," Wolf told him, starting up the worn stone steps. "Watch that one," he said about halfway up, pointing at one of the steps. "The stone is loose."

"Why don't you fix it?" Garion asked, stepping up over the loose stone.

"I've been meaning to, but I just haven't gotten around to

it. It's been that way for a long time. I'm so used to it now that I never seem to think of fixing it when I'm here."

The chamber at the top of the tower was round and very cluttered. A thick coat of dust lay over everything. There were several tables in various parts of the room, covered with rolls and scraps of parchment, strange-looking implements and models, bits and pieces of rock and glass, and a couple of birds' nests; on one, a curious stick was so wound and twisted and coiled that Garion's eye could not exactly follow its convolutions. He picked it up and turned it over in his hands, trying to trace it out. "What's this, Grandfather?" he asked.

"One of Polgara's toys," the old man said absently, staring around at the dusty chamber.

"What's it supposed to do?"

"It kept her quiet when she was a baby. It's only got one end. She spent five years trying to figure it out."

Garion pulled his eyes off the fascinatingly compelling piece of wood. "That's a cruel sort of thing to do to a child."

"I had to do something," Wolf answered. "She had a penetrating voice as a child. Beldaran was a quiet, happy little girl, but your Aunt never seemed satisfied."

"Beldaran?"

"Your Aunt's twin sister." The old man's voice trailed off, and he looked sadly out of one of the windows for a few moments. Finally he sighed and turned back to the round room. "I suppose I ought to clean this up a bit," he said, looking around at the dust and litter.

"Let me help," Garion offered.

"Just be careful not to break anything," the old man warned. "Some of those things took me centuries to make." He began moving around the chamber, picking things up and setting them down again, blowing now and then on them to clear away a bit of the dust. His efforts didn't really seem to be getting anywhere.

Finally he stopped, staring at a low, rough-looking chair with the rail along its back, scarred and gashed as if it had been continually grasped by strong claws. He sighed again.

"What's wrong?" Garion asked.

"Poledra's chair," Wolf said. "—My wife. She used to perch there and watch me—sometimes for years on end."

"Perch?"

"She was fond of the shape of the owl."

"Oh." Garion had somehow never thought of the old man as ever having been married, although he obviously had to have been at some time, since Aunt Pol and her twin sister were his daughters. The shadowy wife's affinity for owls, however, explained Aunt Pol's own preference for that shape. The two women, Poledra and Beldaran, were involved rather intimately in his own background, he realized, but quite irrationally he resented them. They had shared a part of the lives of his Aunt and his grandfather that he would never—could never know.

The old man moved a parchment and picked up a peculiar-looking device with a sighting glass in one end of it. "I thought I'd lost you," he told the device, touching it with a familiar fondness. "You've been under that parchment all this time."

"What is it?" Garion asked him.

"A thing I made when I was trying to discover the reason for mountains."

"The reason?"

"Everything has a reason." Wolf raised the instrument. "You see, what you do is—" He broke off and laid the device back on the table. "It's much too complicated to explain. I'm not even sure if I remember exactly how to use it myself. I haven't touched it since before Belzedar came to the Vale. When he arrived, I had to lay my studies aside to train him." He looked around at the dust and clutter. "This is useless," he said. "The dust will just come back anyway."

"Were you alone here before Belzedar came?"

"My Master was here. That's his tower over there." Wolf pointed through the north window at a tall, slender stone structure about a mile away.

"Was he really here?" Garion asked. "I mean, not just his spirit?"

"No. He was really here. That was before the Gods departed."

"Did you live here always?"

"No. I came like a thief, looking for something to steal—well, that's not actually true, I suppose. I was about your age when I came here, and I was dying at the time."

"Dying?" Garion was startled.

"Freezing to death. I'd left the village I was born in the year before—after my mother died—and spent my first winter in the camp of the Godless Ones. They were very old by then."

"Godless Ones?"

"Ulgos—or rather the ones who decided not to follow Gorim to Prolgu. They stopped having children after that, so they were happy to take me in. I couldn't understand their language at the time, and all their pampering got on my nerves, so I ran away in the spring. I was on my way back the next fall, but I got caught in an early snowstorm not far from here. I lay down against the side of my Master's tower to die—I didn't know it was a tower at first. With all the snow swirling around, it just looked like a pile of rock. As I recall, I was feeling rather sorry for myself at the time."

"I can imagine." Garion shivered at the thought of being alone and dying.

"I was sniveling a bit, and the sound disturbed my Master. He let me in—probably more to quiet me than for any other reason. As soon as I got inside, I started looking for things to steal."

"But he made you a sorcerer instead."

"No. He made me a servant—a slave. I worked for him for five years before I even found out who he was. Sometimes I think I hated him, but I had to do what he told me to—I didn't really know why. The last straw came when he told me to move a big rock out of his way. I tried with all my strength, but I couldn't budge it. Finally I got angry enough to move it with my mind instead of my back. That's what he'd been waiting for, of course. After that we got along better. He changed my name from Garath to Belgarath, and he made me his pupil."

"And his disciple?"

"That took a little longer. I had a lot to learn. I was ex-amining the reason that certain stars fell at the time he first called me his disciple—and he was working on a round, gray stone he'd picked up by the riverbank."

"Did you ever discover the reason—that stars fall, I mean?"

"Yes. It's not all that complicated. It has to do with balance. The world needs a certain weight to keep it turning. When it starts to slow down, a few nearby stars fall. Their weight makes up the difference."

"I never thought of that."

"Neither did I—not for quite some time."

"The stone you mentioned. Was it—"

"The Orb," Wolf confirmed. "Just an ordinary rock until my Master touched it. Anyway, I learned the secret of the Will and the Word—which isn't really that much of a secret, after all. It's there in all of us—or did I say that before?"

"I think so."

"Probably so. I tend to repeat myself." The old man picked up a roll of parchment and glanced at it, then laid it aside again. "So much that I started and haven't finished." He sighed.

"Grandfather?"

"Yes, Garion?"

"This—thing of ours—how much can you actually do with it?"

"That depends on your mind, Garion. The complexity of it lies in the complexity of the mind that puts it to use. Quite obviously, it can't do something that can't be imagined by the mind that focuses it. That was the purpose of our studies—to expand our minds so that we could use the power more fully."

"Everybody's mind is different, though." Garion was struggling toward an idea.

"Yes."

"Wouldn't that mean that—this thing—" He shied away from the word "power." "What I mean is, is it different? Sometimes you do things, and other times you have Aunt Pol do them."

Wolf nodded. "It's different in each one of us. There are certain things we can all do. We can all move things, for example."

"Aunt Pol called it trans—" Garion hesitated, not remembering the word.

"Translocation," Wolf supplied. "Moving something from one place to another. It's the simplest thing you can do—usually the thing you do first—and it makes the most noise."

"That's what she told me." Garion remembered the slave he had jerked from the river at Sthiss Tor—the slave who had died.

"Polgara can do things that I can't," Wolf continued. "Not because she's any stronger than I am, but because she thinks differently than I do. We're not sure how much you can do yet, because we don't know exactly how your mind works. You seem to be able to do certain things quite easily that I wouldn't even attempt. Maybe it's because you don't realize how difficult they are."

"I don't quite understand what you mean."

The old man looked at him. "Perhaps you don't, at that. Remember the crazy monk who tried to attack you in that village in northern Tolnedra just after we left Arendia?"

Garion nodded.

"You cured his madness. That doesn't sound like much until you realize that in the instant you cured him, you had to understand fully the nature of his insanity. That's an extremely difficult thing, and you did it without even thinking about it. And then, of course, there was the colt."

Garion glanced down through the window at the little horse friskily running through the field surrounding the tower.

"The colt was dead, but you made him start to breathe. In order for you to do that, you had to be able to understand death."

"It was just a wall," Garion explained. "All I did was reach through it."

"There's more to it than that, I think. What you seem to be able to do is to visualize extremely difficult ideas in very simple terms. That's a rare gift, but there are some dangers involved in it that you should be aware of."

"Dangers? Such as what?"

"Don't *over*simplify. If a man's dead, for example, he's

usually dead for a very good reason—like a sword through the heart. If you bring him back, he'll only die immediately again anyway. As I said before, just because you *can* do something doesn't necessarily mean that you *should*."

Garion sighed. "I'm afraid this is going to take a very long time, Grandfather," he said. "I have to learn how to keep myself under control; I have to learn what I can't do, so I don't kill myself trying to do something impossible; I have to learn what I can do and what I should do. I wish this had never happened to me."

"We all do sometimes," the old man told him. "The decision wasn't ours to make, though. I haven't always liked some of the things I've had to do, and neither has your Aunt; but what we're doing is more important than we are, so we do what's expected of us—like it or not."

"What if I just said, 'No. I won't do it'?"

"You *could* do that, I suppose, but you won't, will you?"

Garion sighed again. "No," he said, "I guess not."

The old sorcerer put his arm around the boy's shoulders. "I thought you might see things that way, Belgarion. You're bound to this the same way we all are."

The strange thrill he always felt at the sound of his other, secret name ran through Garion. "Why do you all insist on calling me that?" he asked.

"Belgarion?" Wolf said mildly. "Think, boy. Think what it means. I haven't been talking to you and telling you stories all these years just because I like the sound of my own voice."

Garion turned it over carefully in his mind. "You were Garath," he mused thoughtfully, "but the God Aldur changed your name to Belgarath. Zedar was Zedar first and then Belzedar—and then he went back to being Zedar again."

"And in my old tribe, Polgara would have just been Gara. Pol is like Bel. The only difference is that she's a woman. Her name comes from mine—because she's my daughter. Your name comes from mine, too."

"Garion—Garath," the boy said. "Belgarath—Belgarion. It all fits together, doesn't it?"

"Naturally," the old man replied. "I'm glad you noticed it."

Garion grinned at him. Then a thought occurred. "But I'm not really Belgarion yet, am I?"

"Not entirely. You still have a way to go."

"I suppose I'd better get started then." Garion said it with a certain ruefulness. "Since I don't really have any choice."

"Somehow I knew that eventually you'd come around," Mister Wolf said.

"Don't you sometimes wish that I was just Garion again, and you were the old storyteller coming to visit Faldor's farm—with Aunt Pol making supper in the kitchen as she did in the old days—and we were hiding under a haystack with a bottle I'd stolen for you?" Garion felt the homesickness welling up in him.

"Sometimes, Garion, sometimes," Wolf admitted, his eyes far away.

"We won't ever be able to go back there again, will we?"

"Not the same way, no."

"I'll be Belgarion, and you'll be Belgarath. We won't even be the same people any more."

"Everything changes, Garion," Belgarath told him.

"Show me the rock," Garion said suddenly.

"Which rock?"

"The one Aldur made you move—the day you first discovered the power."

"Oh," Belgarath said, "*that* rock. It's right over there—the white one. The one the colt's sharpening his hooves on."

"It's a very big rock."

"I'm glad you appreciate that," Belgarath replied modestly. "I thought so myself."

"Do you suppose *I* could move it?"

"You never know until you try, Garion," Belgarath told him.

Chapter Eleven

THE NEXT MORNING when Garion awoke, he knew immediately that he was not alone.

"Where have you been?" he asked silently.

"I've been watching," the other consciousness in his mind said. *"I see that you've finally come around."*

"What choice did I have?"

"None. You'd better get up. Aldur's coming."

Garion quickly rolled out of his blankets. *"Here? Are you sure?"*

The voice in his mind didn't answer.

Garion put on a clean tunic and hose and wiped off his half-boots with a certain amount of care. Then he went out of the tent he shared with Silk and Durnik.

The sun was just coming up over the high mountains to the east, and the line between sunlight and shadow moved with a stately ponderousness across the dewy grass of the Vale. Aunt Pol and Belgarath stood near the small fire where a pot was just beginning to bubble. They were talking quietly, and Garion joined them.

"You're up early," Aunt Pol said. She reached out and smoothed his hair.

"I was awake," he replied. He looked around, wondering from which direction Aldur would come.

"Your grandfather tells me that the two of you had a long talk yesterday."

119

Garion nodded. "I understand a few things a little better now. I'm sorry I've been so difficult."

She drew him to her and put her arms around him. "It's all right, dear. You had some hard decisions to make."

"You're not angry with me, then?"

"Of course not, dear."

The others had begun to get up, coming out of their tents, yawning and stretching and rumpled-looking.

"What do we do today?" Silk asked, coming to the fire and rubbing the sleep from his eyes.

"We wait," Belgarath told him. "My Master said he'd meet us here."

"I'm curious to see him. I've never met a God before."

"Thy curiosity, methinks, will soon be satisfied, Prince Kheldar," Mandorallen said. "Look there."

Coming across the meadow not far from the great tree beneath which they had pitched their tents, a figure in a blue robe was approaching. A soft nimbus of blue light surrounded the figure, and the immediate sense of presence made it instantly clear that what approached was not a man. Garion was not prepared for the impact of that presence. His meeting with the Spirit of Issa in Queen Salmissra's throne room had been clouded by the narcotic effects of the things the Serpent Queen had forced him to drink. Similarly, half his mind had slept during the confrontation with Mara in the ruins of Mar Amon. But now, fully awake in the first light of morning, he found himself in the presence of a God.

Aldur's face was kindly and enormously wise. His long hair and beard were white—from conscious choice, Garion felt, rather than from any result of age. The face was very familiar to him somehow. It bore a startling resemblance to Belgarath's, but Garion perceived immediately, with a sudden curious inversion of his original notion, that it was Belgarath who resembled Aldur—as if their centuries of association had stamped Aldur's features upon the face of the old man. There were differences, of course. That certain mischievous roguishness was not present on the calm face of Aldur. That quality was Belgarath's own, the last remnant, perhaps, of the face of the

thieving boy Aldur had taken into his tower on a snowy day
some seven thousand years ago.

"Master," Belgarath said, bowing respectfully as Aldur approached.

"Belgarath," the God acknowledged. His voice was very
quiet. "I have not seen thee in some time. The years have not
been unkind to thee."

Belgarath shrugged wryly. "Some days I feel them more
than others, Master. I carry a great number of years with me."

Aldur smiled and turned to Aunt Pol. "My beloved daughter,"
he said fondly, reaching out to touch the white lock at her
brow. "Thou art as lovely as ever."

"And thou as kind, Master," she replied, smiling and inclining her head.

There passed among the three of them a kind of intensely
personal linkage, a joining of minds that marked their reunion.
Garion could feel the edges of it with his own mind, and he
was somewhat wistful at being excluded—though he realized
at once that there was no intent to exclude him. They were
merely reestablishing an eons-old companionship—shared ex-
periences that stretched back into antiquity.

Aldur then turned to look at the others. "And so you have
come together at last, as it hath been foretold from the beginning
of days you should. You are the instruments of destiny, and
my blessing goes with each as you move toward that awful day
when the universe will become one again."

The faces of Garion's companions were awed and puzzled
by Aldur's enigmatic blessing. Each, however, bowed with
profound respect and humility.

And then Ce'Nedra emerged from the tent she shared with
Aunt Pol. The tiny girl stretched luxuriantly and ran her fingers
through the tumbled mass of her flaming hair. She was dressed
in a Dryad tunic and sandals.

"Ce'Nedra," Aunt Pol called her, "come here."

"Yes, Lady Polgara," the little princess replied obediently.
She crossed to the fire, her feet seeming barely to touch the
ground. Then she saw Aldur standing with the others and
stopped, her eyes wide.

"This is our Master, Ce'Nedra," Aunt Pol told her. "He wanted to meet you."

The princess stared at the glowing presence in confusion. Nothing in her life had prepared her for such a meeting. She lowered her eyelashes and then looked up shyly, her tiny face artfully and automatically assuming its most appealing expression.

Aldur smiled gently. "She's like a flower that charms without knowing it." His eyes looked deeply into those of the princess. "There is steel in this one, however. She is fit for her task. My blessings upon thee, my child."

Ce'Nedra responded with an instinctively graceful curtsey. It was the first time Garion had ever seen her bow to anyone.

Aldur turned then to look full at Garion. A brief, unspoken acknowledgment passed between the God and the consciousness that shared Garion's thoughts. There was in that momentary meeting a sense of mutual respect and of shared responsibility. And then Garion felt the massive touch of Aldur's mind upon his own and knew that the God had instantly seen and understood his every thought and feeling.

"Hail, Belgarion," Aldur said gravely.

"Master," Garion replied. He dropped to one knee, not really knowing why.

"We have awaited thy coming since time's beginning. Thou art the vessel of all our hopes." Aldur raised his hand. "My blessing, Belgarion. I am well pleased with thee."

Garion's entire being was suffused with love and gratitude as the warmth of Aldur's benediction filled him.

"Dear Polgara," Aldur said to Aunt Pol, "thy gift to us is beyond value. Belgarion has come at last, and the world trembles at his coming."

Aunt Pol bowed again.

"Let us now go apart," Aldur said to Belgarath and Aunt Pol. "Your task is well begun, and I must now provide you with that instruction I promised when first I set your steps upon this path. That which was once clouded becomes clearer, and we now can see what lies before us. Let us look toward that day we have all awaited and make our preparations."

The three of them moved away from the fire, and it seemed to Garion that, as they went, the glowing nimbus which had surrounded Aldur now enclosed Aunt Pol and his grandfather as well. Some movement or sound distracted his eye for a moment, and when he looked back, the three had vanished.

Barak let out his breath explosively. "Belar! That was something to see!"

"We have been favored, I think, beyond all men," Mandorallen said.

They all stood staring at each other, caught up in the wonder of what they had just witnessed. Ce'Nedra, however, broke the mood. "All right," she ordered peremptorily, "don't just stand there gaping. Move away from the fire."

"What are you going to do?" Garion asked her.

"The Lady Polgara's going to be busy," the little girl said loftily, "so *I'm* going to make breakfast." She moved toward the fire with a businesslike bustling.

The bacon was not too badly burned, but Ce'Nedra's attempt to toast slices of bread before the open fire turned out disastrously, and her porridge had lumps in it as solid as clods in a sun-baked field. Garion and the others, however, ate what she offered without comment, prudently avoiding the direct gaze she leveled at them, as if daring them to speak so much as one word of criticism.

"I wonder how long they're going to be," Silk said after breakfast.

"Gods, I think, have little notion of time," Barak replied sagely, stroking at his beard. "I don't expect them back until sometime this afternoon at the earliest."

"It is a good time to check over the horses," Hettar decided. "Some of them have picked up a few burrs along the way, and I'd like to have a look at their hooves—just to be on the safe side."

"I'll help you," Durnik offered, getting up.

Hettar nodded, and the two went off to the place where the horses were picketed.

"And I've got a nick or two in my sword edge," Barak

remembered, fishing a piece of polishing stone out of his belt and laying his heavy blade across his lap.

Mandorallen went to his tent and brought out his armor. He laid it out on the ground and began a minute inspection for dents and spots of rust.

Silk rattled a pair of dice hopefully in one hand, looking inquiringly at Barak.

"If it's all the same to you, I think I'd like to enjoy the company of my money for a while longer," the big man told him.

"This whole place absolutely *reeks* of domesticity," Silk complained. Then he sighed, put away his dice, and went to fetch a needle and thread and a tunic he'd torn on a bush up in the mountains.

Ce'Nedra had returned to her communion with the vast tree and was scampering among the branches, taking what Garion felt to be inordinate risks as she jumped from limb to limb with a catlike unconcern. After watching her for a few moments, he fell into a kind of reverie, thinking back to the awesome meeting that morning. He had met the Gods Issa and Mara already, but there was something special about Aldur. The affinity Belgarath and Aunt Pol showed so obviously for this God who had always remained aloof from men spoke loudly to Garion. The devotional activities of Sendaria, where he had been raised, were inclusive rather than exclusive. A good Sendar prayed impartially, and honored all the Gods—even Torak. Garion now, however, felt a special closeness and reverence for Aldur, and the adjustment in his theological thinking required a certain amount of thought.

A twig dropped out of the tree onto his head, and he glanced up with annoyance.

Ce'Nedra, grinning impishly, was directly over his head. "Boy," she said in her most superior and insulting tone, "the breakfast dishes are getting cold. The grease is going to be difficult to wash off if you let it harden."

"I'm not your scullion," he told her.

"Wash the dishes, Garion," she ordered him, nibbling at the tip of a lock of hair.

"Wash them yourself."

She glared down at him, biting rather savagely at the unoffending lock.

"Why do you keep chewing on your hair like that?" he asked irritably.

"What are you talking about?" she demanded, removing the lock from between her teeth.

"Every time I look at you, you've got your hair stuck in your mouth."

"I do *not*," she retorted indignantly. "Are you going to wash the dishes?"

"No." He squinted up at her. The short Dryad tunic she was wearing seemed to expose an unseemly amount of leg. "Why don't you go put on some clothes?" he suggested. "Some of us don't appreciate the way you run around half-naked all the time."

The fight got under way almost immediately after that.

Finally Garion gave up his efforts to get in the last word and stamped away in disgust.

"Garion!" she screamed after him. "Don't you *dare* go off and leave me with all these dirty dishes!"

He ignored her and kept walking.

After a short distance, he felt a familiar nuzzling at his elbow and he rather absently scratched the colt's ears. The small animal quivered with delight and rubbed against him affectionately. Then, unable to restrain himself any more, the colt galloped off into the meadow to pester a family of docilely feeding rabbits. Garion found himself smiling. The morning was just too beautiful to allow the squabble with the princess to spoil it.

There was, it seemed, something rather special about the Vale. The world around grew cold with the approach of winter and was buffetted by storms and dangers, but here it seemed as if the hand of Aldur stretched protectively above them, filling this special place with warmth and peace and a kind of eternal and magical serenity. Garion, at this trying point in his life, needed all the warmth and peace he could get. There were things that had to be worked out, and he needed a time, however brief, without storms and dangers to deal with them.

He was halfway to Belgarath's tower before he realized that it had been there that he had been going all along. The tall grass was wet with dew, and his boots were soon soaked, but even that did not spoil the day.

He walked around the tower several times, gazing up at it. Although he found the stone that marked the door quite easily, he decided not to open it. It would not be proper to go uninvited into the old man's tower; and beyond that, he was not entirely certain that the door would respond to any voice but Belgarath's.

He stopped quite suddenly at that last thought and started searching back, trying to find the exact instant when he had ceased to think of his grandfather as Mister Wolf and had finally accepted the fact that he was Belgarath. The changeover seemed significant—a kind of turning point.

Still lost in thought, he turned then and walked across the meadow toward the large, white rock the old man had pointed out to him from the tower window. Absently he put one hand on it and pushed. The rock didn't budge.

Garion set both hands on it and pushed again, but the rock remained motionless. He stepped back and considered it. It wasn't really a vast boulder. It was rounded and white and not quite as high as his waist—heavy, certainly, but it should not be so inflexibly solid. He bent over to look at the bottom, and then he understood. The underside of the rock was flat. It would never roll. The only way to move it would be to lift one side and tip it over. He walked around the rock, looking at it from every angle. He judged that it was marginally movable. If he exerted every ounce of his strength, he might be able to lift it. He sat down and looked at it, thinking hard. As he sometimes did, he talked to himself, trying to lay out the problem.

"The first thing to do is to *try* to move it," he concluded. "It doesn't really look totally impossible. Then, if that doesn't work, we'll try it the other way."

He stood up, stepped purposefully to the rock, wormed his fingers under the edge of it and heaved. Nothing happened.

"Have to try a little harder," he told himself. He spread his feet and set himself. He began to lift again, straining, the cords standing out in his neck. For the space of about ten heartbeats he tried as hard as he could to lift the stubborn rock—not to roll it over; he'd given that up after the first instant—but simply to make it budge, to acknowledge his existence. Though the ground was not particularly soft there, his feet actually sank a fraction of an inch or so as he strained against the rock's weight.

His head was swimming, and little dots seemed to swirl in front of his eyes as he released the rock and collapsed, gasping, against it. He lay against the cold, gritty surface for several minutes, recovering.

"All right," he said finally, "now we know that *that* won't work." He stepped back and sat down.

Each time he'd done something with his mind before, it had been on impulse, a response to some crisis. He had never sat down and deliberately worked himself up to it. He discovered almost at once that the entire set of circumstances was completely different. The whole world seemed suddenly filled with distractions. Birds sang. A breeze brushed his face. An ant crawled across his hand. Each time he began to bring his will to bear, something pulled his attention away.

There was a certain feeling to it, he knew that, a tightness in the back of his head and a sort of pushing out with his forehead. He closed his eyes, and that seemed to help. It was coming. It was slow, but he felt the will begin to build in him. Remembering something, he reached inside his tunic and put the mark on his palm against the amulet. The force within him, amplified by that touch, built to a great roaring crescendo. He kept his eyes closed and stood up. Then he opened his eyes and looked hard at the stubborn white rock. "You *will* move," he muttered. He kept his right hand on the amulet and held out his left hand, palm up.

"Now!" he said sharply and slowly began to raise his left hand in a lifting motion. The force within him surged, and the roaring sound inside his head became deafening.

Slowly the edge of the rock came up out of the grass. Worms and burrowing grubs who had lived out their lives in the safe, comfortable darkness under the rock flinched as the morning sunlight hit them. Ponderously, the rock raised, obeying Garion's inexorably lifting hand. It teetered for a second on its edge, then toppled slowly over.

The exhaustion he had felt after trying to lift the rock with his back was nothing compared to the bone-deep weariness that swept over him after he let the clenching of his will relax. He folded his arms on the grass and let his head sink down on them.

After a moment or two, that peculiar fact began to dawn on him. He was still standing, but his arms were folded comfortably in front of him on the grass. He jerked his head up and looked around in confusion. He had moved the rock, certainly. That much was obvious, since the rock now lay on its rounded top with its damp underside turned up. Something else had also happened, however. Though he had not touched the rock, its weight had nonetheless been upon him as he had lifted it, and the force he had directed at it had not all gone at the rock.

With dismay, Garion realized that he had sunk up to his armpits in the firm soil of the meadow.

"Now what do I do?" he asked himself helplessly. He shuddered away from the idea of once again mustering his will to pull himself out of the ground. He was too exhausted even to consider it. He tried to wriggle, thinking that he might be able to loosen the earth around him and work his way up an inch at a time, but he could not so much as budge.

"Look what you've done," he accused the rock.

The rock ignored him.

A thought occurred to him. "Are *you* in there?" he asked that awareness that seemed always to have been with him.

The silence in his mind was profound.

"Help!" he shouted.

A bird, attracted by the exposed worms and bugs that had been under the rock, cocked one eye at him and then went back to its breakfast.

Garion heard a light step behind him and craned around, trying to see. The colt was staring at him in amazement. Hesitantly, the small horse thrust out his nose and nuzzled Garion's face.

"Good horse," Garion said, relieved not to be alone, at least. An idea came to him. "You're going to have to go get Hettar," he told the colt.

The colt pranced about and nuzzled his face again.

"Stop that," Garion commanded. "This is serious." Cautiously, he tried to push his mind into the colt's thoughts. He tried a dozen different ways until he finally struck the right combination by sheer accident. The colt's mind flitted from here to there without purpose or pattern. It was a baby's mind, vacant of thought, receiving only sense impressions. Garion caught flickering images of green grass and running and clouds in the sky and warm milk. He also felt the sense of wonder in the little mind, and the abiding love the colt had for him.

Slowly, painfully, Garion began constructing a picture of Hettar in the colt's wandering thoughts. It seemed to take forever.

"Hettar," Garion said over and over. "Go get Hettar. Tell him that I'm in trouble."

The colt scampered around and came back to stick his soft nose in Garion's ear.

"Please pay attention," Garion cried. *"Please!"*

Finally, after what seemed hours, the colt seemed to understand. He went several paces away, then came back to nuzzle Garion again.

"Go—get—Hettar," Garion ordered, stressing each word.

The colt pawed at the ground, then turned and galloped away—going in the wrong direction. Garion started to swear. For almost a year now he had been exposed to some of the more colorful parts of Barak's vocabulary. After he had repeated all the phrases he remembered six or eight times, he began to extemporize.

A flickering thought came back to him from the now-vanished colt. The little beast was chasing butterflies. Garion pounded the ground with his fists, wanting to howl with frustration.

The sun rose higher, and it started to get hot.

It was early afternoon when Hettar and Silk, following the prancing little colt, found him.

"How in the world did you manage to do that?" Silk asked curiously.

"I don't want to talk about it," Garion muttered, somewhere between relief and total embarrassment.

"He probably can do many things that we can't," Hettar observed, climbing down from his horse and untying Durnik's shovel from his saddle. "The thing I can't understand, though, is *why* he'd want to do it."

"I'm positive he had a good reason for it," Silk assured him.

"Do you think we should ask him?"

"It's probably very complicated," Silk replied. "I'm sure simple men like you and me wouldn't be able to understand it."

"Do you suppose he's finished with whatever it is he's doing?"

"We could ask him, I suppose."

"I wouldn't want to disturb him," Hettar said. "It could be very important."

"It almost has to be," Silk agreed.

"Will you *please* get me out of here?" Garion begged.

"Are you sure you're finished?" Silk asked politely. "We can wait if you're not done yet."

"Please," Garion asked, almost in tears.

Chapter Twelve

"WHY DID YOU try to *lift* it?" Belgarath asked Garion the next morning after he and Aunt Pol had returned and Silk and Hettar had solemnly informed them of the predicament in which they had found the young man the afternoon before.

"It seemed like the best way to tip it over," Garion answered. "You know, kind of get hold of it from underneath and then roll it—sort of."

"Why didn't you just push against it—close to the top? It would have rolled over if you'd done it that way."

"I didn't think of it."

"Don't you realize that soft earth won't accept that kind of pressure?" Aunt Pol asked.

"I do now," Garion replied. "But wouldn't pushing on it have just moved me backward?"

"You have to brace yourself," Belgarath explained. "That's part of the whole trick. As much of your will goes to holding yourself immobile as it does to pushing against the object you're trying to move. Otherwise all you do is just shove yourself away."

"I didn't know that," Garion admitted. "It's the first time I've ever tried to do anything unless it was an emergency... Will you *stop* that?" he demanded crossly of Ce'Nedra, who had collapsed into gales of laughter as soon as Silk had finished telling them about Garion's blunder.

She laughed even harder.

"I think you're going to have to explain a few things to him, father," Aunt Pol said. "He doesn't seem to have even the most rudimentary idea about the way forces react against each other." She looked at Garion critically. "It's lucky you didn't decide to throw it," she told him. "You might have flung yourself halfway back to Maragor."

"I really don't think it's all that funny," Garion told his friends, who were all grinning openly at him. "This isn't as easy as it looks, you know." He realized that he had just made a fool of himself and he was not sure if he were more embarrassed or hurt by their amusement.

"Come with me, boy," Belgarath said firmly. "It looks as if we're going to have to start at the very beginning."

"It's not my fault I didn't know," Garion protested. "You should have told me."

"I didn't know you were planning to start experimenting so soon," the old man replied. "Most of us have sense enough to wait for guidance before we start rearranging local geography."

"Well, at least I *did* manage to move it," Garion said defensively as he followed the old man across the meadow toward the tower.

"Splendid. Did you put it back the way you found it?"

"Why? What difference does it make?"

"We don't move things here in the Vale. Everything that's here is here for a reason, and they're all supposed to be exactly where they are."

"I didn't know," Garion apologized.

"You do now. Let's go put it back where it belongs."

They trudged along in silence.

"Grandfather?" Garion said finally.

"Yes?"

"When I moved the rock, it seemed that I was getting the strength to do it from all around me. It seemed just to flow in from everyplace. Does that mean anything?"

"That's the way it works," Belgarath explained. "When we do something, we take the power to do it from our surroundings. When you burned Chamdar, for example, you drew the heat from all around you—from the air, from the ground, and from everyone who was in the area. You drew a little heat from everything to build the fire. When you tipped the rock over, you took the force to do it from everything nearby."

"I thought it all came from inside."

"Only when you create things," the old man replied. "That force has to come from within us. For anything else, we borrow. We gather up a little power from here and there and put it all together and then turn it loose all at one spot. Nobody's big enough to carry around the kind of force it would take to do even the simplest sort of thing."

"Then that's what happens when somebody tries to unmake something," Garion said intuitively. "He pulls in all the force, but then he can't let it go, and it just—" He spread his hands and jerked them suddenly apart.

Belgarath looked narrowly at him. "You've got a strange sort of mind, boy. You understand the difficult things quite easily, but you can't seem to get hold of the simple ones. There's the rock." He shook his head. "That will never do. Put it back where it belongs, and try not to make so much noise this time. That racket you raised yesterday echoed all over the Vale."

"What do I do?" Garion asked.

"Gather in the force," Belgarath told him. "Take it from everything around."

Garion tried that.

"Not from *me*!" the old man exclaimed sharply.

Garion excluded his grandfather from his field of reaching out and pulling in. After a moment or two, he felt as if he were tingling all over and that his hair was standing on end. "Now what?" he asked, clenching his teeth to hold it in.

"Push out behind you and push at the rock at the same time."

"What do I push at behind me?"

"Everything—and at the rock as well. It has to be simultaneous."

"Won't I get—sort of squeezed in between?"

"Tense yourself up."

"We'd better hurry, Grandfather," Garion said. "I feel like I'm going to fly apart."

"Hold it in. Now put your will on the rock, and say the word."

Garion put his hands out in front of him and straightened his arms. "Push," he commanded. He felt the surge and the roaring.

With a resounding thud, the rock teetered and then rolled back smoothly to where it had been the morning before. Garion suddenly felt bruised all over, and he sank to his knees in exhaustion.

"Push?" Belgarath said incredulously.

"You said to say push."

"I said to push. I didn't say to *say* push."

"It went over. What difference does it make what word I used?"

"It's a question of style," the old man said with a pained look. "Push sounds so—so babyish."

Weakly, Garion began to laugh.

"After all, Garion, we do have a certain dignity to maintain," the old man said loftily. "If we go around saying 'push' or 'flop' or things like that, no one's ever going to take us seriously."

Garion wanted to stop laughing, but he simply couldn't.

Belgarath stalked away indignantly, muttering to himself.

When they returned to the others, they found that the tents had been struck and the packhorses loaded.

"There's no point in staying here," Aunt Pol told them, "and the others are waiting for us. Did you manage to make him understand anything, father?"

Belgarath grunted, his face set in an expression of profound disapproval.

"Things didn't go well, I take it."

"I'll explain later," he said shortly.

During Garion's absence, Ce'Nedra, with much coaxing and a lapful of apples from their stores, had seduced the little colt into a kind of ecstatic subservience. He followed her about shamelessly, and the rather distant look he gave Garion showed not the slightest trace of guilt.

"You're going to make him sick," Garion accused her.

"Apples are good for horses," she replied airily.

"Tell her, Hettar," Garion said.

"They won't hurt him," the hook-nosed man answered. "It's a customary way to gain the trust of a young horse."

Garion tried to think of another suitable objection, but without success. For some reason the sight of the little animal nuzzling at Ce'Nedra offended him, though he couldn't exactly put his finger on why.

"Who are these others, Belgarath?" Silk asked as they rode. "The ones Polgara mentioned."

"My brothers," the old sorcerer replied. "Our Master's advised them that we're coming."

"I've heard stories about the Brotherhood of Sorcerers all my life. Are they as remarkable as everyone says?"

"I think you're in for a bit of a disappointment," Aunt Pol told him rather primly. "For the most part, sorcerers tend to be crochety old men with a wide assortment of bad habits. I grew up amongst them, so I know them all rather well." She turned her face to the thrush perched on her shoulder, singing adoringly. "Yes," she said to the bird, "I know."

Garion pulled closer to his Aunt and began to listen very hard to the birdsong. At first it was merely noise—pretty, but without sense. Then, gradually, he began to pick up scraps of meaning—a bit here, a bit there. The bird was singing of nests and small, speckled eggs and sunrises and the overwhelming joy of flying. Then, as if his ears had suddenly opened, Garion began to understand. Larks sang of flying and singing. Sparrows chirped of hidden little pockets of seeds. A hawk, soaring overhead, screamed its lonely song of riding the wind alone and the fierce joy of the kill. Garion was awed as the air around him suddenly came alive with words.

Aunt Pol looked at him gravely. "It's a beginning," she said without bothering to explain.

Garion was so caught up in the world that had just opened to him that he did not see the two silvery-haired men at first. They stood together beneath a tall tree, waiting as the party rode nearer. They wore identical blue robes, and their white hair was quite long, though they were clean-shaven. When

Garion looked at them for the first time, he thought for a moment that his eyes were playing tricks. The two were so absolutely identical that it was impossible to tell them apart.

"Belgarath, our brother," one of them said, "it's been such—"

"—a terribly long time," the other finished.

"Beltira," Belgarath said. "Belkira." He dismounted and embraced the twins.

"Dearest little Polgara," one of them said then.

"The Vale has been—" the other started.

"—empty without you," the second completed. He turned to his brother. "That was very poetic," he said admiringly.

"Thank you," the first replied modestly.

"These are my brothers, Beltira and Belkira," Belgarath informed the members of the party who had begun to dismount. "Don't bother to try to keep them separate. Nobody can tell them apart anyway."

"We can," the two said in unison.

"I'm not even sure of that," Belgarath responded with a gentle smile. "Your minds are so close together that your thoughts start with one and finish with the other."

"You always complicate it so much, father," Aunt Pol said. "This is Beltira." She kissed one of the sweet-faced old men. "And this is Belkira." She kissed the other. "I've been able to tell them apart since I was a child."

"Polgara knows—"

"—all our secrets." The twins smiled. "And who are—"

"—your companions?"

"I think you'll recognize them," Belgarath answered. "Mandorallen, Baron of Vo Mandor."

"The Knight Protector," the twins said in unison, bowing.

"Prince Kheldar of Drasnia."

"The Guide," they said.

"Barak, Earl of Trellheim."

"The Dreadful Bear." They looked at the big Cherek apprehensively.

Barak's face darkened, but he said nothing.

"Hettar, son of Cho-Hag of Algaria."

"The Horse Lord."

"And Durnik of Sendaria."

"The One with Two Lives," they murmured with profound respect.

Durnik looked baffled at that.

"Ce'Nedra, Imperial Princess of Tolnedra."

"The Queen of the World," they replied with another deep bow.

Ce'Nedra laughed nervously.

"And this—"

"—can only be Belgarion," they said, their faces alive with joy, "the Chosen One." The twins reached out in unison and laid their right hands on Garion's head. Their voices sounded within his mind. *"Hail, Belgarion, Overlord and Champion, hope of the world."*

Garion was too surprised at this strange benediction to do more than awkwardly nod his head.

"If this gets any more cloying, I think I'll vomit," a new voice, harsh and rasping, announced. The speaker, who had just stepped out from behind the tree, was a squat, misshapen old man, dirty and profoundly ugly. His legs were bowed and gnarled like oak trunks. His shoulders were huge, and his hands dangled below his knees. There was a large hump in the middle of his back, and his face was twisted into a grotesque caricature of a human countenance. His straggly, iron-gray hair and beard were matted, and twigs and bits of leaves were caught in the tangles. His hideous face wore an expression of perpetual contempt and anger.

"Beldin," Belgarath said mildly, "we weren't sure you would come."

"I shouldn't have, you bungler," the ugly man snapped. "You've made a mess of things as usual, Belgarath." He turned to the twins. "Get me something to eat," he told them peremptorily.

"Yes, Beldin," they said quickly and started away.

"And don't be all day," he shouted after them.

"You seem to be in a good humor today, Beldin," Belgarath said with no trace of sarcasm. "What's made you so cheerful?"

The ugly dwarf scowled at him, then laughed, a short, barking sound. "I saw Belzedar. He looked like an unmade bed. Something had gone terribly wrong for him, and I enjoy that sort of thing."

"Dear Uncle Beldin," Aunt Pol said fondly, putting her arms around the filthy little man. "I've missed you so much."

"Don't try to charm me, Polgara," he told her, though his eyes seemed to soften slightly. "This is as much your fault as it is your father's. I thought you were going to keep an eye on him. How did Belzedar get his hands on our Master's Orb?"

"We think he used a child," Belgarath answered seriously. "The Orb won't strike an innocent."

The dwarf snorted. "There's no such thing as an innocent. All men are born corrupt." He turned his eyes back to Aunt Pol and looked appraisingly at her. "You're getting fat," he said bluntly. "Your hips are as wide as an ox cart."

Durnik immediately clenched his fists and went for the hideous little man.

The dwarf laughed, and one of his big hands caught the front of the smith's tunic. Without any seeming effort, he lifted the surprised Durnik and threw him several yards away. "You can start your second life right now if you want," he growled threateningly.

"Let me handle this, Durnik," Aunt Pol told the smith. "Beldin," she said coolly, "how long has it been since you've had a bath?"

The dwarf shrugged. "It rained on me a couple months ago."

"Not hard enough, though. You smell like an uncleaned pigsty."

Beldin grinned at her. "That's my girl." He chortled. "I was afraid the years had taken off your edge."

The two of them then began to trade the most hair-raising insults Garion had ever heard in his life. Graphic, ugly words passed back and forth between them, almost sizzling in the air. Barak's eyes widened in astonishment, and Mandorallen's face blanched often. Ce'Nedra, her face flaming, bolted out of earshot.

The worse the insults, however, the more the hideous Beldin

smiled. Finally Aunt Pol delivered an epithet so vile that Garion actually cringed, and the ugly little man collapsed on the ground, roaring with laughter and hammering at the dirt with his great fists. "By the Gods, I've missed you, Pol!" he gasped. "Come here and give us a kiss."

She smiled, kissing his dirty face affectionately. "Mangy dog."

"Big cow." He grinned, catching her in a crushing embrace.

"I'll need my ribs more or less in one piece, uncle," she told him.

"I haven't cracked any of your ribs in years, my girl."

"I'd like to keep it that way."

The twins hurried across to the dwarf Beldin, carrying a large plate of steaming stew and a huge tankard. The ugly man looked curiously at the plate, then casually dumped the stew on the ground and tossed the plate away. "Doesn't smell too bad." He squatted and began to stuff the food into his mouth with both hands, pausing only now and then to spit out some of the larger pebbles that clung to the chunks of meat. When he had finished, he swilled down the contents of the tankard, belched thunderously, and sat back, scratching at his matted hair with gravy-smeared fingers. "Let's get down to business," he said.

"Where have you been?" Belgarath asked him.

"Central Cthol Murgos. I've been sitting on a hilltop since the Battle of Vo Mimbre, watching the cave where Belzedar took Torak."

"Five hundred years?" Silk gasped.

Beldin shrugged. "More or less," he replied indifferently. "Somebody had to keep an eye on Burnt-Face, and I wasn't doing anything that couldn't be interrupted."

"You said you saw Belzedar," Aunt Pol said.

"About a month ago. He came to the cave as if he had a demon on his tail and pulled Torak out. Then he changed himself into a vulture and flew off with the body."

"That must have been right after Ctuchik caught him at the Nyissan border and took the Orb away from him," Belgarath mused.

"I wouldn't know about that. That was part of your responsibility, not mine. All I was supposed to do was keep watch over Torak. Did any of the ashes fall on you?"

"Which ashes?" one of the twins asked.

"When Belzedar took Torak out of the cave, the mountain exploded—blew its guts out. I imagine it had something to do with the force surrounding One-Eye's body. It was still blowing when I left."

"We wondered what had caused the eruption," Aunt Pol commented. "It put ash down an inch deep all over Nyissa."

"Good. Too bad it wasn't deeper."

"Did you see any signs—"

"—of Torak stirring?" the twins asked.

"Can't you two ever talk straight?" Beldin demanded.

"We're sorry—"

"—it's our nature."

The ugly little man shook his head with disgust. "Never mind. No. Torak didn't move once in the whole five hundred years. There was mold on him when Belzedar dragged him out of the cave."

"Did you follow Belzedar?" Belgarath asked.

"Naturally."

"Where did he take Torak?"

"Now where do you think, idiot? To the ruins of Cthol Mishrak in Mallorea, of course. There are only a few places on earth that will bear Torak's weight, and that's one of them. Belzedar will have to keep Ctuchik and the Orb away from Torak, and that's the only place he *could* go. The Mallorean Grolims refuse to accept Ctuchik's authority, so Belzedar will be safe there. It will cost him a great deal to pay for their aid, but they'll keep Ctuchik out of Mallorea—unless he raises an army of Murgos and invades."

"That's something we could hope for," Barak said.

"You're supposed to be a bear, not a donkey," Beldin told him. "Don't base your hopes on the impossible. Neither Ctuchik nor Belzedar would start that sort of war at this particular time—not with Belgarion here stalking through the world like an earthquake." He scowled at Aunt Pol. "Can't you teach him to be a little quieter? Or are your wits getting as flabby as your behind?"

"Be civil, uncle," she replied. "The boy's just coming into his strength. We were all a bit clumsy at first."

"He doesn't have time to be a baby, Pol. The stars are dropping into southern Cthol Murgos like poisoned roaches, and dead Grolims are moaning in their tombs from Rak Cthol to Rak Hagga. The time's on us, and he has to be ready."

"He'll be ready, uncle."

"Maybe," the filthy man said sourly.

"Are you going back to Cthol Mishrak?" Belgarath asked.

"No. Our Master told me to stay here. The twins and I have work to do and we don't have much time."

"He spoke to—"

"—us, too."

"Stop that!" Beldin snapped. He turned back to Belgarath. "Are you going to Rak Cthol now?"

"Not yet. We've got to go to Prolgu first. I have to talk to the Gorim, and we've got to pick up another member of the party."

"I noticed that your group wasn't complete yet. What about the last one?"

Belgarath spread his hands. "That's the one that worries me. I haven't been able to find any trace of her—and I've been looking for three thousand years."

"You spent too much time looking in alehouses."

"I noticed the same thing, uncle," Aunt Pol said with a sweet little smile.

"Where do we go after Prolgu?" Barak asked.

"I think that then we'll go to Rak Cthol," Belgarath replied rather grimly. "We've got to get the Orb back from Ctuchik, and I've been meaning to have a rather pointed discussion with the magician of the Murgos for a long, long time, now."

Part Three

ULGO

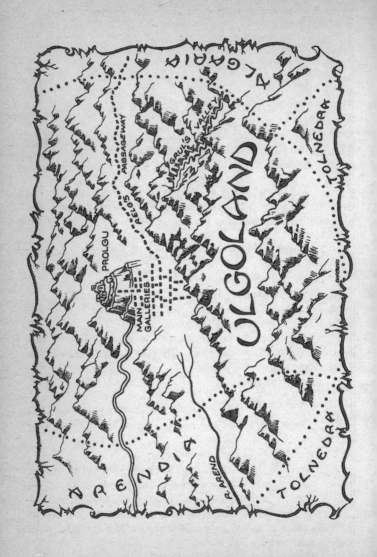

Chapter Thirteen

THE FOLLOWING MORNING they turned northwest and rode toward the stark, white peaks of the mountains of Ulgo, glittering in the morning sun above the lush meadows of the Vale.

"Snow up there," Barak observed. "It could be a difficult trip."

"It always is," Hettar told him.

"Have you been to Prolgu before?" Durnik asked.

"A few times. We keep communications open with the Ulgos. Our visits are mostly ceremonial."

Princess Ce'Nedra had been riding beside Aunt Pol, her tiny face troubled. "How can you *stand* him, Lady Polgara?" she burst out finally. "He's so *ugly*."

"Who's that, dear?"

"That awful dwarf."

"Uncle Beldin?" Aunt Pol looked mildly surprised. "He's always been like that. You have to get to know him, that's all."

"But he says such terrible things to you."

"It's the way he hides his real feelings," Aunt Pol explained. "He's a very gentle person, really, but people don't expect that—coming from him. When he was a child, his people drove him out because he was so deformed and hideous. When he finally came to the Vale, our Master saw past the ugliness to the beauty in his mind."

"But does he have to be so *dirty*?"

Aunt Pol shrugged slightly. "He hates his deformed body, so he ignores it." She looked at the princess, her eyes calm. "It's the easiest thing in the world to judge things by appearances, Ce'Nedra," she said, "and it's usually wrong. Uncle Beldin and I are very fond of each other. That's why we take the trouble to invent such elaborate insults. Compliments would be hypocrisy—he *is*, after all, very ugly."

"I just don't understand." Ce'Nedra sounded baffled.

"Love can show itself in many strange ways," Aunt Pol told her. Her tone was offhand, but the look she directed at the tiny princess was penetrating.

Ce'Nedra flickered one quick look at Garion, and then averted her eyes, blushing slightly.

Garion considered the exchange between his Aunt Pol and the princess as he rode. It was quite obvious that Aunt Pol had been telling the little girl something important, but whatever it was escaped him.

They rode for several days across the Vale and then moved up into the foothills which clustered along the flanks of the ragged peaks that formed the land of the Ulgos. Once again the seasons changed as they rode. It was early autumn as they crested the first low range, and the valleys beyond were aflame with crimson leaves. At the top of a second, higher range, the trees had been swept bare, and the wind had the first bite of winter in it as it whistled down from the peaks. The sky grew overcast, and tendrils of cloud seeped down the rocky gorges above them. Spits of intermittent snow and rain pelted them as they climbed higher up the rocky slopes.

"I suppose we'd better begin keeping an eye out for Brill," Silk said hopefully one snowy afternoon. "It's about time for him to show up again."

"Not very likely," Belgarath replied. "Murgos avoid Ulgoland even more than they avoid the Vale. Ulgos dislike Angaraks intensely."

"So do Alorns."

"Ulgos can see in the dark, though," the old man told him. "Murgos who come into these mountains tend not to wake up from their first night's sleep up here. I don't think we need to worry about Brill."

"Pity," Silk remarked with a certain disappointment.

"It won't hurt to keep our eyes open, though. There are worse things than Murgos in the mountains of Ulgo."

Silk scoffed. "Aren't those stories exaggerated?"

"No. Not really."

"The region abounds with monsters, Prince Kheldar," Mandorallen assured the little man. "Some years back, a dozen foolish young knights of my acquaintance rode into these mountains to test their bravery and prowess against the unseemly beasts. Not one returned."

When they crested the next ridge, the full force of a winter gale struck them. Snow, which had grown steadily heavier as they climbed, drove horizontally in the howling wind.

"We'll have to take cover until this blows over, Belgarath," Barak shouted above the wind, fighting to keep his flapping bearskin cape around him.

"Let's drop down into this next valley," Belgarath replied, also struggling with his cloak. "The trees down there should break the wind."

They crossed the ridge and angled down toward the pines clustered at the bottom of the basin ahead. Garion pulled his cloak tighter and bowed his head into the shrieking wind.

The thick stand of sapling pine in the basin blocked the force of the gale, but the snow swirled about them as they reined in.

"We're not going to get much farther today, Belgarath," Barak declared, trying to brush the snow out of his beard. "We might as well hole up here and wait for morning."

"What's that?" Durnik asked sharply, cocking his head to one side.

"The wind," Barak shrugged.

"No. Listen."

Above the howling of the wind, a shrill whinnying sound came to them.

"Look there." Hettar pointed.

Dimly they saw a dozen horselike animals crossing the ridge

behind them. Their shapes were blurred by the thickly falling snow, and their line as they moved seemed almost ghostly. On a rise just above them stood a huge stallion, his mane and tail tossing in the wind. His neigh was almost a shrill scream.

"Hrulgin!" Belgarath said sharply.

"Can we outrun them?" Silk asked hopefully.

"I doubt it," Belgarath replied. "Besides, they've got our scent now. They'll dog our trail from here to Prolgu if we try to run."

"Then we must teach them to fear our trail and avoid it," Mandorallen declared, tightening the straps on his shield. His eyes were very bright.

"You're falling back into your old habits, Mandorallen," Barak observed in a grumpy voice.

Hettar's face had assumed that curiously blank expression it usually did when he was communicating with his horses. He shuddered finally, and his eyes went sick with revulsion.

"Well?" Aunt Pol asked him.

"They aren't horses," he began.

"We know that, Hettar," she replied. "Can you do anything with them? Frighten them off perhaps?"

He shook his head. "They're hungry, Polgara," he told her, "and they have our scent. The herd stallion seems to have much more control over them than he would if they were horses. I might be able to frighten one or two of the weaker ones—if it weren't for him."

"Then we'll have to fight them all," Barak said grimly, buckling on his shield.

"I don't think so," Hettar replied, his eyes narrowing. "The key seems to be the stallion. He dominates the whole herd. I think that if we kill him, the rest will turn and run."

"All right," Barak said, "we try for the stallion then."

"We might want to make some kind of noise," Hettar suggested. "Something that sounds like a challenge. That might make him come out to the front to answer it. Otherwise, we'll have to go through the whole herd to get to him."

"Mayhap this will provoke him," Mandorallen said. He

lifted his horn to his lips and blew a brassy note of ringing defiance that was whipped away by the gale.

The stallion's shrill scream answered immediately.

"It sounds as if it's working," Barak observed. "Blow it again, Mandorallen."

Mandorallen sounded his horn again, and again the stallion shrilled his reply. Then the great beast plunged down from the ridgetop and charged furiously through the herd toward them. When he reached the forefront, he shrieked again and reared up on his hind legs, his front claws flashing in the snowy air.

"That did it," Barak barked. "Let's go!" He jammed his spurs home, and his big gray leaped forward, spraying snow behind him. Hettar and Mandorallen swept out to flank him, and the three plunged forward through the thickly falling snow toward the screaming Hrulga stallion. Mandorallen set his lance as he charged, and a strange sound drifted back on the wind as he thundered toward the advancing Hrulgin. Mandorallen was laughing.

Garion drew his sword and pulled his horse in front of Aunt Pol and Ce'Nedra. He realized that it was probably a futile gesture, but he did it anyway.

Two of the Hrulgin, perhaps at the herd stallion's unspoken command, bounded forward to cut off Barak and Mandorallen while the stallion himself moved to meet Hettar as if recognizing the Algar as the greatest potential danger to the herd. As the first Hrulga reared, his fangs bared in a catlike snarl and his clawed feet widespread, Mandorallen lowered his lance and drove it through the snarling monster's chest. Bloody froth burst from the Hrulga's mouth, and he toppled over backward, clawing the broken shaft of Mandorallen's lance into splinters as he fell.

Barak caught a clawed swipe on his shield and split open the head of the second Hrulga with a vast overhand swing of his heavy sword. The beast collapsed, his convulsions churning the snow.

Hettar and the herd stallion stalked each other in the swirling snow. They moved warily, circling, their eyes locked on each other with a deadly intensity. Suddenly the stallion reared and lunged all in one motion, his great forelegs wide and his claws outspread. But Hettar's horse, his mind linked with his rider's, danced clear of the furious charge. The Hrulga spun and charged again, and once again Hettar's horse jumped to one side. The infuriated stallion screamed his frustration and lunged in, his claws flailing. Hettar's horse sidestepped the enraged beast, then darted in, and Hettar launched himself from his saddle and landed on the stallion's back. His long, powerful legs locked about the Hrulga's ribs and his right hand gathered a great fistful of the animal's mane.

The stallion went mad as he felt for the first time in the entire history of his species the weight of a rider on his back. He plunged and reared and shrieked, trying to shake Hettar off. The rest of the herd, which had been moving to the attack, faltered and stared in uncomprehending horror at the stallion's wild attempts to dislodge his rider. Mandorallen and Barak reined in, dumbfounded, as Hettar rode the raging stallion in circles through the blizzard. Then, grimly, Hettar slid his left hand down his leg and drew a long, broad dagger from his boot. He knew horses, and he knew where to strike.

His first thrust was lethal. The churned snow turned red. The stallion reared one last time, screaming and with blood pouring out of his mouth, and then he dropped back to stand on shuddering legs. Slowly his knees buckled and he toppled to one side. Hettar jumped clear.

The herd of Hrulgin turned and fled, squealing, back into the blizzard.

Hettar grimly cleaned his dagger in the snow and resheathed it in his boot. Briefly he laid one hand on the dead stallion's neck, then turned to look through the trampled snow for the sabre he had discarded in his wild leap onto the stallion's back.

When the three warriors returned to the shelter of the trees, Mandorallen and Barak were staring at Hettar with a look of profound respect.

"It's a shame they're mad," the Algar said with a distant look on his face. "There was a moment—just a moment—when I almost got through to him, and we moved together. Then the madness came back, and I had to kill him. If they could be tamed—" He broke off and shook his head. "Oh, well." He shrugged regretfully.

"You wouldn't actually ride something like that?" Durnik's voice was shocked.

"I've never had an animal like that under me," Hettar said quietly. "I don't think I'll ever forget what it was like." The tall man turned and walked some distance away and stood staring out into the swirling snow.

They set up for the night in the shelter of the pines. The next morning the wind had abated, although it was still snowing heavily when they set out again. The snow was already knee-deep, and the horses struggled as they climbed.

They crossed yet another ridge and started down into the next valley. Silk looked dubiously around at the thick-falling snow settling through the silent air. "If it gets much deeper, we're going to bog down, Belgarath," he said glumly. "Particularly if we have to keep climbing like this."

"We'll be all right now," the old man assured him. "We follow a series of valleys from here. They lead right up to Prolgu, so we can avoid the peaks."

"Belgarath," Barak said back over his shoulder from his place in the lead, "there are some fresh tracks up here." He pointed ahead at a line of footprints plowed through the new snow across their path.

The old man moved ahead and stopped to examine the tracks. "Algroth," he said shortly. "We'd better keep our eyes open."

They rode warily down into the valley where Mandorallen paused long enough to cut himself a fresh lance.

"I'd be a little dubious about a weapon that keeps breaking," Barak observed as the knight remounted.

Mandorallen shrugged, his armor creaking. "There are always trees about, my Lord," he replied.

Back among the pines that carpeted the valley floor, Garion heard a familiar barking. "Grandfather," he warned.

"I hear them," Belgarath answered.

"How many, do you think?" Silk asked.

"Perhaps a dozen," Belgarath said.

"Eight," Aunt Pol corrected firmly.

"If they are but eight, will they dare attack?" Mandorallen asked. "Those we met in Arendia seemed to seek courage in numbers."

"Their lair's in this valley, I think," the old man replied. "Any animal tries to defend its lair. They're almost certain to attack."

"We must seek them out, then," the knight declared confidently. "Better to destroy them now on ground of our own choosing than to be surprised in some ambush."

"He's definitely backsliding," Barak observed sourly to Hettar.

"He's probably right this time, though," Hettar replied.

"Have you been drinking, Hettar?" Barak asked suspiciously.

"Come, my Lords," Mandorallen said gaily. "Let us rout the brutes so that we may continue our journey unmolested." He plowed off through the snow in search of the barking Algroths.

"Coming, Barak?" Hettar invited as he drew his sabre.

Barak sighed. "I guess I'd better," he answered mournfully. He turned to Belgarath. "This shouldn't take long. I'll try to keep our bloodthirsty friends out of trouble."

Hettar laughed.

"You're getting to be as bad as he is," Barak accused as the two of them moved into a gallop in Mandorallen's wake.

Garion and the others sat waiting tensely in the sifting snowfall. Then the barking sounds off in the woods suddenly turned into yelps of surprise. The sound of blows began to ring through the trees, and there were shrieks of pain and shouts as the three warriors called to each other. After perhaps a quarter of an hour, they came galloping back with the deep snow spraying out from their horses' hooves.

"Two of them got away," Hettar reported regretfully.

"What a shame," Silk replied.

"Mandorallen," Barak said with a pained look, "you've

picked up a bad habit somewhere. Fighting's a serious business, and all this giggling and laughing of yours smacks of frivolity."

"Doth it offend thee, my Lord?"

"It's not so much that it offends me, Mandorallen. It's more a distraction. It breaks my concentration."

"I shall strive to moderate my laughter in future, then."

"I'd appreciate it."

"How did it go?" Silk asked.

"It wasn't much of a fight," Barak replied. "We caught them completely by surprise. I hate to admit it, but our chortling friend there was right for once."

Garion thought about Mandorallen's changed behavior as they rode on down the valley. Back at the cave where the colt had been born, Durnik had told Mandorallen that fear could be conquered by laughing at it, and, though Durnik had probably not meant it in precisely that way, Mandorallen had taken his words quite literally. The laughter which so irritated Barak was not directed at the foes he met, but rather at the enemy within him. Mandorallen was laughing at his own fear as he rode to each attack.

"It's unnatural," Barak was muttering to Silk. "That's what bothers me so much. Not only that, it's a breach of etiquette. If we ever get into a serious fight, it's going to be terribly embarrassing to have him giggling and carrying on like that. What will people think?"

"You're making too much of it, Barak," Silk told him. "Actually, I think it's rather refreshing."

"You think it's *what*?"

"Refreshing. An Arend with a sense of humor is a novelty, after all—sort of like a talking dog."

Barak shook his head in disgust. "There's absolutely no point in ever trying to discuss anything seriously with you, Silk, do you know that? This compulsion of yours to make clever remarks turns everything into a joke."

"We all have our little shortcomings," Silk admitted blandly.

Chapter Fourteen

THE SNOW GRADUALLY slackened throughout the rest of the day and by evening only a few solitary flakes drifted down through the darkening air as they set up for the night in a grove of dense spruces. During the night, however, the temperature fell, and the air was bitterly cold when they arose the next morning.

"How much farther to Prolgu?" Silk asked, standing close to the fire with his shivering hands stretched out to its warmth.

"Two more days," Belgarath replied.

"I don't suppose you'd consider doing something about the weather?" the little man asked hopefully.

"I prefer not to do that unless I absolutely have to," the old man told him. "It disrupts things over a very wide area. Besides, the Gorim doesn't like us to tamper with things in his mountains. The Ulgos have reservations about that sort of thing."

"I was afraid you might look at it that way."

Their route that morning twisted and turned so often that by noon Garion was completely turned around. Despite the biting cold, the sky was overcast, a solid lead-gray. It seemed somehow as if the cold had frozen all color from the world. The sky was gray; the snow was a flat, dead white; and the tree trunks were starkly black. Even the rushing water in the streams they followed flowed black between snow-mounded banks. Belgarath moved confidently, pointing their direction as each succeeding valley intersected with another.

"Are you sure?" the shivering Silk asked him at one point.

"We've been going upstream all day, now you say we go down."

"We'll hit another valley in a few miles. Trust me, Silk. I've been here before."

Silk pulled his heavy cloak tighter. "It's just that I get nervous on unfamiliar ground," he objected, looking at the dark water of the river they followed.

From far upstream came a strange sound, a kind of mindless hooting that was almost like laughter. Aunt Pol and Belgarath exchanged a quick look.

"What is it?" Garion asked.

"Rock-wolf," Belgarath answered shortly.

"It doesn't sound like a wolf."

"It isn't." The old man looked around warily. "They're scavengers for the most part and, if it's just a wild pack, they probably won't attack. It's too early in the winter for them to be that desperate. If it's one of the packs that has been raised by the Eldrakyn, though, we're in for trouble." He stood up in his stirrups to look ahead. "Let's pick up the pace a bit," he called to Mandorallen, "and keep your eyes open."

Mandorallen, his armor glittering with frost, glanced back, nodded, and moved out at a trot, following the seething black water of the mountain river.

Behind them the shrill, yelping laughter grew louder.

"They're following us, father," Aunt Pol said.

"I can hear that." The old man began searching the sides of the valley with his eyes, his face creased with a worried frown. "You'd better have a look, Pol. I don't want any surprises."

Aunt Pol's eyes grew distant as she probed the thickly forested sides of the valley with her mind. After a moment, she gasped and then shuddered. "There's an Eldrak out there, father. He's watching us. His mind is a sewer."

"They always are," the old man replied. "Could you pick up his name?"

"Grul."

"That's what I was afraid of. I knew we were getting close to his range." He put his fingers to his lips and whistled sharply.

Barak and Mandorallen halted to wait while the rest caught up with them. "We've got trouble," Belgarath told them all seriously. "There's an Eldrak out there with a pack of rock-wolves. He's watching us right now. It's only a question of time until he attacks."

"What's an Eldrak?" Silk asked.

"The Eldrakyn are related to Algroths and Trolls, but they're more intelligent—and much bigger."

"But only one?" Mandorallen asked.

"One's enough. I've met this one. His name is Grul. He's big, quick, and as cruel as a hook-pointed knife. He'll eat anything that moves, and he doesn't really care if it's dead or not before he starts to eat."

The hooting laughter of the rock-wolves drew closer.

"Let's find an open place and build a fire," the old man said. "The rock-wolves are afraid of fire, and there's no point in fighting with them *and* Grul if we don't have to."

"There?" Durnik suggested, pointing to a broad, snow-covered bar protruding out into the dark water of the river. The bar was joined to the near bank by a narrow neck of gravel and sand.

"It's defensible, Belgarath," Barak approved, squinting at the bar. "The river will keep them off our backs, and they can only come at us across that one narrow place."

"It will do," Belgarath agreed shortly. "Let's go."

They rode out onto the snow-covered bar and quickly scraped an area clear with their feet while Durnik worked to build a fire under a large, gray driftwood snag that half-blocked the narrow neck of the bar. Within a few moments, orange flames began to lick up around the snag. Durnik fed the fire with sticks until the snag was fully ablaze. "Give me a hand," the smith said, starting to pile larger pieces of wood on the fire. Barak and Mandorallen went to the jumbled mass of driftwood piled against the upstream edge of the gravel and began hauling limbs and chunks of log to the fire. At the end of a quarter of an hour they had built a roaring bonfire that stretched across the narrow neck of sand, cutting them off completely from the dark trees on the riverbank.

"It's the first time I've been warm all day." Silk grinned, backing up to the fire.

"They're coming," Garion warned. Back among the dark tree trunks, he had caught a few glimpses of furtive movements.

Barak peered through the flames. "Big brutes, aren't they?" he observed grimly.

"About the size of a donkey," Belgarath confirmed.

"Are you sure they're afraid of fire?" Silk asked nervously.

"Most of the time."

"*Most* of the time?"

"Once in a while they get desperate—or Grul could drive them toward us. They'd be more afraid of him than of the fire."

"Belgarath," the weasel-faced little man objected, "sometimes you've got a nasty habit of keeping things to yourself."

One of the rock-wolves came out onto the riverbank just upstream from the bar and stood sniffing the air and looking nervously at the fire. Its forelegs were noticeably longer than its hind ones, giving it a peculiar, half-erect stance, and there was a large, muscular hump across its shoulders. Its muzzle was short, and it seemed snub-faced, almost like a cat. Its coat was a splotchy black and white, marked with a pattern hovering somewhere between spots and stripes. It paced nervously back and forth, staring at them with a dreadful intensity and yelping its high-pitched, hooting laugh. Soon another came out to join it, and then another. They spread out along the bank, pacing and hooting, but staying well back from the fire.

"They don't look like dogs exactly," Durnik said.

"They're not," Belgarath replied. "Wolves and dogs are related, but rock-wolves belong to a different family."

By now ten of the ugly creatures lined the bank, and their hooting rose in a mindless chorus.

Then Ce'Nedra screamed, her face deathly pale and her eyes wide with horror.

The Eldrak shambled out of the trees and stood in the middle of the yelping pack. It was about eight feet tall and covered with shaggy black fur. It wore an armored shirt that had been made of large scraps of chainmail tied together with thongs;

over the mail, also held in place with thongs, was a rusty breastplate that appeared to have been hammered out with rocks until it was big enough to fit around the creature's massive chest. A conical steel helmet, split up the back to make it fit, covered the brute's head. In its hand the Eldrak held a huge, steel-wrapped club, studded with spikes. It was the face, however, that had brought the scream to Ce'Nedra's lips. The Eldrak had virtually no nose, and its lower jaw jutted, showing two massive, protruding tusks. Its eyes were sunk in deep sockets beneath a heavy ridge of bone across its brow, and they burned with a hideous hunger.

"That's far enough, Grul," Belgarath warned the thing in a cold, deadly voice.

"'Grat come back to Grul's mountains?" the monster growled. Its voice was deep and hollow, chilling.

"It talks?" Silk gasped incredulously.

"Why are you following us, Grul?" Belgarath demanded.

The creature stared at them, its eyes like fire. "Hungry, 'Grat," it growled.

"Go hunt something else," the old man told the monster.

"Why? Horses here—men. Plenty to eat."

"But not easy food, Grul," Belgarath replied.

A hideous grin spread across Grul's face. "Fight first," he said, "then eat. Come 'Grat. Fight again."

"Grat?" Silk asked.

"He means me. He can't pronounce my name—it has to do with the shape of his jaw."

"You *fought* that thing?" Barak sounded stunned.

Belgarath shrugged. "I had a knife up my sleeve. When he grabbed me, I sliced him open. It wasn't much of a fight."

"Fight!" Grul roared. He hammered on his breastplate with his huge fist. "Iron," he said. "Come, 'Grat. Try to cut Grul's belly again. Now Grul wear iron—like men wear." He began to pound on the frozen ground with his steel-shod club. "Fight!" he bellowed. "Come, 'Grat. Fight!"

"Maybe if we all go after him at once, one of us might get in a lucky thrust," Barak said, eyeing the monster speculatively.

"Thy plan is flawed, my Lord," Mandorallen told him. "We must lose several companions should we come within range of that club."

Barak looked at him in astonishment. "Prudence, Mandorallen? Prudence from you?"

"It were best, I think, should *I* undertake this alone," the knight stated gravely. "My lance is the only weapon that can seek out the monster's life with safety."

"There's something to what he says," Hettar agreed.

"Come fight!" Grul roared, still beating on the ground with his club.

"All right," Barak agreed dubiously. "We'll distract him then—come at him from two sides to get his attention. Then Mandorallen can make his charge."

"What about the rock-wolves?" Garion asked.

"Let me try something," Durnik said. He took up a burning stick and threw it, spinning and flaring, at the nervous pack surrounding the monster. The rock-wolves yelped and shied quickly away from the tumbling brand. "They're afraid of the fire, all right," the smith said. "I think that if we all throw at once and keep throwing, their nerve will break and they'll run."

They all moved to the fire.

"Now!" Durnik shouted sharply. They began throwing the blazing sticks as fast as they could. The rock-wolves yelped and dodged, and several of them screamed in pain as the tumbling firebrands singed them.

Grul roared in fury as the pack dodged and scurried around his feet, trying to escape the sudden deluge of fire. One of the singed beasts, maddened by pain and fright, tried to leap at him. The Eldrak jumped out of its way with astonishing agility and smashed the rock-wolf to the ground with his great club.

"He's quicker than I thought," Barak said. "We'll have to be careful."

"They're running!" Durnik shouted, throwing another fiery stick.

The pack had broken under the rain of burning brands and

turned to flee howling back into the woods, leaving the infuriated Grul standing alone on the riverbank, hammering at the
snow-covered ground with his spiked club. "Come fight!" he
roared again. "Come fight!" He advanced one huge step and
smashed his club at the snow again.

"We'd better do whatever we're going to do now," Silk said
tensely. "He's getting himself worked up. We'll have him out
here on the bar with us in another minute or two."

Mandorallen nodded grimly and turned to mount his charger.

"Let the rest of us distract him first," Barak said. He drew
his heavy sword. "Let's go!" he shouted and leaped over the
fire. The others followed him, spreading out in a half-circle in
front of the towering Grul.

Garion reached for his sword.

"Not you," Aunt Pol snapped. "You stay here."

"But—"

"Do as I say."

One of Silk's daggers, skilfully thrown from several yards
away, sank into Grul's shoulder while the creature was advancing on Barak and Durnik. Grul howled and turned to charge
Silk and Hettar, swinging his vast club. Hettar dodged, and
Silk danced back out of reach. Durnik began pelting the monster
with fist-sized rocks from the riverbank. Grul turned back,
raging now, with flecks of foam dripping from his pointed
tusks.

"Now, Mandorallen!" Barak shouted.

Mandorallen couched his lance and spurred his warhorse.
The huge armored animal leaped forward, its hooves churning
gravel, jumped the fire, and bore down on the astonished Grul.
For a moment it looked as if their plan might work. The deadly,
steel-pointed lance was leveled at Grul's chest, and it seemed
that nothing could stop it from plunging through his huge body.
But the monster's quickness again astonished them all. He
leaped to one side and smashed his spiked club down on Mandorallen's lance, shattering the stout wood.

The force of Mandorallen's charge, however, could not be
stopped. Horse and man crashed into the great brute with a

deafening impact. Grul reeled back, dropping his club, tripping, falling with Mandorallen and his warhorse on top of him.

"Get him!" Barak roared, and they all dashed forward to attack the fallen Grul with swords and axes. The monster, however, levered his legs under Mandorallen's thrashing horse and thrust the big animal off. A great, flailing fist caught Mandorallen in the side, throwing him for several yards. Durnik spun and dropped, felled by a glancing blow to the head even as Barak, Hettar, and Silk swarmed over the fallen Grul.

"Father!" Aunt Pol cried in a ringing voice.

There was suddenly a new sound directly behind Garion— first a deep, rumbling snarl followed instantly by a hair-raising howl. Garion turned quickly and saw the huge wolf he had seen once before in the forests of northern Arendia. The old gray wolf bounded across the fire and entered the fight, his great teeth flashing and tearing.

"Garion, I need you!" Aunt Pol was shaking off the panic-stricken princess and pulling her amulet out of her bodice. "Take out your medallion—quickly!"

He did not understand, but he drew his amulet out from under his tunic. Aunt Pol reached out, took his right hand, and placed the mark on his palm against the figure of the owl on her own talisman; at the same time, she took his medallion in her other hand. "Focus your will," she commanded.

"On what?"

"On the amulets. Quickly!"

Garion brought his will to bear, feeling the power building in him tremendously, amplified somehow by his contact with Aunt Pol and the two amulets. Polgara closed her eyes and raised her face to the leaden sky. *"Mother!"* she cried in a voice so loud that the echo rang like a trumpet note in the narrow valley.

The power surged out of Garion in so vast a rush that he collapsed to his knees, unable to stand. Aunt Pol sank down beside him.

Ce'Nedra gasped.

As Garion weakly raised his head, he saw that there were *two* wolves attacking the raging Grul—the gray old wolf he knew to be his grandfather, and another, slightly smaller wolf that seemed surrounded by a strange, flickering blue light.

Grul had struggled to his feet and was laying about him with his huge fists as the men attacking him chopped futilely at his armored body. Barak was flung out of the fight and fell to his hands and knees, shaking his head groggily. Grul brushed Hettar aside, his eyes alight with dreadful glee as he lunged toward Barak with both huge arms raised. But the blue wolf leaped snarling at his face. Grul swung his fist and gaped with astonishment as it passed directly through the flickering body. Then he shrieked with pain and began to topple backward as Belgarath, darting in from behind to employ the wolf's ancient tactic, neatly hamstrung him with great, ripping teeth. The towering Grul, howling, fell and struck the earth like some vast tree.

"Keep him down!" Barak roared, stumbling to his feet and staggering forward.

The wolves were ripping at Grul's face, and he flailed his arms, trying to beat them away. Again and again his hands passed through the body of the strange, flickering blue wolf. Mandorallen, his feet spread wide apart and holding the hilt of his broadsword with both hands, chopped steadily at the monster's body, his great blade shearing long rents in Grul's breastplate. Barak swung huge blows at Grul's head, his sword striking sparks from the rusty steel helmet. Hettar crouched at one side, eyes intent, sabre ready, waiting. Grul raised his arm to ward off Barak's blows, and Hettar lunged, thrusting his sabre through the exposed armpit and into the huge chest. A bloody froth spouted from Grul's mouth as the sabre ripped through his lungs. He struggled to a half-sitting position.

Then Silk, who had lurked just at the edge of the fight, darted in, set the point of his dagger against the back of Grul's neck and smashed a large rock against the dagger's pommel. With a sickening crunch, the dagger drove through bone, angling up into the monster's brain. Grul shuddered convulsively. Then he collapsed.

In the moment of silence that followed, the two wolves looked at each other across the monster's dead face. The blue wolf seemed to wink once; in a voice which Garion could hear quite clearly—a woman's voice—she said, "How remarkable." With a seeming smile and one last flicker, she vanished.

The old gray wolf raised his muzzle and howled, a sound of such piercing anguish and loss that Garion's heart wrenched within him. Then the old wolf seemed to shimmer, and Belgarath knelt in his place. He rose slowly to his feet and walked back toward the fire, tears streaming openly down his grizzled cheeks.

Chapter Fifteen

"Is HE GOING to be all right?" Barak asked anxiously, hovering over the still unconscious Durnik as Aunt Pol examined the large purple contusion on the side of the smith's face.

"It's nothing serious," she replied in a voice seeming to droop with a great weariness.

Garion sat nearby with his head in his hands. He felt as if all the strength had been wrenched out of his body.

Beyond the heaped coals of the rapidly dying bonfire, Silk and Hettar were struggling to remove Mandorallen's dented breastplate. A deep crease running diagonally from shoulder to hip gave mute evidence of the force of Grul's blow and placed so much stress on the straps beneath the shoulder plates that they were almost impossible to unfasten.

"I think we're going to have to cut them," Silk said.

"I pray thee, Prince Kheldar, avoid that if possible," Mandorallen answered, wincing as they wrenched at the fastenings. "Those straps are crucial to the fit of the armor, and are most difficult to replace properly."

"This one's coming now," Hettar grunted, prying at a buckle with a short iron rod. The buckle released suddenly and the taut breastplate rang like a softly struck bell.

"Now I can get it," Silk said, quickly loosening the other shoulder buckle.

Mandorallen sighed with relief as they pulled off the dented breastplate. He took a deep breath and winced again.

"Tender right here?" Silk asked, putting his fingers lightly to the right side of the knight's chest. Mandorallen grunted with pain, and his face paled visibly. "I think you've got some cracked ribs, my splendid friend," Silk told him. "You'd better have Polgara take a look."

"In a moment," Mandorallen said. "My horse?"

"He'll be all right," Hettar replied. "A strained tendon in his right foreleg is all."

Mandorallen let out a sigh of relief. "I had feared for him."

"I feared for us all there for a while," Silk said. "Our over-sized playmate there was almost more than we could handle."

"Good fight, though," Hettar remarked.

Silk gave him a disgusted look, then glanced up at the scudding gray clouds overhead. He jumped across the glowing coals of their fire and went over to where Belgarath sat staring into the icy river. "We're going to have to get off this bar, Belgarath," he urged. "The weather's going bad on us again, and we'll all freeze to death if we stay out here in the middle of the river tonight."

"Leave me alone," Belgarath muttered shortly, still staring at the river.

"Polgara?" Silk turned to her.

"Just stay away from him for a while," she told him. "Go find a sheltered place for us to stay for a few days."

"I'll go with you," Barak offered, hobbling toward his horse.

"You'll stay here," Aunt Pol declared firmly. "You creak like a wagon with a broken axle. I want to have a look at you before you get a chance to damage yourself permanently."

"I know a place," Ce'Nedra said, rising and pulling her cloak about her shoulders. "I saw it when we were coming down the river. I'll show you."

Silk looked inquiringly at Aunt Pol.

"Go ahead," she told him. "It's safe enough now. Nothing else would live in the same valley with an Eldrak."

Silk laughed. "I wonder why? Coming, Princess?" The two of them mounted and rode off through the snow.

"Shouldn't Durnik be coming around?" Garion asked his Aunt.

"Let him sleep," she replied wearily. "He'll have a blinding headache when he wakes up."

"Aunt Pol?"

"Yes?"

"Who was the other wolf?"

"My mother, Poledra."

"But isn't she—"

"Yes. It was her spirit."

"You can do *that*?" Garion was stunned by the enormity of it.

"Not alone," she said. "You had to help me."

"Is that why I feel so—" It was an effort even to talk.

"It took everything we could both raise to do it. Don't ask so many questions just now, Garion. I'm very tired and I still have many things to do."

"Is Grandfather all right?"

"He'll come around. Mandorallen, come here."

The knight stepped over the coals at the neck of the bar and walked slowly toward her, his hand pressed lightly against his chest.

"You'll have to take off your shirt," she told him. "And please sit down."

About a half-hour later Silk and the princess returned. "It's a good spot," Silk reported. "A thicket in a little ravine. Water, shelter—everything we need. Is anybody seriously hurt?"

"Nothing permanent." Aunt Pol was applying a salve to Barak's hairy leg.

"Do you suppose you could hurry, Polgara?" Barak asked. "It's a little chilly for standing around half-dressed."

"Stop being such a baby," she said heartlessly.

The ravine to which Silk and Ce'Nedra led them was a short way back upriver. A small mountain brook trickled from its mouth, and a dense thicket of spindly pines filled it seemingly from wall to wall. They followed the brook for a few hundred yards until they came to a small clearing in the center of the thicket. The pines around the inner edge of the clearing, pressed by the limbs of the others in the thicket, leaned inward, almost touching above the center of the open area.

"Good spot." Hettar looked around approvingly. "How did you find it?"

"She did." Silk nodded at Ce'Nedra.

"The trees told me it was here," she said. "Young pine trees babble a lot." She looked at the clearing thoughtfully. "We'll build our fire there," she decided, pointing at a spot near the brook at the upper end of the clearing, "and set up our tents along the edge of the trees just back from it. You'll need to pile rocks around the fire and clear away all the twigs from the ground near it. The trees are very nervous about the fire. They promised to keep the wind off us, but only if we keep our fire strictly under control. I gave them my word."

A faint smile flickered across Hettar's hawklike face.

"I'm serious," she said, stamping her little foot.

"Of course, your Highness," he replied, bowing.

Because of the incapacity of the others, the work of setting up the tents and building the firepit fell largely upon Silk and Hettar. Ce'Nedra commanded them like a little general, snapping out her orders in a clear, firm voice. She seemed to be enjoying herself immensely.

Garion was sure that it was some trick of the fading light, but the trees almost seemed to draw back when the fire first flared up, though after a while they seemed to lean back in again to arch protectively over the little clearing. Wearily he got to his feet and began to gather sticks and dead limbs for firewood.

"Now," Ce'Nedra said, bustling about the fire in a thoroughly businesslike way, "what would you all like for supper?"

They stayed in their protected little clearing for three days while their battered warriors and Mandorallen's horse recuperated from the encounter with the Eldrak. The exhaustion which had fallen upon Garion when Aunt Pol had summoned all his strength to help call the spirit of Poledra was largely gone after one night's sleep, though he tired easily during the next day. He found Ce'Nedra's officiousness in her domain near the fire almost unbearable, so he passed some time helping Durnik hammer the deep crease out of Mandorallen's breastplate; after that, he spent as much time as possible with the horses. He began teaching the little colt a few simple tricks, though he had never attempted training animals before. The colt seemed to enjoy it, although his attention wandered frequently.

The incapacity of Durnik, Barak, and Mandorallen was easy to understand, but Belgarath's deep silence and seeming indifference to all around him worried Garion. The old man appeared to be sunk in a melancholy reverie that he could not or would not shake off.

"Aunt Pol," Garion said finally on the afternoon of the third day, "you'd better do something. We'll be ready to leave soon, and Grandfather has to be able to show us the way. Right now I don't think he even cares where he is."

Aunt Pol looked across at the old sorcerer, who sat on a rock, staring into the fire. "Possibly you're right. Come with me." She led the way around the fire and stopped directly in front of the old man. "All right, father," she said crisply, "I think that's about enough."

"Go away, Polgara," he told her.

"No, father," she replied. "It's time for you to put it away and come back to the real world."

"That was a cruel thing to do, Pol," he said reproachfully.

"To mother? She didn't mind."

"How do you know that? You never knew her. She died when you were born."

"What's that got to do with it?" She looked at him directly.

"Father," she declared pointedly, "you of all people should know that mother was extremely strong-minded. She's always been with me, and we know each other very well."

He looked dubious.

"She has her part to play in this just the same as the rest of us do. If you'd been paying attention all these years, you'd have realized that she's never really been gone."

The old man looked around a little guiltily.

"Precisely," Aunt Pol said with just the hint of a barb in her voice. "You really should have behaved yourself, you know. Mother's very tolerant for the most part, but there were times when she was quite vexed with you."

Belgarath coughed uncomfortably.

"Now it's time for you to pull yourself out of this and stop feeling sorry for yourself," she continued crisply.

His eyes narrowed. "That's not entirely fair, Polgara," he replied.

"I don't have time to be fair, father."

"Why did you choose that particular form?" he asked with a hint of bitterness.

"I didn't, father. She did. It's her natural form, after all."

"I'd almost forgotten that," he mused.

"She didn't."

The old man straightened and drew back his shoulders. "Is there any food around?" he asked suddenly.

"The princess has been doing the cooking," Garion warned him. "You might want to think it over before you decide to eat anything she's had a hand in."

The next morning under a still-threatening sky, they struck their tents, packed their gear again, and rode down along the narrow bed of the brook back into the river valley.

"Did you thank the trees, dear?" Aunt Pol asked the princess.

"Yes, Lady Polgara," Ce'Nedra replied. "Just before we left."

"That's nice," Aunt Pol said.

The weather continued to threaten for the next two days, and finally the blizzard broke in full fury as they approached a strangely pyramidal peak. The sloping walls of the peak were

steep, rising sharply up into the swirling snow, and they seemed
to have none of the random irregularities of the surrounding
mountains. Though he rejected the idea immediately, Garion
could not quite overcome the notion that the curiously angular
peak had somehow been constructed—that its shape was the
result of a conscious design.

"Prolgu," Belgarath said, pointing at the peak with one hand
while he clung to his wind-whipped cloak with the other.

"How do we get up there?" Silk asked, staring at the steep
walls dimly visible in the driving snow.

"There's a road," the old man replied. "It starts over there."
He pointed to a vast pile of jumbled rock to one side of the
peak.

"We'd better hurry then, Belgarath," Barak said. "This storm
isn't going to improve much."

The old man nodded and moved his horse into the lead.
"When we get up there," he shouted back to them over the
sound of the shrieking wind, "we'll find the city. It's abandoned, but you may see a few things lying about—broken
pots, some other things. Don't touch any of them. The Ulgos
have some peculiar beliefs about Prolgu. It's a very holy place
to them, and everything there is supposed to stay just where it
is."

"How do we get down into the caves?" Barak asked.

"The Ulgos will let us in," Belgarath assured him. "They
already know we're here."

The road that led to the mountaintop was a narrow ledge,
inclining steeply up and around the sides of the peak. They
dismounted before they started up and led their horses. The
wind tugged at them as they climbed, and the driving snow,
more pellets than flakes, stung their faces.

It took them two hours to wind their way to the top, and
Garion was numb with cold by the time they got there. The
wind seemed to batter at him, trying to pluck him off the ledge,
and he made a special point of staying as far away from the
edge as possible.

Though the wind had been brutal on the sides of the peak,
once they reached the top it howled at them with unbroken

force. They passed through a broad, arched gate into the deserted city of Prolgu with snow swirling about them and the wind shrieking insanely in their ears.

There were columns lining the empty streets, tall, thick columns reaching up into the dancing snow. The buildings, all unroofed by time and the endless progression of the seasons, had a strange, alien quality about them. Accustomed to the rigid rectangularity of the structures in the other cities he had seen, Garion was unprepared for the sloped corners of Ulgo architecture. Nothing seemed exactly square. The complexity of the angles teased at his mind, suggesting a subtle sophistication that somehow just eluded him. There was a massiveness about the construction that seemed to defy time, and the weathered stones sat solidly, one atop the other, precisely as they had been placed thousands of years before.

Durnik seemed also to have noticed the peculiar nature of the structures, and his expression was one of disapproval. As they all moved behind a building to get out of the wind and to rest for a moment from the exertions of the climb, he ran his hand up one of the slanted corners. "Hadn't they ever heard of a plumb line?" he muttered critically.

"Where do we go to find the Ulgos?" Barak asked, pulling his bearskin cloak even tighter about him.

"It isn't far," Belgarath answered.

They led their horses back out into the blizzard-swept streets, past the strange, pyramidal buildings.

"An eerie place," Mandorallen said, looking around him. "How long hath it been abandoned thus?"

"Since Torak cracked the world," Belgarath replied. "About five thousand years."

They trudged across a broad street through the deepening snow to a building somewhat larger than the ones about it and passed inside through a wide doorway surmounted by a huge stone lintel. Inside, the air hung still and calm. A few flakes of snow drifted down through the silent air, sifting through the narrow opening at the top where the roof had been and lightly dusting the stone floor.

Belgarath moved purposefully to a large black stone in the

precise center of the floor. The stone was cut in such a way as to duplicate the truncated pyramid shape of the buildings in the city, angling up to a flat surface about four feet above the floor. "Don't touch it," he warned them, carefully stepping around the stone.

"Is it dangerous?" Barak asked.

"No," Belgarath said. "It's holy. The Ulgos don't want it profaned. They believe that UL himself placed it here." He studied the floor intently, scraping away the thin dusting of snow with his foot in several places. "Let's see." He frowned slightly. Then he uncovered a single flagstone that seemed a slightly different color from those surrounding it. "Here we are," he grunted. "I always have to look for it. Give me your sword, Barak."

Wordlessly the big man drew his sword and handed it to the old sorcerer.

Belgarath knelt beside the flagstone he'd uncovered and rapped sharply on it three times with the pommel of Barak's heavy sword. The sound seemed to echo hollowly from underneath.

The old man waited for a moment, then repeated his signal. Nothing happened.

A third time Belgarath hammered his three measured strokes on the echoing flagstone. A slow grinding sound started in one corner of the large chamber.

"What's that?" Silk demanded nervously.

"The Ulgos," Belgarath replied, rising to his feet and dusting off his knees. "They're opening the portal to the caves."

The grinding continued and a line of faint light appeared suddenly about twenty feet out from the east wall of the chamber. The line became a crack and then slowly yawned wider as a huge stone in the floor tilted up, rising with a ponderous slowness. The light from below seemed very dim.

"Belgarath," a deep voice echoed from beneath the slowly tilting stone, *"Yad ho, groja UL."*

"Yad ho, groja UL. Vad mar ishum," Belgarath responded formally.

"*Veed mo*, Belgarath. *Mar ishum Ulgo*," the unseen speaker said.

"What was that?" Garion asked in perplexity.

"He invited us into the caves," the old man said. "Shall we go down now?"

Chapter Sixteen

IT TOOK ALL of Hettar's force of persuasion to start the horses moving down the steeply inclined passageway that led into the dimness of the caves of Ulgo. Their eyes rolled nervously as they took step after braced step down the slanting corridor, and they all flinched noticeably as the grinding stone boomed shut behind them. The colt walked so close to Garion that they frequently bumped against each other, and Garion could feel the little animal's trembling with every step.

At the end of the corridor two figures stood, each with his face veiled in a kind of filmy cloth. They were short men, shorter even than Silk, but their shoulders seemed bulky beneath their dark robes. Just beyond them an irregularly shaped chamber opened out, faintly lighted by a dim, reddish glow.

Belgarath moved toward the two, and they bowed respectfully to him as he approached. He spoke with them briefly, and they bowed again, pointing toward another corridor opening on the far side of the chamber. Garion nervously looked around for the source of the faint red light, but it seemed lost in the strange, pointed rocks hanging from the ceiling.

"We go this way," Belgarath quietly told them, crossing

the chamber toward the corridor the two veiled men had indicated to him.

"Why are their faces covered?" Durnik whispered.

"To protect their eyes from the light when they opened the portal."

"But it was almost dark inside that building up there," Durnik objected.

"Not to an Ulgo," the old man replied.

"Don't any of them speak our language?"

"A few—not very many. They don't have much contact with outsiders. We'd better hurry. The Gorim is waiting for us."

The corridor they entered ran for a short distance and then opened abruptly into a cavern so vast that Garion could not even see the other side of it in the faint light that seemed to pervade the caves.

"How extensive are these caverns, Belgarath?" Mandorallen asked, somewhat awed by the immensity of the place.

"No one knows for sure. The Ulgos have been exploring the caves since they came down here, and they're still finding new ones."

The passageway they had followed from the portal chamber had emerged high up in the wall of the cavern near the vaulted roof, and a broad ledge sloped downward from the opening, running along the sheer wall. Garion glanced once over the edge. The cavern floor was lost in the gloom far below. He shuddered and stayed close to the wall after that.

As they descended, they found that the huge cavern was not silent. From what seemed infinitely far away there was the cadenced sound of chanting by a chorus of deep male voices, the words blurred and confused by the echoes reverberating from the stone walls and seeming to die off, endlessly repeated. Then, as the last echoes of the chant faded, the chorus began to sing, their song strangely disharmonic and in a mournful, minor key. In a peculiar fashion, the disharmony of the first phrases echoing back joined the succeeding phrases and merged with them, moving inexorably toward a final harmonic resolution so profound that Garion felt his entire being moved by it. The echoes merged as the chorus ended its song, and the caves of Ulgo sang on alone, repeating that final chord over and over.

"I've never heard anything like that," Ce'Nedra whispered softly to Aunt Pol.

"Few people have," Polgara replied, "though the sound lingers in some of these galleries for days."

"What were they singing?"

"A hymn to UL. It's repeated every hour, and the echoes keep it alive. These caves have been singing that same hymn for five thousand years now."

There were other sounds as well, the scrape of metal against metal, snatches of conversation in the guttural language of the Ulgos, and an endless chipping sound, coming, it seemed, from a dozen places.

"There must be a lot of them down there," Barak observed, peering over the edge.

"Not necessarily," Belgarath told him. "Sound lingers in these caves, and the echoes keep coming back over and over again."

"Where does the light come from?" Durnik asked, looking puzzled. "I don't see any torches."

"The Ulgos grind two different kinds of rock to powder," Belgarath replied. "When you mix them, they give off a glow."

"It's pretty dim light," Durnik observed, looking down toward the floor of the cavern.

"Ulgos don't need all that much light."

It took them almost half an hour to reach the cavern floor. The walls around the bottom were pierced at regular intervals with the openings of corridors and galleries radiating out into the solid rock of the mountain. As they passed, Garion glanced down one of the galleries. It was very long and dimly lighted with openings along its walls and a few Ulgos moving from place to place far down toward the other end.

In the center of the cavern lay a large, silent lake, and they skirted the edge of it as Belgarath moved confidently, seeming to know precisely where he was going. Somewhere from far out on the dim lake, Garion heard a faint splash, a fish perhaps or the sound of a dislodged pebble from far above falling into the water. The echo of the singing they had heard when they entered the cavern still lingered, curiously loud in some places and very faint in others.

Two Ulgos waited for them near the entrance to one of the galleries. They bowed and spoke briefly to Belgarath. Like the men who had met them in the portal chamber, both were short and heavy-shouldered. Their hair was very pale and their eyes large and almost black.

"We'll leave the horses here," Belgarath said. "We have to go down some stairs. These men will care for them."

The colt, still trembling, had to be told several times to stay with his mother, but he finally seemed to understand. Then Garion hurried to catch up to the others, who had already entered the mouth of one of the galleries.

There were doors in the walls of the gallery they followed, doors opening into small cubicles, some of them obviously workshops of one kind or another and others just as obviously arranged for domestic use. The Ulgos inside the cubicles continued at their tasks, paying no attention to the party passing in the gallery. Some of the pale-haired people were working with metal, some with stone, a few with wood or cloth. An Ulgo woman was nursing a small baby.

Behind them in the cavern they had first entered, the sound of the chanting began again. They passed a cubicle where seven Ulgos, seated in a circle, were reciting something in unison.

"They spend a great deal of time in religious observances," Belgarath remarked as they passed the cubicle. "Religion's the central fact of Ulgo life."

"Sounds dull," Barak grunted.

At the end of the gallery a flight of steep, worn stairs descended sharply, and they went down, their hands on the wall to steady themselves.

"It would be easy to get turned around down here," Silk observed. "I've lost track of which direction we're going."

"Down," Hettar told him.

"Thanks," Silk replied dryly.

At the bottom of the stairs they entered another cavern, once again high up in the wall, but this time the cavern was spanned by a slender bridge, arching across to the other side. "We cross that," Belgarath told them and led them out onto the bridge that arched through the half light to the other side.

Garion glanced down once and saw a myriad of gleaming openings dotting the cavern walls far below. The openings did not appear to have any systematic arrangement, but rather seemed scattered randomly. "There must be a lot of people living here," he said to his grandfather.

The old man nodded. "It's the home cave of one of the major Ulgo tribes," he replied.

The first disharmonic phrases of the ancient hymn to UL drifted up to them as they neared the other end of the bridge. "I wish they'd find another tune," Barak muttered sourly. "That one's starting to get on my nerves."

"I'll mention that to the first Ulgo I meet," Silk told him lightly. "I'm sure they'll be only too glad to change songs for you."

"Very funny," Barak said.

"It probably hasn't occurred to them that their song isn't universally admired."

"Do you mind?" Barak asked acidly.

"They've only been singing it for five thousand years now."

"That'll do, Silk," Aunt Pol told the little man.

"Anything you say, great lady," Silk answered mockingly.

They entered another gallery on the far side of the cavern and followed it until it branched. Belgarath firmly led them to the left.

"Are you sure?" Silk asked. "I could be wrong, but it seems like we're going in a circle."

"We are."

"I don't suppose you'd care to explain that."

"There's a cavern we wanted to avoid, so we had to go around it."

"Why did we have to avoid it?"

"It's unstable. The slightest sound there might bring the roof down."

"Oh."

"That's one of the dangers down here."

"You don't really need to go into detail, old friend," Silk said, looking nervously at the roof above. The little man seemed to be talking more than usual, and Garion's own sense of oppression at the thought of all the rock surrounding him gave him a quick insight into Silk's mind. The sense of being closed in was unbearable to some men, and Silk, it appeared, was one of them. Garion glanced up also, and seemed to feel the weight of the mountain above pressing down firmly on him. Silk, he decided, might not be the only one disturbed by the thought of all that dreadful mass above them.

The gallery they followed opened out into a small cavern with a glass-clear lake in its center. The lake was very shallow and it had a white gravel bottom. An island rose from the center of the lake, and on the island stood a building constructed in the same curiously pyramidal shape as the buildings in the ruined city of Prolgu far above. The building was surrounded by a ring of columns, and here and there benches were carved from white stone. Glowing crystal globes were suspended on long chains from the ceiling of the cavern about thirty feet overhead, and their light, while still faint, was noticeably brighter than that in the galleries through which they had passed. A white marble causeway crossed to the island, and a very old man stood at its end, peering across the still water toward them as they entered the cavern.

"*Yad ho*, Belgarath," the old man called. "*Groja UL.*"

"Gorim," Belgarath replied with a formal bow. "*Yad ho, groja UL.*"

He led them across the marble causeway to the island in the center of the lake and warmly clasped the old man's hand, speaking to him in the guttural Ulgo language.

The Gorim of Ulgo appeared to be very old. He had long, silvery hair and beard, and his robe was snowy white. There was a kind of saintly serenity about him that Garion felt immediately, and the boy knew, without knowing how he knew, that he was approaching a holy man—perhaps the holiest on earth.

The Gorim extended his arms fondly to Aunt Pol, and she

embraced him affectionately as they exchanged the ritual greeting, "*Yad ho, groja UL.*"

"Our companions don't speak your language, old friend," Belgarath said to the Gorim. "Would it offend you if we conversed in the language of the outside?"

"Not at all, Belgarath," the Gorim replied. "UL tells us that it's important for men to understand one another. Come inside, all of you. I've had food and drink prepared for you." As the old man looked at each of them, Garion noticed that his eyes, unlike those of the other Ulgos he had seen, were a deep, almost violet blue. Then the Gorim turned and led them along a path to the doorway of the pyramid-shaped building.

"Has the child come yet?" Belgarath asked the Gorim as they passed through the massive stone doorway.

The Gorim sighed. "No, Belgarath, not yet, and I am very weary. There's hope at each birth. But after a few days, the eyes of the child darken. It appears that UL is not finished with me yet."

"Don't give up hope, Gorim," Belgarath told his friend. "The child will come—in UL's own time."

"So we are told." The Gorim sighed again. "The tribes are growing restless, though, and there's bickering—and worse— in some of the farther galleries. The zealots grow bolder in their denunciations, and strange aberrations and cults have begun to appear. Ulgo needs a new Gorim. I've outlived my time by three hundred years."

"UL still has work for you," Belgarath replied. "His ways are not ours, Gorim, and he sees time in a different way."

The room they entered was square but had, nonetheless, the slightly sloping walls characteristic of Ulgo architecture. A stone table with low benches on either side sat in the center of the room, and there were a number of bowls containing fruit sitting upon it. Among the bowls sat several tall flasks and round crystal cups. "I'm told that winter has come early to our mountains," the Gorim said to them. "The drink should help to warm you."

"It's chilly outside," Belgarath admitted.

They sat down on the benches and began to eat. The fruit

was tangy and wild-tasting, and the clear liquid in the flasks was fiery and brought an immediate warm glow that radiated out from the stomach.

"Forgive us our customs, which may seem strange to you," the Gorim said, noting that Barak and Hettar in particular approached the meal of fruit with a distinct lack of enthusiasm. "We are a people much tied to ceremony. We begin our meals with fruit in remembrance of the years we spent wandering in search of UL. The meat will come in due time."

"Where do you obtain such food in these caves, Holy One?" Silk asked politely.

"Our gatherers go out of the caves at night," the Gorim replied. "They tell us that the fruits and grains they bring back with them grow wild in the mountains, but I suspect that they have long since taken up the cultivation of certain fertile valleys. They also maintain that the meat they carry down to us is the flesh of wild cattle, taken in the hunt, but I have my doubts about that as well." He smiled gently. "I permit them their little deceptions."

Perhaps emboldened by the Gorim's geniality, Durnik raised a question that had obviously been bothering him since he had entered the city on the mountaintop above. "Forgive me, your Honor," he began, "but why do your builders make everything crooked? What I mean is, nothing seems to be square. It all leans over."

"It has to do with weight and support, I understand," the Gorim replied. "Each wall is actually falling down; but since they're all falling against each other, none of them can move so much as a finger's width—and, of course, their shape reminds us of the tents we lived in during our wanderings."

Durnik frowned thoughtfully, struggling with the alien idea.

"And have you as yet recovered Aldur's Orb, Belgarath?" the Gorim inquired then, his face growing serious.

"Not yet," Belgarath replied. "We chased Zedar as far as Nyissa, but when he crossed over into Cthol Murgos, Ctuchik was waiting and took the Orb away from him. Ctuchik has it now—at Rak Cthol."

"And Zedar?"

"He escaped Ctuchik's ambush and carried Torak off to Cthol Mishrak in Mallorea to keep Ctuchik from raising him with the Orb."

"Then you'll have to go to Rak Cthol."

Belgarath nodded as an Ulgo servingman brought in a huge, steaming roast, set it on the table, and left with a respectful bow.

"Has anyone found out how Zedar was able to take the Orb without being struck down?" the Gorim asked.

"He used a child," Aunt Pol told him. "An innocent."

"Ah." The Gorim stroked his beard thoughtfully. "Doesn't the prophecy say, 'And the child shall deliver up the birthright unto the Chosen One'?"

"Yes," Belgarath replied.

"Where's the child now?"

"So far as we know, Ctuchik has him at Rak Cthol."

"Will you assault Rak Cthol, then?"

"I'd need an army, and it could take years to reduce that fortress. There's another way, I think. A certain passage in the Darine Codex speaks of caves under Rak Cthol."

"I know that passage, Belgarath. It's very obscure. It *could* mean that, I suppose, but what if it doesn't?"

"It's confirmed by the Mrin Codex," Belgarath said a little defensively.

"The Mrin Codex is even worse, old friend. It's obscure to the point of being gibberish."

"I somehow have the feeling that when we look back at it—after all this is over—we're going to find that the Mrin Codex is the most accurate version of all. I do have certain other verification, however. Back during the time when the Murgos were constructing Rak Cthol, a Sendarian slave escaped and made his way back to the West. He was delirious when he was found, but he kept talking of caves under the mountain before he died. Not only that, Anheg of Cherek found a copy of *The Book of Torak* that contains a fragment of a very old Grolim prophecy—'Guard well the temple, above and beneath, for Cthrag Yaska will summon foes down from the air or up from the earth to bear it away again.'"

"That's even more obscure," the Gorim objected.

"Grolim prophecies usually are, but it's all I've got to work with. If I reject the notion of caves under Rak Cthol, I'll have to lay siege to the place. It would take all the armies of the West to do that, and then Ctuchik would summon the Angarak armies to defend the city. Everything points to some final battle, but I'd prefer to pick the time and place—and the Wasteland of Murgos is definitely *not* one of the places I'd choose."

"You're leading someplace with this, aren't you?"

Belgarath nodded. "I need a diviner to help me find the caves beneath Rak Cthol and to lead me up through them to the city."

The Gorim shook his head. "You're asking the impossible, Belgarath. The diviners are all zealots—mystics. You'll never persuade one of them to leave the holy caverns here beneath Prolgu—particularly not now. All of Ulgo is waiting for the coming of the child, and every zealot is firmly convinced that he will be the one to discover the child and reveal him to the tribes. I couldn't even order one of them to accompany you. The diviners are regarded as holy men, and I have no authority over them."

"It may not be as hard as you think, Gorim." Belgarath pushed back his plate and reached for his cup. "The diviner I need is one named Relg."

"Relg? He's the worst of the lot. He's gathered a following and he preaches to them by the hour in some of the far galleries. He believes that he's the most important man in Ulgo just now. You'll never persuade him to leave these caves."

"I don't think I'll have to, Gorim. I'm not the one who selected Relg. That decision was made for me long before I was born. Just send for him."

"I'll send for him if you want," the Gorim said doubtfully. "I don't think he'll come, though."

"He'll come," Aunt Pol told him confidently. "He won't know why, but he'll come. And he *will* go with us, Gorim. The same power that brought us all together will bring him as well. He doesn't have any more choice in the matter than we do."

Chapter Seventeen

IT ALL SEEMED so tedious. The snow and cold they
had endured on the journey to Prolgu had numbed Ce'Nedra,
and the warmth here in the caverns made her drowsy. The
endless, obscure talk of Belgarath and the strange, frail old
Gorim seemed to pull her toward sleep. The peculiar singing
began again somewhere, echoing endlessly through the caves,
and that too lulled her. Only a lifetime of training in the involved etiquette of court behavior kept her awake.

The journey had been ghastly for Ce'Nedra. Tol Honeth
was a warm city, and she was not accustomed to cold weather.
It seemed that her feet would never be warm again. She had
also discovered a world filled with shocks, terrors, and unpleasant surprises. At the Imperial Palace in Tol Honeth, the
enormous power of her father, the Emperor, had shielded her
from danger of any kind, but now she felt vulnerable. In a rare
moment of absolute truth with herself, she admitted that much
of her spiteful behavior toward Garion had grown out of her
dreadful new sense of insecurity. Her safe, pampered little
world had been snatched away from her, and she felt exposed,
unprotected, and afraid.

Poor Garion, she thought. He was such a nice boy. She felt
a little ashamed that he had been the one who'd had to suffer
from her bad temper. She promised herself that soon—very
soon—she would sit down with him and explain it all. He was
a sensible boy, and he'd be sure to understand. That, of course,

would immediately patch up the rift which had grown between them.

Feeling her eyes on him, he glanced once at her and then looked away with apparent indifference. Ce'Nedra's eyes hardened like agates. How *dared* he? She made a mental note of it and added it to her list of his many imperfections.

The frail-looking old Gorim had sent one of the strange, silent Ulgos to fetch the man he and Belgarath and Lady Polgara had been discussing, and then they turned to more general topics. "Were you able to pass through the mountains unmolested?" the Gorim asked.

"We had a few encounters," Barak, the big, red-beared Earl of Trellheim, replied with what seemed to Ce'Nedra gross understatement.

"But thanks to UL you're all safe," the Gorim declared piously. "Which of the monsters are still abroad at this season? I haven't been out of the caves in years, but as I recall most of them seek their lairs when the snow begins."

"We encountered Hrulgin, Holy One," Baron Mandorallen informed him, "and some Algroths. And there was an Eldrak."

"The Eldrak was troublesome," Silk said dryly.

"Understandably. Fortunately there aren't very many Eldrakyn. They're fearsome monsters."

"We noticed that," Silk said.

"Which one was it?"

"Grul," Belgarath replied. "He and I had met before, and he seemed to hold a grudge. I'm sorry, Gorim, but we had to kill him. There wasn't any other way."

"Ah," the Gorim said with a slight note of pain in his voice. "Poor Grul."

"I personally don't miss him very much," Barak said. "I'm not trying to be forward, Holy One, but don't you think it might be a good idea to exterminate some of the more troublesome beasts in these mountains?"

"They're the children of UL, even as we," the Gorim explained.

"But if they weren't out there, you could return to the world above," Barak pointed out.

The Gorim smiled at that. "No," he said gently. "Ulgo will never leave the caves now. We've dwelt here for five millennia and, over the years, we've changed. Our eyes could not bear the sunlight now. The monsters above cannot reach us here, and their presence in the mountains keeps strangers out of Ulgo. We're not at ease with strangers, really, so it's probably for the best."

The Gorim was sitting directly across the narrow stone table from Ce'Nedra. The subject of the monsters obviously pained him, and he looked at her for a moment, then gently reached out his frail old hand and cupped her little chin in it, lifting her face to the dim light of the hanging globe suspended above the table. "All of the alien creatures are not monsters," he said, his large, violet eyes calm and very wise. "Consider the beauty of this Dryad."

Ce'Nedra was a little startled—not by his touch, certainly, for older people had responded to her flowerlike face with that same gesture for as long as she could remember—but rather by the ancient man's immediate recognition of the fact that she was not entirely human.

"Tell me, child," the Gorim asked, "do the Dryads still honor UL?"

She was completely unprepared for the question. "I-I'm sorry, Holy One," she floundered. "Until quite recently, I'd not even heard of the God UL. For some reason, my tutors have very little information about your people or your God."

"The princess was raised as a Tolnedran," Lady Polgara explained. "She's a Borune—I'm sure you've heard of the link between that house and the Dryads. As a Tolnedran, her religious affiliation is to Nedra."

"A serviceable God," the Gorim said. "Perhaps a bit stuffy for my taste, but certainly adequate. The Dryads themselves, though—do they still know their God?"

Belgarath coughed a bit apologetically. "I'm afraid not, Gorim. They've drifted away, and the eons have erased what they knew of UL. They're flighty creatures anyway, not much given to religious observances."

The Gorim's face was sad. "What God do they honor now?"

"None, actually," Belgarath admitted. "They have a few sacred groves—a rough idol or two fashioned from the root of a particularly venerated tree. That's about it. They don't really have any clearly formulated theology."

Ce'Nedra found the whole discussion a trifle offensive. Rising to the occasion, she drew herself up slightly and smiled winsomely at the old Gorim. She knew exactly how to charm an elderly man. She'd practiced for years on her father. "I feel the shortcomings of my education most keenly, Holy One," she lied. "Since mysterious UL is the hereditary God of the Dryads, I should know him. I hope that someday soon I may receive instruction concerning him. It may be that I—unworthy though I am—can be the instrument of renewing the allegiance of my sisters to their rightful God."

It was an artful little speech, and on the whole Ce'Nedra was rather proud of it. To her surprise, however, the Gorim was not satisfied to accept a vague expression of interest and let it go at that. "Tell your sisters that the core of our faith is to be found in *The Book of Ulgo*," he told her seriously.

"*The Book of Ulgo*," she repeated. "I must remember that. As soon as I return to Tol Honeth, I'll obtain a copy and deliver it to the Wood of the Dryads personally." That, she thought, should satisfy him.

"I'm afraid that such copies as you'd find in Tol Honeth would be much corrupted," the Corim told her. "The tongue of my people is not easily understood by strangers, and translations are difficult." Ce'Nedra definitely felt that the dear old man was becoming just a bit tiresome about the whole thing. "As is so often the case with scriptures," he was saying, "our Holy Book is bound up in our history. The wisdom of the Gods is such that their instruction is concealed within stories. Our minds delight in the stories, and the messages of the Gods are implanted thus. All unaware, we are instructed even as we are entertained."

Ce'Nedra was familiar with the theory. Master Jeebers, her tutor, had lectured her tediously concerning it. She cast about rather desperately, trying to find some graceful way to change the subject.

"Our story is very old," the Gorim continued inexorably. "Would you like to hear it?"

Caught by her own cleverness, Ce'Nedra could only nod helplessly.

And so the Gorim began: "At the Beginning of Days when the World was spun out of darkness by the wayward Gods, there dwelt in the silences of the heavens a spirit known only as UL."

In utter dismay, Ce'Nedra realized that he fully intended to recite the *entire* book to her. After a few moments of chagrin, however, she began to feel the strangely compelling quality of his story. More than she would have cared to admit, she was moved by the first Gorim's appeal to the indifferent spirit that appeared to him at Prolgu. What manner of man would thus dare to accuse a God?

As she listened, a faint flicker seemed to tug at the corner of her eye. She glanced toward it and saw a soft glow somewhere deep within the massive rocks that formed one of the walls of the chamber. The glow was peculiarly different from the dim light of the hanging crystal globes.

"Then the heart of Gorim was made glad," the old man continued his recitation, "and he called the name of the high place where all this had come to pass Prolgu, which is Holy Place. And he departed from Prolgu and returned unto—"

"*Ya! Garach tek*, Gorim!" The words were spat out in the snarling Ulgo language, and the harsh voice that spoke them was filled with outrage.

Ce'Nedra jerked her head around to look at the intruder. Like all Ulgos, he was short, but his arms and shoulders were so massively developed that he seemed almost deformed. His colorless hair was tangled and unkempt. He wore a hooded leather smock, stained and smeared with some kind of mud, and his large black eyes burned with fanaticism. Crowded behind him were a dozen or more other Ulgos, their faces set in expressions of shock and righteous indignation. The fanatic in the leather smock continued his stream of crackling vituperation.

The Gorim's face set, but he endured the abuse from the

wild-eyed man at the door patiently. Finally, when the fanatic paused for breath, the frail old man turned to Belgarath. "This is Relg," he said a bit apologetically. "You see what I mean about him? Trying to convince him of anything is impossible."

"What use would he be to us?" Barak demanded, obviously irritated by the newcomer's attitude. "He can't even speak a civilized tongue."

Relg glared at him. "I speak your language, foreigner," he said with towering contempt, "but I choose not to defile the holy caverns with its unsanctified mouthings." He turned back to Gorim. "Who gave you the right to speak the words of the Holy Book to unbelieving foreigners?" he demanded.

The gentle old Gorim's eyes hardened slightly. "I think that's about enough, Relg," he said firmly. "Whatever idiocies you babble in out-of-the-way galleries to those gullible enough to listen is your concern, but what you say to me in my house is mine. I am still Gorim in Ulgo, whatever you may think, and I am not required to answer to you." He looked past Relg at the shocked faces of the zealot's followers. "This is not a general audience," he informed Relg. "You were summoned here; they were not. Send them away."

"They came to be sure you intended me no harm," Relg replied stiffly. "I have spoken the truth about you, and powerful men fear the truth."

"Relg," the Gorim said in an icy voice, "I don't think you could even begin to realize how indifferent I am to anything you might have said about me. Now send them away—or would you rather have me do it?"

"They won't obey you," Relg sneered. "*I* am their leader."

The Gorim's eyes narrowed, and he rose to his feet. Then he spoke in the Ulgo tongue directly to Relg's adherents. Ce'Nedra could not understand his words, but she did not really need to. She recognized the tone of authority instantly, and she was a bit startled at how absolutely the saintly old Gorim used it. Not even her father would have dared speak in that tone.

The men crowded behind Relg looked nervously at each other and began to back away, their faces frightened. The

Gorim barked one final command, and Relg's followers turned and fled.

Relg scowled after them and seemed for a moment on the verge of raising his voice to call them back, but apparently thought better of it. "You go too far, Gorim," he accused. "*That* authority is not meant to be used in worldly matters."

"That authority is *mine*, Relg," the Gorim replied, "and it's up to me to decide when it's required. You've chosen to confront me on theological ground, therefore I needed to remind your followers—and you—just who I am."

"Why have you summoned me here?" Relg demanded. "The presence of these unsanctified ones is an affront to my purity."

"I require your service, Relg," the Gorim told him. "These strangers go to battle against our Ancient Foe, the one accursed above all others. The fate of the world hangs upon their quest, and your aid is needed."

"What do I care about the world?" Relg's voice was filled with contempt. "And what do I care about maimed Torak? I am safe within the hand of UL. He has need of me here, and I will not go from the holy caverns to risk defilement in the lewd company of unbelievers and monsters."

"The entire world will be defiled if Torak gains dominion over it," Belgarath pointed out, "and if we fail, Torak *will* become king of the world."

"He will not reign in Ulgo," Relg retorted.

"How little you know him," Polgara murmured.

"I will not leave the caves," Relg insisted. "The coming of the child is at hand, and I have been chosen to reveal him to Ulgo and to guide and instruct him until he is ready to become Gorim."

"How interesting," the Gorim observed dryly. "Just who was it who advised you of your election?"

"UL spoke to me," Relg declared.

"Odd. The caverns respond universally to the voice of UL. All Ulgo would have heard his voice."

"He spoke to me in my heart," Relg replied quickly.

"What a curious thing for him to do," the Gorim answered mildly.

"All of this is beside the point," Belgarath said brusquely. "I'd prefer to have you join us willingly, Relg; but willing or not, you *will* join us. A power greater than any of us commands it. You can argue and resist as much as you like, but when we leave here, you'll be going with us."

Relg spat. "Never! I will remain here in the service of UL and of the child who will become Gorim of Ulgo. And if you try to compel me, my followers will not permit it."

"Why do we need this blind mole, Belgarath?" Barak asked. "He's just going to be an aggravation to us. I've noticed that men who spend all their time congratulating themselves on their sanctity tend to be very poor companions, and what can this one do that I can't?"

Relg looked at the red-bearded giant with disdain. "Big men with big mouths seldom have big brains," he said. "Watch closely, hairy one." He walked over to the sloping wall of the chamber. "Can you do this?" he asked and slowly pushed his hand directly into the rock as if he were sinking it into water.

Silk whistled with amazement and moved quickly over to the wall beside the fanatic. As Relg pulled his hand out of the rock, Silk reached out to put his own hand on the precise spot. "How did you do that?" he demanded, shoving at the stones.

Relg laughed harshly and turned his back.

"That's the ability that makes him useful to us, Silk," Belgarath explained. "Relg's a diviner. He finds caves, and we need to locate the caves under Rak Cthol. If necessary, Relg can walk through solid rock to find them for us."

"How could anyone do that?" Silk asked, still staring at the spot where Relg had sunk his hand into the wall.

"It has to do with the nature of matter," the sorcerer replied. "What we see as solid isn't really all that impenetrable."

"Either something's solid or it's not," Silk insisted, his face baffled.

"Solidity's an illusion," Belgarath told him. "Relg can slip the bits and pieces that make up his substance through the spaces that exist between the bits and pieces that make up the substance of the rock."

"Can *you* do it?" Silk demanded skeptically.

Belgarath shrugged. "I don't know. I've never had occasion to try. Anyway, Relg can smell caves, and he goes straight to them. He probably doesn't know himself how he does it."

"I am led by my sanctity," Relg declared arrogantly.

"Perhaps that's it," the sorcerer agreed with a tolerant smile.

"The holiness of the caves draws me, since I am drawn to all holy things," Relg rasped on, "and for me to leave the caverns of Ulgo would be to turn my back on holiness and move toward defilement."

"We'll see," Belgarath told him.

The glow in the rock wall which Ce'Nedra had noticed before began to shimmer and pulsate, and the princess seemed to see a dim shape within the rocks. Then, as if the stones were only air, the shape became distinct and stepped out into the chamber. For just a moment, it seemed that the figure was an old man, bearded and robed like the Gorim, although much more robust. Then Ce'Nedra was struck by an overpowering sense of something more than human. With an awed shudder, she realized that she was in the presence of divinity.

Relg gaped at the bearded figure, and he began to tremble violently. With a strangled cry he prostrated himself.

The figure looked calmly at the groveling zealot. "Rise, Relg," it said in a soft voice that seemed to carry all the echoes of eternity in it, and the caverns outside rang with the sound of that voice. "Rise, Relg, and serve thy God."

Chapter Eighteen

CE'NEDRA HAD received an exquisite education. She had been so thoroughly trained that she knew instinctively all the niceties of etiquette and all the proper forms to be observed upon coming into the presence of an emperor or a king, but the physical presence of a God still baffled and even frightened her. She felt awkward, even gauche, like some ignorant farm girl. She found herself trembling and, for one of the few times in her life, she hadn't the faintest idea what to do.

UL was still looking directly into Relg's awe-struck face. "Thy mind hath twisted what I told thee, my son," the God said gravely. "Thou hast turned my words to make them conform to thy desire, rather than to my will."

Relg flinched, and his eyes were stricken.

"I told thee that the child who will be Gorim will come to Ulgo through thee," UL continued, "and that thou must prepare thyself to nurture him and see to his rearing. Did I tell thee to exalt thyself by reason of this?"

Relg began to shake violently.

"Did I tell thee to preach sedition? Or to stir Ulgo against the Gorim whom I have chosen to guide them?"

Relg collapsed. "Forgive me, O my God," he begged, groveling again on the floor.

"Rise, Relg," UL told him sternly. "I am not pleased with thee, and thine obeisance offends me, for thy heart is filled with pride. I will bend thee to my will, Relg, or I will break thee. I will purge thee on this overweening esteem thou hast for thyself. Only then wilt thou be worthy of the task to which I have set thee."

Relg stumbled to his feet, his face filled with remorse. "O my God—" He choked.

"Hearken unto my words, Relg, and obey me utterly. It is my command that thou accompany Belgarath, Disciple of Aldur, and render unto him all aid within thy power. Thou wilt obey him even as if he were speaking in my voice. Dost thou understand this?"

"Yes, O my God," Relg replied humbly.

"And wilt thou obey?"

"I will do as thou hast commanded me, O my God—though it cost me my life."

"It shall not cost thee thy life, Relg, for I have need of thee. Thy reward for this shall be beyond thy imagining."

Relg bowed in mute acceptance.

The God then turned to the Gorim. "Abide yet a while, my son," he said, "though the years press heavily upon thee. It shall not be long until thy burden shall be lifted. Know that I am pleased with thee."

The Gorim bowed in acceptance.

"Belgarath," UL greeted the sorcerer. "I have watched thee at thy task, and I share thy Master's pride in thee. The prophecy moves through thee and Polgara thy daughter toward that moment we have all awaited."

Belgarath also bowed. "It's been a long time, Most Holy," he replied, "and there were twists and turns to it that none of us could see at the beginning."

"Truly," UL agreed. "It hath surprised us all upon occasion. Hath Aldur's gift to the world come into his birthright as yet?"

"Not entirely, Most Holy," Polgara answered gravely. "He's touched the edges of it, however, and what he's shown us so far gives us hope for his success."

"Hail then, Belgarion," UL said to the startled young man. "Take my blessing with thee and know that I will join with Aldur to be with thee when thy great task begins."

Garion bowed—rather awkwardly, Ce'Nedra noticed. She decided that soon—very soon—she'd have to give him some schooling in such matters. He'd resist, naturally—he was impossibly stubborn—but she knew that if she nagged and badgered him enough, he'd eventually come around. And it was for his own good, after all.

UL seemed to be still looking at Garion, but there was a subtle difference in his expression. It seemed to Ce'Nedra that he was communicating wordlessly to some *other* presence—something that was a part of Garion and yet not a part of him. He nodded gravely then, and turned his gaze directly upon the princess herself.

"She seems but a child," he observed to Polgara.

"She's of a suitable age, Most Holy," Polgara replied. "She's a Dryad, and they're all quite small."

UL smiled gently at the princess, and she felt herself suddenly glowing in the warmth of that smile. "She is like a flower, is she not?" he said.

"She still has a few thorns, Most Holy," Belgarath replied wryly, "and a bit of bramble in her nature."

"We will value her all the more for that, Belgarath. The time will come when her fire and her brambles will serve our cause far more than her beauty." UL glanced once at Garion, and a strange, knowing smile crossed his face. For some reason, Ce'Nedra felt herself beginning to blush, then lifted her chin as if daring the blush to go any further.

"It is to speak with thee that I have come, my daughter," UL said directly to her then, and his tone and face grew serious. "Thou must abide here when thy companions depart. Do not venture into the kingdom of the Murgos, for if it should come to pass that thou makest this journey unto Rak Cthol, thou shalt surely die, and without thee the struggle against the darkness must fail. Abide here in the safety of Ulgo until thy companions return."

This was the kind of thing Ce'Nedra completely understood. As a princess, she knew the need for instant submission to authority. Though she had wheedled, coaxed, and teased her father all her life to get her own way, she had seldom directly rebelled. She bowed her head. "I will do as thou hast commanded, Most Holy," she replied without even thinking of the implications of the God's words.

UL nodded with satisfaction. "Thus is the prophecy protected," he declared. "Each of you hath his appointed tasks in this work of ours—and I have mine as well. I will delay you no longer, my children. Fare you all well in this. We will meet again." Then he vanished.

The sounds of his last words echoed in the caverns of Ulgo. After a moment of stunned silence, the hymn of adoration burst forth again in a mighty chorus, as every Ulgo raised his voice in ecstasy at this divine visitation.

"Belar!" Barak breathed explosively. "Did you *feel* it?"

"UL has a commanding presence," Belgarath agreed. He turned to look at Relg, one eyebrow cocked rather whimsically. "I take it you've had a change of heart," he observed.

Relg's face had gone ashen, and he was still trembling violently. "I will obey my God," he vowed. "Where he has commanded me, I will go."

"I'm glad that's been settled," Belgarath told him. "At the moment he wants you to go to Rak Cthol. He may have other plans for you later, but right now Rak Cthol's enough to worry about."

"I will obey you without question," the fanatic declared, "even as my God has commanded me."

"Good," Belgarath replied, and then he went directly to the point. "Is there a way to avoid the weather and the difficulties above?"

"I know a way," Relg answered. "It's difficult and long, but it will lead us to the foothills above the land of the horse people."

"You see," Silk observed to Barak, "he's proving useful already."

Barak grunted, still not looking entirely convinced.

"May I know why we must go to Rak Cthol?" Relg asked, his entire manner changed by his meeting with his God.

"We have to reclaim the Orb of Aldur," Belgarath told him.

"I've heard of it," Relg admitted.

Silk was frowning. "Are you sure you'll be able to find the

caves under Rak Cthol?" he asked Relg. "Those caves won't be the caverns of UL, you know, and in Cthol Murgos they're not likely to be holy—quite the opposite, most probably."

"I can find any cave—anywhere," Relg stated confidently.

"All right then," Belgarath continued. "Assuming that all goes well, we'll go up through the caves and enter the city unobserved. We'll find Ctuchik and take the Orb away from him."

"Won't he try to fight?" Durnik asked.

"I certainly hope so," Belgarath replied fervently.

Barak laughed shortly. "You're starting to sound like an Alorn, Belgarath."

"That's not necessarily a virtue," Polgara pointed out.

"I'll deal with the magician of Rak Cthol when the time comes," the sorcerer said grimly. "At any rate, once we've recovered the Orb, we'll go back down through the caves and make a run for it."

"With all of Cthol Murgos hot on our heels," Silk added. "I've had dealings occasionally with Murgos. They're a persistent sort of people."

"That could be a problem," Belgarath admitted. "We don't want their pursuit gaining too much momentum. If an army of Murgos inadvertently follows us into the West, it will be viewed as an invasion, and that will start a war we aren't ready for yet. Any ideas?" He looked around.

"Turn them all into frogs," Barak suggested with a shrug.

Belgarath gave him a withering look.

"It was just a thought," Barak said defensively.

"Why not just stay in the caves under the city until they give up the search?" Durnik offered.

Polgara shook her head firmly. "No," she said. "There's a place we have to be at a certain time. We'll barely make it there as it is. We can't afford to lose a month or more hiding in some cave in Cthol Murgos."

"Where do we have to be, Aunt Pol?" Garion asked her.

"I'll explain later," she evaded, throwing a quick glance at Ce'Nedra. The princess perceived immediately that the appointment the Lady spoke of concerned *her*, and curiosity began to gnaw at her.

Mandorallen, his face thoughtful and his fingers lightly touching the ribs that had been cracked in his encounter with Grul, cleared his throat. "Does there perchance happen to be a map of the region we must enter somewhere nearby, Holy Gorim?" he asked politely.

The Gorim thought for a moment. "I believe I have one somewhere," he replied. He tapped his cup lightly on the table and an Ulgo servingman immediately entered the chamber. The Gorim spoke briefly to him, and the servingman went out. "The map I recall is very old," the Gorim told Mandorallen, "and I'm afraid it won't be very accurate. Our cartographers have difficulty comprehending the distances involved in the world above."

"The distances do not matter so much," Mandorallen assured him. "I wish but to refresh my memory concerning the contiguity of certain other realms upon the borders of Cthol Murgos. I was at best an indifferent student of geography as a schoolboy."

The servingman returned and handed a large roll of parchment to the Gorim. The Gorim in turn passed the roll to Mandorallen.

The knight carefully unrolled the chart and studied it for a moment. "It is as I recalled," he said. He turned to Belgarath. "Thou hast said, ancient friend, that no Murgo will enter the Vale of Aldur?"

"That's right," Belgarath replied.

Mandorallen pointed at the map. "The closest border from Rak Cthol is that which abuts Tolnedra," he showed them. "Logic would seem to dictate that our route of escape should lie in that direction—toward the nearest frontier."

"All right," Belgarath conceded.

"Let us then seem to make all haste toward Tolnedra, leaving behind us abundant evidence of our passage. Then, at some point where rocky ground would conceal signs of our change of direction, let us turn and strike out to the northwest toward the Vale. Might this not confound them? May we not confidently anticipate that they will continue to pursue our imagined course? In time, certainly, they will realize their error, but by then we will be many leagues ahead of them. Pursuing far to our rear, might not the further discouragement of the prohibited Vale cause them to abandon the chase entirely?"

They all looked at the map.

"I like it," Barak said, effusively slapping one huge hand on the knight's shoulder.

Mandorallen winced and put his hand to his injured ribs.

"Sorry, Mandorallen," Barak apologized quickly. "I forgot."

Silk was studying the map intently. "It's got a lot to recommend it, Belgarath," he urged, "and if we angle up to here—" He pointed. "—we'll come out on top of the eastern escarpment. We should have plenty of time to make the descent, but they'll definitely want to think twice before trying it. It's a good mile straight down at that point."

"We could send word to Cho-Hag," Hettar suggested. "If a few clans just happened to be gathered at the foot of the escarpment there, the Murgos would think more than twice before starting down."

Belgarath scratched at his beard. "All right," he decided after a moment, "we'll try it that way. As soon as Relg leads us out of Ulgo, you go pay your father a visit, Hettar. Tell him what we're going to do and invite him to bring a few thousand warriors down to the Vale to meet us."

The lean Algar nodded, his black scalp lock bobbing. His face, however, showed a certain disappointment.

"Forget it, Hettar," the old man told him bluntly. "I never had any intention of taking you into Cthol Murgos. There'd be too many opportunities there for you to get yourself in trouble."

Hettar sighed somewhat mournfully.

"Don't take it so hard, Hettar," Silk bantered. "Murgos are a fanatic race. You can be practically certain that a few of them at least will try the descent—no matter what's waiting for them at the bottom. You'd almost have to make an example of them, wouldn't you?"

Hettar's face brightened at that thought.

"Silk," Lady Polgara said reprovingly.

The little man turned an innocent face to her. "We have to discourage pursuit, Polgara," he protested.

"Of course," she replied sarcastically.

"It wouldn't do to have Murgos infesting the Vale, would it?"

"Do you mind?"

"I'm not really all that bloodthirsty, you know."

She turned her back on him.

Silk sighed piously. "She always thinks the worst of me."

By now Ce'Nedra had had sufficient time to consider the implications of the promise she had so unhesitatingly given to UL. The others would soon leave, and she must remain behind. Already she was beginning to feel isolated, cut off from them, as they made plans which did not include her. The more she thought about it, the worse it became. She felt her lower lip beginning to quiver.

The Gorim of the Ulgos had been watching her, his wise old face sympathetic. "It's difficult to be left behind," he said gently, almost as if his large eyes had seen directly into her thoughts, "and our caves are strange to you—dark and seemingly filled with gloom."

Wordlessly she nodded her agreement.

"In a day or so, however," he continued, "your eyes will become accustomed to the subdued light. There are beauties here which no one from the outside has ever seen. While it's true that we have no flowers, there are hidden caverns where gems bloom on the floors and walls like wild blossoms. No trees or foliage grow in our sunless world, but I know a cave wall where vines of pure gold twist in ropey coils down from the ceiling and spill out across the floor."

"Careful, Holy Gorim," Silk warned. "The Princess is Tolnedran. If you show her that kind of wealth, she may go into hysterics right before your eyes."

"I don't find that particularly amusing, Prince Kheldar," Ce'Nedra told him in a frosty tone.

"I'm overcome with remorse, your Imperial Highness," he apologized with towering hypocrisy and a florid bow.

In spite of herself, the princess laughed. The rat-faced little Drasnian was so absolutely outrageous that she found it impossible to remain angry with him.

"You'll be as my beloved granddaughter while you stay in Ulgo, Princess," the Gorim told her. "We can walk together beside our silent lakes and explore long forgotten caves. And we can talk. The world outside knows little of Ulgo. It may well be that you will become the very first stranger to understand us."

Ce'Nedra impulsively reached out to take his frail old hand in hers. He was such a dear old man. "I'll be honored, Holy Gorim," she told him with complete sincerity.

They stayed that night in comfortable quarters in the Gorim's pyramid-shaped house—though the terms night and day had no meaning in this strange land beneath the earth. The following morning several Ulgos led the horses into the Gorim's cavern, traveling, the princess assumed, by some longer route than the one the party had followed, and her friends made their preparations to leave. Ce'Nedra sat to one side, feeling terribly alone already. Her eyes moved from face to face as she tried to fix each of them in her memory. When she came at last to Garion, her eyes brimmed.

Irrationally, she had already begun to worry about him. He was so impulsive. She knew that he'd do things that would put him in danger once he was out of her sight. To be sure, Polgara would be there to watch over him, but it wasn't the same. She felt quite suddenly angry with him for all the foolish things he was going to do and for the worry his careless behavior was going to cause her. She glared at him, wishing that he would do something for which she could scold him.

She had determined that she would not follow them out of the Gorim's house—that she would not stand forlornly at the edge of the water staring after them as they departed—but as they all filed out through the heavy-arched doorway, her resolution crumbled. Without thinking she ran after Garion and caught his arm.

He turned with surprise, and she stretched up on her tiptoes, took his face between her tiny hands and kissed him. "You *must* be careful," she commanded. Then she kissed him again, spun and ran sobbing back into the house, leaving him staring after her in baffled astonishment.

Part Four

CTHOL MURGOS

Chapter Nineteen

THEY HAD BEEN in the darkness for days. The single dim light Relg carried could only provide a point of reference, something to follow. The darkness pressed against Garion's face, and he stumbled along the uneven floor with one hand thrust out in front of him to keep himself from banging his head into unseen rocks. It was not only the musty-smelling darkness, however. He could sense the oppressive weight of the mountains above him and on all sides. The stone seemed to push in on him; he was closed in, sealed up in miles of solid rock. He fought continually with the faint, fluttering edges of panic and he often clenched his teeth to keep from screaming.

There seemed to be no purpose to the twisting, turning route Relg followed. At the branching of passageways, his choices seemed random, but always he moved with steady confidence through the dark, murmuring caves where the memory of sounds whispered in the dank air, voices out of the past echoing endlessly, whispering, whispering. Relg's air of confidence as he led them was the only thing that kept Garion from giving in to unreasoning panic.

At one point the zealot stopped.

"What's wrong?" Silk asked sharply, his voice carrying that same faint edge of panic that Garion felt gnawing at his own awareness.

"I have to cover my eyes here," Relg replied. He was wearing a peculiarly fashioned shirt of leaf-mail, a strange garment formed of overlapping metal scales, belted at the waist and with a snug-fitting hood that left only his face exposed. From his belt hung a heavy, hook-pointed knife, a weapon that made Garion cold just to look at it. He drew a piece of cloth out from under his mail shirt and carefully tied it over his face.

"Why are you doing that?" Durnik asked him.

"There's a vein of quartz in the cavern just ahead," Relg told him. "It reflects sunlight down from the outside. The light is very bright."

"How can you tell which way to go if you're blindfolded?" Silk protested.

"The cloth isn't that thick. I can see through it well enough. Let's go."

They rounded a corner in the gallery they were following, and Garion saw light ahead. He resisted an impulse to run toward it. They moved on, the hooves of the horses Hettar was leading clattering on the stone floor. The lighted cavern was huge, and it was filled with a glittering crystal light. A gleaming band of quartz angled across the ceiling, illuminating the cavern with a blazing radiance. Great points of stone hung like icicles from the ceiling, and other points rose from the floor to meet them. In the center of the cavern another underground lake stretched, its surface rippled by a tiny waterfall trickling down into its upper end with an endless tinkling sound that echoed in the cave like a little silver bell and joined harmoniously with the faint, remembered sigh of the singing of the Ulgos miles behind. Garion's eyes were dazzled by color that seemed to be everywhere. The prisms in the crystalline quartz twisted the light, breaking it into colored fragments and filling the cave with the multihued light of the rainbow. Garion found himself quite suddenly wishing that he could show the dazzling cave to Ce'Nedra, and the thought puzzled him.

"Hurry," Relg urged them, holding one hand across his brow as if to further shade his already veiled eyes.

"Why not stop here?" Barak suggested. "We need some rest, and this looks like a good place."

"It's the worst place in all the caves," Relg told him. "Hurry."

"Maybe *you* like the dark," Barak said, "but the rest of us aren't that fond of it." He looked around at the cave.

"Protect your eyes, you fool," Relg snapped.

"I don't care for your tone, friend."

"You'll be blind once we get past this place if you don't. It's taken your eyes two days to get used to the dark. You'll lose all of that if you stay here too long."

Barak stared hard at the Ulgo for a moment. Then he grunted and nodded shortly. "Sorry," he said. "I didn't understand." He reached out to put his hand on Relg's shoulder in apology.

"Don't touch me!" Relg cried, shrinking away from the big hand.

"What's the matter?"

"Just don't touch me—not ever." Relg hurried on ahead.

"What's the matter with him?" Barak demanded.

"He doesn't want you to defile him," Belgarath explained.

"Defile him? *Defile* him?"

"He's very concerned about his personal purity. The way he sees it, any kind of touch can soil him."

"Soil? He's as dirty as a pig in a wallow."

"It's a different kind of dirt. Let's move on."

Barak strode along behind the rest of them, grumbling and sputtering in outrage. They moved into another dark passageway, and Garion looked longingly back over his shoulder at the fading light from the glowing cavern behind. Then they rounded a corner and the light was gone.

There was no way to keep track of time in the murmuring darkness. They stumbled on, pausing now and then to eat or to rest, though Garion's sleep was filled with nightmares about mountains crushing in on him. He had almost given up all hope of ever seeing the sky again when the first faint cobweb touch of moving air brushed his cheek. It had been, as closely as he could judge, five days since they had left the last dimly lighted gallery of the Ulgos behind and plunged into this eternal night. At first he thought the faint hint of warmer air might only be his imagination, but then he caught the scent of trees and grass in the musty air of the cave, and he knew that somewhere ahead there lay an opening—a way out.

The touch of warmer outside air grew stronger, and the smell of grass began to fill the passageway along which they crept. The floor began to slope upward, and imperceptibly it grew less dark. It seemed somehow that they moved up out of endless night toward the light of the first morning in the history of the world. The horses, plodding along at the rear, had also caught the scent of fresh air, and their pace quickened. Relg, however, moved slower, and then slower still. Finally he stopped altogether. The faint metallic rustling of his leaf-mail shirt spoke loudly to him. Relg was trembling, bracing himself for what lay ahead. He bound his veil across his face again, mumbling something over and over in the snarling language of the Ulgos, fervent, almost pleading. Once his eyes were covered, he moved on again, reluctantly, his feet almost dragging.

Then there was golden light ahead. The mouth of the passageway was a jagged, irregular opening with a stiff tangle of limbs sharply outlined in front of it. With a sudden clatter of little hooves, the colt, ignoring Hettar's sharp command, bolted for the opening and plunged out into the light.

Belgarath scratched at his whiskers, squinting after the little animal. "Maybe you'd better take him and his mother with you when we separate," he said to Hettar. "He seems to have a little trouble taking things seriously, and Cthol Murgos is a very serious place."

Hettar nodded gravely.

"I can't," Relg blurted suddenly, turning his back to the light and pressing himself against the rock wall of the passageway. "I can't do it."

"Of course you can," Aunt Pol said comfortingly to him. "We'll go out slowly so you can get used to it a little at a time."

"Don't touch me," Relg replied almost absently.

"That's going to get very tiresome," Barak growled.

Garion and the rest of them pushed ahead eagerly, their hunger for light pulling at them. They shoved their way roughly through the tangle of bushes at the mouth of the cave and, blinking and shading their eyes, they emerged into the sunlight. The light at first stabbed Garion's eyes painfully; but after a few moments, he found that he could see again. The partially concealed entrance to the caves was near the midpoint of a rocky hillside. Behind them, the snow-covered mountains of Ulgo glittered in the morning sun, outlined against the deep blue sky, and a vast plain spread before them like a sea. The tall grass was golden with autumn, and the morning breeze touched it into long, undulating waves. The plain reached to the horizon, and Garion felt as if he had just awakened from a nightmare.

Just inside the mouth of the cave behind them, Relg knelt with his back to the light, praying and beating at his shoulders and chest with his fists.

"*Now* what's he doing?" Barak demanded.

"It's a kind of purification ritual," Belgarath explained. "He's trying to purge himself of all unholiness and draw the essence of the caves into his soul. He thinks it may help to sustain him while he's outside."

"How long's he going to be at it?"

"About an hour, I'd imagine. It's a fairly complicated ritual."

Relg stopped praying long enough to bind a second veil across his face on top of the first one.

"If he wraps any more cloth around his head, he's likely to smother," Silk observed.

"I'd better get started," Hettar said, tightening the straps on his saddle. "Is there anything else you wanted me to tell Cho-Hag?"

"Tell him to pass the word along to the others about what's happened so far," Belgarath answered. "Things are getting to the point where I'd like everybody to be more or less alert."

Hettar nodded.

"Do you know where you are?" Barak asked him.

"Of course." The tall man looked out at the seemingly featureless plain before him.

"It's probably going to take us at least a month to get to Rak Cthol and back," Belgarath advised. "If we get a chance, we'll light signal fires on top of the eastern escarpment before we start down. Tell Cho-Hag how important it is for him to be waiting for us. We don't want Murgos blundering into Algaria. I'm not ready for a war just yet."

"We'll be there," Hettar replied, swinging up into his saddle. "Be careful in Cthol Murgos." He turned his horse and started down the hill toward the plain with the mare and the colt tagging along behind him. The colt stopped once to look back at Garion, gave a forlorn little whinny, then turned to follow his mother.

Barak shook his head sombrely. "I'm going to miss Hettar," he rumbled.

"Cthol Murgos wouldn't be a good place for Hettar," Silk pointed out. "We'd have to put a leash on him."

"I know that." Barak sighed. "But I'll miss him all the same."

"Which direction do we take?" Mandorallen asked, squinting out at the grassland.

Belgarath pointed to the southeast. "That way. We'll cross the upper end of the Vale to the escarpment and then go through the southern tip of Mishrak ac Thull. The Thulls don't put out patrols as regularly as the Murgos do."

"Thulls don't do much of anything unless they have to," Silk noted. "They're too preoccupied with trying to avoid Grolims."

"When do we start?" Durnik asked.

"As soon as Relg finishes his prayers," Belgarath replied.

"We'll have time for breakfast then," Barak said dryly.

They rode all that day across the flat grassland of southern Algaria beneath the deep blue autumn sky. Relg, wearing an old hooded tunic of Durnik's over his mail shirt, rode badly, with his legs sticking out stiffly. He seemed to be concentrating more on keeping his face down than on watching where he was going.

Barak watched sourly, with disapproval written plainly on his face. "I'm not trying to tell you your business, Belgarath," he said after several hours, "but that one's going to be trouble before we're finished with this."

"The light hurts his eyes, Barak," Aunt Pol told the big man, "and he's not used to riding. Don't be so quick to criticize."

Barak clamped his mouth shut, his expression still disparaging.

"At least we'll be able to count on his staying sober," Aunt Pol observed primly. "Which is more than I can say about *some* members of this little group."

Barak coughed uncomfortably.

They set up for the night on the treeless bank of a meandering stream. Once the sun had gone down, Relg seemed less apprehensive, though he made an obvious point of not looking directly at the driftwood fire. Then he looked up and saw the first stars in the evening sky. He gaped up at them in horror, his unveiled face breaking out in a glistening sweat. He covered his head with his arms and collapsed face down on the earth with a strangled cry.

"Relg!" Garion exclaimed, jumping to the stricken man's side and putting his hands on him without thinking.

"Don't touch me," Relg gasped automatically.

"Don't be stupid. What's wrong? Are you sick?"

"The sky," Relg croaked in despair. "The sky! It terrifies me!"

"The sky?" Garion was baffled. "What's wrong with the sky?" He looked up at the familiar stars.

"There's no end to it," Relg groaned. "It goes up forever."

Quite suddenly Garion understood. In the caves *he* had been afraid—unreasoningly afraid—because he had been closed in. Out here under the open sky, Relg suffered from the same kind of blind terror. Garion realized with a kind of shock that quite probably Relg had never been outside the caves of Ulgo in his entire life. "It's all right," he assured him comfortingly. "The sky can't hurt you. It's just up there. Don't pay any attention to it."

"I can't bear it."

"Don't look at it."

"I still know it's there—all that emptiness."

Garion looked helplessly at Aunt Pol. She made a quick gesture that told him to keep talking. "It's not empty," he floundered. "It's full of things—all kinds of things—clouds, birds, sunlight, stars—"

"What?" Relg lifted his face up out of his hands. "What are those?"

"Clouds? Everyone knows what—" Garion stopped. Obviously Relg did *not* know what clouds were. He'd never seen a cloud in his life. Garion tried to rearrange his thoughts to take that into account. It was not going to be easy to explain. He took in a deep breath. "All right. Let's start with clouds, then."

It took a long time, and Garion was not really sure that Relg understood or if he was simply clinging to the words to avoid thinking about the sky. After clouds, birds were a bit easier, although feathers were very hard to explain.

"UL spoke to you," Relg interrupted Garion's description of wings. "He called you Belgarion. Is that your name?"

"Well—" Garion replied uncomfortably. "Not really. Actually my name is Garion, but I think the other name is supposed to be mine too—sometime later, I believe—when I'm older."

"UL knows all things," Relg declared. "If he called you Belgarion, that's your true name. I will call you Belgarion."

"I really wish you wouldn't."

"My God rebuked me," Relg groaned, his voice sunk into a kind of sick self-loathing. "I have failed him."

Garion couldn't quite follow that. Somehow, even in the midst of his panic, Relg had been suffering the horrors of a theological crisis. He sat on the ground with his face turned away from the fire and his shoulders slumped in an attitude of absolute despair.

"I'm unworthy," he said, his voice on the verge of a sob. "When UL spoke in the silence of my heart, I felt that I had been exalted above all other men, but now I am lower than dirt." In his anguish he began to beat the sides of his head with his fists.

"Stop that!" Garion said sharply. "You'll hurt yourself. What's this all about?"

"UL told me that I was to reveal the child to Ulgo. I took his words to mean that I had found special grace in his eyes."

"What child are we talking about?"

"*The* child. The new Gorim. It's UL's way to guide and protect his people. When an old Gorim's work is done, UL places a special mark upon the eyes of the child who is to succeed him. When UL told me that I had been chosen to bring the child to Ulgo, I revealed his words to others, and they revered me and asked me to speak to them in the words of UL. I saw sin and corruption all around me and I denounced it, and the people listened to me—but the words were mine, not UL's. In my pride, I presumed to speak for UL. I ignored my own sins to accuse the sins of others." Relg's voice was harsh with fanatic self-accusation. "I am filth," he declared, "an abomination. UL should have raised his hand against me and destroyed me."

"That's forbidden," Garion told him without thinking.

"Who has the power to forbid anything to UL?"

"I don't know. All I know is that unmaking is forbidden— even to the Gods. It's the very first thing we learn."

Relg looked up sharply, and Garion knew instantly that he had made a dreadful mistake. "You know the secrets of the Gods?" the fanatic demanded incredulously.

"The fact that they're Gods doesn't have anything to do with it," Garion replied. "The rule applies to everybody."

Relg's eyes burned with a sudden hope. He drew himself up onto his knees and bowed forward until his face was in the dirt. "Forgive me my sins," he intoned.

"What?"

"I have exalted myself when I was unworthy."

"You made a mistake—that's all. Just don't do it anymore. Please get up, Relg."

"I'm wicked and impure."

"You?"

"I've had impure thoughts about women."

Garion flushed with embarrassment. "We all have those kinds of thoughts once in a while," he said with a nervous cough.

"My thoughts are wicked—wicked," Relg groaned with guilt. "I burn with them."

"I'm sure that UL understands. Please get up, Relg. You don't have to do this."

"I have prayed with my mouth when my mind and heart were not in my prayers."

"Relg—"

"I have sought out hidden caves for the joy of finding them rather than to consecrate them to UL. I have thus defiled the gift given me by my God."

"Please, Relg—"

Relg began to beat his head on the ground. "Once I found a cave where the echoes of UL's voice lingered. I did not reveal it to others, but kept the sound of UL's voice for myself."

Garion began to become alarmed. The fanatic Relg was working himself into a frenzy.

"Punish me, Belgarion," Relg pleaded. "Lay a hard penance on me for my iniquity."

Garion's mind was very clear as he answered. He knew exactly what he had to say. "I can't do that, Relg," he said gravely. "I can't punish you—any more than I can forgive you. If you've done things you shouldn't have, that's between you and UL. If you think you need to be punished, you'll have to do it yourself. I can't. I won't."

Relg lifted his stricken face out of the dirt and stared at Garion. Then with a strangled cry he lurched to his feet and fled wailing into the darkness.

"Garion!" Aunt Pol's voice rang with that familiar note.

"I didn't do anything," he protested almost automatically.

"What did you say to him?" Belgarath demanded.

"He said that he'd committed all kinds of sins," Garion explained. "He wanted me to punish him and forgive him."

"So?"

"I couldn't do that, Grandfather."

"What's so hard about it?"

Garion stared at him.

"All you had to do was lie to him a little. Is that so difficult?"

"Lie? About something like that?" Garion was horrified at the thought.

"I *need* him, Garion, and he can't function if he's incapacitated by some kind of religious hysteria. Use your head, boy."

"I can't do it, Grandfather," Garion repeated stubbornly. "It's too important to him for me to cheat him about it."

"You'd better go find him, father," Aunt Pol said.

Belgarath scowled at Garion. "You and I aren't finished with this yet, boy," he said, pointing an angry finger. Then, muttering irritably to himself, he went in search of Relg.

With a cold certainty Garion suddenly knew that the journey to Cthol Murgos was going to be very long and uncomfortable.

Chapter Twenty

THOUGH SUMMER THAT year had lingered in the lowlands and on the plains of Algaria, autumn was brief. The blizzards and squalls they had encountered in the mountains above Maragor and again among the peaks of Ulgo had hinted that winter would be early and severe, and there was already a chill to the nights as they rode day after day across the open grassland toward the eastern escarpment.

Belgarath had recovered from his momentary fit of anger over Garion's failure to deal with Relg's attack of guilt, but then, with inescapable logic, he had placed an enormous burden squarely on Garion's shoulders. "For some reason he trusts you," the old man observed, "so I'm going to leave him entirely in your hands. I don't care what you have to do, but keep him from flying apart again."

At first, Relg refused to respond to Garion's efforts to draw him out; but after a while, one of the waves of panic caused by the thought of the open sky above swept over the zealot, and he began to talk—haltingly at first but then finally in a great rush. As Garion had feared, Relg's favorite topic was sin. Garion was amazed at the simple things that Relg considered sinful. Forgetting to pray before a meal, for example, was a major transgression. As the fanatic's gloomy catalogue of his faults expanded, Garion began to perceive that most of his sins were sins of thought rather than of action. The one matter that kept cropping up again and again was the question of lustful thoughts about women. To Garion's intense discomfort, Relg insisted on describing these lustful thoughts extensively.

"Women are not the same as we are, of course," the zealot confided one afternoon as they rode together. "Their minds and hearts are not drawn to holiness the way ours are, and they set out deliberately to tempt us with their bodies and draw us into sin."

"Why do you suppose that is?" Garion asked carefully.

"Their hearts are filled with lust," Relg declared adamantly. "They take particular delight in tempting the righteous. I tell you truly, Belgarion, you would not believe the subtlety of the creatures. I have seen the evidence of this wickedness in the soberest of matrons—the wives of some of my most devout followers. They're forever touching—brushing as if by accident—and they take great pains to allow the sleeves of their robes to slip up brazenly to expose their rounded arms—and the hems of their garments always seem to be hitching up to display their ankles."

"If it bothers you, don't look," Garion suggested.

Relg ignored that. "I have even considered banning them from my presence, but then I thought that it might be better if I kept my eyes on them so that I could protect my followers from their wickedness. I thought for a time that I should forbid marriage among my followers, but some of the older ones told me that I might lose the young if I did that. I still think it might not be a bad idea."

"Wouldn't that sort of eliminate your followers altogether?" Garion asked him. "I mean, if you kept it up long enough? No marriage, no children. You get my point?"

"That's the part I haven't worked out yet," Relg admitted.

"And what about the child—the new Gorim? If two people are supposed to get married so they can have a child—that particular, special child—and you persuade them not to, aren't you interfering with something that UL wants to happen?"

Relg drew in a sharp breath as if he had not considered that. Then he groaned. "You see? Even when I'm trying my very hardest, I always seem to stumble straight into sin. I'm cursed, Belgarion, cursed. Why did UL choose me to reveal the child when I am so corrupt?"

Garion quickly changed the subject to head off that line of thought.

For nine days they crossed the endless sea of grass toward the eastern escarpment, and for nine days the others, with a callousness that hurt Garion to the quick, left him trapped in the company of the ranting zealot. He grew sulky and frequently cast reproachful glances at them, but they ignored him.

Near the eastern edge of the plain, they crested a long hill and stared for the first time at the immense wall of the eastern escarpment, a sheer basalt cliff rising fully a mile above the rubble at its base and stretching off into the distance in either direction.

"Impossible," Barak stated flatly. "We'll never be able to climb that."

"We won't have to," Silk told him confidently. "I know a trail."

"A secret trail, I suppose?"

"Not exactly a secret," Silk replied. "I don't imagine too many people know about it, but it's right out in plain sight—if you know where to look. I had occasion to leave Mishrak ac Thull in a hurry once, and I stumbled across it."

"One gets the feeling that you've had occasion to leave just about every place in a hurry at one time or another."

Silk shrugged. "Knowing when it's time to run is one of the most important things people in my profession ever learn."

"Will the river ahead not prove a barrier?" Mandorallen asked, looking at the sparkling surface of the Aldur River lying between them and the grim, black cliff. He was running his fingertips lightly over his side, testing for tender spots.

"Mandorallen, stop that," Aunt Pol told him. "They'll never heal if you keep poking at them."

"Methinks, my Lady, that they are nearly whole again," the knight replied. "Only one still causes me any discomfort."

"Well, leave it alone."

"There's a ford a few miles upstream," Belgarath said in answer to the question. "The river's down at this time of year, so we won't have any difficulty crossing." He started out again, leading them down the gradual slope toward the Aldur. They forded late that afternoon and pitched their tents on the far side. The next morning they moved out to the foot of the escarpment.

"The trail's just a few miles south," Silk told them, leading the way along the looming black cliff.

"Do we have to go up along the face of it?" Garion asked apprehensively, craning his neck to look up the towering wall.

Silk shook his head. "The trail's a streambed. It cuts down through the cliff. It's a little steep and narrow, but it will get us safely to the top."

Garion found that encouraging.

The trail appeared to be little more than a crack in the stupendous cliff, and a trickle of water ran out of the opening to disappear into the jumble of rocky debris along the base of the escarpment. "Are you sure it goes all the way to the top?" Barak asked, eyeing the narrow chimney suspiciously.

"Trust me," Silk assured him.

"Not if I can help it."

The trail was awful, steep and strewn with rock. At times it was so narrow that the packhorses had to be unloaded before they could make it through and they had to be literally man-handled up over basalt boulders that had fractured into squares, almost like huge steps. The trickle of water running down the cut made everything slick and muddy. To make matters even worse, thin, high clouds swept in from the west and a bitterly cold draft spilled down the narrow cut from the arid plains of Mishrak ac Thull, lying high above.

It took them two days, and by the time they reached the top, a mile or so back from the brink of the escarpment, they were all exhausted.

"I feel as if somebody's been beating me with a stick,"

Barak groaned, sinking to the ground in the brushy gully at the top of the cut. "A very big, dirty stick."

They all sat on the ground among the prickly thornbushes in the gully, recovering from the dreadful climb. "I'll have a look around," Silk said after only a few moments. The small man had the body of an acrobat—supple, strong, and quick to restore itself. He crept up to the rim of the gully, ducking low under the thornbushes and worming his way the last few feet on his stomach to peer carefully over the top. After several minutes, he gave a low whistle, and they saw him motion sharply for them to join him.

Barak groaned again and stood up. Durnik, Mandorallen, and Garion also got stiffly to their feet.

"See what he wants," Belgarath told them. "I'm not ready to start moving around just yet."

The four of them started up the slope through the loose gravel toward the spot where Silk lay peering out from under a thornbush, crawling the last few feet as he had done.

"What's the trouble?" Barak asked the little man as they came up beside him.

"Company," Silk replied shortly, pointing out over the rocky, arid plain lying brown and dead under the flat gray sky.

A cloud of yellow dust, whipped low to the ground by the stiff, chill wind, gave evidence of riders.

"A patrol?" Durnik asked in a hushed voice.

"I don't think so," Silk answered. "Thulls aren't comfortable on horses. They usually patrol on foot."

Garion peered out across the arid waste. "Is that somebody out in front of them?" he asked, pointing at a tiny, moving speck a half mile or so in front of the riders.

"Ah," Silk said with a peculiar kind of sadness.

"What is it?" Barak asked. "Don't keep secrets, Silk. I'm not in the mood for it."

"They're Grolims," Silk explained. "The one they're chasing is a Thull trying to escape being sacrificed. It happens rather frequently."

"Should Belgarath be warned?" Mandorallen suggested.

"It's probably not necessary," Silk replied. "The Grolims

around here are mostly low-ranking. I doubt that any of them would have any skill at sorcery."

"I'll go tell him anyway," Durnik said. He slid back away from the edge of the gully, rose, and went back down to where the old man rested with Aunt Pol and Relg.

"As long as we stay out of sight, we'll probably be all right," Silk told them. "It looks as if there are only three of them, and they're concentrating on the Thull."

The running man had moved closer. He ran with his head down and his arms pumping at his sides.

"What happens if he tries to hide here in the gully?" Barak asked.

Silk shrugged. "The Grolims will follow him."

"We'd have to take steps at that point, wouldn't we?"

Silk nodded with a wicked little smirk.

"We could call him, I suppose," Barak suggested, loosening his sword in its sheath.

"The same thought had just occurred to me."

Durnik came back up the slope, his feet crunching in the gravel. "Wolf says to keep an eye on them," he reported, "but he says not to do anything unless they actually start into the gully."

"What a shame!" Silk sighed regretfully.

The running Thull was clearly visible now. He was a thick-bodied man in a rough tunic, belted at the waist. His hair was shaggy and mud-colored, and his face was contorted into an expression of brutish panic. He passed the place where they hid, perhaps thirty paces out on the flats, and Garion could clearly hear his breath whistling in his throat as he pounded past. He was whimpering as he ran—an animal-like sound of absolute despair.

"They almost never try to hide," Silk said in a soft voice tinged with pity. "All they do is run." He shook his head.

"They'll overtake him soon," Mandorallen observed. The pursuing Grolims wore black, hooded robes and polished steel masks.

"We'd better get down," Barak advised.

They all ducked below the gully rim. A few moments later,

the three horses galloped by, their hooves thudding on the hard earth.

"They'll catch him in a few more minutes," Garion said. "He's running right for the edge. He'll be trapped."

"I don't think so," Silk replied somberly.

A moment later they heard a long, despairing shriek, fading horribly into the gulf below.

"I more or less expected that," Silk said.

Garion's stomach wrenched at the thought of the dreadful height of the escarpment.

"They're coming back," Barak warned. "Get down."

The three Grolims rode back along the edge of the gully. One of them said something Garion could not quite hear, and the other two laughed.

"The world might be a brighter place with three less Grolims in it," Mandorallen suggested in a grim whisper.

"Attractive thought," Silk agreed, "but Belgarath would probably disapprove. I suppose it's better to let them go. We wouldn't want anybody looking for them."

Barak looked longingly after the three Grolims, then sighed with deep regret.

"Let's go back down," Silk said.

They all turned and crawled back down into the brushy gully.

Belgarath looked up as they returned. "Are they gone?"

"They're riding off," Silk told him.

"What was that cry?" Relg asked.

"Three Grolims chased a Thull off the edge of the escarpment," Silk replied.

"Why?"

"He'd been selected for a certain religious observance, and he didn't want to participate."

"He refused?" Relg sounded shocked. "He deserved his fate then."

"I don't think you appreciate the nature of Grolim ceremonies, Relg," Silk said.

"One must submit to the will of one's God," Relg insisted.

There was a sanctimonious note to his voice. "Religious obligations are absolute."

Silk's eyes glittered as he looked at the Ulgo fanatic. "How much do you know about the Angarak religion, Relg?" he asked.

"I concern myself only with the religion of Ulgo."

"A man ought to know what he's talking about before he makes judgments."

"Let it lie, Silk," Aunt Pol told him.

"I don't think so, Polgara. Not this time. A few facts might be good for our devout friend here. He seems to lack perspective." Silk turned back to Relg. "The core of the Angarak religion is a ritual most men find repugnant. Thulls devote their entire lives to avoiding it. That's the central reality of Thullish life."

"An abominable people." Relg's denunciation was harsh.

"No. Thulls are stupid—even brutish—but they're hardly abominable. You see, Relg, the ritual we're talking about involves human sacrifice."

Relg pulled the veil from his eyes to stare incredulously at the rat-faced little man.

"Each year two thousand Thulls are sacrificed to Torak," Silk went on, his eyes boring into Relg's stunned face. "The Grolims permit the substitution of slaves, so a Thull spends his whole life working in order to get enough money to buy a slave to take his place on the altar if he's unlucky enough to be chosen. But slaves die sometimes—or they escape. If a Thull without a slave is chosen, he usually tries to run. Then the Grolims chase him—they've had a lot of practice, so they're very good at it. I've never heard of a Thull actually getting away."

"It's their duty to submit," Relg maintained stubbornly, though he seemed a bit less sure of himself.

"How are they sacrificed?" Durnik asked in a subdued voice. The Thull's willingness to hurl himself off the escarpment had obviously shaken him.

"It's a simple procedure," Silk replied, watching Relg closely. "Two Grolims bend the Thull backward over the altar, and a third cuts his heart out. Then they burn the heart in a little fire. Torak isn't interested in the whole Thull. He only wants the heart."

Relg flinched at that.

"They sacrifice women, too," Silk pressed. "But women have a simpler means of escape. The Grolims won't sacrifice a pregnant woman—it confuses their count—so Thullish women try to stay pregnant constantly. That explains why there are so many Thulls and why Thullish women are notorious for their indiscriminate appetite."

"Monstrous." Relg gasped. "Death would be better than such vile corruption."

"Death lasts for a long time, Relg," Silk said with a cold little smile. "A little corruption can be forgotten rather quickly if you put your mind to it. That's particularly true if your life depends on it."

Relg's face was troubled as he struggled with the blunt description of the horror of Thullish life. "You're a wicked man," he accused Silk, though his voice lacked conviction.

"I know," Silk admitted.

Relg appealed to Belgarath. "Is what he says true?"

The sorcerer scratched thoughtfully at his beard. "He doesn't seem to have left out very much," he replied. "The word religion means different things to different people, Relg. It depends on the nature of one's God. You ought to try to get that sorted out in your mind. It might make some of the things you'll have to do a bit easier."

"I think we've just about exhausted the possibilities of this conversation, father," Aunt Pol suggested, "and we have a long way to go."

"Right," he agreed, getting to his feet.

They rode down through the arid jumble of rock and scrubby bushes that spread across the western frontier of the land of the Thulls. The continual wind that swept up across the escarpment was bitterly cold, though there were only a few patches of thin snow lying beneath the somber gray sky.

Relg's eyes adjusted to the subdued light, and the clouds appeared to quiet the panic the open sky had caused him. But this was obviously a difficult time for him. The world here aboveground was alien, and everything he encountered seemed to shatter his preconceptions. It was also a time of personal religious turmoil, and the crisis goaded him into peculiar fluctuations of speech and action. At one moment he would sanctimoniously denounce the sinful wickedness of others, his face set in a stern expression of righteousness; and in the next, he would be writhing in an agony of self-loathing, confessing his sin and guilt in an endless, repetitious litany to any who would listen. His pale face and huge, dark eyes, framed by the hood of his leaf-mail shirt, contorted in the tumult of his emotions. Once again the others—even patient, good-hearted Durnik— drew away from him, leaving him entirely to Garion. Relg stopped often for prayers and obscure little rituals that always seemed to involve a great deal of groveling in the dirt.

"It's going to take us all year to get to Rak Cthol at this rate," Barak rumbled sourly on one such occasion, glaring with open dislike at the ranting fanatic kneeling in the sand beside the trail.

"We need him," Belgarath replied calmly, "and he needs this. We can live with it if we have to."

"We're getting close to the northern edge of Cthol Murgos," Silk said, pointing ahead at a low range of hills. "We won't be able to stop like this once we cross the border. We'll have to ride as hard as we can until we get to the South Caravan Route. The Murgos patrol extensively, and they disapprove of side trips. Once we get to the track, we'll be all right, but we don't want to be stopped before we get there."

"Will we not be questioned even on the caravan route, Prince Kheldar?" Mandorallen asked. "Our company is oddly assorted, and Murgos are suspicious."

"They'll watch us," Silk admitted, "but they won't interfere as long as we don't stray from the track. The treaty between Taur Urgas and Ran Borune guarantees freedom of travel along the caravan route, and no Murgo alive would be foolish enough to embarrass his king by violating it. Taur Urgas is very severe with people who embarrass him."

They crossed into Cthol Murgos shortly after noon on a

cold, murky day and immediately pushed into a gallop. After about a league or so, Relg began to pull in his horse.

"Not now, Relg," Belgarath told him sharply. "Later."

"But—"

"UL's a patient God. He'll wait. Keep going."

They galloped on across the high, barren plain toward the caravan route, their cloaks streaming behind them in the biting wind. It was midafternoon when they reached the track and reined in. The South Caravan Route was not precisely a road, but centuries of travel had clearly marked its course. Silk looked around with satisfaction. "Made it," he said. "Now we become honest merchants again, and no Murgo in the world is going to interfere with us." He turned his horse eastward then and led the way with a great show of confidence. He squared his shoulders, seeming to puff himself up with a kind of busy self-importance, and Garion knew that he was making mental preparations involved in assuming a new role. When they encountered the well-guarded packtrain of a Tolnedran merchant moving west, Silk had made his transition and he greeted the merchant with the easy camaraderie of a man of trade.

"Good day, Grand High Merchant," he said to the Tolnedran, noting the other's marks of rank. "If you can spare a moment, I thought we might exchange information about the trail. You've come from the east, and I've just come over the route to the west of here. An exchange might prove mutually beneficial."

"Excellent idea," the Tolnedran agreed. The Grand High Merchant was a stocky man with a high forehead and wore a fur-lined cloak pulled tightly about him to ward off the icy wind.

"My name is Ambar," Silk said. "From Kotu."

The Tolnedran nodded in polite acknowledgment. "Kalvor," he introduced himself, "of Tol Horb. You've picked a hard season for the journey east, Ambar."

"Necessity," Silk said. "My funds are limited, and the cost of winter lodgings in Tol Honeth would have devoured what little I have."

"The Honeths are rapacious," Kalvor concurred. "Is Ran Borune still alive?"

"He was when I left."

Kalvor made a face. "And the squabble over the succession goes on?"

Silk laughed. "Oh, yes."

"Is that swine Kador from Tol Vordue still dominant?"

"Kador fell upon hard times, I understand. I heard that he made an attempt on the life of Princess Ce'Nedra. I imagine that the Emperor's going to take steps to remove him from the race."

"What splendid news," Kalvor said, his face brightening.

"How's the trail to the east?" Silk asked.

"There's not much snow," Kalvor told him. "Of course there never is in Cthol Murgos. It's a very dry kingdom. It's cold, though. It's bitter in the passes. What about the mountains in eastern Tolnedra?"

"It was snowing when we came through."

"I was afraid of that," Kalvor said with a gloomy look.

"You probably should have waited until spring, Kalvor. The worst part of the trip's still ahead of you."

"I had to get out of Rak Goska." Kalvor looked around almost as if expecting to see someone listening. "You're headed toward trouble, Ambar," he said seriously.

"Oh?"

"This is not the time to go to Rak Goska. The Murgos have gone insane there."

"Insane?" Silk said with alarm.

"There's no other explanation. They're arresting honest merchants on the flimsiest charges you ever heard of, and everyone from the West is followed constantly. It's certainly not the time to take a lady to that place."

"My sister," Silk replied, glancing at Aunt Pol. "She's invested in my venture, but she doesn't trust me. She insisted on coming along to make sure I don't cheat her."

"I'd stay out of Rak Goska," Kalvor advised.

"I'm committed now," Silk said helplessly. "I don't have any other choice, do I?"

"I'll tell you quite honestly, Ambar, it's as much as a man's life is worth to go to Rak Goska just now. A good merchant I know was actually accused of violating the women's quarters in a Murgo household."

"Well, I suppose that happens sometimes. Murgo women are reputed to be very handsome."

"Ambar," Kalvor said with a pained expression, "the man was seventy-three years old."

"His sons can be proud of his vitality then." Silk laughed. "What happened to him?"

"He was condemned and impaled," Kalvor said with a shudder. "The soldiers rounded us all up and made us watch. It was ghastly."

Silk frowned. "There's no chance that the charges were true?"

"Seventy-three years old, Ambar," Kalvor repeated. "The charges were obviously false. If I didn't know better, I'd guess that Taur Urgas is trying to drive all western merchants out of Cthol Murgos. Rak Goska simply isn't safe for us any more."

Silk grimaced. "Who can ever say what Taur Urgas is thinking?"

"He profits from every transaction in Rak Goska. He'd have to be insane to drive us out deliberately."

"I've met Taur Urgas," Silk said grimly. "Sanity's not one of his major failings." He looked around with a kind of desperation on his face. "Kalvor, I've invested everything I own and everything I can borrow in this venture. If I turn back now, I'll be ruined."

"You could turn north after you get through the mountains," Kalvor suggested. "Cross the river into Mishrak ac Thull and go to Thull Mardu."

Silk made a face. "I hate dealing with Thulls."

"There's another possibility," the Tolnedran said. "You know where the halfway point between Tol Honeth and Rak Goska is?"

Silk nodded.

"There's always been a Murgo resupply station there—food, spare horses, other necessities. Anyway, since the troubles in Rak Goska, a few enterprising Murgos have come out there and are buying whole caravan loads—horses and all. Their prices aren't as attractive as the prices in Rak Goska, but it's a chance for *some* profit, and you don't have to put yourself in danger to make it."

"But that way you have no goods for the return journey," Silk objected. "Half the profit's lost if you come back with nothing to sell in Tol Honeth."

"You'd have your life, Ambar," Kalvor said pointedly. He looked around again nervously, as if expecting to be arrested. "I'm not coming back to Cthol Murgos," he declared in a firm voice. "I'm as willing as any man to take risks for a good profit, but all the gold in the world isn't worth another trip to Rak Goska."

"How far is it to the halfway point?" Silk asked, seemingly troubled.

"I've ridden for three days since I left there," Kalvor replied. "Good luck, Ambar—whatever you decide." He gathered up his reins. "I want to put a few more leagues behind me before I stop for the night. There may be snow in the Tolnedran mountains, but at least I'll be out of Cthol Murgos and out from under the fist of Taur Urgas." He nodded briefly and moved off to the west at a fast trot, with his guards and his packtrain following after him.

Chapter Twenty-one

THE SOUTH CARAVAN ROUTE wound through a series of high, arid valleys that ran in a generally east-west direction. The surrounding peaks were high—higher probably than the mountains to the west, but their upper slopes were only faintly touched with snow. The clouds overhead turned the sky a dirty slate-gray, but what moisture they held did not fall on this desiccated wilderness of sand, rock, and scrubby thorn. Though it did not snow, it was nonetheless bitterly cold. The wind blew continually, and its edge was like a knife.

They rode east, making good time.

"Belgarath," Barak said back over his shoulder, "there's a Murgo on that ridgeline ahead—just to the south of the track."

"I see him."

"What's he doing?"

"Watching us. He won't do anything as long as we stay on the caravan route."

"They always watch like that," Silk stated. "The Murgos like to keep a close watch on everybody in their kingdom."

"That Tolnedran—Kalvor," Barak said. "Do you think he was exaggerating?"

"No," Belgarath replied. "I'd guess that Taur Urgas is looking for an excuse to close the caravan route and expel all the westerners from Cthol Murgos."

"Why?" Durnik asked.

Belgarath shrugged. "The war is coming. Taur Urgas knows that a good number of the merchants who take this route to

227

Rak Goska are spies. He'll be bringing armies up from the south soon, and he'd like to keep their numbers and movements a secret."

"What manner of army could be gathered from so bleak and uninhabited a realm?" Mandorallen asked.

Belgarath looked around at the high, bleak desert. "This is only the little piece of Cthol Murgos we're permitted to see. It stretches a thousand leagues or more to the south, and there are cities down there that no westerner has ever seen—we don't even know their names. Here in the north, the Murgos play a very elaborate game to conceal the real Cthol Murgos."

"Is it thy thought then that the war will come soon?"

"Next summer perhaps," Belgarath replied. "Possibly the summer following."

"Are we going to be ready?" Barak asked.

"We're going to try to be."

Aunt Pol made a brief sound of disgust.

"What's wrong?" Garion asked her quickly.

"Vultures," she said. "Filthy brutes."

A dozen heavy-bodied birds were flapping and squawking over something on the ground to one side of the caravan track.

"What are they feeding on?" Durnik asked. "I haven't seen any animals of any kind since we left the top of the escarpment."

"A horse, probably—or a man," Silk said. "There's nothing else up here."

"Would a man be left unburied?" the smith asked.

"Only partially," Silk told him. "Sometimes certain brigands decide that the pickings along the caravan route might be easy. The Murgos give them plenty of time to realize how wrong they were."

Durnik looked at him questioningly.

"The Murgos catch them," Silk explained, "and then they bury them up to the neck and leave them. The vultures have learned that a man in that situation is helpless. Often they get impatient and don't bother to wait for the man to finish dying before they start to eat."

"That's one way to deal with bandits," Barak said, almost

approvingly. "Even a Murgo can have a good idea once in a while."

"Unfortunately, Murgos automatically assume that anybody who isn't on the track itself is a bandit."

The vultures brazenly continued to feed, refusing to leave their dreadful feast as the party passed no more than twenty yards from their flapping congregation. Their wings and bodies concealed whatever it was they were feeding on, a fact for which Garion was profoundly grateful. Whatever it was, however, was not very large.

"We should stay quite close to the track when we stop for the night, then," Durnik said, averting his eyes with a shudder.

"That's a very good idea, Durnik," Silk agreed.

The information the Tolnedran merchant had given them about the makeshift fair at the halfway point proved to be accurate. On the afternoon of the third day, they came over a rise and saw a cluster of tents surrounding a solid stone building set to one side of the caravan track. The tents looked small in the distance and they billowed and flapped in the endless wind that swept down the valley.

"What do you think?" Silk asked Belgarath.

"It's late," the old man replied. "We're going to have to stop for the night soon anyway, and it would look peculiar if we didn't stop."

Silk nodded.

"We're going to have to try to keep Relg out of sight, though," Belgarath continued. "Nobody's going to believe we're ordinary merchants if they see an Ulgo with us."

Silk thought a moment. "We'll wrap him in a blanket," he suggested, "and tell anybody who asks that he's sick. People stay away from sick men."

Belgarath nodded. "Can you act sick?" he asked Relg.

"I *am* sick," the Ulgo said without any attempt at humor. "Is it always this cold up here?" He sneezed.

Aunt Pol pulled her horse over beside his and reached out to put her hand on his forehead.

"Don't touch me." Relg cringed away from her hand.

"Stop that," she told him. She briefly touched his face and

looked at him closely. "He's coming down with a cold, father," she announced. "As soon as we get settled, I'll give him something for it. Why didn't you tell me?" she asked the fanatic.

"I will endure what UL chooses to send me," Relg declared. "It's his punishment for my sins."

"No," she told him flatly. "It has nothing to do with sin or punishment. It's a cold—nothing more."

"Am I going to die?" Relg asked calmly.

"Of course not. Haven't you ever had a cold before?"

"No. I've never been sick in my life."

"You won't be able to say that again," Silk said lightly, pulling a blanket out of one of the packs and handing it to him. "Wrap this around your shoulders and pull it up over your head. Try to look like you're suffering."

"I am," Relg said, starting to cough.

"But you have to *look* like it," Silk told him. "Think about sin—that ought to make you look miserable."

"I think about sin all the time," Relg replied, still coughing.

"I know," Silk said, "but try to think about it a little harder."

They rode down the hill toward the collection of tents with the dry, icy wind whipping at them as they rode. Very few of the assembled merchants were outside their tents, and those who were moved quickly about their tasks in the biting chill.

"We should stop by the resupply station first, I suppose," Silk suggested, gesturing toward the square stone building squatting among the tents. "That would look more natural. Let me handle things."

"Silk, you mangy Drasnian thief!" a coarse voice roared from a nearby tent.

Silk's eyes widened slightly, and then he grinned. "I seem to recognize the squeals of a certain Nadrak hog," he said, loud enough to be heard by the man in the tent.

A rangy Nadrak in a belted, ankle-length, black felt overcoat and a snug-fitting fur cap strode out of the tent. He had coarse, black hair and a thin, scraggly beard. His eyes had the peculiar angularity to them that was a characteristic of all Angaraks; but unlike the dead eyes of the Murgos, this Nadrak's eyes were alive with a kind of wary friendship. "Haven't they caught you yet, Silk?" he demanded raucously. "I was sure that by now someone would have peeled off your hide."

"Drunk as usual, I see." Silk grinned viciously. "How many days has it been this time, Yarblek?"

"Who counts?" The Nadrak laughed, swaying slightly on his feet. "What are you doing in Cthol Murgos, Silk? I thought your fat king needed you in Gar og Nadrak."

"I was getting to be a little too well-known on the streets of Yar Nadrak," Silk replied. "It was getting to the point that people were avoiding me."

"Now I wonder just why that could be," Yarblek retorted with heavy sarcasm. "You cheat at trade, you switch dice, you make free with other men's wives, and you're a spy. That shouldn't be any reason for men not to admire your good points—whatever they are."

"Your sense of humor's as overpowering as ever, Yarblek."

"It's my only failing," the slightly tipsy Nadrak admitted. "Get down off that horse, Silk. Come inside my tent and we'll get drunk together. Bring your friends." He lurched back inside the tent.

"An old acquaintance," Silk explained quickly, sliding out of his saddle.

"Can he be trusted?" Barak asked suspiciously.

"Not entirely, but he's all right. He's not a bad fellow, really—for a Nadrak. He'll know everything that's going on, and if he's drunk enough, we might be able to get some useful information out of him."

"Get in here, Silk," Yarblek roared from inside his gray felt tent.

"Let's see what he has to say," Belgarath said.

They all dismounted, tied their horses to a picket line at the side of the Nadrak's tent, and trooped inside. The tent was large, and the floor and walls were covered with thick crimson carpets. An oil lamp hung from the ridgepole, and an iron brazier snimmered out waves of heat.

Yarblek was sitting cross-legged on the carpeting at the back of the tent, with a large black keg conveniently beside him.

"Come in. Come in," he said brusquely. "Close the flap. You're letting out all the heat."

"This is Yarblek," Silk said by way of introduction, "an adequate merchant and a notorious drunkard. We've known each other for a long time now."

"My tent is yours." Yarblek hiccuped indifferently. "It's not much of a tent, but it's yours anyway. There are cups over there in that pile of things by my saddle—some of them are even clean. Let's all have a drink."

"This is Mistress Pol, Yarblek," Silk introduced her.

"Good-looking woman," Yarblek observed, looking at her boldly. "Forgive me for not getting up, Mistress, but I feel a bit giddy at the moment—probably something I ate."

"Of course," she agreed with a dry little smile. "A man should always be careful about what he puts in his stomach."

"I've made that exact point myself a thousand times." He squinted at her as she pulled back her hood and unfastened her cape. "That's a remarkably handsome woman, Silk," he declared. "I don't suppose you'd care to sell her."

"You couldn't afford me, Yarblek," she told him without seeming to take the slightest offense.

Yarblek stared at her and then roared with laughter. "By One-Eye's nose, I'd bet that I couldn't, at that—and you've probably got a dagger somewhere under your clothes, too. You'd slice open my belly if I tried to steal you, wouldn't you?"

"Naturally."

"What a woman!" Yarblek chortled. "Can you dance, too?"

"Like you've never seen before, Yarblek," she replied. "I could turn your bones to water."

Yarblek's eyes burned. "After we all get drunk, maybe you'll dance for us."

"We'll see," she said with a hint of promise. Garion was stunned at this uncharacteristic boldness. It was obviously the way Yarblek expected a woman to behave, but Garion wondered just when Aunt Pol had learned the customs of the Nadraks so well that she could respond without the slightest hint of embarrassment.

"This is Mister Wolf," Silk said, indicating Belgarath.

"Never mind names." Yarblek waved his hand. "I'd just forget them anyway." He did, however, look rather shrewdly at each of them. "As a matter of fact," he continued, sounding suddenly not nearly as drunk as he appeared, "it might be just as well if I didn't know your names. What a man doesn't know, he can't reveal, and you're too well-mixed a group to be in stinking Cthol Murgos on honest business. Fetch yourselves cups. This keg is almost full, and I've got another chilling out back of the tent."

At Silk's gesture, they each took a cup from the heap of cookware piled beside a well-worn saddle and joined Yarblek on the carpet near the keg.

"I'd pour for you like a proper host," Yarblek told them, "but I spill too much that way. Dip out your own."

Yarblek's ale was a very dark brown and had a rich, almost fruity flavor.

"Interesting taste," Barak said politely.

"My brewer chops dried apples into his vats," the Nadrak replied. "It smooths out some of the bite." He turned to Silk. "I thought you didn't like Murgos."

"I don't."

"What are you doing in Cthol Murgos, then?"

Silk shrugged. "Business."

"Whose? Yours or Rhodar's?"

Silk winked at him.

"I thought as much. I wish you luck, then. I'd even offer to help, but I'd probably better keep my nose out of it. Murgos distrust us even more than they distrust you Alorns—not that I can really blame them. Any Nadrak worth the name would go ten leagues out of his way for the chance to cut a Murgo's throat."

"Your affection for your cousins touches my heart." Silk grinned.

Yarblek scowled. "Cousins!" he spat. "If it weren't for the Grolims, we'd have exterminated the whole cold-blooded race generations ago." He dipped out another cup of ale, lifted it and said, "Confusion to the Murgos."

"I think we've found something we can drink to together," Barak said with a broad smile. "Confusion to the Murgos."

"And may Taur Urgas grow boils on his behind," Yarblek added. He drank deeply, scooped another cupful of ale from the open keg and drank again. "I'm a little drunk," he admitted.

"We'd never have guessed," Aunt Pol told him.

"I like you, girl." Yarblek grinned at her. "I wish I could afford to buy you. I don't suppose you'd consider running away?"

She sighed a mocking little sigh. "No," she refused. "I'm afraid not. That gives a woman a bad reputation, you know."

"Very true," Yarblek agreed owlishly. He shook his head sadly. "As I was saying," he went on, "I'm a little drunk. I probably shouldn't say anything about this, but it's not a good time for westerners to be in Cthol Murgos—Alorns particularly. I've been hearing some strange things lately. Word's been filtering out of Rak Cthol that Murgoland is to be purged of outsiders. Taur Urgas wears the crown and plays king in Rak Goska, but the old Grolim at Rak Cthol has his hand around Taur Urgas' heart. The king of the Murgos knows that one squeeze from Ctuchik will leave his throne empty."

"We met a Tolnedran a few leagues west of here who said the same sort of thing," Silk said seriously. "He told us that merchants from the West were being arrested all over Rak Goska on false charges."

Yarblek nodded. "That's only the first step. Murgos are always predictable—they have so little imagination. Taur Urgas isn't quite ready to offend Ran Borune openly by butchering every western merchant in the kingdom, but it's getting closer. Rak Goska's probably a closed city by now. Taur Urgas is free to turn his attention to the outlands. I'd imagine that's why he's coming here."

"He's *what*?" Silk's face paled visibly.

"I thought you knew," Yarblek told him. "Taur Urgas is marching toward the frontier with his army behind him. My guess is that he plans to close the border."

"How far away is he?" Silk demanded.

"I was told that he was seen this morning not five leagues from here," Yarblek said. "What's wrong?"

"Taur Urgas and I have had some serious fallings out," Silk answered quickly, his face filled with consternation. "I can't be here when he arrives." He jumped to his feet.

"Where are you going?" Belgarath asked quickly.

"Some place safe. I'll catch up with you later." He turned then and bolted out of the tent. A moment later they heard the pounding of his horse's hooves.

"Do you want me to go with him?" Barak asked Belgarath.

"You'd never catch him."

"I wonder what he did to Taur Urgas," Yarblek mused. He chuckled then. "It must have been something pretty awful, the way the little thief ran out of here."

"Is it safe for him to go away from the caravan track?" Garion asked, remembering the vultures at their grisly feast beside the trail.

"Don't worry about Silk," Yarblek replied confidently.

From a great distance away, a slow thudding sound began to intrude itself. Yarblek's eyes narrowed with hate. "It looks like Silk left just in time," he growled.

The thudding became louder and turned into a hollow, booming sound. Dimly, behind the booming, they could hear a kind of groaning chant of hundreds of voices in a deep, minor key.

"What's that?" Durnik asked.

"Taur Urgas," Yarblek answered and spat. "That's the war song of the king of the Murgos."

"War?" Mandorallen demanded sharply.

"Taur Urgas is always at war," Yarblek replied with heavy contempt. "Even when there isn't anybody to be at war with. He sleeps in his armor, even in his own palace. It makes him smelly, but all Murgos stink anyway, so it doesn't really make any difference. Maybe I'd better go see what he's up to." He got heavily to his feet. "Wait here," he told them. "This is a Nadrak tent, and there are certain courtesies expected between Angaraks. His soldiers won't come in here, so you'll be safe as long as you stay inside." He lurched toward the door of the tent, an expression of icy hatred on his face.

The chanting and the measured drumbeats grew louder. Shrill fifes picked up a discordant, almost jigging accompaniment, and then there was a sudden blaring of deep-throated horns.

"What do you think, Belgarath?" Barak rumbled. "This Yarblek seems like a good enough fellow, but he's still an Angarak. One word from him, and we'll have a hundred Murgos in here with us."

"He's right, father," Aunt Pol agreed. "I know Nadraks well enough to know that Yarblek wasn't nearly as drunk as he pretended to be."

Belgarath pursed his lips. "Maybe it isn't too good an idea to gamble all that much on the fact that Nadraks despise Murgos," he conceded. "We might be doing Yarblek an injustice, but perhaps it would be better just to slip away before Taur Urgas has time to put guards around the whole place anyway. There's no way of knowing how long he's going to stay here; and once he settles in, we might have trouble leaving." ·

Durnik pulled aside the red carpeting that hung along the back wall, reached down, and tugged out several tent pegs. He lifted the canvas. "I think we can crawl out here."

"Let's go, then," Belgarath decided.

One by one, they rolled out of the tent into the chill wind.

"Get the horses," Belgarath said quietly. He looked around, his eyes narrowing. "That gully over there." He pointed at a wash opening out just beyond the last row of tents. "If we keep the tents between us and the main caravan track, we should be able to get into it without being seen. Most likely everybody here's going to be watching the arrival of Taur Urgas."

"Would the Murgo king know thee, Belgarath?" Mandorallen asked.

"He might. We've never met, but my description's been noised about in Cthol Murgos for a long time now. It's best not to take any chances."

They led their horses along the back of the tents and gained the cover of the gully without incident.

"This wash comes down off the back side of that hill there."
Barak pointed. "If we follow it, we'll be out of sight all the
way, and once we get the hill between us and the camp, we'll
be able to ride away without being seen."

"It's almost evening." Belgarath looked up at the lowering
sky. "Let's go up a ways and then wait until after dark."

They moved on up the gully until they were behind the
shoulder of the hill.

"Better keep an eye on things," Belgarath said.

Barak and Garion scrambled up out of the gully and moved
at a crouch to the top of the hill, where they lay down behind
a scrubby bush. "Here they come," Barak muttered.

A steady stream of grim-faced Murgo soldiers marched eight
abreast into the makeshift fair to the cadenced beat of great
drums. In their midst, astride a black horse and under a flapping
black banner, rode Taur Urgas. He was a tall man with heavy,
sloping shoulders and an angular, merciless face. The thick
links of his mail shirt had been dipped in molten red gold,
making it almost appear as if he were covered with blood. A
thick metal belt encircled his waist, and the scabbard of the
sword he wore on his left hip was jewel-encrusted. A pointed
steel helmet sat low over his black eyebrows, and the blood-
red crown of Cthol Murgos was riveted to it. A kind of chainmail hood covered the back and sides of the king's neck and
spread out over his shoulders.

When he reached the open area directly in front of the square
stone supply post, Taur Urgas reined in his horse. "Wine!" he
commanded. His voice, carried by the icy wind, seemed star-
tlingly close. Garion squirmed a bit lower under the bush.

The Murgo who ran the supply post scurried inside and
came back out, carrying a flagon and a metal goblet. Taur
Urgas took the goblet, drank, and then slowly closed his big
fist around it, crushing it in his grip. Barak snorted with contempt.

"What was that about?" Garion whispered.

"Nobody drinks from a cup once Taur Urgas has used it,"
the red-bearded Cherek replied. "If Anheg behaved like that,
his warriors would dunk him in the bay at Val Alorn."

"Have you the names of all foreigners here?" the king demanded of the Murgo storekeeper, his wind-carried voice distinct in Garion's ears.

"As you commanded, dread king," the storekeeper replied with an obsequious bow. He drew a roll of parchment out of one sleeve and handed it up to his ruler.

Taur Urgas unrolled the parchment and glanced at it. "Summon the Nadrak, Yarblek," he ordered.

"Let Yarblek of Gar og Nadrak approach," an officer at the king's side bellowed.

Yarblek, his felt overcoat flapping stiffly in the wind, stepped forward.

"Our cousin from the north," Taur Urgas greeted him coldly.

"Your Majesty," Yarblek replied with a slight bow.

"It would be well if you departed, Yarblek," the king told him. "My soldiers have certain orders, and some of them might fail to recognize a fellow Angarak in their eagerness to obey my commands. I cannot guarantee your safety if you remain, and I would be melancholy if something unpleasant befell you."

Yarblek bowed again. "My servants and I will leave at once, your Majesty."

"If they are Nadraks, they have our permission to go," the king said. "All foreigners, however, must remain. You're dismissed, Yarblek."

"I think we got out of that tent just in time," Barak muttered.

Then a man in a rusty mail shirt covered with a greasy brown vest stepped out of the supply post. He was unshaven, and the white of one of his eyes gleamed unwholesomely.

"Brill!" Garion exclaimed.

Barak's eyes went flat.

Brill bowed to Taur Urgas with an unexpected grace. "Hail, Mighty King," he said. His tone was neutral, carrying neither respect nor fear.

"What are you doing here, Kordoch?" Taur Urgas demanded coldly.

"I'm on my master's business, dread king," Brill replied.

"What business would Ctuchik have in a place like this?"

"Something personal, Great King," Brill answered evasively.

"I like to keep track of you and the other Dagashi, Kordoch. When did you come back to Cthol Murgos?"

"A few months ago, Mighty Arm of Torak. If I'd known you were interested, I'd have sent word to you. The people my master wants me to deal with know I'm following them, so my movements aren't secret."

Taur Urgas laughed shortly, a sound without any warmth. "You must be getting old, Kordoch. Most Dagashi would have finished the business by now."

"These are rather special people." Brill shrugged. "It shouldn't take me much longer, however. The game is nearly over. Incidentally, Great King, I have a gift for you." He snapped his fingers sharply, and two of his henchmen came out of the building, dragging a third man between them. There was blood on the front of the captive's tunic, and his head hung down as if he were only semiconscious. Barak's breath hissed between his teeth.

"I thought you might like a bit of sport," Brill suggested.

"I'm the king of Cthol Murgos, Kordoch," Taur Urgas replied coldly. "I'm not amused by your attitude and I'm not in the habit of doing chores for the Dagashi. If you want him dead, kill him yourself."

"This would hardly be a chore, your Majesty," Brill said with an evil grin. "The man's an old friend of yours." He reached out, roughly grasped the prisoner's hair, and jerked his head up for the king to see.

It was Silk. His face was pale, and a deep cut on one side of his forehead trickled blood down the side of his face.

"Behold the Drasnian spy Kheldar." Brill smirked. "I make a gift of him to your Majesty."

Taur Urgas began to smile then, his eyes lighting with a dreadful pleasure. "Splendid," he said. "You have the gratitude of your king, Kordoch. Your gift is beyond price." His smile grew broader. "Greetings, Prince Kheldar," he said, almost purring. "I've been waiting for the chance to see you again for a long time now. We have many old scores to settle, don't we?"

Silk seemed to stare back at the Murgo king, but Garion could not be sure if he were conscious enough even to comprehend what was happening to him.

"Abide here a bit, Prince of Drasnia," Taur Urgas gloated. "I'll want to give some special thought to your final entertainment, and I'll want to be sure you're fully awake to appreciate it. You deserve something exquisite, I think—probably lingering—and I certainly wouldn't want to disappoint you by rushing into it."

Chapter Twenty-two

BARAK AND GARION slid back down into the gully with the gravel rattling down the steep bank around them.

"They've got Silk," Barak reported quietly. "Brill's there. It looks as if he and his men caught Silk while he was trying to leave. They turned him over to Taur Urgas."

Belgarath stood up slowly, a sick look on his face. "Is he—" He broke off.

"No," Barak answered. "He's still alive. It looks as if they roughed him up a little, but he seemed to be all right."

Belgarath let out a long, slow breath. "That's something, anyway."

"Taur Urgas seemed to know him," Barak continued. "It sounded as if Silk had done something that offended the king pretty seriously, and Taur Urgas looks like the kind of man who holds grudges."

"Are they holding him someplace where we can get to him?" Durnik asked.

"We couldn't tell," Garion answered. "They all talked for a while, and then several soldiers took him around behind that building down there. We couldn't see where they took him from there."

"The Murgo who runs the place said something about a pit," Barak added.

"We have to do something, father," Aunt Pol said.

"I know, Pol. We'll come up with something." He turned to Barak again. "How many soldiers did Taur Urgas bring with him?"

"A couple of regiments at least. They're all over the place down there."

"We can translocate him, father," Aunt Pol suggested.

"That's a long way to lift something, Pol," he objected. "Besides, we'd have to know exactly where he's being held."

"I'll find that out." She reached up to unfasten her cloak.

"Better wait until after dark," he told her. "There aren't many owls in Cthol Murgos, and you'd attract attention in the daylight. Did Taur Urgas have any Grolims with him?" he asked Garion.

"I think I saw a couple."

"That's going to complicate things. Translocation makes an awful noise. We'll have Taur Urgas right on our heels when we leave."

"Do you have any other ideas, father?" Aunt Pol asked.

"Let me work on it," he replied. "At any rate, we can't do anything until it gets dark."

A low whistle came from some distance down the gully.

"Who's that?" Barak's hand went to his sword.

"Ho, Alorns." It was a hoarse whisper.

"Methinks it is the Nadrak Yarblek," Mandorallen said.

"How did he know we're here?" Barak demanded.

There was the crunching sound of footsteps in the gravel, and Yarblek came around a bend in the gully. His fur cap was low over his face, and the collar of his felt overcoat was pulled up around his ears. "There you are," he said, sounding relieved.

"Are you alone?" Barak's voice was heavy with suspicion.

"Of course I'm alone," Yarblek snorted. "I told my servants to go on ahead. You certainly left in a hurry."

"We didn't feel like staying to greet Taur Urgas," Barak replied.

"It's probably just as well. I'd have had a great deal of trouble getting you out of that mess back there. The Murgo soldiers inspected every one of my people to be sure they were all Nadraks before they'd let me leave. Taur Urgas has Silk."

"We know," Barak said. "How did you find us?"

"You left the pegs pulled up at the back of my tent, and this hill's the closest cover on this side of the fair. I guessed which way you'd go, and you left a track here and there to confirm it." The Nadrak's coarse face was serious, and he showed no signs of his extended bout at the ale barrel. "We're going to have to get you out of here," he said. "Taur Urgas will be putting out patrols soon, and you're almost in his lap."

"We must rescue our companion first," Mandorallen told him.

"Silk? You'd better forget that. I'm afraid my old friend has switched his last pair of dice." He sighed. "I liked him, too."

"He's not dead, is he?" Durnik's voice was almost sick.

"Not yet," Yarblek replied, "but Taur Urgas plans to correct that when the sun comes up in the morning. I couldn't even get close enough to that pit to drop a dagger to him so he could open a vein. I'm afraid his last morning's going to be a bad one."

"Why are you trying to help us?" Barak asked bluntly.

"You'll have to excuse him, Yarblek," Aunt Pol said. "He's not familiar with Nadrak customs." She turned to Barak. "He invited you into his tent and offered you his ale. That makes you the same as his brother until sunrise tomorrow."

Yarblek smiled briefly at her. "You seem to know us quite well, girl," he observed. "I never got to see you dance, did I?"

"Perhaps another time," she replied.

"Perhaps so." He squatted and pulled a curved dagger from

beneath his overcoat. He smoothed a patch of sand with his other hand and began sketching rapidly with his dagger point. "The Murgos are going to watch me," he said, "so I can't add half a dozen or so more people to my party without having them all over me. I think the best thing would be for you to wait here until dark. I'll move out to the east and stop a league or so on up the caravan track. As soon as it gets dark, you slip around and catch up with me. We'll work something out after that."

"Why did Taur Urgas tell you to leave?" Barak asked him.

Yarblek looked grim. "There's going to be a large accident tomorrow. Taur Urgas will immediately send an apology to Ran Borune—something about inexperienced troops chasing a band of brigands and mistaking honest merchants for bandits. He'll offer to pay reparation, and things will all be smoothed over. Pay is a magic word when you're dealing with Tolnedrans."

"He's going to massacre the whole camp?" Barak sounded stunned.

"That's his plan. He wants to clean all the westerners out of Cthol Murgos and he seems to think that a few such accidents will do the job for him."

Relg had been standing to one side, his large eyes lost in thought. Suddenly he stepped across the gully to where Yarblek's sketch was. He smoothed it out of the sand. "Can you show me exactly where this pit in which they're holding our friend is located?" he asked.

"It won't do you any good," Yarblek told him. "It's guarded by a dozen men. Silk's got quite a reputation, and Taur Urgas doesn't want him to get away."

"Just show me," Relg insisted.

Yarblek shrugged. "We're here on the north side." He roughed in the fair and the caravan route. "The supply station is here." He pointed with his dagger. "The pit's just beyond it at the base of that big hill on the south side."

"What kind of walls does it have?"

"Solid stone."

"Is it a natural fissure in the rock, or has it been dug out?"

"What difference does it make?"

"I need to know."

"I didn't see any tool marks," Yarblek replied, "and the opening at the top is irregular. It's probably just a natural hole."

Relg nodded. "And the hill behind it—is it rock or dirt?"

"Mostly rock. All of stinking Cthol Murgos is mostly rock."

Relg stood up. "Thank you," he said politely.

"You're not going to be able to tunnel through to him, if that's what you're thinking," Yarblek said, also standing and brushing the sand off the skirts of his overcoat. "You don't have time."

Belgarath's eyes were narrowed with thought. "Thanks, Yarblek," he said. "You've been a good friend."

"Anything to irritate the Murgos," the Nadrak said. "I wish I could do something for Silk."

"Don't give up on him yet."

"There isn't much hope, I'm afraid. I'd better be going. My people will wander off if I'm not there to watch them."

"Yarblek," Barak said, holding out his hand, "someday we'll have to get together and finish getting drunk."

Yarblek grinned at him and shook his hand. Then he turned and caught Aunt Pol in a rough embrace. "If you ever get bored with these Alorns, girl, my tent flap is always open to you."

"I'll keep that in mind, Yarblek," she replied demurely.

"Luck," Yarblek told them. "I'll wait for you until midnight." Then he turned and strode off down the gully.

"That's a good man there," Barak said. "I think I could actually get to like him."

"We must make plans for Prince Kheldar's rescue," Mandorallen declared, beginning to take his armor out of the packs strapped to one of the horses. "All else failing, we must of necessity resort to main force."

"You're backsliding again, Mandorallen," Barak said.

"That's already been taken care of," Belgarath told them.

Barak and Mandorallen stared at him.

"Put your armor away, Mandorallen," the old man instructed the knight. "You're not going to need it."

"Who's going to get Silk out of there?" Barak demanded.

"I am," Relg answered quietly. "How much longer is it going to be before it gets dark?"

"About an hour. Why?"

"I'll need some time to prepare myself."

"Have you got a plan?" Durnik asked.

Relg shrugged. "There isn't any need. We'll just circle around until we're behind that hill on the other side of the encampment. I'll go get our friend, and then we can leave."

"Just like that?" Barak asked.

"More or less. Please excuse me." Relg started to turn away.

"Wait a minute. Shouldn't Mandorallen and I go with you?"

"You wouldn't be able to follow me," Relg told him. He walked up the gully a short distance. After a moment, they could hear him muttering his prayers.

"Does he think he can pray him out of that pit?" Barak sounded disgusted.

"No," Belgarath replied. "He's going to go through the hill and carry Silk back out. That's why he was asking Yarblek all those questions."

"He's going to *what*?"

"You saw what he did at Prolgu—when he stuck his arm into the wall?"

"Well, yes, but—"

"It's quite easy for him, Barak."

"What about Silk? How's he going to pull *him* through the rock?"

"I don't really know. He seems quite sure he can do it, though."

"If it doesn't work, Taur Urgas is going to have Silk roasting over a slow fire first thing tomorrow morning. You know that, don't you?"

Belgarath nodded somberly.

Barak shook his head. "It's unnatural," he grumbled.

"Don't let it upset you so much," Belgarath advised.

The light began to fade, and Relg continued to pray, his voice rising and falling in formal cadences. When it was fully dark, he came back to where the others waited. "I'm ready," he said quietly. "We can leave now."

"We'll circle to the west," Belgarath told them. "We'll lead the horses and stay under cover as much as we can."

"It will take us a couple hours," Durnik said.

"That's all right. It will give the soldiers time to settle down. Pol, see what the Grolims Garion saw are up to."

She nodded, and Garion felt the gentle push of her probing mind. "It's all right, father," she stated after a few moments. "They're preoccupied. Taur Urgas has them conducting services for him."

"Let's go, then," the old man said.

They moved carefully down the gully, leading the horses. The night was murky, and the wind bit at them as they came out from between the protecting gravel banks. The plain to the east of the fair was dotted with a hundred fires whipping in the wind and marking the vast encampment of the army of Taur Urgas.

Relg grunted and covered his eyes with his hands.

"What's wrong?" Garion asked him.

"Their fires," Relg said. "They stab at my eyes."

"Try not to look at them."

"My God has laid a hard burden on me, Belgarion." Relg sniffed and wiped at his nose with his sleeve. "I'm not meant to be out in the open like this."

"You'd better have Aunt Pol give you something for that cold. It will taste awful, but you'll feel better after you drink it."

"Perhaps," Relg said, still shielding his eyes from the dim flicker of the Murgo watch fires.

The hill on the south side of the fair was a low outcropping of granite. Although eons of constant wind had covered it for the most part with a thick layer of blown sand and dirt, the rock itself lay solid beneath its covering mantle. They stopped behind it, and Relg began carefully to brush the dirt from a sloping granite face.

"Wouldn't it be closer if you started over there?" Barak asked quietly.

"Too much dirt," Relg replied.

"Dirt or rock—what's the difference?"

"A great difference. You wouldn't understand." He leaned forward and put his tongue to the granite face, seeming actually to taste the rock. "This is going to take a while," he said. He drew himself up, began to pray, and slowly pushed himself directly into the rock.

Barak shuddered and quickly averted his eyes.

"What ails thee, my Lord?" Mandorallen asked.

"It makes me cold all over just watching that," Barak replied.

"Our new friend is perhaps not the best of companions," Mandorallen said, "but if his gift succeeds in freeing Prince Kheldar, I will embrace him gladly and call him brother."

"If it takes him very long, we're going to be awfully close to this spot when morning comes and Taur Urgas finds out that Silk's gone," Barak mentioned.

"We'll just have to wait and see what happens," Belgarath told him.

The night dragged by interminably. The wind moaned and whistled around the rocks on the flanks of the stony hill, and the sparse thornbushes rustled stiffly. They waited. A growing fear oppressed Garion as the hours passed. More and more, he became convinced that they had lost Relg as well as Silk. He felt that same sick emptiness he had felt when it had been necessary to leave the wounded Lelldorin behind back in Arendia. He realized, feeling a bit guilty about it, that he hadn't thought about Lelldorin in months. He began to wonder how well the young hothead had recovered from his wound—or even *if* he had recovered. His thoughts grew bleaker as the minutes crawled.

Then, with no warning—with not even a sound—Relg stepped out of the rock face he had entered hours before. Astride his broad back and clinging desperately to him was Silk. The rat-faced little man's eyes were wide with horror, and his hair seemed to be actually standing on end.

They all crowded around the two, trying to keep their jubilation quiet, conscious of the fact that they were virtually on top of an army of Murgos.

"I'm sorry it took so long," Relg said, jerking his shoulders uncomfortably until Silk finally slid off his back. "There's a different kind of rock in the middle of the hill. I had to make certain adjustments."

Silk stood, gasping and shuddering uncontrollably. Finally he turned on Relg. "Don't *ever* do that to me again," he blurted. "Not ever."

"What's the trouble?" Barak asked.

"I don't want to talk about it."

"I had feared we had lost thee, my friend," Mandorallen said, grasping Silk's hand.

"How did Brill catch you?" Barak asked.

"I was careless. I didn't expect him to be here. His men threw a net over me as I was galloping through a ravine. My horse fell and broke his neck."

"Hettar's not going to like that."

"I'll cut the price of the horse out of Brill's skin—someplace close to the bone, I think."

"Why does Taur Urgas hate you so much?" Barak asked curiously.

"I was in Rak Goska a few years ago. A Tolnedran agent made a few false charges against me—I never found out exactly why. Taur Urgas sent some soldiers out to arrest me. I didn't particularly feel like being arrested, so I argued with the soldiers a bit. Several of them died during the argument—those things happen once in a while. Unfortunately, one of the casualties was Taur Urgas' oldest son. The king of the Murgos took it personally. He's very narrow-minded sometimes."

Barak grinned. "He'll be terribly disappointed in the morning when he finds out that you've left."

"I know," Silk replied. "He'll probably take this part of Cthol Murgos apart stone by stone trying to find me."

"I think it's time we left," Belgarath agreed.

"I thought you'd never get around to that," Silk said.

Chapter Twenty-three

THEY RODE HARD through the rest of the night and for most of the following day. By evening their horses were stumbling with exhaustion, and Garion was as numb with weariness as with the biting cold.

"We'll have to find shelter of some kind," Durnik said as they reined in to look for a place to spend the night. They had moved up out of the series of connecting valleys through which the South Caravan Route wound and had entered the ragged, barren wilderness of the mountains of central Cthol Murgos. It had grown steadily colder as they had climbed into that vast jumble of rock and sand, and the endless wind moaned among the treeless crags. Durnik's face was creased with fatigue, and the gritty dust that drove before the wind had settled into the creases, etching them deeper. "We can't spend the night in the open," he declared. "Not with this wind."

"Go that way," Relg said, pointing toward a rockfall on the steep slope they were climbing. His eyes were squinted almost shut, though the sky was still overcast and the fading daylight was pale. "There's shelter there—a cave."

They had all begun to look at Relg in a somewhat different light since his rescue of Silk. His demonstration that he could, when necessary, take decisive action made him seem less an encumbrance and more like a companion. Belgarath had finally convinced him that he could pray on horseback just as well as he could on his knees, and his frequent devotions no longer interrupted their journey. His praying thus had become less an inconvenience and more a personal idiosyncrasy—somewhat like Mandorallen's archaic speech or Silk's sardonic witticisms.

"You're sure there's a cave?" Barak asked him.

Relg nodded. "I can feel it."

They turned and rode toward the rockfall. As they drew closer, Relg's eagerness became more obvious. He pushed his horse into the lead and nudged the tired beast into a trot, then a canter. At the edge of the rockslide, he swung down from his horse, stepped behind a large boulder, and disappeared.

"It looks as if he knew what he was talking about," Durnik observed. "I'll be glad to get out of this wind."

The opening to the cave was narrow, and it took some pushing and dragging to persuade the horses to squeeze through; but once they were inside, the cave widened out into a large, low-ceilinged chamber.

Durnik looked around with approval. "Good place." He unfastened his axe from the back of his saddle. "We'll need firewood."

"I'll help you," Garion said.

"I'll go, too," Silk offered quickly. The little man was looking around at the stone walls and ceiling nervously, and he seemed obviously relieved as soon as the three of them were back outside.

"What's wrong?" Durnik asked him.

"After last night, closed-in places make me a little edgy," Silk replied.

"What was it like?" Garion asked him curiously. "Going through stone, I mean?"

Silk shuddered. "It was hideous. We actually seeped into the rock. I could feel it sliding through me."

"It got you out, though," Durnik reminded him.

"I think I'd almost rather have stayed." Silk shuddered again. "Do we have to talk about it?"

Firewood was difficult to find on that barren mountainside and even more difficult to cut. The tough, springy thornbushes resisted the blows of Durnik's axe tenaciously. After an hour, as darkness began to close in on them, they had gathered only three very scanty armloads.

"Did you see anybody?" Barak asked as they reentered the cave.

"No," Silk replied.

"Taur Urgas is probably looking for you."

"I'm sure of it." Silk looked around. "Where's Relg?"

"He went back into the cave to rest his eyes," Belgarath told him. "He found water—ice actually. We'll have to thaw it before we can water the horses."

Durnik's fire was tiny, and he fed it with twigs and small bits of wood, trying to conserve their meager fuel supply. It proved to be an uncomfortable night.

In the morning Aunt Pol looked critically at Relg. "You don't seem to be coughing any more," she told him. "How do you feel?"

"I'm fine," he replied, being careful not to look directly at her. The fact that she was a woman seemed to make him terribly uncomfortable, and he tried to avoid her as much as possible.

"What happened to that cold you had?"

"I don't think it could go through the rock. It was gone when I brought him out of the hillside last night."

She looked at him gravely. "I'd never thought of that," she mused. "No one's ever been able to cure a cold before."

"A cold isn't really that serious a thing, Polgara," Silk told her with a pained look. "I'll guarantee you that sliding through rock is never going to be a popular cure."

It took them four days to cross the mountains to reach the vast basin Belgarath referred to as the Wasteland of Murgos and another half day to make their way down the steep basalt face to the black sand of the floor.

"What hath caused this huge depression?" Mandorallen asked, looking around at the barren expanse of scab-rock, black sand and dirty gray salt flats.

"There was an inland sea here once," Belgarath replied. "When Torak cracked the world, the upheaval broke away the eastern edge and all the water drained out."

"That must have been something to see," Barak said.

"We had other things on our minds just then."

"What's that?" Garion asked in alarm, pointing at something

sticking out of the sand just ahead of them. The thing had a huge head with a long, sharp-toothed snout. Its eye sockets, as big as buckets, seemed to stare balefully at them.

"I don't think it has a name," Belgarath answered calmly. "They lived in the sea before the water escaped. They've all been dead now for thousands of years."

As they passed the dead sea monster, Garion could see that it was only a skeleton. Its ribs were as big as the rafters of a barn, and its vast, bleached skull larger than a horse. The vacant eye sockets watched them as they rode past.

Mandorallen, dressed once again in full armor, stared at the skull. "A fearsome beast," he murmured.

"Look at the size of the teeth," Barak said in an awed voice. "It could bite a man in two with one snap."

"That happened a few times," Belgarath told him, "until people learned to avoid this place."

They had moved only a few leagues out into the wasteland when the wind picked up, scouring along the black dunes under the slate-gray sky. The sand began to shift and move and then, as the wind grew even stronger, it began to whip off the tops of the dunes, stinging their faces.

"We'd better take shelter," Belgarath shouted over the shrieking wind. "This sandstorm's going to get worse as we move out farther from the mountains."

"Are there any caves around?" Durnik asked Relg.

Relg shook his head. "None that we can use. They're all filled with sand."

"Over there." Barak pointed at a pile of scab-rock rising from the edge of a salt flat. "If we go to the leeward side, it will keep the wind off us."

"No," Belgarath shouted. "We have to stay to the windward. The sand will pile up at the back. We could be buried alive."

They reached the rock pile and dismounted. The wind tore at their clothing, and the sand billowed across the wasteland like a vast, black cloud.

"This is poor shelter, Belgarath," Barak roared, his beard whipping about his shoulders. "How long is this likely to last?"

"A day—two days—sometimes as long as a week."

Durnik had bent to pick up a piece of broken scab-rock. He looked at it carefully, turning it over in his hands. "It's fractured into square pieces," he said, holding it up. "It will stack well. We can build a wall to shelter us."

"That will take quite a while," Barak objected.

"Did you have something else to do?"

By evening they had the wall up to shoulder height, and by anchoring the tents to the top of it and higher up on the side of the rock-pile, they were able to get in out of the worst of the wind. It was crowded, since they had to shelter the horses as well, but at least it was out of the storm.

They huddled in their cramped shelter for two days with the wind shrieking insanely around them and the taut tent canvas drumming overhead. Then, when the wind finally blew itself out and the black sand began to settle slowly, the silence seemed almost oppressive.

As they emerged, Relg glanced up once, then covered his face and sank to his knees, praying desperately. The clearing sky overhead was a bright, chilly blue. Garion moved over to stand beside the praying fanatic. "It will be all right, Relg," he told him. He reached out his hand without thinking.

"Don't touch me," Relg said and continued to pray.

Silk stood, beating the dust and sand out of his clothing. "Do these storms come up often?" he asked.

"It's the season for them," Belgarath replied.

"Delightful," Silk said sourly.

Then a deep rumbling sound seemed to come from deep in the earth beneath them, and the ground heaved. "Earthquake!" Belgarath warned sharply. "Get the horses out of there!"

Durnik and Barak dashed back inside the shelter and led the horses out from behind the trembling wall and onto the salt flat.

After several moments the heaving subsided. "Is Ctuchik doing that?" Silk demanded. "Is he going to fight us with earthquakes and sandstorms?"

Belgarath shook his head. "No. Nobody's strong enough to do that. That's what's causing it." He pointed to the south. Far across the wasteland they could make out a line of dark peaks.

A thick plume was rising from one of them, towering into the air, boiling up in great black billows as it rose. "Volcano," the old man said. "Probably the same one that erupted last summer and dropped all the ash on Sthiss Tor."

"A fire-mountain?" Barak rumbled, staring at the great cloud that was growing up out of the mountaintop. "I've never seen one before."

"That's fifty leagues away, Belgarath," Silk stated. "Would it make the earth shake even here?"

The old man nodded. "The earth's all one piece, Silk. The force that's causing that eruption is enormous. It's bound to cause a few ripples. I think we'd better get moving. Taur Urgas' patrols will be out looking for us again, now that the sandstorm's blown over."

"Which way do we go?" Durnik asked, looking around, trying to get his bearings.

"That way." Belgarath pointed toward the smoking mountain.

"I was afraid you were going to say that," Barak grumbled.

They rode at a gallop for the rest of the day, pausing only to rest the horses. The dreary wasteland seemed to go on forever. The black sand had shifted and piled into new dunes during the sandstorm, and the thick-crusted salt flats had been scoured by the wind until they were nearly white. They passed a number of the huge, bleached skeletons of the sea monsters which had once inhabited this inland ocean. The bony shapes appeared almost to be swimming up out of the black sand, and the cold, empty eye sockets seemed somehow hungry as they galloped past.

They stopped for the night beside another shattered outcropping of scab-rock. Although the wind had died, it was still bitterly cold, and firewood was scanty.

The next morning as they set out again, Garion began to smell a strange, foul odor. "What's that stink?" he asked.

"The Tarn of Cthok," Belgarath replied. "It's all that's left of the sea that used to be here. It would have dried out centuries ago, but it's fed by underground springs."

"It smells like rotten eggs," Barak said.

"There's quite a bit of sulfur in the ground water around here. I wouldn't drink from the lake."

"I wasn't planning to." Barak wrinkled his nose.

The Tarn of Cthok was a vast, shallow pond filled with oily-looking water that reeked like all the dead fish in the world. Its surface steamed in the icy air, and the wisps of steam gagged them with the dreadful stink. When they reached the southern tip of the lake, Belgarath signalled for a halt. "This next stretch is dangerous," he told them soberly. "Don't let your horses wander. Be sure you stay on solid rock. Ground that looks firm quite often won't be, and there are some other things we'll need to watch out for. Keep your eyes on me and do what I do. When I stop, you stop. When I run, you run." He looked thoughtfully at Relg. The Ulgo had bound another cloth across his eyes, partially to keep out the light and partially to hide the expanse of the sky above him.

"I'll lead his horse, Grandfather," Garion offered.

Belgarath nodded. "It's the only way, I suppose."

"He's going to have to get over that eventually," Barak said.

"Maybe, but this isn't the time or place for it. Let's go." The old man moved forward at a careful walk.

The region ahead of them steamed and smoked as they approached it. They passed a large pool of gray mud that bubbled and fumed, and beyond it a sparkling spring of clear water, boiling merrily and cascading a scalding brook down into the mud. "At least it's warmer," Silk observed.

Mandorallen's face was streaming perspiration beneath his heavy helmet. "Much warmer," he agreed.

Belgarath had been riding slowly, his head turned slightly as he listened intently. "Stop!" he said sharply.

They all reined in.

Just ahead of them another pool suddenly erupted as a dirty gray geyser of liquid mud spurted thirty feet into the air. It continued to spout for several minutes, then gradually subsided.

"Now!" Belgarath barked. "Run!" He kicked his horse's flanks, and they galloped past the still-heaving surface of the pool, the hooves of their horses splashing in the hot mud that had splattered across their path. When they had passed, the old man slowed again and once more rode with his ear cocked toward the ground.

"What's he listening for?" Barak asked Polgara.

"The geysers make a certain noise just before they erupt," she answered.

"I didn't hear anything."

"You don't know what to listen for."

Behind them the mud geyser spouted again.

"Garion!" Aunt Pol snapped as he turned to look back at the mud plume rising from the pool. "Watch where you're going!"

He jerked his eyes back. The ground ahead of him looked quite ordinary.

"Back up," she told him. "Durnik, get the reins of Relg's horse."

Durnik took the reins, and Garion began to turn his mount.

"I said to back up," she repeated.

Garion's horse put one front hoof on the seemingly solid ground, and the hoof sank out of sight. The horse scrambled back and stood trembling as Garion held him in tightly. Then, carefully, step by step, Garion backed to the solid rock of the path they followed.

"Quicksand," Silk said with a sharp intake of his breath.

"It's all around us," Aunt Pol agreed. "Don't wander off the path—any of you."

Silk stared with revulsion at the hoofprint of Garion's horse, disappearing on the surface of the quicksand. "How deep is it?"

"Deep enough," Aunt Pol replied.

They moved on, carefully picking their way through the quagmires and quicksand, stopping often as more geysers—some of mud, some of frothy, boiling water—shot high into the air. By late afternoon, when they reached a low ridge of hard, solid rock beyond the steaming bog, they were all exhausted from the effort of the concentration it had taken to pass through the hideous region.

"Do we have to go through any more like that?" Garion asked.

"No," Belgarath replied. "It's just around the southern edges of the Tarn."

"Can one not go around it, then?" Mandorallen inquired.

"It's much longer if you do, and the bog helps to discourage pursuit."

"What's that?" Relg cried suddenly.

"What's what?" Barak asked him.

"I heard something just ahead—a kind of click, like two pebbles knocking together."

Garion felt a quick kind of wave against his face, almost like an unseen ripple in the air, and he knew that Aunt Pol was searching ahead of them with her mind.

"Murgos!" she said.

"How many?" Belgarath asked her.

"Six—and a Grolim. They're waiting for us just behind the ridge."

"Only six?" Mandorallen said, sounding a little disappointed.

Barak grinned tightly. "Light entertainment."

"You're getting to be as bad as he is," Silk told the big Cherek.

"Thinkest thou that we might need some plan, my Lord?" Mandorallen asked Barak.

"Not really," Barak replied. "Not for just six. Let's go spring their trap."

The two warriors moved into the lead, unobtrusively loosening their swords in their scabbards.

"Has the sun gone down yet?" Relg asked Garion.

"It's just setting."

Relg pulled the binding from around his eyes and tugged down the dark veil. He winced and squinted his large eyes almost shut.

"You're going to hurt them," Garion told him. "You ought to leave them covered until it gets dark."

"I might need them," Relg said as they rode up the ridge toward the waiting Murgo ambush.

The Murgos gave no warning. They rode out from behind a large pile of black rock and galloped directly at Mandorallen and Barak, their swords swinging. The two warriors, however, were waiting for them and reacted without that instant of frozen surprise which might have made the attack successful. Mandorallen swept his sword from its sheath even as he drove his warhorse directly into the mount of one of the charging Murgos. He rose in his stirrups and swung a mighty blow downward, splitting the Murgo's head with his heavy blade. The horse, knocked off his feet by the impact, fell heavily backward on top of his dying rider. Barak, also charging at the attackers, chopped another Murgo out of the saddle with three massive blows, spattering bright red blood on the sand and rock around them.

A third Murgo sidestepped Mandorallen's charge and struck at the knight's back, but his blade clanged harmlessly off the steel armor. The Murgo desperately raised his sword to strike again, but stiffened and slid from his saddle as Silk's skilfully thrown dagger sank into his neck, just below the ear.

A dark-robed Grolim in his polished steel mask had stepped out from behind the rocks. Garion could quite clearly feel the priest's exultation turning to dismay as Barak and Mandorallen systematically chopped his warriors to pieces. The Grolim drew himself up, and Garion sensed that he was gathering his will to strike. But it was too late. Relg had already closed on him. The zealot's heavy shoulders surged as he grasped the front of the Grolim's robe with his knotted hands. Without apparent effort he lifted and pushed the man back against the flattened face of a house-sized boulder.

At first it appeared that Relg only intended to hold the Grolim pinned against the rock until the others could assist him with the struggling captive, but there was a subtle difference. The set of his shoulders indicated that he had not finished the action he had begun with lifting the man from his feet. The Grolim hammered at Relg's head and shoulders with his fists, but Relg pushed at him inexorably. The rock against which the Grolim was pinned seemed to shimmer slightly around him.

"Relg—no!" Silk's cry was strangled.

The dark-robed Grolim began to sink into the stone face, his arms flailing wildly as Relg pushed him in with a dreadful slowness. As he went deeper into the rock, the surface closed smoothly over him. Relg continued to push, his arms sliding into the stone as he sank the Grolim deeper and deeper. The priest's two protruding hands continued to twitch and writhe, even after the rest of his body had been totally submerged. Then Relg drew his arms out of the stone, leaving the Grolim behind. The two hands sticking out of the rock opened once in mute supplication, then stiffened into dead claws.

Behind him, Garion could hear the muffled sound of Silk's retching.

Barak and Mandorallen had by now engaged two of the remaining Murgos, and the sound of clashing sword blades rang in the chill air. The last Murgo, his eyes wide with fright, wheeled his horse and bolted. Without a word, Durnik jerked his axe free of his saddle and galloped after him. Instead of striking the man down, however, Durnik cut across in front of his opponent's horse, turning him, driving him back. The panic-stricken Murgo flailed at his horse's flanks with the flat of his sword, turning away from the grim-faced smith, and plunged at a dead run back up over the ridge with Durnik close behind him.

The last two Murgos were down by then, and Barak and Mandorallen, both wild-eyed with the exultation of battle, were looking around for more enemies. "Where's that last one?" Barak demanded.

"Durnik's chasing him," Garion said.

"We can't let him get away. He'll bring others."

"Durnik's going to take care of it," Belgarath told him.

Barak fretted. "Durnik's a good man, but he's not really a warrior. Maybe I'd better go help him."

From beyond the ridge there was a sudden scream of horror, then another. The third cut off quite suddenly, and there was silence.

After several minutes, Durnik came riding back alone, his face somber.

"What happened?" Barak asked. "He didn't get away, did he?"

Durnik shook his head. "I chased him into the bog, and he ran into some quicksand."

"Why didn't you cut him down with your axe?"

"I don't really like hitting people," Durnik replied.

Silk was staring at Durnik, his face still ashen. "So you just chased him into quicksand instead and then stood there and watched him go down? Durnik, that's monstrous!"

"Dead is dead," Durnik told him with uncharacteristic bluntness. "When it's over, it doesn't really matter how it happened, does it?" He looked a bit thoughtful. "I *am* sorry about the horse, though."

Chapter Twenty-four

THE NEXT MORNING they followed the ridgeline that angled off toward the east. The wintry sky above them was an icy blue, and there was no warmth to the sun. Relg kept his eyes veiled against the light and muttered prayers as he rode to ward off his panic. Several times they saw dust clouds far out on the desolation of sand and salt flats to the south, but they were unable to determine whether the clouds were caused by Murgo patrols or vagrant winds.

About noon, the wind shifted and blew in steadily from the south. A ponderous cloud, black as ink, blotted out the jagged line of peaks lying along the southern horizon. It moved toward them with a kind of ominous inexorability, and flickers of lightning glimmered in its sooty underbelly.

"That's a bad storm coming, Belgarath," Barak rumbled, staring at the cloud.

Belgarath shook his head. "It's not a storm," he replied. "It's ashfall. That volcano out there is erupting again, and the wind's blowing the ash this way."

Barak made a face, then shrugged. "At least we won't have to worry about being seen, once it starts," he said.

"The Grolims won't be looking for us with their eyes, Barak," Aunt Pol reminded him.

Belgarath scratched at his beard. "We'll have to take steps to deal with that, I suppose."

"This is a large group to shield, father," Aunt Pol pointed out, "and that's not even counting the horses."

"I think you can manage it, Pol. You were always very good it it."

"I can hold up my side as long as you can hold up yours, Old Wolf."

"I'm afraid I'm not going to be able to help you, Pol. Ctuchik himself is looking for us. I've felt him several times already, and I'm going to have to concentrate on him. If he decides to strike at us, he'll come very fast. I'll have to be ready for him, and I can't do that if I'm all tangled up in a shield."

"I can't do it alone, father," she protested. "Nobody can enclose this many men and horses without help."

"Garion can help you."

"Me?" Garion jerked his eyes off the looming cloud to stare at his grandfather.

"He's never done it before, father," Aunt Pol pointed out.

"He's going to have to learn sometime."

"This is hardly the time or place for experimentation."

"He'll do just fine. Walk him through it a time or two until he gets the hang of it."

"Exactly what is it I'm supposed to do?" Garion asked apprehensively.

Aunt Pol gave Belgarath a hard look and then turned to Garion. "I'll show you dear," she said. "The first thing you have to do is stay calm. It really isn't all that difficult."

"But you just said—"

"Never mind what I said, dear. Just pay attention."

"What do you want me to do?" he asked doubtfully.

"The first thing is to relax," she replied, "and think about sand and rock."

"That's all?"

"Just do that first. Concentrate."

He thought about sand and rock.

"No, Garion, not *white* sand. *Black* sand—like the sand all around us."

"You didn't say that."

"I didn't think I had to."

Belgarath started to laugh.

"Do *you* want to do this, father?" she demanded crossly. Then she turned back to Garion. "Do it again, dear. Try to get it right this time."

He fixed it in his mind.

"That's better," she told him. "Now, as soon as you get sand and rock firmly in your mind, I want you to sort of push the idea out in a half-circle so that it covers your entire right side. I'll take care of the left."

He strained with it. It was the hardest thing he had ever done.

"Don't push quite so hard, Garion. You're wrinkling it, and it's very hard for me to make the seams match when you do that. Just keep it steady and smooth."

"I'm sorry." He smoothed it out.

"How does it look, father?" she asked the old man.

Garion felt a tentative push against the idea he was holding.

"Not bad, Pol," Belgarath replied. "Not bad at all. The boy's got talent."

"Just exactly what are we doing?" Garion asked. In spite of the chill, he felt sweat standing out on his forehead.

"You're making a shield," Belgarath told him. "You enclose yourself in the idea of sand and rock, and it merges with the real sand and rock all around us. When Grolims go looking for things with their minds, they're looking for men and horses. They'll sweep right past us, because all they'll see here is more sand and more rock."

"That's all there is to it?" Garion was quite pleased with how simple it was.

"There's a bit more, dear," Aunt Pol said. "We're going to extend it now so that it covers all of us. Go out slowly, a few feet at a time."

That was much less simple. He tore the fabric of the idea several times before he got it pushed out as far as Aunt Pol wanted it. He felt a strange merging of his mind with hers along the center of the idea where the two sides joined.

"I think we've got it now, father," Aunt Pol said.

"I told you he could do it, Pol."

The purple-black cloud was rolling ominously up the sky toward them, and faint rumbles of thunder growled along its leading edge.

"If that ash is anything like what it was in Nyissa, we're going to be wandering blind out here, Belgarath," Barak said.

"Don't worry about it," the sorcerer replied. "I've got a lock on Rak Cthol. The Grolims aren't the only ones who can locate things that way. Let's move out."

They started along the ridge again as the cloud blotted out the sky overhead. The thunder shocks were a continuous rumble, and lightning seethed in the boiling cloud. The lightning had an arid, crackling quality about it as the billions of tiny particles seethed and churned, building enormous static discharges. Then the first specks of drifting ash began to settle down through the icy air, as Belgarath led them down off the ridge and out onto the sand flats.

By the end of the first hour, Garion found that holding the image in his mind had grown easier. It was no longer necessary to concentrate all his attention on it as it had been at first. By the end of the second hour, it had become no more than tedious. To relieve the boredom of it as they rode through the thickening ashfall, he thought about one of the huge skeletons they had passed when they had first entered the wasteland. Painstakingly he constructed one of them and placed it in the image he was holding. On the whole he thought it looked rather good, and it gave him something to do.

"Garion," Aunt Pol said crisply, "please don't try to be creative."

"What?"

"Just stick to sand. The skeleton's very nice, but it looks a bit peculiar with only one side."

"One side?"

"There wasn't a skeleton on my side of the image—just yours. Keep it simple, Garion. Don't embellish."

They rode on, their faces muffled to keep the choking ash out of their mouths and noses. Garion felt a tentative push against the image he was holding. It seemed to flutter against his mind, feeling almost like the wriggling touch of the tadpoles he had once caught in the pond at Faldor's farm.

"Hold it steady, Garion," Aunt Pol warned. "That's a Grolim."

"Did he see us?"

"No. There—he's moving on now." And the fluttering touch was gone.

They spent the night in another of the piles of broken rock that dotted the wasteland. Durnik once again devised a kind of low, hollowed-out shelter of piled rock and anchored-down tent cloth. They took a cold supper of bread and dried meat and built no fire. Garion and Aunt Pol took turns holding the image of empty sand over them like an umbrella. He discovered that it was much easier when they weren't moving.

The ash was still falling the next morning, but the sky was no longer the inky black it had been the day before. "I think it's thinning out, Belgarath," Silk said as they saddled their horses. "If it blows over, we'll have to start dodging patrols again."

The old man nodded. "We'd better hurry," he agreed. "There's a place I know of where we can hide—about five miles north of the city. I'd like to get there before this ashfall subsides. You can see for ten leagues in any direction from the walls of Rak Cthol."

"Are the walls so high, then?" Mandorallen asked.

"Higher than you can imagine."

"Higher even than the walls of Vo Mimbre?"

"Ten times higher—fifty times higher. You'll have to see it to understand."

They rode hard that day. Garion and Aunt Pol held their

shield of thought in place, but the searching touches of the Grolims came more frequently now. Several times the push against Garion's mind was very strong and came without warning.

"They know what we're doing, father," Aunt Pol told the old man. "They're trying to penetrate the screen."

"Hold it firm," he replied. "You know what to do if one of them breaks through."

She nodded, her face grim.

"Warn the boy."

She nodded again, then turned to Garion. "Listen to me carefully, dear," she said gravely. "The Grolims are trying to take us by surprise. The best shield in the world can be penetrated if you hit it quickly enough and hard enough. If one of them does manage to break through, I'm going to tell you to stop. When I say stop, I want you to erase the image immediately and put your mind completely away from it."

"I don't understand."

"You don't have to. Just do exactly as I say. If I tell you to stop, pull your thought out of contact with mine instantly. I'll be doing something that's very dangerous, and I don't want you getting hurt."

"Can't I help?"

"No, dear. Not this time."

They rode on. The ashfall grew even thinner, and the sky overhead turned a hazy, yellowish blue. The ball of the sun, pale and round like a full moon, appeared not far above the southwestern horizon.

"Garion, stop!"

What came was not a push but a sharp stab. Garion gasped and jerked his mind away, throwing the image of sand from him. Aunt Pol stiffened, and her eyes were blazing. Her hand flicked a short gesture, and she spoke a single world. The surge Garion felt as her will unleashed was overpowering. With a momentary dismay, he realized that his mind was still linked to hers. The merging that had held the image together was too strong, too complete to break. He felt himself drawn with her as their still-joined minds lashed out like a whip. They flashed back along the faint trail of thought that had stabbed at the shield and they found its origin. They touched another mind, a mind filled with the exultation of discovery. Then, sure of her target now, Aunt Pol struck with the full force of her will. The mind they had touched flinched back, trying to break off the contact, but it was too late for that now. Garion could feel the other mind swelling, expanding unbearably. Then it suddenly burst, exploding into gibbering insanity, shattering as horror upon horror overwhelmed it. There was flight then, blind shrieking flight across dark stones of some kind, a flight with the single thought of a dreadful, final escape. The stones were gone, and there was a terrible sense of falling from some incalculable height. Garion wrenched his mind away from it.

"I told you to get clear," Aunt Pol snapped at him.

"I couldn't help it. I couldn't get loose."

"What happened?" Silk's face was startled.

"A Grolim broke through," she replied.

"Did he see us?"

"For a moment. It doesn't matter. He's dead now."

"You killed him? How?"

"He forgot to defend himself. I followed his thought back."

"He went crazy," Garion said in a choked voice, still filled with the horror of the encounter. "He jumped off something very high. He wanted to jump. It was the only way he could escape from what was happening to him." Garion felt sick.

"It was awfully noisy, Pol," Belgarath said with a pained expression. "You haven't been that clumsy in years."

"I had this passenger." She gave Garion an icy look.

"It wasn't my fault," Garion protested. "You were holding on so tight I couldn't break loose. You had us all tied together."

"You do that sometimes, Pol," Belgarath told her. "The contact gets a little too personal, and you seem to want to take up permanent residence. It has to do with love, I imagine."

"Do you have any idea what they're talking about?" Barak asked Silk.

"I wouldn't even want to guess."

Aunt Pol was looking thoughtfully at Garion. "Perhaps it was my fault," she admitted finally.

"You're going to have to let go someday, Pol," Belgarath said gravely.

"Perhaps—but not just yet."

"You'd better put the screen back up," the old man suggested. "They know we're out here now, and there'll be others looking for us."

She nodded. "Think about sand again, Garion."

The ash continued to settle as they rode through the afternoon, obscuring less and less with each passing mile. They were able to make out the shapes of the jumbled piles of rock around them and a few rounded spires of basalt thrusting up out of the sand. As they approached another of the low rock ridges that cut across the wasteland at regular intervals, Garion saw something dark and enormously high looming in the haze ahead.

"We can hide here until dark," Belgarath said, dismounting behind the ridge.

"Are we there?" Durnik asked, looking around.

"That's Rak Cthol." The old man pointed at the ominous shadow.

Barak squinted at it. "I thought that was just a mountain."

"It is. Rak Cthol's built on top of it."

"It's almost like Prolgu then, isn't it?"

"The locations are similar, but Ctuchik the magician lives here. That makes it quite different from Prolgu."

"I thought Ctuchik was a sorcerer," Garion said, puzzled. "Why do you keep calling him a magician?"

"It's a term of contempt," Belgarath replied. "It's considered a deadly insult in our particular society."

They picketed their horses among some large rocks on the back side of the ridge and climbed the forty or so feet to the top, where they took cover to watch and wait for nightfall.

As the settling ash thinned even more, the peak began to emerge from the haze. It was not so much a mountain as a rock pinnacle towering up out of the wasteland. Its base, surrounded by a mass of shattered rubble, was fully five miles around, and its sides were sheer and black as night.

"How high doth it reach?" Mandorallen asked, his voice dropping almost unconsciously into a half-whisper.

"Somewhat more than a mile," Belgarath replied.

A steep causeway rose sharply from the floor of the wasteland to encircle the upper thousand or so feet of the black tower. "I imagine that took a while to build," Barak noted.

"About a thousand years," Belgarath answered. "While it was under construction, the Murgos bought every slave the Nyissans could put their hands on."

"A grim business," Mandorallen observed.

"It's a grim place," Belgarath agreed.

As the chill breeze blew off the last of the haze, the shape of the city perched atop the crag began to emerge. The walls were as black as the sides of the pinnacle, and black turrets jutted out from them, seemingly at random. Dark spires rose within the walls, stabbing up into the evening sky like spears. There was a foreboding, evil air about the black city of the Grolims. It perched, brooding, atop its peak, looking out over the savage wasteland of sand, rock, and sulfur-reeking bogs that encircled it. The sun, sinking into the banks of cloud and ash along the jagged western rim of the wasteland, bathed the grim fortress above them in a sooty crimson glow. The walls of Rak Cthol seemed to bleed. It was as if all the blood that had been spilled on all the altars of Torak since the world began had been gathered together to stain the dread city above them and that all the oceans of the world would not be enough to wash it clean again.

Chapter Twenty-five

As the last trace of light slid from the sky, they moved carefully down off the ridge and crossed the ash-covered sand toward the rock tower looming above them. When they reached the shattered scree at its base, they dismounted, left the horses with Durnik and climbed up the steeply sloped rubble to the rock face of the basalt pinnacle that blotted out the stars. Although Relg had been shuddering and hiding his eyes a moment before, he moved almost eagerly now. He stopped and then carefully placed his hands and forehead against the icy rock.

"Well?" Belgarath asked after a moment, his voice hushed but carrying a note of dreadful concern. "Was I right? Are there caves?"

"There are open spaces," Relg replied. "They're a long way inside."

"Can you get to them?"

"There's no point. They don't go anywhere. They're just closed-in hollows."

"Now what?" Silk asked.

"I don't know," Belgarath admitted, sounding terribly disappointed.

"Let's try a little farther around," Relg suggested. "I can feel some echoes here. There might be something off in that direction." He pointed.

"I want one thing clearly understood right here and now," Silk announced, planting his feet firmly. "I'm not going to go through any more rock. If there's going to be any of that, I'll stay behind."

"We'll come up with something," Barak told him.

Silk shook his head stubbornly. "No passing through rock," he declared adamantly.

Relg was already moving along the face, his fingers lightly touching the basalt. "It's getting stronger," he told them. "It's large and it goes up." He moved on another hundred yards or so, and they followed, watching him intently. "It's right through here," he said finally, patting the rock face with one hand. "It might be the one we want. Wait here." He put his hands against the rock and pushed them slowly into the basalt.

"I can't stand this," Silk said, turning his back quickly. "Let me know once he's inside."

With a kind of dreadful determination, Relg pushed his way into the rock.

"Is he gone yet?" Silk asked.

"He's going in," Barak replied clinically. "Only half of him's still sticking out."

"Please, Barak, don't tell me about it."

"Was it really *that* bad?" the big man asked.

"You have no idea. You have absolutely no idea." The rat-faced man was shivering uncontrollably.

They waited in the chill darkness for half an hour or more. Somewhere high above them there was a scream.

"What was that cry?" Mandorallen asked.

"The Grolims are busy," Belgarath answered grimly. "It's the season of the wounding—when the Orb burned Torak's hand and face. A large number of sacrifices are called for at this time of year—usually slaves. Torak doesn't seem to insist on Angarak blood. As long as it's human, it seems to satisfy him."

There was a faint sound of steps somewhere along the cliff, and a few moments later Relg rejoined them. "I found it," he told them. "The opening's about a half-mile farther along. It's partially blocked."

"Does it go all the way up?" Belgarath demanded.

Relg shrugged. "It goes up. I can't say how far. The only

way to find out for sure is to follow it. The whole series of caves is fairly extensive, though."

"Do we really have any choice, father?" Aunt Pol asked.

"No. I suppose not."

"I'll go get Durnik," Silk said. He turned and disappeared into the darkness.

The rest of them followed Relg until they reached a small hole in the rock face just above the tumbled scree. "We'll have to move some of this rubble if we're going to get your animals inside," he told them.

Barak bent and lifted a large stone block. He staggered under its weight and dropped it to one side with a clatter.

"Quietly!" Belgarath told him.

"Sorry," Barak mumbled.

For the most part, the stones were not large, but there were a great many of them. When Silk and Durnik joined them, they all fell to clearing the rubble out of the cave mouth. It took them nearly an hour to remove enough rock to make it possible for the horses to squeeze through.

"I wish Hettar was here," Barak grunted, putting his shoulder against the rump of a balky packhorse.

"Talk to him, Barak," Silk suggested.

"I am talking."

"Try it without all the curse words."

"There's going to be some climbing involved," Relg told them after they had pushed the last horse inside and stood in the total blackness of the cave. "As nearly as I can tell, the galleries run vertically, so we'll have to climb from level to level."

Mandorallen leaned against one of the walls, and his armor clinked.

"That's not going to work," Belgarath told him. "You wouldn't be able to climb in armor anyway. Leave it here with the horses, Mandorallen."

The knight sighed and began removing his armor.

A faint glow appeared as Relg mixed powders in a wooden bowl from two leather pouches he carried inside his mail shirt.

"That's better," Barak approved, "but wouldn't a torch be brighter?"

"Much brighter," Relg agreed, "but then I wouldn't be able to see. This will give you enough light to see where you're going."

"Let's get started," Belgarath said.

Relg handed the glowing bowl to Barak and turned to lead them up a dark gallery.

After they had gone a few hundred yards, they came to a steep slope of rubble rising up into darkness. "I'll look," Relg said and scrambled up the slope out of sight. After a moment or so, they heard a peculiar popping sound, and tiny fragments of rock showered down onto the rubble from above. "Come up now," Relg's voice came to them.

Carefully they climbed the rubble until they reached a sheer wall. "To your right," Relg said, still above them. "You'll find some holes in the rock you can use to climb up."

They found the holes, quite round and about six inches deep. "How did you make these?" Durnik asked, examining one of the holes.

"It's a bit difficult to explain," Relg replied. "There's a ledge up here. It leads to another gallery."

One by one they climbed the rock face to join Relg on the ledge. As he had told them, the ledge led to a gallery that angled sharply upward. They followed it toward the center of the peak, passing several passageways opening to the sides.

"Shouldn't we see where they go?" Barak asked after they had passed the third or fourth passageway.

"They don't go anyplace," Relg told him.

"How can you be sure?"

"A gallery that goes someplace feels different. That one we just passed comes to a blank wall about a hundred feet in."

Barak grunted dubiously.

They came to another sheer face, and Relg stopped to peer up into the blackness.

"How high is it?" Durnik asked.

"Thirty feet or so. I'll make some holes so we can climb up." Relg knelt and slowly pushed one hand into the face of the rock. Then he tensed his shoulder and twisted his arm slightly. The rock popped with a sharp little detonation; when Relg pulled his hand out, a shower of fragments came with it. He brushed the rest of the debris out of the hole he had made, stood up and sank his other hand into the rock about two feet above the first hole.

"Clever," Silk admired.

"It's a very old trick," Relg told him.

They followed Relg up the face and squeezed through a narrow crack at the top. Barak muttered curses as he wriggled through, leaving a fair amount of skin behind.

"How far have we come?" Silk asked. His voice had a certain apprehension in it, and he looked about nervously at the rock which seemed to press in all around them.

"We're about eight hundred feet above the base of the pinnacle," Relg replied. "We go that way now." He pointed up another sloping passageway.

"Isn't that back in the direction we just came?" Durnik asked.

"The cave zigzags," Relg told him. "We have to keep following the galleries that lead upward."

"Do they go all the way to the top?"

"They open out somewhere. That's all I can tell for sure at this point."

"What's that?" Silk cried sharply.

From somewhere along one of the dark passageways, a voice floated out at them, singing. There seemed to be a deep sadness in the song, but the echoes made it impossible to pick out the words. About all they could be sure of was the fact that the singer was a woman.

After a moment, Belgarath gave a startled exclamation.

"What's wrong?" Aunt Pol asked him.

"Marag!" the old man said.

"That's impossible."

"I know the song, Pol. It's a Marag funeral song. Whoever she is, she's very close to dying."

The echoes in the twisting passageways made it very difficult to pinpoint the singer's exact location; but as they moved, the sound seemed to be getting closer.

"Down here," Silk said finally, stopping with his head cocked to one side in front of an opening.

The singing stopped abruptly. "No closer," the unseen woman warned sharply. "I have a knife."

"We're friends," Durnik called to her.

She laughed bitterly at that. "I have no friends. You're not going to take me back. My knife is long enough to reach my heart."

"She thinks we're Murgos," Silk whispered.

Belgarath raised his voice, speaking in a language Garion had never heard before. After a moment, the woman answered haltingly, as if trying to remember words she had not spoken for years.

"She thinks it's a trick," the old man told them quietly. "She says she's got a knife right against her heart, so we're going to have to be careful." He spoke again into the dark passageway, and the woman answered him. The language they were speaking was liquid, musical.

"She says she'll let one of us go to her," Belgarath said finally. "She still doesn't trust us."

"I'll go," Aunt Pol told him.

"Be careful, Pol. She might decide at the last minute to use her knife on you instead of herself."

"I can handle it, father." Aunt Pol took the light from Barak and moved slowly on down the passageway, speaking calmly as she went.

The rest of them stood in the darkness, listening intently to the murmur of voices coming from the passageway, as Aunt Pol talked quietly to the Marag woman. "You can come now," she called to them finally, and they went down the passageway toward her voice.

The woman was lying beside a small pool of water. She was dressed only in scanty rags, and she was very dirty. Her hair was a lustrous black, but badly tangled, and her face had a resigned, hopeless look on it. She had wide cheekbones, full lips, and huge, violet eyes framed with sooty black lashes. The few pitiful rags she wore exposed a great deal of her pale skin. Relg drew in a sharp breath and immediately turned his back.

"Her name is Taiba," Aunt Pol told them quietly. "She escaped from the slave pens under Rak Cthol several days ago."

Belgarath knelt beside the exhausted woman. "You're a Marag, aren't you?" he asked her intently.

"My mother told me I was," she confirmed. "She's the one who taught me the old language." Her dark hair fell across one of her pale cheeks in a shadowy tangle.

"Are there any other Marags in the slave pens?"

"A few, I think. It's hard to tell. Most of the other slaves have had their tongues cut out."

"She needs food," Aunt Pol said. "Did anyone think to bring anything?"

Durnik untied a pouch from his belt and handed it to her. "Some cheese," he said, "and a bit of dried meat."

Aunt Pol opened the pouch.

"Have you any idea how your people came to be here?" Belgarath asked the slave woman. "Think. It could be very important."

Taiba shrugged. "We've always been here." She took the food Aunt Pol offered her and began to eat ravenously.

"Not too fast," Aunt Pol warned.

"Have you ever heard anything about how Marags wound up in the slave pens of the Murgos?" Belgarath pressed.

"My mother told me once that thousands of years ago we lived in a country under the open sky and that we weren't slaves then," Taiba replied. "I didn't believe her, though. It's the sort of story you tell children."

"There are some old stories about the Tolnedran campaign in Maragor, Belgarath," Silk remarked. "Rumors have been floating around for years that some of the legion commanders sold their prisoners to the Nyissan slavers instead of killing them. It's the sort of thing a Tolnedran would do."

"It's a possibility, I suppose," Belgarath replied, frowning.

"Do we have to stay here?" Relg demanded harshly. His back was still turned, and there was a rigidity to it that spoke his outrage loudly.

"Why is he angry with me?" Taiba asked, her voice dropping wearily from her lips in scarcely more than a whisper.

"Cover your nakedness, woman," Relg told her. "You're an affront to decent eyes."

"Is that all?" She laughed, a rich, throaty sound. "These are all the clothes I have." She looked down at her lush figure. "Besides, there's nothing wrong with my body. It's not deformed or ugly. Why should I hide it?"

"Lewd woman!" Relg accused her.

"If it bothers you so much, don't look," she suggested.

"Relg has a certain religious problem," Silk told her dryly.

"Don't mention religion," she said with a shudder.

"You see," Relg snorted. "She's completely depraved."

"Not exactly," Belgarath told him. "In Rak Cthol the word religion means the altar and the knife."

"Garion," Aunt Pol said, "give me your cloak."

He unfastened his heavy wool cloak and handed it to her. She started to cover the exhausted slave woman with it, but stopped suddenly and looked closely at her. "Where are your children?" she asked.

"The Murgos took them," Taiba replied in a dead voice. "They were two baby girls—very beautiful—but they're gone now."

"We'll get them back for you," Garion promised impulsively.

She gave a bitter little laugh. "I don't think so. The Murgos gave them to the Grolims, and the Grolims sacrificed them on the altar of Torak. Ctuchik himself held the knife."

Garion felt his blood run cold.

"This cloak is warm," Taiba said gratefully, her hands smoothing the rough cloth. "I've been cold for such a long time." She sighed with a sort of weary contentment.

Belgarath and Aunt Pol were looking at each other across Taiba's body. "I must be doing something right," the old man remarked cryptically after a moment. "To stumble across her like this after all these years of searching!"

"Are you sure she's the right one, father?"

"She almost has to be. Everything fits together too well—

right down to the last detail." He drew in a deep breath and then let it out explosively. "That's been worrying me for a thousand years." He suddenly looked enormously pleased with himself. "How did you escape from the slave pens, Taiba?" he asked gently.

"One of the Murgos forgot to lock a door," she replied, her voice drowsy. "After I slipped out, I found this knife. I was going to try to find Ctuchik and kill him with it, but I got lost. There are so many caves down here—so many. I wish I could kill him before I die, but I don't suppose there's much hope for that now." She sighed regretfully. "I think I'd like to sleep now. I'm so very tired."

"Will you be all right here?" Aunt Pol asked her. "We have to leave, but we'll be back. Do you need anything?"

"A little light, maybe." Taiba sighed. "I've lived in the dark all my life. I think I'd like it to be light when I die."

"Relg," Aunt Pol said, "make her some light."

"We might need it ourselves." His voice was still stiffly offended.

"She needs it more."

"Do it, Relg," Belgarath told the zealot in a firm voice.

Relg's face hardened, but he mixed some of the contents of his two pouches together on a flat stone and dribbled a bit of water on the mixture. The pasty substance began to glow.

"Thank you," Taiba said simply.

Relg refused to answer or even to look at her.

They went back up the passageway, leaving her beside the small pool with her dim little light. She began to sing again, quite softly this time and in a voice near the edge of sleep.

Relg led them through the dark galleries, twisting and changing course frequently, always climbing. Hours dragged by, though time had little meaning in the perpetual darkness. They climbed more of the sheer faces and followed passageways that wound higher and higher up into the vast rock pillar. Garion lost track of direction as they climbed, and found himself wondering if even Relg knew which way he was going. As they rounded another corner in another gallery, a faint breeze seemed to touch their faces. The breeze carried a dreadful odor with it.

"What's that stink?" Silk asked, wrinkling his sharp nose.

"The slave pens, most likely," Belgarath replied. "Murgos are lax about sanitation."

"The pens are under Rak Cthol, aren't they?" Barak asked. Belgarath nodded.

"And they open up into the city itself?"

"As I remember it, they do."

"You've done it, Relg," Barak said, clapping the Ulgo on the shoulder.

"Don't touch me," Relg told him.

"Sorry, Relg."

"The slave pens are going to be guarded," Belgarath told them. "We'll want to be very quiet now."

They crept on up the passageway, being careful where they put their feet. Garion was not certain at what point the gallery began to show evidence of human construction. Finally they passed a partially open iron door. "Is there anybody in there?" he whispered to Silk.

The little man sidled up to the opening, his dagger held low and ready. He glanced in, his head making a quick, darting movement. "Just some bones," he reported somberly.

Belgarath signalled for a halt. "These lower galleries have probably been abandoned," he told them in a very quiet voice. "After the causeway was finished, the Murgos didn't need all those thousands of slaves. We'll go on up, but be quiet and keep your eyes open."

They padded silently up the gradual incline of the gallery, passing more of the rusting iron doors, all standing partially ajar. At the top of the slope, the gallery turned back sharply on itself, still angling upward. Some words were crudely lettered on the wall in a script Garion could not recognize. "Grandfather," he whispered, pointing at the words.

Belgarath glanced at the lettering and grunted. "Ninth level," he muttered. "We're still some distance below the city."

"How far do we go before we start running into Murgos?"

Barak rumbled, looking around with his hand on his sword hilt.

Belgarath shrugged slightly. "It's hard to say. I'd guess that only the top two or three levels are occupied."

They followed the gallery upward until it turned sharply, and once again there were words written on the wall in the alien script. "Eighth level," Belgarath translated. "Keep going."

The smell of the slave pens grew stronger as they progressed upward through the succeeding levels.

"Light ahead," Durnik warned sharply, just before they turned the corner to enter the fourth level.

"Wait here," Silk breathed and melted around the corner, his dagger held close against his leg.

The light was dim and seemed to be bobbing slightly, growing gradually brighter as the moments dragged by. "Someone with a torch," Barak muttered.

The torchlight suddenly flickered, throwing gyrating shadows. Then it grew steady, no longer bobbing. After a few moments, Silk came back, carefully wiping his dagger. "A Murgo," he told them. "I think he was looking for something. The cells up there are still empty."

"What did you do with him?" Barak asked.

"I dragged him into one of the cells. They won't stumble over him unless they're looking for him."

Relg was carefully veiling his eyes.

"Even that little bit of light?" Durnik asked him.

"It's the color of it," Relg explained.

They rounded the corner into the fourth level and started up again. A hundred yards up the gallery a torch was stuck into a crack in the wall, burning steadily. As they approached it, they could see a long smear of fresh blood on the uneven, littered floor.

Belgarath stopped outside the cell door, scratching at his beard. "What was he wearing?" he asked Silk.

"One of those hooded robes," Silk replied. "Why?"

"Go get it."

Silk looked at him briefly, then nodded. He went back into

the cell and came out a moment later carrying a black Murgo robe. He handed it to the old man.

Belgarath held up the robe, looking critically at the long cut running up the back. "Try not to put such big holes in the rest of them," he told the little man.

Silk grinned at him. "Sorry. I guess I got a bit overenthusiastic. I'll be more careful from now on." He glanced at Barak. "Care to join me?" he invited.

"Naturally. Coming, Mandorallen?"

The knight nodded gravely, loosening his sword in its sheath.

"We'll wait here, then," Belgarath told them. "Be careful, but don't take any longer than you have to."

The three men moved stealthily on up the gallery toward the third level.

"Can you guess at the time, father?" Aunt Pol asked quietly after they had disappeared.

"Several hours after midnight."

"Will we have enough time left before dawn?"

"If we hurry."

"Maybe we should wait out the day here and go up when it gets dark again."

He frowned. "I don't think so, Pol. Ctuchik's up to something. He knows I'm coming—I've felt that for the last week— but he hasn't made a move of his own yet. Let's not give him any more time than we have to."

"He's going to fight you, father."

"It's long overdue anyway," he replied. "Ctuchik and I have been stepping around each other for thousands of years because the time was never just exactly right. Now it's finally come down to this." He looked off into the darkness, his face bleak. "When it starts, I want you to stay out of it, Pol."

She looked at the grim-faced old man for a long moment, then nodded. "Whatever you say, father," she said.

Chapter Twenty-six

THE MURGO ROBE was made of coarse, black cloth and it had a strange red emblem woven into the fabric just over Garion's heart. It smelled of smoke and of something else even more unpleasant. There was a small ragged hole in the robe just under the left armpit, and the cloth around the hole was wet and sticky. Garion's skin cringed away from that wetness.

They were moving rapidly up through the galleries of the last three levels of the slave pens with the deep-cowled hoods of the Murgo robes hiding their faces. Though the galleries were lighted by sooty torches, they encountered no guards, and the slaves locked behind the pitted iron doors made no sound as they passed. Garion could feel the dreadful fear behind those doors.

"How do we get up into the city?" Durnik whispered.

"There's a stairway at the upper end of the top gallery," Silk replied softly.

"Is it guarded?"

"Not any more."

An iron-barred gate, chained and locked, blocked the top of the stairway, but Silk bent and drew a slim metal implement from one boot, probed inside the lock for a few seconds, then grunted with satisfaction as the lock clicked open in his hand. "I'll have a look," he whispered and slipped out.

Beyond the gate Garion could see the stars and, outlined against them, the looming buildings of Rak Cthol. A scream, agonized and despairing, echoed through the city, followed after a moment by the hollow sound of some unimaginably huge iron gong. Garion shuddered.

A few moments later, Silk slipped back through the gate. "There doesn't seem to be anybody about," he murmured softly. "Which way do we go?"

Belgarath pointed. "That way. We'll go along the wall to the Temple."

"The Temple?" Relg asked sharply.

"We have to go through it to get to Ctuchik," the old man replied. "We're going to have to hurry. Morning isn't far off."

Rak Cthol was not like other cities. The vast buildings had little of that separateness that they had in other places. It was as if the Murgos and Grolims who lived here had no sense of personal possession, so that their structures lacked that insularity of individual property to be found among the houses in the cities of the West. There were no streets in the ordinary sense of the word, but rather interconnecting courtyards and corridors that passed between and quite often through the buildings.

The city seemed deserted as they crept silently through the dark courtyards and shadowy corridors, yet there was a kind of menacing watchfulness about the looming, silent black walls around them. Peculiar-looking turrets jutted from the walls in unexpected places, leaning out over the courtyards, brooding down at them as they passed. Narrow windows stared accusingly at them, and the arched doorways were filled with lurking shadows. An oppressive air of ancient evil lay heavily on Rak Cthol, and the stones themselves seemed almost to gloat as Garion and his friends moved deeper and deeper into the dark maze of the Grolim fortress.

"Are you sure you know where you're going?" Barak whispered nervously to Belgarath.

"I've been here before, using the causeway," the old man told him quietly. "I like to keep an eye on Ctuchik from time to time. We go up those stairs. They'll take us to the top of the city wall."

The stairway was narrow and steep, with massive walls on either side and a vaulted roof overhead. The stone steps were worn by centuries of use. They climbed silently. Another scream echoed through the city, and the huge gong sounded its iron note once more.

When they emerged from the stairway, they were atop the outer wall. It was as broad as a highway and encircled the entire city. A parapet ran along its outer edge, making the brink of the dreadful precipice that dropped away to the floor of the rocky wasteland a mile or more below. Once they emerged from the shelter of the buildings, the chill air bit at them, and the black flagstones and rough-hewn blocks of the outer parapet glittered with frost in the icy starlight.

Belgarath looked at the open stretch lying along the top of the wall ahead of them and at the shadowy buildings looming several hundred yards ahead. "We'd better spread out," he whispered. "Too many people in one place attract attention in Rak Cthol. We'll go across here two at a time. Walk—don't run or crouch down. Try to look as if you belong here. Let's go." He started along the top of the wall with Barak at his side, the two of them walking purposefully, but not appearing to hurry. After a few moments, Aunt Pol and Mandorallen followed.

"Durnik," Silk whispered. "Garion and I'll go next. You and Relg follow in a minute or so." He peered at Relg's face, shadowed beneath the Murgo hood. "Are you all right?" he asked.

"As long as I don't look up at the sky," Relg answered tightly. His voice sounded as if it were coming from between clenched teeth.

"Come along, then, Garion," Silk murmured.

It required every ounce of Garion's self-control to walk at a normal pace across the frosty stones. It seemed somehow that eyes watched from every shadowy building and tower as he and the little Drasnian crossed the open section atop the wall. The air was dead calm and bitterly cold, and the stone blocks of the outer parapet were covered with a lacy filigree of rime frost.

There was another scream from the Temple lying somewhere ahead.

The corner of a large tower jutted out at the end of the open stretch of wall, obscuring the walkway beyond. "Wait here a moment," Silk whispered as they stepped gratefully into its shadow and he slipped around the jutting corner.

Garion stood in the icy dark, straining his ears for any sound. He glanced once toward the parapet. Far out on the desolate wasteland below, a small fire was burning. It twinkled in the dark like a small red star. He tried to imagine how far away it might be.

Then there was a slight scraping sound somewhere above him. He spun quickly, his hand going to his sword. A shadowy figure dropped from a ledge on the side of the tower several yards over his head and landed with catlike silence on the flagstones directly in front of him. Garion caught a familiar sour, acid reek of stale perspiration.

"It's been a long time, hasn't it, Garion?" Brill said quietly with an ugly chuckle.

"Stay back," Garion warned, holding his sword with its point low as Barak had taught him.

"I knew that I'd catch you alone someday," Brill said, ignoring the sword. He spread his hands wide and crouched slightly, his cast eye gleaming in the starlight.

Garion backed away, waving his sword threateningly. Brill bounded to one side, and Garion instinctively followed him with the sword point. Then, so fast that Garion could not follow, Brill dodged back and struck his hand down sharply on the boy's forearm. Garion's sword skittered away across the icy flagstones. Desperately, Garion reached for his dagger.

Then another shadow flickered in the darkness at the corner of the tower. Brill grunted as a foot caught him solidly in the side. He fell, but rolled quickly across the stones and came back up onto his feet, his stance wide and his hands moving slowly in the air in front of him.

Silk dropped his Murgo robe behind him, kicked it out of the way, and crouched, his hands also spread wide.

Brill grinned. "I should have known you were around somewhere, Kheldar."

"I suppose I should have expected you too, Kordoch," Silk replied. "You always seem to show up."

Brill flicked a quick hand toward Silk's face, but the little man easily avoided it. "How do you keep getting ahead of us?" he asked, almost conversationally. "That's a habit of yours that's starting to irritate Belgarath." He launched a quick kick at Brill's groin, but the cast-eyed man jumped back agilely.

Brill laughed shortly. "You people are too tender-hearted with horses," he said. "I've had to ride quite a few of them to death chasing you. How did you get out of that pit?" He sounded interested. "Taur Urgas was furious the next morning."

"What a shame."

"He had the guards flayed."

"I imagine a Murgo looks a bit peculiar without his skin."

Brill dove forward suddenly, both hands extended, but Silk side-stepped the lunge and smashed his hand sharply down in the middle of Brill's back. Brill grunted again, but rolled clear farther out on the stones atop the wall. "You might be just as good as they say," he admitted grudgingly.

"Try me, Kordoch," Silk invited, with a nasty grin. He moved out from the wall of the tower, his hands in constant motion. Garion watched the two circling each other with his heart in his mouth.

Brill jumped again, with both feet lashing out, but Silk dove under him. They both rolled to their feet again. Silk's left hand flashed out, even as he came to his feet, catching Brill high on the head. Brill reeled from the blow, but managed to kick Silk's knee as he spun away. "Your technique's defensive, Kheldar," he grated, shaking his head to clear the effects of Silk's blow. "That's a weakness."

"Just a difference of style, Kordoch," Silk replied.

Brill drove a gouging thumb at Silk's eye, but Silk blocked it and slammed a quick counterblow to the pit of his enemy's stomach. Brill scissored his legs as he fell, sweeping Silk's legs out from under him. Both men tumbled across the frosty stones and sprang to their feet again, their hands flickering blows faster than Garion's eyes could follow them.

The mistake was a simple one, so slight that Garion could

not even be sure it *was* a mistake. Brill flicked a jab at Silk's face that was an ounce or two harder than it should have been and traveled no more than a fraction of an inch too far. Silk's hands flashed up and caught his opponent's wrist with a deadly grip and rolled backward toward the parapet, his legs coiling, even as the two of them fell. Jerked off balance, Brill seemed almost to dive forward. Silk's legs straightened suddenly, launching the cast-eyed man up and forward with a tremendous heave. With a strangled exclamation Brill clutched desperately at one of the stone blocks of the parapet as he sailed over, but he was too high and his momentum was too great. He hurtled over the parapet, plunging out and down into the darkness below the wall. His scream faded horribly as he fell, lost in the sound of yet another shriek from the Temple of Torak.

Silk rose to his feet, glanced once over the edge, and then came back to where Garion stood trembling in the shadows by the tower wall.

"Silk!" Garion exclaimed, catching the little man's arm in relief.

"What was that?" Belgarath asked, coming back around the corner.

"Brill," Silk replied blandly, pulling his Murgo robe back on.

"Again?" Belgarath demanded with exasperation. "What was he doing this time?"

"Trying to fly, last time I saw him." Silk smirked.

The old man looked puzzled.

"He wasn't doing it very well," Silk added.

Belgarath shrugged. "Maybe it'll come to him in time."

"He doesn't really have all that much time." Silk glanced out over the edge.

From far below—terribly far below—there came a faint, muffled crash; then, after several seconds, another. "Does bouncing count?" Silk asked.

Belgarath made a wry face. "Not really."

"Then I'd say he didn't learn in time," Silk said blithely. He looked around with a broad smile. "What a beautiful night this is," he remarked to no one in particular.

"Let's move along," Belgarath suggested, throwing a quick, nervous glance at the eastern horizon. "It will start to lighten up over there any time now."

They joined the others in the deep shadows beside the high wall of the Temple some hundred yards farther down the wall and waited tensely for Relg and Durnik to catch up.

"What kept you?" Barak whispered as they waited.

"I met an old friend of ours," Silk replied quietly. His grin was a flash of white teeth in the shadows.

"It was Brill," Garion told the rest of them in a hoarse whisper. "He and Silk fought with each other, and Silk threw him over the edge."

Mandorallen glanced toward the frosty parapet. "'Tis a goodly way down," he observed.

"Isn't it, though?" Silk agreed.

Barak chuckled and put his big hand wordlessly on Silk's shoulder.

Then Durnik and Relg came along the top of the wall to join them in the shadows.

"We have to go through the Temple," Belgarath told them in a quiet voice. "Pull your hoods as far over your faces as you can and keep your heads down. Stay in single file and mutter to yourselves as if you were praying. If anybody speaks to us, let me do the talking; and each time the gong sounds, turn toward the altar and bow." He led them then to a thick door bound with weathered iron straps. He looked back once to be sure they were all in line, then put his hand to the latch and pushed the door open.

The inside of the temple glowed with smoky red light, and a dreadful, charnel-house reek filled it. The door through which they entered led onto a covered balcony that curved around the back of the dome of the Temple. A stone balustrade ran along the edge of the balcony, with thick pillars at evenly spaced intervals. The openings between the pillars were draped with the same coarse, heavy cloth from which the Murgo robes were woven. Along the back wall of the balcony were a number of doors, set deep in the stone. Garion surmised that the balcony was largely used by Temple functionaries going to and fro on various errands.

As soon as they started along the balcony, Belgarath crossed his hands on his chest and led them at a slow, measured pace, chanting in a deep, loud voice.

A scream echoed up from below, piercing, filled with terror and agony. Garion involuntarily glanced through the parted drapery toward the altar. For the rest of his life he wished he had not.

The circular walls of the Temple were constructed of polished black stone, and directly behind the altar was an enormous face forged of steel and buffed to mirror brightness—the face of Torak and the original of the steel masks of the Grolims. The face was beautiful—there was no question of that—yet there was a kind of brooding evil in it, a cruelty beyond human ability to comprehend the meaning of the word. The Temple floor facing the God's image was densely packed with Murgos and Grolim priests, kneeling and chanting an unintelligible rumble in a dozen dialects. The altar stood on a raised dais directly beneath the glittering face of Torak. A smoking brazier on an iron post stood at each front corner of the blood-smeared altar, and a square pit opened in the floor immediately in front of the dais. Ugly red flames licked up out of the pit, and black, oily smoke rolled from it toward the dome high above.

A half dozen Grolims in black robes and steel masks were gathered around the altar, holding the naked body of a slave. The victim was already dead, his chest gaping open like the chest of a butchered hog, and a single Grolim stood in front of the altar, facing the image of Torak with raised hands. In his right, he held a long, curved knife; in his left, a dripping human heart. "Behold our offering, Dragon God of Angarak!" he cried in a huge voice, then turned and deposited the heart in one of the smoking braziers. There was a burst of steam and smoke from the brazier and a hideous sizzle as the heart dropped into the burning coals. From somewhere beneath the Temple floor, the huge iron gong sounded, its vibration shimmering in the air. The assembled Murgos and their Grolim overseers groaned and pressed their faces to the floor.

Garion felt a hand nudge his shoulder. Silk, already turned, was bowing toward the bloody altar. Awkwardly, sickened by the horror below, Garion also bowed.

The six Grolims at the altar lifted the lifeless body of the slave almost contemptuously and cast it into the pit before the dais. Flames belched up and sparks rose in the thick smoke as the body fell into the fire below.

A dreadful anger welled up in Garion. Without even thinking, he began to draw in his will, fully intent upon shattering that vile altar and the cruel image hovering above it into shards and fragments in a single, cataclysmic unleashing of naked force.

"Belgarion!" the voice within his mind said sharply. *"Don't interfere. This isn't the time."*

"I can't stand it," Garion raged silently. *"I've got to do something."*

"You can't. Not now. You'll rouse the whole city. Unclench your will, Belgarion."

"Do as he says, Garion," Aunt Pol's voice sounded quietly in his mind. The unspoken recognition passed between Aunt Pol's mind and that strange other mind as Garion helplessly let the anger and the will drain out of him.

"This abomination won't stand much longer, Belgarion," the voice assured him. *"Even now the earth gathers to rid itself of it."* And then the voice was gone.

"What are you doing up here?" a harsh voice demanded. Garion jerked his eyes away from the hideous scene below. A masked and robed Grolim stood in front of Belgarath, blocking their way.

"We are the servants of Torak," the old man replied in an accent that perfectly matched the gutturals of Murgo speech.

"All in Rak Cthol are the servants of Torak," the Grolim said. "You aren't attending the ritual of sacrifice. Why?"

"We're pilgrims from Rak Hagga," Belgarath explained, "only just arrived in the dread city. We were commanded to present ourselves to the Hierarch of Rak Hagga in the instant of our arrival. That stern duty prevents our participation in the celebration."

The Grolim grunted suspiciously.

"Could the revered priest of the Dragon God direct us to the chambers of our Hierarch? We are unfamiliar with the dark Temple."

There was another shriek from below. As the iron gong boomed, the Grolim turned and bowed toward the altar. Belgarath gave a quick jerk of his head to the rest of them, turned and also bowed.

"Go to the last door but one," the Grolim instructed, apparently satisfied by their gestures of piety. "It will lead you down to the halls of the Hierarchs."

"We are endlessly grateful to the priest of the Dark God," Belgarath thanked him, bowing. They filed past the steel-masked Grolim, their heads down and their hands crossed on their breasts, muttering to themselves as if in prayer.

"Vile!" Relg was strangling. "Obscenity! Abomination!"

"Keep your head down!" Silk whispered. "There are Grolims all around us."

"As UL gives me strength, I won't rest until Rak Cthol is laid waste," Relg vowed in a fervent mutter.

Belgarath had reached an ornately carved door near the end of the balcony, and he swung it open cautiously. "Is the Grolim still watching us?" he whispered to Silk.

The little man glanced back at the priest standing some distance behind them. "Yes. Wait—there he goes. The balcony's clear now."

The sorcerer let the door swing shut and stepped instead to the last door on the balcony. He tugged the latch carefully, and the door opened smoothly. He frowned. "It's always been locked before," he muttered.

"Do you think it's a trap?" Barak rumbled, his hand dipping under the Murgo robe to find his sword hilt.

"It's possible, but we don't have much choice." Belgarath pulled the door open the rest of the way, and they all slipped through as another shriek came from the altar. The door slowly closed behind them as the gong shuddered the stones of the Temple. They started down the worn stone steps beyond the door. The stairway was narrow and poorly lighted, and it went down sharply, curving always to the right.

"We're right up against the outer wall, aren't we?" Silk asked, touching the black stones on his left.

Belgarath nodded. "The stairs lead down to Ctuchik's private place." They continued down until the walls on either side changed from blocks to solid stone.

"He lives below the city?" Silk asked, surprised.

"Yes," Belgarath replied. "He built himself a sort of hanging turret out from the rock of the peak itself."

"Strange idea," Durnik said.

"Ctuchik's a strange sort of person," Aunt Pol told him grimly.

Belgarath stopped them. "The stairs go down about another hundred feet," he whispered. "There'll be two guards just outside the door to the turret. Not even Ctuchik could change that—no matter what he's planning."

"Sorcerers?" Barak asked softly.

"No. The guards are ceremonial more than functional. They're just ordinary Grolims."

"We'll rush them then."

"That won't be necessary. I can get you close enough to deal with them, but I want it quick and quiet." The old man reached inside his Murgo robe and drew out a roll of parchment bound with a strip of black ribbon. He started down again with Barak and Mandorallen close behind him.

The curve of the stairway brought a lighted area into view as they descended. Torches illuminated the bottom of the stone steps and a kind of antechamber hewn from the solid rock. Two Grolim priests stood in front of a plain black door, their arms folded. "Who approaches the Holy of Holies?" one of them demanded, putting his hand to his sword hilt.

"A messenger," Belgarath announced importantly. "I bear a message for the Master from the Hierarch of Rak Goska." He held the rolled parchment above his head.

"Approach, messenger."

"Praise the name of the Disciple of the Dragon God of Angarak," Belgarath boomed as he marched down the steps with Mandorallen and Barak flanking him. He reached the bottom of the stairs and stopped in front of the steel-masked guards. "Thus have I performed my appointed task," he declared, holding out the parchment.

One of the guards reached for it, but Barak caught his arm in a huge fist. The big man's other hand closed swiftly about the surprised Grolim's throat.

The other guard's hand flashed toward his sword hilt, but he grunted and doubled over sharply as Mandorallen thrust a long, needle-pointed poniard up into his belly. With a kind of deadly concentration the knight twisted the hilt of the weapon, probing with the point deep inside the Grolim's body. The guard shuddered when the blade reached his heart and collapsed with a long, gurgling sigh.

Barak's massive shoulder shifted, and there was a grating crunch as the bones in the first Grolim's neck came apart in his deadly grip. The guard's feet scraped spasmodically on the floor for a moment, and then he went limp. "I feel better already," Barak muttered, dropping the body.

"You and Mandorallen stay here," Belgarath told him. "I don't want to be disturbed once I'm inside."

"We'll see to it," Barak promised. "What about these?" He pointed at the two dead guards.

"Dispose of them, Relg," Belgarath said shortly to the Ulgo.

Silk turned his back quickly as Relg knelt between the two bodies and took hold of them, one with each hand. There was a sort of muffled slithering as he pushed down, sinking the bodies into the stone floor.

"You left a foot sticking out," Barak observed in a detached tone.

"Do you *have* to talk about it?" Silk demanded.

Belgarath took a deep breath and put his hand to the iron door handle. "All right," he said to them quietly, "let's go, then." He pushed open the door.

Chapter Twenty-seven

THE WEALTH OF empires lay beyond the black door. Heaps of bright yellow coins—gold beyond counting—lay in heaps on the floor; carelessly scattered among the coins were rings, bracelets, chains, and crowns, gleaming richly. Blood-red bars from the mines of Angarak stood in stacks along the wall, interspersed here and there by open chests filled to overflowing with fist-sized diamonds that glittered like ice. A large table sat in the center of the room, littered with rubies, sapphires, and emeralds as big as eggs. Ropes and strings of pearls, pink, rosy gray, and even some of jet held back the deep crimson drapes that billowed heavily before the windows.

Belgarath moved like a stalking animal, showing no sign of his age, his eyes everywhere. He ignored the riches around him and crossed the deep-carpeted floor to a room filled with learning, where tightly rolled scrolls lay in racks reaching to the ceiling and the leather backs of books marched like battalions along dark wooden shelves. The tables in the second room were covered with the curious glass apparatus of chemical experiment and strange machines of brass and iron, all cogs and wheels and pulleys and chains.

In yet a third chamber stood a massive gold throne backed by drapes of black velvet. An ermine cape lay across one arm of the throne, and a scepter and a heavy gold crown lay upon the seat. Inlaid in the polished stones of the floor was a map that depicted, so far as Garion could tell, the entire world.

"What sort of place is this?" Durnik whispered in awe.

"Ctuchik amuses himself here," Aunt Pol replied with an expression of repugnance. "He has many vices and he likes to keep each one separate."

"He's not down here," Belgarath muttered. "Let's go up to the next level." He led them back the way they had come and started up a flight of stone steps that curved along the rounded wall of the turret.

The room at the top of the stairs was filled with horror. A rack stood in the center of it, and whips and flails hung on the walls. Cruel implements of gleaming steel lay in orderly rows on a table near the wall—hooks, needle-pointed spikes, and dreadful things with saw-edges that still had bits of bone and flesh caught between their teeth. The entire room reeked of blood.

"You and Silk go ahead, father," Aunt Pol said. "There are things in the other rooms on this level that Garion, Durnik, and Relg shouldn't see."

Belgarath nodded and went through a doorway with Silk behind him. After a few moments they returned by way of another door. Silk's face looked slightly sick. "He has some rather exotic perversions, doesn't he?" he remarked with a shudder.

Belgarath's face was bleak. "We go up again," he said quietly. "He's on the top level. I thought he might be, but I needed to be sure." They mounted another stairway.

As they neared the top, Garion felt a peculiar tingling glow beginning somewhere deep within him, and a sort of endless singing seemed to draw him on. The mark on the palm of his right hand burned.

A black stone altar stood in the first room on the top level of the turret, and the steel image of the face of Torak brooded from the wall behind it. A gleaming knife, its hilt crusted with dried blood, lay on the altar, and bloodstains had sunk into the very pores of the rock. Belgarath was moving quickly now, his face intent and his stride catlike. He glanced through one door in the wall beyond the altar, shook his head and moved on to a closed door in the far wall. He touched his fingers lightly to the wood, then nodded. "He's in here," he murmured with satisfaction. He drew in a deep breath and grinned suddenly. "I've been waiting for this for a long time," he said.

"Don't dawdle, father," Aunt Pol told him impatiently. Her eyes were steely, and the white lock at her brow glittered like frost.

"I want you to stay out of it when we get inside, Pol," he reminded her. "You too, Garion. This is between Ctuchik and me."

"All right, father," Aunt Pol replied.

Belgarath put out his hand and opened the door. The room beyond was plain, even bare. The stone floor was uncarpeted, and the round windows looking out into the darkness were undraped. Simple candles burned in sconces on the walls, and a plain table stood in the center of the room. Seated at the table with his back to the door sat a man in a hooded black robe who seemed to be gazing into an iron cask. Garion felt his entire body throbbing in response to what was in the casks, and the singing in his mind filled him.

A little boy with pale blond hair stood in front of the table, and he was also staring at the cask. He wore a smudged linen smock and dirty little shoes. Though his expression seemed devoid of all thought, there was a sweet innocence about him that caught at the heart. His eyes were blue, large, and trusting, and he was quite the most beautiful child Garion had ever seen.

"What took you so long, Belgarath?" the man at the table asked, not even bothering to turn around. His voice sounded dusty. He closed the iron box with a faint click. "I was almost beginning to worry about you."

"A few minor delays, Ctuchik," Belgarath replied. "I hope we didn't keep you waiting too long."

"I managed to keep myself occupied. Come in. Come in— all of you." Ctuchik turned to look at them. His hair and beard were a yellowed white and were very long. His face was deeply lined, and his eyes glittered in their sockets. It was a face filled with an ancient and profound evil. Cruelty and arrogance had eroded all traces of decency or humanity from it, and a towering egotism had twisted it into a perpetual sneer of contempt for every other living thing. His eyes shifted to Aunt Pol. "Polgara," he greeted her with a mocking inclination of his head. "You're as lovely as ever. Have you come finally then to submit yourself to the will of my Master?" His leer was vile.

"No, Ctuchik," she replied coldly. "I came to see justice."

"Justice?" He laughed scornfully. "There's no such thing, Polgara. The strong do what they like; the weak submit. My Master taught me that."

"And his maimed face did not teach you otherwise?"

The High Priest's face darkened briefly, but he shrugged off his momentary irritation. "I'd offer you all a place to sit and some refreshment, perhaps," he continued in that same dusty voice, "but you won't be staying that long, I'm afraid." He glanced at the rest of them, his eyes noting each in turn. "Your party seems diminished, Belgarath," he observed. "I hope you haven't lost any of them along the way."

"They're all well, Ctuchik," Belgarath assured him. "I'm certain that they'll appreciate your concern, however."

"All?" Ctuchik drawled. "I see the Nimble Thief and the Man with Two Lives and the Blind Man, but I don't see the others. Where's the Dreadful Bear and the Knight Protector? The Horse Lord and the Bowman? And the ladies? Where are they—the Queen of the World and the Mother of the Race That Died?"

"All well, Ctuchik," Belgarath replied. "All well."

"How extraordinary. I was almost certain that you'd have lost one or two at least by now. I admire your dedication, old man—to keep intact for all these centuries a prophecy that would have collapsed if one single ancestor had died at the wrong time." His eyes grew distant momentarily. "Ah," he said. "I see. You left them below to stand guard. You didn't have to do that, Belgarath. I left orders that we weren't to be disturbed."

The High Priest's eyes stopped then on Garion's face. "Belgarion," he said almost politely. Despite the singing that still thrilled in his veins, Garion felt a chill as the evil force of the High Priest's mind touched him. "You're younger than I expected."

Garion stared defiantly at him, gathering his will to ward off any surprise move by the old man at the table.

"Would you pit your will against mine, Belgarion?" Ctuchik seemed amused. "You burned Chamdar, but he was a fool. You'll find me a bit more difficult. Tell me, boy, did you enjoy it?"

"No," Garion replied, still holding himself ready.

"In time you'll learn to enjoy it," Ctuchik said with an evil grin. "Watching your enemy writhe and shriek in your mind's grip is one of the more satisfying rewards of power." He turned his eyes back to Belgarath. "And so you've come at last to destroy me?" he said mockingly.

"If it comes down to that, yes. It's been a long time coming, Ctuchik."

"Hasn't it, though? We're very much alike, Belgarath. I've been looking forward to this meeting almost as much as you have. Yes, we're very much alike. Under different circumstances, we might even have been friends."

"I doubt that. I'm a simple man, and some of your amusements are a bit sophisticated for my taste."

"Spare me that, please. You know as well as I do that we're both beyond all restriction."

"Perhaps, but I prefer to choose my friends a bit more carefully."

"You're growing tiresome, Belgarath. Tell the others to come up." Ctuchik raised one eyebrow sardonically. "Don't you want to have them watch while you destroy me? Think of how sweet their admiration will be."

"They're fine just where they are," Belgarath told him.

"Don't be tedious. Surely you're not going to deny me the opportunity to pay homage to the Queen of the World." Ctuchik's voice was mocking. "I yearn to behold her exquisite perfection before you kill me."

"I doubt that she'd care much for you, Ctuchik. I'll convey your respects, however."

"I insist, Belgarath. It's a small request—easily granted. If you don't summon her, I will."

Belgarath's eyes narrowed, and then he suddenly grinned.

"So that's it," he said softly. "I wondered why you'd gone to all the trouble to let us get through so easily."

"It doesn't really matter now, you know," Ctuchik almost purred. "You've made your last mistake, old man. You've brought her to Rak Cthol, and that's all I really needed. Your prophecy dies here and now, Belgarath—and you with it, I'd imagine." The High Priest's eyes flashed triumphantly, and Garion felt the evil force of Ctuchik's mind reaching out, searching with a terrible purpose.

Belgarath exchanged a quick look with Aunt Pol and slyly winked.

Ctuchik's eyes widened suddenly as his mind swept through the lower levels of his grim turret and found it empty. "Where is she?" he demanded wildly in a voice that was almost a scream.

"The princess wasn't able to come with us," Belgarath replied blandly. "She sends her apologies, though."

"You're lying, Belgarath! You wouldn't have dared to leave her behind. There's no place in the world where she'd be safe."

"Not even in the caves of Ulgo?"

Ctuchik's face blanched. "Ulgo?" he gasped.

"Poor old Ctuchik," Belgarath said, shaking his head in mock regret. "You're slipping badly, I'm afraid. It wasn't a bad plan you had, but didn't it occur to you to make sure that the princess was actually with us before you let me get this close to you?"

"One of the others will do just as well," Ctuchik asserted, his eyes blazing with fury.

"No," Belgarath disagreed. "The others are all unassailable. Ce'Nedra's the only vulnerable one, and she's at Prolgu—under the protection of UL himself. You can attempt *that* if you'd like, but I wouldn't really advise it."

"Curse you, Belgarath!"

"Why don't you just give me the Orb now, Ctuchik?" Belgarath suggested. "You know I can take it away from you if I have to."

Ctuchik struggled to gain control of himself. "Let's not be hasty, Belgarath," he said after a moment. "What are we going to gain by destroying each other? We have Cthrag Yaska in our possession. We could divide the world between us."

"I don't want half the world, Ctuchik."

"You want it all for yourself?" A brief, knowing smile crossed Ctuchik's face. "So did I—at first—but I'll settle for half."

"Actually, I don't want any of it."

Ctuchik's expression became a bit desperate. "What *do* you want, Belgarath?"

"The Orb," Belgarath replied inexorably. "Give it to me, Ctuchik."

"Why don't we join forces and use the Orb to destroy Zedar?"

"Why?"

"You hate him as much as I do. He betrayed your Master. He stole Cthrag Yaska from you."

"He betrayed himself, Ctuchik, and I think that haunts him sometimes. His plan to steal the Orb was clever, though." Belgarath looked thoughtfully at the little boy standing in front of the table, his large eyes fixed on the iron cask. "I wonder where he found this child," he mused. "Innocence and purity are not exactly the same thing, of course, but they're very close. It must have cost Zedar a great deal of effort to raise a total innocent. Think of all the impulses he had to suppress."

"That's why I let *him* do it," Ctuchik said.

The little blond boy, seeming to know that they were discussing him, looked at the two old men, his eyes filled with absolute trust.

"The whole point is that I still have Cthrag Yaska—the Orb," Ctuchik said, leaning back in his chair and laying one hand on the cask. "If you try to take it, I'll fight you. Neither of us knows for sure how that would turn out. Why take chances?"

"What good is it doing you? Even if it would submit to you, what then? Would you raise Torak and surrender it to *him*?"

"I might think about it. But Torak's been asleep for five centuries now, and the world's run fairly well without him. I don't imagine there's all that much point in disturbing him just yet."

"Which would leave you in possession of the Orb."

Ctuchik shrugged. "Someone has to have it. Why not me?"

He was still leaning back in his chair, seeming almost completely at ease. There was no warning movement or even a flicker of emotion across his face as he struck.

It came so quickly that it was not a surge but a blow, and the sound of it was not the now-familiar roaring in the mind but a thunderclap. Garion knew that, had it been directed at him, it would have destroyed him. But it was not directed at him. It lashed instead at Belgarath. For a dreadful instant Garion saw his grandfather engulfed in a shadow blacker than night itself. Then the shadow shattered like a goblet of delicate crystal, scattering shards of darkness as it blew apart. Now grim-faced, Belgarath still faced his ancient enemy. "Is that the best you can do, Ctuchik?" he asked, even as his own will struck.

A searing blue light suddenly surrounded the Grolim, closing in upon him, seeming to crush him with its intensity. The stout chair upon which he sat burst into chunks and splinters, as if a sudden vast weight had settled down upon it. Ctuchik fell among the fragments of his chair and pushed back the blue incandescence with both hands. He lurched to his feet and answered with flames. For a dreadful instant Garion remembered Asharak, burning in the Wood of the Dryads, but Belgarath brushed the fire away and, despite his once-stated assertion that the Will and Word needed no gesture, he raised his hand and smashed at Ctuchik with lightning.

The sorcerer and the magician faced each other in the center of the room, surrounded by blazing lights and waves of flame and darkness. Garion's mind grew numb under the repeated detonations of raw energy as the two struggled. He sensed that their battle was only partially visible and that blows were being struck which he could not see—could not even imagine. The air in the turret room seemed to crackle and hiss. Strange images appeared and vanished, flickering at the extreme limits of visibility—vast faces, enormous hands, and things Garion could not name. The turret itself trembled as the two dreadful old men ripped open the fabric of reality itself to grasp weapons of imagination or delusion.

Without even thinking, Garion began to gather his will, drawing his mind into focus. He had to stop it. The edges of the blows were smashing at him and at the others. Beyond thought now, Belgarath and Ctuchik, consumed with their hatred for each other, were unleashing forces that could kill them all.

"Garion! Stay out of it!" Aunt Pol told him in a voice so harsh that he could not believe it was hers. "They're at the limit. If you throw anything else into it, you'll destroy them both." She gestured sharply to the others. "Get back—all of you. The air around them is alive."

Fearfully, they all backed toward the rear wall of the turret room.

The sorcerer and the magician stood no more than a few feet apart now, their eyes blazing and their power surging back and forth in waves. The air sizzled around them, and their robes smoked.

Then Garion's eyes fell upon the little boy. He stood watching with calm, uncomprehending eyes. He neither started nor flinched at the dreadful sounds and sights that crashed around him. Garion tensed himself to dash forward and yank the child to safety, but at that moment the little boy turned toward the table. Quite calmly, he walked through a sudden wall of green flame that shot up in front of him. Either he did not see the fire, or he did not fear it. He reached the table, stood on his tiptoes and, raising the lid, he put his hand into the iron cask over which Ctuchik had been gloating. He lifted a round, polished, gray stone out of the cask. Garion instantly felt that strange tingling glow again, so strong now that it was almost overwhelming, and his ears filled with the haunting song.

He heard Aunt Pol gasp.

Holding the gray stone in both hands like a ball, the little boy turned and walked directly toward Garion, his eyes filled with trust and the expression on his small face confident. The polished stone reflected the flashing lights of the terrible conflict raging in the center of the room, but there was another light within it as well. Deep within it stood an intense azure glow—a light that neither flickered nor changed, a light that grew steadily stronger as the boy approached Garion. The child stopped and raised the stone in his hands, offering it to Garion. He smiled and spoke a single word, "Errand."

An instant image filled Garion's mind, an image of a dreadful fear. He knew that he was looking directly into the mind of Ctuchik. There was a picture in Ctuchik's mind—a picture of Garion holding the glowing stone in his hand—and that picture terrified the Grolim. Garion felt waves of fear spilling out toward him. Deliberately and quite slowly he reached his right hand toward the stone the child was offering. The mark on his palm yearned toward the stone, and the chorus of song in his mind swelled to a mighty crescendo. Even as he stretched out his hand, he felt the sudden, unthinking, animal panic in Ctuchik.

The Grolim's voice was a hoarse shriek. *"Be not!"* he cried out desperately, directing all his terrible power at the stone in the little boy's hands.

For a shocking instant, a deadly silence filled the turret. Even Belgarath's face, drawn by his terrible struggle, was shocked and unbelieving.

The blue glow within the heart of the stone seemed to contract. Then it flared again.

Ctuchik, his long hair and beard disheveled, stood gaping in wide-eyed and openmouthed horror. "I didn't mean it!" he howled. "I didn't—I—"

But a new and even more stupendous force had already entered the round room. The force flashed no light, nor did it push against Garion's mind. It seemed instead to pull out, drawing at him as it closed about the horrified Ctuchik.

The High Priest of the Grolims shrieked mindlessly. Then he seemed to expand, then contract, then expand again. Cracks appeared on his face as if he had suddenly solidified into stone and the stone was disintegrating under the awful force welling up within him. Within those hideous cracks Garion saw, not flesh and blood and bone, but blazing energy. Ctuchik began to glow, brighter and brighter. He raised his hands imploringly. "Help me!" he screamed. He shrieked out a long, despairing,

"NO!" And then, with a shattering sound that was beyond noise, the Disciple of Torak exploded into nothingness.

Hurled to the floor by that awesome blast, Garion tumbled against the wall. Without thinking, he caught the little boy, who was flung against him like a rag doll. The round stone clattered as it bounced against the rocks of the wall. Garion reached out to catch it, but Aunt Pol's hand closed on his wrist. "No!" she said. "Don't touch it. It's the Orb."

Garion's hand froze.

The little boy squirmed out of his grasp and ran after the rolling Orb. "Errand." He laughed triumphantly as he caught it.

"What happened?" Silk muttered, struggling to his feet and shaking his head.

"Ctuchik destroyed himself," Aunt Pol replied, also rising. "He tried to unmake the Orb. The Mother of the Gods will not permit unmaking." She looked quickly at Garion. "Help me with your grandfather."

Belgarath had been standing almost in the center of the explosion that had destroyed Ctuchik. The blast had thrown him halfway across the room, and he lay in a stunned heap, his eyes glazed and his hair and beard singed.

"Get up, father," Aunt Pol said urgently, bending over him.

The turret began to shudder, and the basalt pinnacle from which it hung swayed. A vast booming sound echoed up out of the earth. Bits of rock and mortar showered down from the walls of the room as the earth quivered in the aftershock of Ctuchik's destruction.

In the rooms below, the stout door banged open and Garion heard pounding feet. "Where are you?" Barak's voice bellowed.

"Up here," Silk shouted down the stairway.

Barak and Mandorallen rushed up the stone stairs. "Get out of here!" Barak roared. "The turret's starting to break away from the rock. The Temple up there's collapsing, and there's a crack two feet wide in the ceiling where the turret joins the rock."

"Father!" Aunt Pol said sharply, "you must get up!"

Belgarath stared at her uncomprehendingly.

"Pick him up," she snapped at Barak.

There was a dreadful tearing sound as the rocks that held the turret against the side of the peak began to rip away under the pressures of the convulsing earth.

"There!" Relg said in a ringing voice. He was pointing at the back wall of the turret where the stones were cracking and shattering. "Can you open it? There's a cave beyond."

Aunt Pol looked up quickly, focused her eyes on the wall and pointed one finger. "Burst!" she commanded. The stone wall blew back into the echoing cave like a wall of straw struck by a hurricane.

"It's pulling loose!" Silk yelled, his voice shrill. He pointed at a widening crack between the turret and the solid face of the peak.

"Jump!" Barak shouted. "Hurry!"

Silk flung himself across the crack and spun to catch Relg, who had followed him blindly. Durnik and Mandorallen, with Aunt Pol between them, leaped across as the groaning crack yawned wider. "Go, boy!" Barak commanded Garion. Carrying the still-dazed Belgarath, the big Cherek was lumbering toward the opening.

The child! the voice in Garion's mind crackled, no longer dry or disinterested. *"Save the child or everything that has ever happened is meaningless!"*

Garion gasped, suddenly remembering the little boy. He turned and ran back into the slowly toppling turret. He swept up the boy in his arms and ran for the hole Aunt Pol had blown in the rock.

Barak jumped across, and his feet scrambled for an awful second on the very edge of the far side. Even as he ran, Garion pulled in his strength. At the instant he jumped, he pushed back with every ounce of his will. With the little boy in his arms he literally flew across the awful gap and crashed directly into Barak's broad back.

The little boy in his arms with the Orb of Aldur cradled protectively against his chest smiled up at him. "Errand?" he asked.

Garion turned. The turret was leaning far out from the basalt wall, its supporting stones cracking, ripping away from the sheer face. Ponderously, it toppled outward. And then, with the shards and fragments of the Temple of Torak hurtling past it, it sheared free of the wall and fell into the awful gulf beneath.

The floor of the cave they had entered was heaving as the earth shuddered and shock after shock reverberated up through the basalt pinnacle. Huge chunks of the walls of Rak Cthol were ripping free and plunging past the cave mouth, flickering down through the red light of the newly risen sun.

"Is everybody here?" Silk demanded, looking quickly around. Then, satisfied that they were all safe, he added, "We'd better get back from the opening a bit. This part of the peak doesn't feel all that stable."

"Do you want to go down now?" Relg asked Aunt Pol. "Or do you want to wait until the shaking subsides?"

"We'd better move," Barak advised. "These caves will be swarming with Murgos as soon as the quake stops."

Aunt Pol glanced at the half-conscious Belgarath and then seemed to gather herself. "We'll go down," she decided firmly. "We still have to stop to pick up the slave woman."

"She's almost certain to be dead," Relg asserted quickly. "The earthquake's probably brought the roof of that cave down on her."

Aunt Pol's eyes were flinty as she looked him full in the face.

No man alive could face that gaze for long. Relg dropped his eyes. "All right," he said sullenly. He turned and led them back into the dark cave with the earthquake rumbling beneath their feet.

Here ends Book Three of *The Belgariad.*
Book Four, *Castle of Wizardry,*
brings Garion and Ce'Nedra to the first realization of their heritage as the Prophecy moves them toward its fulfillment, and Garion discovers there are powers more difficult than sorcery.

About the Author

David Eddings was born in Spokane, Washington, in 1931, and was raised in the Puget Sound area north of Seattle. He received a Bachelor of Arts degree from Reed College in Portland, Oregon, in 1954 and a Master of Arts degree from the University of Washington in 1961. He has served in the United States Army, worked as a buyer for the Boeing Company, has been a grocery clerk, and has taught college English. He has lived in many parts of the United States.

His first novel, *High Hunt* (published by Putnam in 1973), was a contemporary adventure story. The field of fantasy has always been of interest to him, however, and he turned to *The Belgariad* in an effort to develop certain technical and philosophical ideas concerning that genre.

Eddings currently resides with his wife, Leigh, in the northwest.

Dear Reader,

Your opinions are very important to us so please take a few moments to tell us your thoughts. It will help us give you more enjoyable DEL REY Books in the future.

1. Where did you obtain this book?

Bookstore	☐1	Department Store ☐4	Airport	☐7	5
Supermarket	☐2	Drug Store ☐5	From A Friend ☐8		
Variety/Discount Store ☐3		Newsstand ☐6	Other_____		

(Write In)

2. On an overall basis, how would you rate this book?

Excellent ☐1   Very Good ☐2   Good ☐3   Fair ☐4   Poor ☐5   6

3. What is the main reason that you purchased this book?

Author ☐1   It Was Recommended To Me ☐3   7
Like The Cover ☐2   Other_____
(Write In)

4. In the same subject category as this book, who are your *two* favorite authors?

_____   8
                                                      9
_____   10
                                                      11

5. Which of the following categories of paperback books have you purchased in the past 3 months?

Adventure/		Biography ☐4	Horror/		Science	
Suspense	☐12-1	Classics ☐5	Terror	☐8	Fiction	☐x
Bestselling		Fantasy ☐6	Mystery	☐9	Self-Help	☐y
Fiction	☐2	Historical	Romance	☐0	War	☐13-
Bestselling		Romance ☐7			Westerns	☐2
Non-Fiction	☐3					

6. What magazines do you subscribe to, or read regularly, that is, 3 out of every 4 issues?

_____   14
                                                      15
_____   16
                                                      17

7. Are you: Male ☐1   Female ☐2   18

8. Please indicate your age group.

| Under 18 | ☐1 | 25-34 | ☐3 | 50 or older ☐5 | 19 |
| 18-24 | ☐2 | 35-49 | ☐4 | | |

9. What is the highest level of education that you have completed?

Post Graduate Degree ☐1	College Graduate ☐3	Some High	20
Some Post Graduate	1-3 Years College ☐4	School	
Schooling ☐2	High School	or Less ☐6	
	Graduate ☐5		

(Optional)

If you would like to learn about future publications and participate in future surveys, please fill in your name and address.

NAME_____

ADDRESS_____

CITY _____ STATE_____ ZIP_____   21

Please mail to: Ballantine Books
                   DEL REY Research, Dept.
                   516 Fifth Avenue — Suite 606
                   New York, N.Y. 10036

F-5

Enchanting fantasies from